THE
ENGLISH
RENDITION

Sharon O. Lightholder

I0597985

Albedo Press
AlbedoPress.com

PB ISBN: 978-0-578-09219-5
HB ISBN: 978-0-578-09715-2

PRINTED IN THE UNITED STATES OF AMERICA

Dedicated to
My Mother,
For a lifetime of encouragement and love

CHAPTER 1

RENDITION

The performance or interpretation of a musical composition.

Emily Finch Montgomery zipped up the jacket of her royal blue warm-up suit as soon as the rain paused just before nine on Thanksgiving morning. She hurried across the deck that jutted out from her Hollywood Hills home, glanced across the Los Angeles basin at the string of lights from the planes approaching LAX, and smiled. If the weather cooperated and the flight arrived on time, her granddaughter and fiancé would arrive by cab about noon. If she hurried, she still could get in violin practice and a long soak in the tub before they arrived. Stepping to the center of the redwood deck, she began her tai chi routine.

Although almost eighty, she had the lean angularity of a model. The wind ruffled her silver hair which was cut as short as a cap and appeared combed whether it had been or not. These were the twenty minutes a day that lubricated her body, peeled away decades, and let her just relax in the present. She considered her tai chi as a dance, called her physical therapist a personal trainer, and the hired help, who did the heavy cleaning and drove her car for her, as personal assistants.

Having completed her exercise, she went to the kitchen, filled the teakettle, set it over the gas flame, and let the sink fill with hot water. She soaked her hands and stretched her fingers and wrists until the kettle steamed. While her tea steeped, she surveyed the long narrow living room for any disorder. The dark oak arms and chocolate leather of the mission style couch and chair were fine. The coffee table between them was freshly dusted and only her latest reading rested on it. The frames of the two California landscapes above the sofa and the small collection of framed family photographs on the mantel were all straight. She glanced over the Mexican tile counter of the small galley kitchen. The glass on the doors to the deck sparkled, her music room had been tidied up, and the powder room scrubbed to a shine. She declared her home ready for guests and poured her tea.

After two cups, she checked the time, showered quickly, and dressed in warm gray wool slacks, a pale gray sweater set and comfortable black loafers. She took her violin from the safe in the music room's closet and played an hour of studies from Mendelssohn's Violin Concerto in E Minor. At eleven thirty-five, she returned her bow and violin to their hard case, checked the weather report on the computer that her daughter had forced her to install in the music room the prior year, and pretended to read a book in the chair near the front door while she listened for the cab.

When it finally arrived just after noon, she was beside the cab before its doors opened. Susan and Ray had a rumpled and too-traveled look. Susan hugged Emily while Ray paid the driver. He grinned as he looked at the two women. "This must be the right place. You look like sisters."

Emily laughed as Ray hurried into the house with the heavy suitcases.

Emily whispered to Susan, "I love him already."

He was a head taller than Susan with a similar runner's leanness and sense of balance. He had dark hair, darker eyes, and an easy smile. He glanced at the photo on the mantel and smiled at Susan.

Ray put their bags just inside the door and ran back to scoop the plastic wrapped *Los Angeles Times* off the driveway. The edge of the bag had torn and the paper was waterlogged. He held it for Emily to see.

"Just as well." She motioned for him to toss it on the corner of the porch. "Saved me an hour of reading about President Clinton's troubles with Saddam Hussein and that woman or another article explaining how El Niño is making 1997 the wettest year in a decade, when any fool in L.A. knows that." The cabbie didn't seem that impressed by the Spanish mission style home. He was used to the opulence. His tires spun on the wet asphalt as the cab lurched up the narrow lane to turn around in the driveway at the top of the hill.

After shutting the door, she pointed to the bags. "Your room is ready, Susan. Why don't you get out of those wet things and freshen up. I'll have coffee ready by the time you get back upstairs."

Susan opened the closet door and hung up their wet raincoats. "Thanks, Gram. Still have my teddy bear in the closet?"

"Of course." Emily looked after them as Ray followed Susan down the stairs.

Emily carefully measured coffee into her new Starbucks coffee maker, tapped the start button, arranged a platter of cranberry muffins and banana bread, and set out cups on saucers. Just as the coffee finished brewing, Susan returned wearing a fresh red turtleneck sweater and black slacks. "Anything I can do?"

"Not a thing, dear."

Susan sat on a bar stool, put her elbows on the counter, and leaned forward in a conspiratorial manner. "Have you practiced yet, Gram?"

"Yes. Why?"

"Darn. I wanted Ray to hear you play. I've played your records for him, and—"

Emily placed the steaming carafe of coffee on the counter. "There is plenty of time for that." Ray arrived and filled the two cups at their places. His red and white tartan plaid shirt was as crisply ironed as his tan slacks.

Holding the carafe, Ray asked, "Coffee, Emily?"

Susan chuckled. "Gram's a loyal tea drinker. Bet you've already had your Earl Gray. Isn't that your morning tea?"

"Yes. Darjeeling is for later in the day"

"And for Thanksgiving, we always had a pot of tea on the table." Susan tore a bit off a muffin and ate it, nodding approval. "You baked these?"

"Yes, but it was a mix."

"Very good," Ray said. "What can we do to help get ready for the feast?"

"Just set the table, later. And open the chardonnay as soon as Barbara gets here, to keep her out from underfoot. Barbara's bringing everything. Should be here by two since she said one."

Susan laughed. "Expect she'll bring enough for an army, as usual."

"Probably. Care for some juice?"

Susan turned to Ray. "Her fresh orange juice spoiled me as a kid. I thought everyone had it."

"They should. It is such a luxury." Emily said pulling a heavy juice press from under the counter. Susan joined her to operate it. Emily selected three oranges from a basket and sliced the oranges in half. Susan slipped them into the press and pulled the handle down. Juice ran easily into the stubby glass under the spout of the juicer."

"They have electric ones now, Gram."

"Yes, I know," Emily said, ending that discussion. "Juice, Ray?"

"Please. This is like a five star hotel, only better."

Susan laughed. "Wait until you taste my mother's turkey dinner. We might drop a star or two."

Ray frowned at her. He sipped his steaming coffee and looked over the rim of the cup at Emily, "How tough is she going to be on me? We've never met, and here I am about to marry her daughter."

Emily frowned briefly before answering. "She'll interview you. She's very…academic." Susan started laughing.

"That's not comforting, Susan," Ray growled. "Is this going to be like a thesis committee over the mashed potatoes?"

"Pretty much. If she remembers to order the potatoes." Susan patted his hand in a comforting manner. "She's really nosey. Any new face at a dinner party gets the third degree. She's just interested in everything, but can come across as pushy. Gram, is pushy a good word for her?"

"Inquisitive, dear."

Ray sat straighter. "Emily? Susan had an idea that I'd like to run by you."

"What is it?"

"We'd like to have the ceremony here. At your home. On New Year's Day."

She grinned at Susan. "Certainly! I know a judge who could perform the…but I am getting ahead of myself. Have you told your mother yet?"

Ray grimaced. "I had hoped to meet her right after we announced our engagement last month, but we couldn't get away. I hope she'll be okay with our new plans."

Emily wondered what Ray would make of her 53-year-old daughter. Barbara was strikingly unlike Emily or Susan. Barbara dyed her permed hair a metallic reddish-brown, which assumed unintended purple highlights in bright sunlight. Susan's auburn hair was long and naturally straight.

Emily had her exercise regimen. Susan ran daily. But Barbara ignored any event that could be characterized as exercise or athletic and retained a uniformly chunky profile and the illusion that black was slimming.

Theirs was a family of women. Emily had outlived Harry. Barbara out-divorced her three husbands. Susan, who was Barbara's only child, considered marriage only with caution at twenty-six. Emily smiled as she thought how she would welcome a male voice in her family again.

As Emily reached for the wineglasses in the cabinet above the counter, she felt an odd sensation, almost like vertigo and grabbed for the edge of the counter. The saucers on the tile jolted and skidded toward her. Susan slid off the barstool and clutched Ray's arm.

CHAPTER 2

ACCIDENTAL

A symbol in a musical notation that changes the key signature for one measure.

"Earthquake! Get in the door frame." Emily pointed to the front door.

The deck groaned and pitched like it did in the Sylmar earthquake. Ray grabbed Emily's arm as they ran to the door. Huddled together, Emily watched the deck undulate and remembered being on it during the Sylmar quake, falling, and watching an orange she was peeling for breakfast tumble over the edge. Out of the blue, she flashed back to the metallic taste of an orange her father brought her from Seville when she was a child and then back to the months of aftershocks.

As they stood in the doorway, Emily tried to sort out the new sounds of wood splintering, metal bending, a car horn, and a sound like a shotgun being fired. She had her palm against the wall next to the door and was holding her breath. The shaking stopped. Ray opened the front door. "Let's get outside and see what's—"

Emily pointed to skid marks on the road and a deep gash on hillside. They followed her as she walked up the narrow road. "The cab? I thought I heard it go back down the road, but—"

Ray jogged ahead of them and suddenly stopped, pointing at the base of the two-story timber supporting the bow of the deck. "It's a car alright, but not the cab."

Emily walked up the hill and traced the black gash of wet soil through the deep green ice plant from the curb to where a black Porsche was wedged under a splintered wood pillar. The pale airbag sagged from the steering wheel. A stocky man in a tan windbreaker and dark slacks sat on the ground beside the car holding his face with both hands.

Ray shouted, "Hey! You okay?"

Emily rubbed her right elbow. "Shall I call nine-one-one for an ambulance?"

He twisted his neck and stood slowly. "Naw, just feels like I got punched in the face. You okay?"

Emily cupped her hands to her mouth. "Seems so. But can you move away from there? That timber on the bonnet of your car appears to be–."

As he took a step up the hill, his thin leather loafers slid on the wet ice plant and he fell. "I'm trying."

"Who are you?" Emily called.

He pointed to the house at the crest of the hill. "Ben Rodman. Just moved in."

"Nice to meet you. I'm Emily Montgomery."

His shoulders dropped. "Oh my God. I thought you looked familiar. You were Emily Finch Montgomery, the English Angel."

She laughed. "Yes, I still am. Emily, that is."

Ray listened to the throaty hum of the car's engine. He pointed down the hill and shouted. "Car's still running. Can you turn it off? I'll meet you down there."

The driver fell twice before getting down to the road and starting his return climb up the street. Ray jogged down the street and returned with Ben.

A clump of mud fell from the sleeve of Ben's windbreaker when he stopped next to Emily, who studied his face. "Have we met?"

"No, I grew up here. Heard you at the Music Center with my parents. I have my dad's record albums." Ben gasped for breath. "Got your *English Angel* solo album. And when you played with the Los Angeles Philharmonic about 1960, and the Four Seasons that you did with...." He fell silent as he looked at her. The lean woman with high cheekbones and dark eyes still resembled her picture on the cover of the *English Angel* record album.

Ben was stocky and only slightly taller than Emily. In contrast to her light California tan, he had an office pallor that made his skin appear skim milk translucent. His short dark hair might have a curl if it were longer. Emily was sure that he was under forty, but the ages between twenty and sixty now blurred. He panted.

Ray took his elbow. "Are you all right, Mr. Rodman?"

He slapped his stomach and muttered, "Ben. Just out of shape. I'm not having a heart attack."

Emily pointed to her home with the rain darkened roof tiles and whitewashed façade. "Come in and we can sort this out."

"But I'm muddy."

"Yes, and you've just been in an auto collision. Stand there while I get a towel for you." After she returned and he brushed mud off his jacket, Emily took the towel and pointed to the open door. "So, you're just now settling in to your new home?"

Ben followed her direction and stomped as much mud off his shoes as possible, then shrugged, slipped out of his loafers, and left them on the porch. "Almost settled. We moved in about a month ago. My wife and I should have introduced ourselves. Guess we've been working too many hours at the firm. She's out of town now. I was just going for a sandwich when…"

Emily pointed to the barstool as she dropped the towel in the sink. "Sit there and collect yourself a moment. May I offer you a water or coffee?"

He noticed that his hand was shaking as he leaned on the counter for balance to get on the high stool. "A water would be—"

Susan went to the counter directly across from him. "Look at me. I want to see if your eyes are in sync. Even though you said you are okay, you're very shaky. I want to see if that's the adrenaline or if you have a concussion."

She stared into his eyes as she held her index finger in front of his nose.

"Are you a doctor?"

"Medical researcher. Quit clinical medicine during my pediatric residency. Follow my finger, please."

Ben leaned his elbows on the counter and obeyed. She nodded and smiled. "Ribs? Think you cracked anything?"

Ben rubbed his left shoulder and collarbone. "Seat belt sure did its job. Just feel bruised."

"Anyone staying with you?"

"No. Why?"

"If you start feeling dizzy or something really hurts, call me. We're visiting my grandmother for a few days."

"Thanks, but I think I'll be fine." He turned to Emily, "Listen, my firm does a lot of construction defect work. We have a slate of engineers that we use. I'll get one out today to see what the damage is and what we need to do right away."

"But it's a holiday. And I have guests."

Ben's raised eyebrow suggested that, holiday or not, the engineer would be out promptly. "This is all my fault, so you can have your carrier get an estimate, or just let me pay for it all. But the faster we see what the damage is, the better chance we have of not letting it get any worse, okay?"

"Yes, of course. Should I call a city building inspector?"

"I'll have my guy put in a call. He's got emergency numbers and they can figure out if this can wait until Monday." Ben said, and then thought that he might be moving too fast for the older woman. "With your permission," he added.

Ray topped off his coffee cup. "Are you in construction?"

"No, I'm a lawyer. Couldn't tell a two-by-four from a six-by-eight without a ruler. But I really think I need to get your deck inspected right away, if you'll let me."

Emily nodded. "Certainly. Go right ahead."

Ben turned toward the deck with his cell phone. "Brad? Sorry to call you at home. It's Ben. My car slid off the road and hit a support timber of my neighbor's deck." He shrugged. "Yeah. I'm okay, but the new car.... Can you call one of your construction experts and get him over to my house ASAP?" He lowered his voice. "I need to know if it is safe for her to stay in her home. There are still four other timbers in place, but I splintered the tallest one. And send someone to put that plastic sheeting stuff on the hill so it won't slide. It's a longer story than I've got time for now. I'll open a file. Charge your time to me, personally. Not the firm. I'll work the details later when I go into the office. Thanks. Oh, Brad....

Give me a call back on my cell phone when you have a name and arrival time. Thanks." Ben clicked the phone off and turned to Emily.

Ray saw the police car crawling up the steep road and shouted to Ben, "Did you call the police?"

"Yes, when I was walking to the road."

Ray started for the front door. "I'll flag them down."

"Thanks."

The patrol car pulled over and Ray motioned them into the house. As Ben went to the open door, she heard him muttering her name. Two patrol officers in dripping yellow slickers stood in Emily's doorway. The taller officer took notes on a clipboard and the other shifted from foot to foot and listened to the radio chatter from the car. Ben gave the two policemen the details quickly. Emily only half listened to the stark facts. She watched the rain brush gray lines over the city. Days like this, Harry would say the city was being cleansed. Starting over. Fresh. Once he said that Los Angeles is a city of dreams and lies where neither can last forever.

The taller officer called to her. "Ma'am?"

Emily turned her head quickly. "Yes?"

"Anyone need any medical attention? Paramedics?"

"No. Why did you think—"

"It's just a part of any accident report. Right now, I got a '97 Porsche with paper plates skidding on a wet road and ramming a house. No injuries. It's a civil matter between you two and the DMV. Do you have anything to add, ma'am?"

"No, thank you."

Ben cleared his throat. "Actually, it's a '98 Porsche. It's next year's model."

The officer wrote over his notes "Okay. Look, with the rain, we're getting about five times the usual calls, so I wouldn't look for this report for a week or so. Criminal and injury reports have to come first. Here's the case number." He printed on the back of his card, pushed it at Ben, and left quickly.

Emily walked into the narrow lane to survey her home as the police car drove down the hill. Nothing was amiss from this perspective.

She always thought it looked like a postcard of some whitewashed adobe hacienda in old California with burnt orange clay roof tiles. Bougainvillea vines planted in the 1920s now splashed halfway down the hill behind the house. The reds floated above the dense green vines like garnets in the rain. Usually, she struggled to find the right name for the red that changed with the light. Early in the day they were almost the color of Merlot, but later in the day the reds shifted between a Chinese red and a nameless red reserved for Matisse. The bougainvillea was vibrant enough for her to see from the road as she turned up the hill from Sunset Boulevard. It had been her beacon home.

She watched the police car pull to the side of the lane to let a landscaper's white pick-up truck pass. It pulled to the curb above Emily's house and three men jumped out of the cab. Two ran to the back and pulled rolls of black plastic out of the bed of the truck while the driver looked down the hill and pushed his ball cap back on his head. He motioned for the others to hurry and pulled a crate of wooden stakes out of the truck.

Ben trotted out to the truck. The men had pegged the sheeting to the edge of the road and covered the pegs with sandbags by the time Ben got to them. The tow truck driver arrived at the top of the hill and started playing out the chain. He radioed for a flat bed truck to go to the bottom of the hill.

The construction expert came by and wrote notes on a steno pad, took some pictures, and told them to stay off the deck until the city inspected it on Monday.

The tow truck driver slipped on the slush of ice plant under the car as he tried to hook the chain to the car's tow ring. This generated bilingual profanity until Ben yelled, "Hey, we got ladies here. Knock it off."

And then the driver swore specifically at Ben until he finished hooking a long cable to the tow ring at the rear bumper. He jiggled levers on the truck, pulled the car up the hill just enough to get the Porsche's nose pointing down the hill, and then lowered the car to the street below. He gave it over to the driver of the flatbed truck, reeled in the chains, and sped away.

Ben walked her toward her front door and handed her the officer's card with the case number on it. "Here. I've memorized it. It's going to be okay."

"I'm sure it will. It's just the timing...."

Ben tipped his head toward her. "Is this the house the newspapers called the White House?

"Not very inventive, were they?"

At the porch, Ben put his hands on his hips and stared at the house. "Seriously? Is this where the Hollywood writers met? The Red Brigade?"

She huffed as she opened her door. "That was long ago."

Ben held up his hand as though to wave as the door shut. As he turned to walk to the street, a dented blue Mercury sped past him, veered into the short driveway and stopped inches from the garage door. The stocky driver wearing a floral patterned scarf and black raincoat hurried to the trunk and unlocked it while waiving at Ben. "Hey. Lend a hand, will you?"

CHAPTER 3

KEY SIGNATURE

The notation at the start of a musical score that identifies which notes will be sharp or flat.

Ben glanced over his shoulder to see if Ray had followed him onto the porch. Once he realized that the woman was addressing him, he went to the trunk where she was handing bags of hot food to him. "Here, Ray. Glad you were out here to help."

She marched toward the door balancing a pie in a white paper box in her left hand. She opened the door and shouted, "Happy Thanksgiving, everyone. Food's here."

Ben trailed after her with a heavy white bag in each hand.

Susan slid off the barstool and reached for the pie that was now being balanced well over the woman's head. "Here, mom, let me take that."

Ray came out of the kitchen and took a bag from Ben. They hoisted the bulging bags onto the counter.

Susan hugged her mother. "You're early. I want you to meet Ray."

Barbara glared at Ben as she handed him her wet raincoat. "Aren't you marrying my daughter?"

Ben laughed. "Think my wife might object, so it must be him. I'm Ben. A neighbor."

"Glad you men are joining us so it won't be just our usual hen party."

Ben looked embarrassed and shrugged.

Emily nodded. "Please do join us, Ben, if you don't have other plans."

Ben looked at his stocking feet and muddy pants. "If I can change first."

Ray laughed. "Sounds like a deal. We'll wait for you."

Emily called after him. "Just let yourself in, we'll be putting dinner on right away."

Ray grabbed one of the three bottles of chardonnay that Emily had put on the counter and opened it easily. He poured the first of the glasses and handed it to Barbara, who settled into the barstool.

Emily glanced at the bags holding Barbara's traditional Thanksgiving meal as prepared by the upscale market du jour. In the sixties and seventies, Jurgenson's catered it. In the eighties, Gelsons did the honors. This year Bristol Farms won her favor.

Barbara picked up the wine glass, leaned back on the stool as the bounty was arranged on serving dishes and platters by Emily and Susan.

Barbara patted the stool next to her. "Come here, Ray. Let's talk while they do that kitchen thing."

"Sure." Ray poured the other glasses and saw that Barbara's was half empty. "Let me top that off for you."

Barbara took a long sip before surrendering her glass to Ray for a refill.

Ben returned in dark slacks and a black Polo shirt. Without asking, he assumed the Sherpa role of carrying platters to the round oak dining table as fast as Susan and Emily filled them. A pale linen tablecloth covered the table that was devoid of turkey or pilgrim figurines.

Barbara cleared her throat and stared at Ray. "Where did you meet?"

Susan rolled her eyes occasionally as Ray answered every question formally and even managed to smile.

Once the table had been covered with steaming dishes and all were seated, Ray held up his glass to Emily. "Thank you for having us."

The inquisition was in full force by the time that the plates were filled and cranberry sauce and relish tray passed. When the plates were about half empty, the conversation shifted to a discussion of the rain, whether El Niño was a shift in weather or just a name for a wet year. Susan took a slow sip of her wine and relaxed slightly. Barbara moved the conversation from weather to celebrity by recounting the television coverage of the recent funeral of Princess Diana, and news that some banker had just bought O. J. Simpson's house. Her theories on the cause of the crash of Flight 800 forced Ray into the kitchen to start coffee. Susan followed him on the pretext of filling the gravy boat and rolled her eyes.

She whispered, "It's half over."

He pointed to the pie and winked. "A third, if that. Don't let your guard down. She's crafty."

"On your way back, take a look at the picture on the mantel."

"Saw it last night. Spotted Emily easily. You *are* right, you do look alike."

When the conversation turned to repairs of the deck, Barbara expressed skepticism that Emily would be able to manage all the details and contracts to get the deck repaired in time for the wedding. Ben explained how he was taking charge of all repairs.

Pie and coffee consumed, inquisition over, Barbara packed most of the leftovers into Tupperware containers that she had brought in her trunk. Only the carcass for soup, enough white meat for a few sandwiches, and a small wedge of pumpkin pie remained. After Ben loaded everything into her car for her, he thanked Emily again, and walked up Linden Lane to his home.

Emily was banished from the kitchen and roosted on the barstool as Susan and Ray chopped vegetables for the turkey soup. They were gentle with each other. Susan was right to wait for him. They complemented each other.

Once the soup pot was simmering, Ray and Susan migrated to the brown leather sofa, held hands, and chatted with Emily who sank into the chair facing them.

Ray stretched. "After Susan got the grant and a research position at Scripps in La Jolla, I figured I better get a job out here too. There was an opening in bio-med research that was perfect for me, so here we are. Expatriates from New York."

Susan patted his hand and interrupted. "So, since we'll be living together now, we thought it made sense to move up the wedding plans and were hoping to be married here."

"What about your family, Ray? Can they—"

"I'm all that's left."

Susan tapped the arm of the sofa. "New Year's Day would have been perfect. But now—"

Emily stretched casually and rubbed her elbow. She looked out at the deck and began mentally arranging the rental chairs. "New Year's Day? I don't see why not. I'm certain that Ben can marshal his troops to accomplish it. He seems well connected and taking charge of the matter quite properly."

Emily balanced a cup of Darjeeling tea on the arm of the chair. "I'm sure the repairs can be completed in time. Ben has someone coming tomorrow to finish the estimates and then get to work next week on it."

"Good. We need to find a Rabbi. And, I still have a few decisions to make," Susan said, laughing.

"A Rabbi?"

"Yes, Ray is Jewish, and I am converting."

"Really? I had no idea," Emily said, leaning forward.

Susan grinned. "We wanted you to be the first to know."

"Thank you, dear."

Ray patted Susan's hand. "She still can't decide what her name is going to be."

"So many young women are keeping their own name now. Perhaps you could consider a hyphenated last name. I know that's common now—"

Susan waved at her. "No, I need to choose my Hebrew name. You have your regular name in the community, but you also have your formal name within the Temple."

Ray saw Emily frown. "As an example, my name is Raymond at work, but at Temple, I am Avraham ben Moshe. Abraham son of Moses. That was my father's name, Moses."

Susan continued, "Naming is important. Usually it's after a beloved and recently deceased relative. Sometimes for the character trait inferred in a name."

Ray added, "Like Ruth, for loyalty."

Emily smiled at her. "Is that what you are considering? Ruth? That's a lovely name."

"No. Rachel. But I wanted your approval first"

"My approval?"

"And your help." She pointed at the photo on the mantel. "Rachel and Isaac were dear friends to you and grandpa. I know that they died in the war. Even though you rarely talked about her, I know that she is important to our family. I want to honor that friendship."

"I don't see what there is for me to...."

"Gram. I need you to think back. Can you remember her Hebrew name?"

Emily was silent for a moment and took a longer than usual sip of tea. "I know that when we met in Geneva, she pronounced her name different than I had heard it before. It wasn't Rachel, like we say in English, like 'Ray Chill'," Emily said very slowly and distinctly. It was more like 'Ruck El', yes, that was how she said it. After that, we just used the English pronunciation, is that what you mean, dear?"

"Partly. Did you know the rest of her name?"

"Her last name?"

Susan went to Emily and put her hand on Emily's shoulder. "No, her father's first name."

Emily looked puzzled. "Why? Why do you need to know that?"

"Because, men take their father's name as a part of their religious name, so do women. Rather than a 'ben' there is a 'bat' between the name of the girl and her father's name. Since my father was not Jewish, I want to adopt Rachel's name and that of her father. A tribute. But I don't know his name."

"Let me think." Emily tapped the fingers of her left hand on the wooden arm of the chair.

"Of course. Take your time, Gram," Susan said, returning to the sofa next to Ray. "No more on this tonight."

"So, is that the last step in your conversion? The name?" Emily asked, with new energy.

"Conversion is not a one-time event, it is a lifetime process. I have been studying and discovered that the kosher laws are less complex than some of mother's diets, and Hebrew is easier than my high school Spanish class," Susan joked. Then she continued seriously, "After real study, for almost two years, I have been in the last of my discussions with Ray's Rabbi for months. This is adding a new dimension, a new depth to my life. And what I did not understand initially is that my conversion is not a denial of my prior life. We believe that there are many paths to one God."

"I see."

"In mid-December, I'm going back to New York to appear before a panel of three Rabbis. They will ask me questions about the responsibilities of the Jewish law, and my intent to fulfill them."

"An exam?"

"More about my commitment than a quiz. Then after their approval, I take a special bath, a *mikvah*. A rebirth with my new name." Ray blinked and tried to hide a yawn.

Emily shooed them with her hand. "It is late. We'll continue this tomorrow. You two get some sleep. I'll be reading for a bit."

Susan hugged Emily and held her hand out to hoist Ray from the sofa.

"Good night, Emily. Thank you for a wonderful day," Ray said as he took Susan's hand and they went down the stairs to the guest room.

Just after nine, the sound of leather shoes scuffing on the flagstone walkway to the front door caught her attention even before the soft knock on the door.

She looked up from the sofa through the narrow panels of leaded glass that bordered the heavy carved oak door. She recognized her neighbor's stocky frame immediately. She wondered why he was at the door again. Folding the back flap of the book's dust jacket to mark her place in the novel, she went to the door.

When Emily opened the door, Ben stood there silently. His hair was mussed, and his collar was half out of his unzipped jacket. "What is it, Ben? Are you feeling ill?"

He ran his hand through his hair. "I'm sorry, but I couldn't sleep and saw your light was still on."

"Couldn't it wait until—"

"Not really." He stood there frowning and gesturing as though looking for an answer. She opened the door.

Ben walked past her to the fireplace and looked at the silver framed black and white photograph on the mantel.

Two men and two women in their early twenties smiled. The men wore dark RAF uniforms. Each had a flat cap folded and slipped under the epaulet on the left shoulder. The men had their dark hair cut so close that it looked shaved above their ears. Both men wore yarmulkes on their heads, almost invisibly. Ben did not touch the framed picture, but he leaned his hand upon the mantel. He looked at her and back at the photograph. "It looks so like you. It could've been taken five years ago, not fifty." His tone was factual, not flattery.

"Almost sixty years ago. January of 1940. Surprised it hasn't turned to dust after all these years."

She expected a comment from him. When people saw the photo they usually said that she looked the same. To this she would simply say thank you. When they commented that she and the other woman looked so much alike. Emily would either ask if they really thought so, or say that everyone looked alike in that awful pageboy haircut. Gray hair was a relief and an escape from the Henna rinse she used when Barbara was young. She had stopped trying to look like her passport picture after Barbara went to college.

Ben said, "I can't tell you how really sorry I am. I just feel terrible."

"Yes, I know you do. But, all of this can be repaired."

Perspiration was glistening on his forehead. "It's not about the deck. It's…."

"Why don't you sit down?" She motioned for him to sit on the sofa where she had been reading. She stood looking at him. He glanced away from her, toward the door.

"Something happened at the office today. I went in after I left here." Ben was looking at his hands and not at her.

"At your law office? Today?"

"Yes. Let me back up. I told you that I work for a law firm. In a firm as large and diverse as ours, we have a section of the office that reviews each client, as well as our personal investments, to be certain that we do not violate any ethical requirements that create a conflict of interest. What I mean to say is that we want to be certain that I don't represent you in a matter in which someone else in my law firm is representing the other side. That's the easiest example, but it can get fairly complex."

She put up her hand to stop him. "I have no idea what you are talking about. Slow down. Would you like a glass of wine with me?"

He nodded. She went to the refrigerator and withdrew the bottle of Chardonnay left from earlier that day. With that in her left hand, she picked up two glasses in her right and went to the oak and glass coffee table in front of the sofa. "Please pour us both a glass."

Ben pulled the cork and poured remarkably equal amounts of pale wine into the large thin globes of glass. He took a large sip. "Well, when I opened a file in my name for damages to your home, I ran your name on our database."

"Why would you have any records on me?"

"We run everyone against our client files, even a web and newspaper search."

"Why ever would you do that?"

"To be sure we can legally represent you. I want to fix this mess without putting my firm at risk or compromising your interests." Ben looked exasperated. "We need to be fair. That's why I need to ask you who your attorney is."

"My what?"

"You're on the list. So I thought that you might already have an attorney who I should be—"

"What list?"

CHAPTER 4

CHROMATIC

The musical scale that moves in half steps.

Ben took another sip of his wine and let its cold bite shiver through him while he gathered his thoughts. He put the glass on the table and leaned forward. She sat crisply upright and returned his stare.

Ben looked at her with amazement. "What list? Don't you know about the dormant Swiss accounts?"

"The what?"

"I figured that you'd seen the notices in the paper." He sighed while deciding where to start. "Some Swiss banks have been actively concealing accounts from owners or their heirs since the war." Ben looked at her to be sure she was following him.

She shrugged. "Wouldn't the money just go to the state, like unclaimed bank accounts here? I have seen *those* notices in the paper about accounts, safe deposit boxes and stock certificates."

"It's different there. American banks are federally chartered. Most Swiss banks are privately held. They don't have to report dormant accounts to anyone. They kept rolling the interest from these accounts into the bank's profit calculations and using the cash as their own since nobody was going to claim it."

"And you believe I have such an account?"

"Yes, my wife is working on the claims against the banks. *Pro bono* for the firm. I know the Swiss Bankers' Association published the list of dormant accounts in July and again in October of this year. That's the list I'm talking about."

"Well, I still don't recall seeing it."

Ben swept his palm across his forehead. "It was on the news. In papers. It's on the Internet." He slapped his knee. "How could you have missed it? You are not like the sort of fuzzy old people at the home in Fairfax where Ellen volunteers."

"Thank you." Emily raised an eyebrow.

Ben ignored her and continued, "Account holders only have until January to file claims. It's usually the account of their parent or grandparent. Sometimes it's an aunt or uncle whose account can be claimed."

"Still, what does that have to do with me?" Emily heard her pulse pounding in her ears and wondered if her face was flushing.

"A lot of the accounts were opened by Jews before the war. I guess I might have assumed that you were Jewish from the picture on the mantel." He motioned toward the photo. "Aren't they wearing yarmulkes?"

"Of course. We were at a Jewish wedding. The strapping lad in the photo is my husband, Harry. He stood up with his friend, Isaac Brod. They were in the RAF together. Harry and I were married much later. That's Yitzhak's…" She paused a moment. "Yes, that was his real name, his Hebrew name, not Isaac like we called him in England. That was Yitzhak's wedding, not Harry's. He married Rachel Havel in a Jewish ceremony." She stared at the photo across the room and felt her gaze blur.

"Emily?"

She blinked and turned to Ben. "Yes?"

"There is a bank account with your name on it that has been earning interest for almost fifty years. The bank never contacted you, even though you're famous. There is a small fortune waiting for you."

"That can't be."

Ben stared at her and his voice went deeper. "It is."

"I'm sure I would know if I had opened an account there."

"But here's the thing. Some of the dormant accounts were family or business accounts whose owners died and the heirs are trying to prove ownership with the few documents they have. Most of the accounts were opened by men who died in concentration camps. The banks required a death certificate to release funds. You see the game."

"I'm certain that there must be some confusion. I did live in

Switzerland when I was at the music conservatory before the war. That was in 1937 and 1938. I was in London by '39. I'm certain that this can't relate to me in any way." She was holding the wine glass in her right hand, cupped so the stem fell loosely between her middle and ring fingers. She never held a glass in her left hand. Not the hand for fingering the strings on her violin. She leaned back and let her elbow rest on the arm of the chair and her forearm float in the air. To the casual observer, she would have appeared calm.

But he was not the casual observer. He watched her hand tremble. He saw ripples in the wine. He knew she was not telling him the truth. But he did not know which part was the lie. "But you were married before the war ended?" Ben wanted the question to sound conversational, but it sounded more like a deposition than a cocktail party.

"In London, 1944." She turned back to him, "Now that you make me think about my time in Switzerland, perhaps I may have forgotten a few Swiss Francs in my account when I left school. But not under my married name."

"I told you, it's not just a few francs," Ben snapped.

"It could not be much, when I left the music conservatory with...." She felt the room getting smaller. She stared at the black and white photograph on the mantel, the small silver frame floating above the dark wood. All she saw was the frame. She started to take a sip of her wine and stopped with the glass at her lips.

"Your father opened it for you," Ben said abruptly. "You're listed as Emily Finch Montgomery. Don't you understand what I'm telling you, Mrs. Montgomery?"

Emily balanced her glass on the arm of the chair as she got up, turned on the stereo, and snapped a new CD out of its jewel case, into the flat tray on the CD player. She pushed three buttons and music filled the room. She turned the volume down after remembering that Susan and Ray were sleeping.

Her music had the structure that allowed her to evade the demons of loss and loneliness. She knew that she could practice and that the sound of her music and the demands of her perfection could silence the voices whispering of loss. She thought once that the form and rigor of her practice was like the plaster cast she had on her ankle after that one skiing episode. Emily still found support in the rigor of practice and in listening to music with a critic's ear. It was the cast on her pain. Her escape. Her form in a formless world. She studied the CD case.

Ben walked toward her. "I'm sorry if I upset you. Maybe I should go."

Turning the CD case over, she nodded.

"Tomorrow? May I come back tomorrow?"

"Why?"

"This is not finished, just because it is uncomfortable for both of us."

She turned over the case and tossed it onto the table by the door. "Call. After six. We'll see."

Ben let himself out the front door and then pulled on the door to confirm that it was locked. She turned and smiled at the photograph on the mantel, paced to it and picked up the frame. She whispered their names. "Emily, Harry, Rachel, Yitzhak. My God, how young we were." She could almost hear the hiss of the flashbulb when Graham took that picture long ago and taste the lemon cake from the reception.

She put the photograph back on the mantel and knew that tomorrow she would send Susan and Ray to the Hotel del Coronado, if they had a vacancy. A little holiday in San Diego while she discovered what Ben really knew about her.

CHAPTER 5

TIME SIGNATURE

The two numbers at the start of a line of music. The top number indicates how many beats per measure. The bottom number indicates which note value receives the one beat.

Friday began with a dull overcast carpet of clouds, which was just enough to wake Emily from a restless sleep. After tying the cord on her white terrycloth robe, she padded upstairs barefoot. Once the kettle was on the fire, she picked up the portable telephone on the kitchen counter, called the Hotel del Coronado, and booked a room overlooking the ocean for two weeks. That would give her guests time to look for an apartment in San Diego and her time to manage the repairs and try to understand Ben. She opened the door to the deck and looked over her city. After a deep breath of the fresh air, she went into her music room, picked up her spare reading glasses from the music stand, and stood by the window.

The music room had the best view of the lights of Los Angeles at night, particularly after a rain had polished the city to its winter shimmer. She let her glasses dangle in her fingertips as she watched the city awaken. The moment when night gave way to day, that was the transition which she loved as much as her friends loved watching a great sunset from her deck. This was her time, when night faded and the hard relief of the day arrived.

If she were a painter, the room would have been her studio. Because she was a violinist, it was her music room. Bookshelves held those musical scores that were bound as books. A cabinet with large long drawers had been built under the window to hold unbound musical scores flat. The room was six inches smaller in each dimension than when she and Harry bought the home. She insisted that it be insulated so that she could practice at any time of the day or night without waking Barbara, who was a small child then, or disturbing Harry or their few neighbors. A love seat sat under the window. A good bright light and a sturdy music stand dominated the center of the room.

She thought that Harry's insistence on having that room air-conditioned was overly extravagant when they first remodeled the room. But, immediately, she saw that he was right. The control of temperature and humidity allowed a consistency of her practice and reliability of her instruments. And then, after she began playing with the Los Angeles Philharmonic, there were occasions in which she would be playing one of the three Stradivarius violins that the Philharmonic owned, including the one that Jack Benny had left the orchestra in his will.

It was so unusual, she thought. They would simply hand her the violin in a hard shell case, have her sign that she had received it, and walk her to her car. The first night that this happened she was certain that she was followed home.

Of course, she wasn't.

After that, she asked the Philharmonic to transport it. That's when Harry had the closet in that room fitted with a tall safe. He told the installer that he went hunting in Wyoming every year and that he wanted a good gun safe. He said he didn't want to be shot with his own ammunition if there were a fire in the house. The workmen laughed at his vision of such an event, and had no idea that the safe would routinely hold a million-dollar violin.

Today, the safe did not hold a Stradivarius. It held the violin made in Prague to finger and sound like a Strad. This was the violin that Emily would not let others play. Three leather bound journals sat on the shelf above it. Four other violins were in the safe as well. They were there for convenience, not security. There wasn't any jewelry. She had sold her good jewelry when her daughter was in the hospital with pneumonia after Harry was blacklisted.

There were two small oils that Harry had painted that year. These landscapes were hung in the living room. California Impressionism. She would put them in the safe if she were leaving the city for an extended trip. "For their value, not their cost," she would tease Harry. She wanted the paintings secure if there were another wildfire in the hills like that one year when she thought they had lost the house.

The kettle began its faint whistle. She dashed to pull it from the burner before its wail woke her guests. She warmed the teapot, emptied it, and started steeping a full pot of tea. As she walked back to the music room, she noticed the empty wine glasses on the coffee table. She could not remember ever leaving glasses out like that. Ever. They were always put in the kitchen, to the right of the sink. Glasses did not get washed until morning. Washing a wine glass after a late evening was a good way to get a cut hand, and a cut hand could end her playing. It was a simple rule. Inflexible. Non-negotiable.

She picked up the wine glasses, washed and dried them quickly.

Taking her tea to the music room, she sat on the love seat. Not formally, with her feet on the ground as she had done in the living room. In her room, she was herself. Softer. She snuggled securely into the corner of the love seat, with her feet tucked under her. She took a very small sip of tea, testing the temperature, and set it down. She seemed less angular now.

She turned to inspect her city. She knew the names of the streets in Hollywood that matched those patterns of delicate webbing into the distance. She knew where the valley began and where the edge of her world touched the Pacific Ocean. Which amber light was gas burning off in a Long Beach refinery and which blue-white glow was the parking lot at the K-Mart in Lakewood.

Downtown was harder to locate now. In the fifties and sixties, it was so simple with the Richfield Tower glowing amber on top at night and shining gold and black in the day. Not subtle, but an effective symbol of black gold. Now, Richfield was ARCO. Its building was gone, replaced by the ARCO Plaza. The skyline was crowded with glassy shining buildings looking too similar on a bright day. She pulled the small crocheted blanket from the back of the love seat and let it fall on her lap. It wasn't that she was cold, she just felt alone.

The cool of the morning came in and freshened her view of the day. Then, a small dark figure appeared on the window ledge by her arm. Almost a hundred feet above the ice plant, the window had a panoramic view but terrified window washers. However, it failed to impress Bernard, the cat who had adopted her. She said that she never liked cats, and in truth she never did, but Bernard was different. He was stout with a white muzzle that contrasted sharply to his black coat.

He was aloof and predictable for his breakfast meeting, whether or not he ate. But he never came for dinner. Some days she would see him working the ice plant like some miniature panther. Bounding through his six-inch high jungle. Getting a mouse now and then. She respected his independence.

Yet, there was something between them. She knew when he was going to arrive. He seemed to know that his robust yowl or his seductive meow outside the window would bring their meeting. If she were in that room, they would rendezvous briefly on the deck, never in the house. What he could not know was that meow was silent. A voice not heard inside the insulated room with the double glass. It was his presence, not his voice that called her.

Sometimes Emily wondered about the sounds that were held in, of her own silent cry to the world. She laughed at herself, tossed back the lap robe and went to the refrigerator. What today? Milk. Just a saucer of milk. No leftover salmon. A cereal bowl with a few ounces of milk. That was their bargain. A bowl that she pushed out to the deck that she could not enter.

She never leaned down to pet him. He never rubbed against her leg or fawned over her. Once she started to pet him. He hissed and disappeared for three long days.

He was wild. She had her doubts about civilization as well. He ate, cleaned and left, his simple presence being thanks enough, they both thought.

The city was stretching now. She went back to the music room intending to read a journal, but worried that her guests might wake early and interrupt her reading, so she left her three journals in the safe. Emily leaned back into the love seat and let Geneva swirl around in her mind, without the structure of the inked words. She shook her head when she thought that over a half a century had passed since they were written.

Spring seemed to come early in 1938 as Rachel packed and re-packed her two suitcases for the conservatory. The breeze was light and sweet from the river. The weather was what Rachel's mother called 'the teasing of the northern spring'. The ice over the river had snapped a few weeks before during a short warm spell. First, there was the moaning of the frozen ice over the river. Then, it broke with one sharp crack that echoed between the buildings like a cannon shot that was heard all the way to the town square, six blocks away. For days, there was the grinding of ice against ice, cracking, snarling, twisting free. The sound was like a train coming at full speed into the station, all rumbles and echoes and power.

After Rachel's train left for Geneva, the charcoal ceiling of clouds pressed down on the city again and delayed the promise of flowers. Eager eyes looking to the hills outside of the city for crocus or daffodil or fresh green buds on the trees were disappointed at the delay.

At the station in Geneva, Rachel discovered a slim English woman holding a small paper on which Rachel's name had been neatly printed in grease pencil, She also held a violin case. Emily introduced herself as the other tenant at Madam Bernard's home. Emily took one of the two small suitcases and they walked the ten blocks to Rachel's new home.

From a distance, they looked alike. Late teens, dark hair, slim figures, conservative clothing, sturdy oxfords for walking the cobble-stone streets, white anklets turned down once, and a violin case in hand. Further inspection would reveal that Rachel was slightly taller; Emily had auburn hair that went to copper in the summer and was almost red in the winter when her skin paled. Rachel's hair was almost coal black.

Emily's eyes were the slightly lighter brown, milk chocolate, while Rachel's were dark chocolate. Both had similar fair skin, pale complexion with the tendency toward a blush of pink after walking in the cool air. And both were the only children of loving families, doted on by their parents and each longing for a younger sister.

After discovering their similarities, they were shocked by their differences. Rachel spoke a dozen languages well enough to converse with any of her father's customers from all over Europe, although she had not traveled away from Prague for more than a few weeks of her entire life.

By contrast, Emily spoke French poorly, Spanish worse, and had failed her German exam in spite of traveling summers and holidays with her parents either on vacation or during the tours that the London Philharmonic scheduled for music competitions and celebrations.

Rachel was quite familiar with English, so their first decision as friends was to speak English while together.

They enjoyed the discovery that each was an only child and that they had been born within a week of each other in the Women's Hospital in Prague. It was the spring music festival that brought Mr. Finch to Prague as a violinist with the London Philharmonic. Anticipating that their child would be born three weeks after the festival concluded, Mrs. Finch joined her husband on the tour. Emily was early. Rachel was late.

Then they discovered the contrasts in their lives. Emily's family had, on her father's side, been English since the Crusades; however, her mother's family had emigrated from Russia a few years before the Revolution in 1917. Both Rachel's mother and father traced their heritage to the city of Prague, inside or outside the wall of the city, depending on the politics of the time.

Emily shook away the memories and returned to the kitchen and refreshed her tea. As she made muffins from a box, she planned how to send Susan and Ray away. Once the muffins were in the oven, she quickly tugged on black slacks, loafers and a heavy Irish fisherman's sweater.

Over breakfast, she told them about the vacation she had arranged for them at the Hotel del Coronado while she supervised the repairs. Ray declined her offer of her car and called Hertz. An hour later, a rental car was delivered to Emily's driveway. Ray signed the paperwork and loaded their bags.

After the tan Ford left, Emily watched three men replanting the ice plant. The stocky men in green gardening uniforms each balanced a flat of plants against the steep hill. They were planting small plugs of ice plant and then moving over six inches to do it again and again until the raw swath was regaining its richness and the dark earth was spattered with green. Their silence and swift completion was a stark contrast to the incessant whine and snarl of the power tools as a truck-load of lumber was shaped to temporarily brace the timbers that held up the corner of the deck. Ben had come home between meetings and walked down the road to where the men were planting. She walked up to him.

He grinned as he loosened his dark blue tie and then shoved his hands deep into the pockets of his suit pants. "It'll be as good as new."

She put her hands on her hips as she watched the planting. "Sometimes, you don't want new, or something 'as good as' anything. You just want time to stand still. But you're too young to know that."

He chuckled. "Glad you're still talking to me."

"You were very upsetting last night. Going back to that time—"

"There are times I want to avoid and others I'd like to be able to put on 'freeze frame' like a video movie and savor."

Emily turned and looked at Ben. "When?"

"When I'm with Ellen. Or the end of a big merger. That's what I do at the firm, M & A. That's mergers and acquisitions. Financial companies mostly. I was a CPA before I went to law school. That's why I volunteered to work with my wife on the Swiss banking case."

"Don't you have clients?"

"My clients are companies, not people-- that's why I volunteered. So did Ellen. She's on half salary for the year. The firm has a strong commitment to do some *pro bono* work. Volunteering. *Pro bono publico.*"

She recalled her Latin from school. "For the public good."

"Right. I put in most of my research time at home on the Internet and have some investigator's time that I get to use at work. I go to the nursing homes in Fairfax and senior centers to tell people about it. In case others missed the notices. Some don't read English. Some just don't read anymore."

"Why get involved in it?"

Ben took her question seriously. "*Tikkun olam.*"

"Excuse me?" Emily leaned forward as though she had not heard him.

"It means 'repairing the world'. Ellen and I think our law practices are a small way to meet that ethical requirement of our faith. It's our world. If it breaks, we need to repair it. Get it right again. Make it better, if we can, in spite of all the lawyer jokes."

Emily looked away, thinking, feeling those words. She looked back at Ben. "I wanted to ask you something. Over Thanksgiving dinner, when we were all talking about our special moments, what we were thankful for. There was a lot of chatter from my family, and Ray. But I never heard you say what you were thankful for."

"Ellen. Any day with her. " Ben laughed at himself. "Can I miss her this much when she's only out of town for a couple weeks? Go figure. I sound like a newly married guy."

"How long?"

"Almost eight years."

"Good for you. That's nice to see."

"You'll love her. She's just a wonderful person." Ben opened the door of his wife's conservative sedan. "Well, I'd better get back to my contract reviews. Just wanted to see how it was going. See you later?" He smiled when Emily nodded.

"Ben?" He turned.

"I'm about to have some tea. Join me? There are leftover muffins."

"Sure."

Emily brewed tea and Ben had a glass of milk with his muffin. He stared at his empty plate, pushing the few crumbs around with the edge of his fork. He was not ready to leave yet not quite ready to talk.

Ben rested the fork on the plate. "I've been thinking about what you must have gone through in the war. I feel that I'm not making your life any easier by talking about this. About the accounts."

"Geneva was beautiful then. So was London. Those were exciting times. Intense times. And at the end, sad times."

"Are you going to file?"

"File?"

"File for the return of your account. We're working on the voluntary return agreement, although there is a class action lawsuit in the Federal District Court for the Eastern District of New York to force recovery."

"I don't know, yet."

"I don't understand why you're hesitating. Why you don't want your own money?"

Emily was quiet for a long time and then looked at him. "I don't know if I can go back. I don't know if I trust myself to let that time become real again."

"I'm sorry about all this. I didn't want to intrude on your visit with your granddaughter and—"

"I've sent them off on a holiday to San Diego while the repairs go on here. I'm not certain that I'm very good company just now."

Emily stood up and stacked the plates on each other and balanced the forks on the top plate. She went to the kitchen sink, pulled up the handle on the faucet and let the water rush over the plates long after the few crumbs were gone. Ben brought the milk glass into the kitchen and set it on the counter beside her. Emily gazed into the rushing water, ignoring him.

"I'm here if you want to talk." Ben turned and let himself out the front door.

When the house was again silent, she checked the lock, and went to her music room. She sat and slowly opened the journal. The scent of old leather and paper rose to her. She inhaled slowly and closed her eyes. Something in the scent stopped her, like testing a newly opened bottle of wine for familiarity, waiting for the scent to seduce you. It was there, the tartness. Perhaps it was the ink. Perhaps it was the leather, which was well worn. That was it. Almost acidic. Maybe it was the aroma of time.

She read the words that she had written when she was another person. She read each of the journals and the handful of letters that she had slipped into the journals over the years. After locking the safe, she went for a brisk walk in the late morning after her tai chi and thought of who she was and who she had been. She saw herself as a schoolgirl again, sharing music, and discovering a new world.

After her exercise, she drew a bath and thought of when she was a child. There were oven-warmed towels in the winter after her bath. She remembered her mother wrapping her in rough white towels.

SHARON O. LIGHTHOLDER

One towel was for her thick hair, one for her body, and then she was tucked into bed to dry. She loved those moments. Her mother always sat with her when she was a small child and told stories to keep her quiet. But she only half listened. She would imagine playing her violin, visualize playing, feel the pressure of the strings against her fingers, and coordinate bow movement to note changes in her mind. And so, mother and daughter were together until her thick hair dried and her mother braided it. These were the moments she called back to herself when the world became too close or the speed of life too fast, or the world too much.

Occasionally, she would try to replicate that moment by bringing towels hot from the dryer to the bathroom just before she showered. Soft, thick, bath sheets. Luxury. When she would wrap in them and go back to bed, she never slept. She used those moments of perfect peace to focus on her music or her daughter's latest challenge during her teen-age years, or the progress of one of her students.

Emily turned off the tap and tossed fresh towels into the dryer. She retrieved the hot towels after a few minutes, filled the tub, and had a long soak. She cocooned in the warm towels, but without the usual feeling of calm or focus. Warm and dry. Safe and sound. She knew all this at some adult level. However, she still had the old feeling, just behind her throat, like a shout that was about to find its way out or that haunting feeling she'd have if she were going to be ill. She had not named it fear, but knew that was the feeling. She had last felt it years before, when she was at the Department of Motor Vehicles for Barbara's first driving test. She shoved the feeling away. As she pulled on the heavy fisherman's sweater and dark slacks again, she thought of a day in Geneva. It was always the same day.

CHAPTER 6

DOLCE

Sweet. The instruction to play sweetly.

Geneva was always pewter and silver in her memory. The old stone city glistened after a spring or summer rain. The cobblestones were rounded and worn over centuries into slippery ruts by the wooden wheels of a thousand carts. In winter, the soft white of snow muffled sounds in the city. It was a city of stone and water.

Only when she recalled a specific event would color become a part of her memory. The color of the lake was her measure of the season. Ink blue water in spring. Blue-black water in winter. Light green on the calmest of summer days when the fountain in the lake, the *Jet d'Eau* near Rue de la Clef, shot a jet of water a hundred meters into the thin pale sky. When the light breeze fanned the spray, the sun spun the water droplets into a rainbow full of intense color. Then a pushcart of Italian frozen ices appeared in summer near the lake.

The room where she lived was embedded deep in a house that had been built of square gray granite blocks before Columbus had received his charter and sailed from Portugal. In the last week of the First World War, Madame Bernard was widowed. Within a month she had converted the bedroom and sitting room on the second floor into two bedrooms with a small bathroom squeezed between them. This provided the rental income allowing Madame Bernard to pretend that she was still wealthy while she lived in the maid's quarters adjoining the spacious kitchen.

The street level had a formal sitting room. An elaborately carved dark wood frame surrounded the worn red velvet of the Victorian settee and side chairs. A white oval of milky marble topped a tea table with a dark pedestal growing out of four carved lion paws. A dried flower arrangement in a small silver bowl sat centered on the marble and collected dust.

Past the sitting room, through a dark door was the large square kitchen. Through the kitchen, there was a small inner courtyard shared with the surrounding homes. Passage through the kitchen to the courtyard was allowed. Making a cup of tea or coffee was allowed. Lingering or cooking was not.

She remembered the rich scent of baguettes fresh from the bakery every afternoon just as she returned from the conservatory. After putting her wet coat on the peg under the stairway, she would greet Madame Bernard in the kitchen, and practice until Madam Bernard announced dinner.

From the street, the homes shared common walls and created a solid gray fortress against the world. The inner courtyard was a relaxed area, paved with flagstones, gone green from years of moss and rain. Around the edges of the courtyard there were clay pots that held a variety of herbs and other larger terra cotta clay pots that held geraniums that seemed to maintain their deep red and orange flowers into the fall.

Within weeks of meeting, Rachel and Emily had developed a pattern as predictable as their attire at the conservatory, which required a light blouse with dark skirt and jacket or sweater. It was as though one had to be at the ready for a concert at any moment. While it did little for Emily's sense of style, it simplified Rachel's life by allowing her limited wardrobe to suffice.

Rachel was usually at practice in her room by the time Emily returned. When the front door rattled and opened with a small crash. Rachel would put down her white horsehair bow, go to the top of the stairs, and stand impatiently as Emily took off her coat, shoved her black kid gloves into a pocket of the heavy wool coat and tossed her gray woolen muffler over the peg. She would turn and give a smile that erased the concern over the crash of the front door into the wall.

Madame Bernard would rattle pans in the kitchen for a bit and then the teakettle would start its slow warble.

Emily would inevitably call down the stairs. "Is that water for tea?"

Madame Bernard would call back. "Soon, soon."

Rachel waited for Emily. "How was your lesson this afternoon?"

Emily shared each and every private violin lesson with Rachel. Emily stretched her neck and rubbed her hands together. "Elliott knows so many small tricks that help so very much in the management of the tremolo."

"Tremolo? I thought we were working on that in a week or so, after the holiday."

"We will, but Elliott wanted to show me a few things to practice."

Rachel begged. "Will you show me?"

Emily shed her dark brown sweater and pulled on a red cable-knit pullover sweater. "Certainly. Like my father said, 'good, better, best; better than all the rest'. That's you, isn't it? You want to be better than all the rest, don't you?"

Rachel blushed. "I want to do my best."

Emily opened her violin case. "You've already surpassed the rest of the class; haven't you noticed that yet?"

"No. No, I still have a much to learn."

"There is no article, there is no 'a' in that sentence. English would say 'I have a great deal to learn, or 'much to learn' but not 'a much to learn'."

"Thank you. Do you ever think I will master this language?"

"No. But then, no one ever has. Even Shakespeare had to make up words and new phrases."

Tea was always delivered during their afternoon practice.

Madame Bernard was a short, wide woman who walked as much from side to side as forward. Emily first thought of her as a metronome, ticking away, making progress at her unique pace. But then she decided that Madame Bernard was a living version of the great round pendulum that ticked off time in the grandfather clock in the living room… although its polished brass was in deep contrast to Madame Bernard's dull monochrome of black dresses and aprons and white hair pulled into a tight bun at the back of her neck.

Emily pushed her sheet music aside and cleared the small oak table in the sitting room upstairs when she heard the click of Madame

Bernard's heels against the plank floor become a small scuffing as she rocked slowly up the carpeted stairs, balancing a tray with a silver teapot, milk pitcher and two cups.

"How went your lesson today?" asked Madame Bernard as she set down the tray. She was interested in a few simple courtesies and rather hoped that the girls didn't really answer her. She was a landlord, not a mother, to her tenants.

"Good. I learned a few things I want to show Rachel after dinner tonight," Emily said, offering to pour the tea by her gestures. Madame Bernard told them that she was meeting a friend of hers for the evening, not making dinner for Emily and Rachel, and that tonight she would treat them to a dinner at *Les Armures* or at Landault's.

Emily knew Geneva's restaurants better than Rachel and took the lead. "I know that you've been to *Les Armures*. The armor maker. Remember, it had the suit of armor in the dining room. We had fondue, that pot of melted cheese that we ate with the bread cubes on those skinny forks. Landault's restaurant is near the University. They have raclette."

"What's that?" Rachel asked.

Emily decided for them with a smile. She told Madame Bernard, "We'll go to Landault's. She must experience their raclette."

Although Landault's had the standard restaurant fare of veal cutlets and fried potatoes cut into slim matchsticks, and carafes of local wine, it was renowned for its raclette which Emily thought of as cheese fondue on a plate.

When they arrived just before eight, Landault's was almost full. Rachel glanced around the open, bright restaurant with brass chandeliers suspended by chains, almost fifty feet above the diners. The light was bright enough for students to read by during meals but not glaring. Most tables had four or six small bistro chairs. There was a bank of dark wood framed booths each of which held four diners. Deep burgundy leather covered the comfortable seats, and hard wood was at the back of these booths that lined the right and left walls of the restaurant as you entered through the double door with the etched glass. The tables did not have tablecloths on them, but were covered with slick white paper, similar to what the butcher would use to wrap meat.

As they took off their wet coats in the entryway, one of the waiters motioned them to the one empty booth. Once their coats were on the brass hook of the dark wood timbers separating the booths, they slid in, facing each other. The waiter arrived promptly, holding menus but not offering them. "Do you wish to order from the menu or have raclette?"

Emily took charge and ordered a carafe of a local white wine and said they would both have raclette. The waiter nodded crisply and disappeared only to return moments later with the liter carafe of wine and two glasses on a silver tray, high over his head. As he set the tray down on the edge of the table, Rachel saw that it also held a white bowl of small steaming red potatoes, a chilled bowl of small pickled white onions and small knobby pickles the size of her little finger.

"Are those really pickles? They are so small."

"Yes, called cornichons," Emily whispered. Without looking at her, the waiter also slid a basket of thinly sliced baguette rounds and a plate of thin slices of ham across the slick paper covering the table.

Rachel looked confused, as there were no plates for the food. Emily told her to look behind her, to the rear of the restaurant, where she saw three large half wheels of pale cheese held on iron racks. Each wheel was the size of an auto tire. The cut face of the wheel of cheese was facing the open fire and softening, just before melting. With each order, the waiter would roll back the half wheel of cheese, run the back of a long chef's knife against the melted face of the wheel. The melted cheese then filled a large white dinner plate, which had been heated by the fire as well. Plates of melted cheese, still steaming in the moist chill of the restaurant, were rushed to the table and placed before the diner. Their waiter brought their steaming white dinner plates from the open kitchen so quickly that the cheese was almost soupy. Without comment, the waiter took a black grease pencil from his black apron and made two slash marks on the paper covering the table before rushing back to the kitchen.

"Enjoy!" Emily said, scooping up the melted cheese on a round of bread. "Or you can get a bit of the melted cheese with your fork with a bit of a potato. I like to nibble the onions or cornichons by hand or put them on the plate and eat them with a knife and fork."

Both Emily and Rachel ate the hot cheese with bread and potato at first, then sipped wine. Rachel left her knife and fork on the rim of the plate. The waiter quickly removed Emily's plate, replaced it with another plate of cheese, and made another mark on the paper covering the table.

Rachel looked after him with some confusion. "Why didn't I get one?"

Emily looked at Rachel's plate and laughed softly. "I seem to have neglected to mention that when you are finished with one plate of raclette, if you place your knife and fork beside the plate, the waiter knows that you are ready for another. Silver on the plate means you do not desire anymore."

"But I do." Rachel quickly removed the silverware from her plate. Before she had finished her next sip of wine, a new plate of raclette arrived. With each delivery, the waiter made a mark on the paper.

Soon, the four strikes had one across them and a sixth mark stood alone. Tallying was transformed from random marks to Roman numerals.

As they finished the next plate of cheese, Emily teased Rachel about leaving her utensils on the plate. The more Emily smiled, the more embarrassed Rachel became.

She folded her napkin, as though to leave. "Do you enjoy my embarrassment?"

"No! That's not it at all. I was remembering how silly I felt my first time eating here."

Rachel lowered her voice. "Are you trying to confuse me or make me feel…I don't know how to say it…lesser? So I won't get a chair in the orchestra?"

"Inferior?" Emily laughed, "Not you. I know that there are only so many chairs in the orchestra and that not all of the students are going to be offered them. But we will."

"How can you be so sure?"

Emily pointed to her napkin. "Put that back on your lap. We haven't finished. Rachel, you must know that no one can play better than you can. I play well enough to compete, thanks in part to my tutor, but you are so far above the rest of us!"

Rachel leaned back against the booth. "How can that be?"

"You never took lessons with others. You were competing against yourself, and adults when you were a child. Your technique now is already world class, you just don't know it."

"Then you aren't trying to run against me?"

"Heavens no. I hope we can be good friends and play in the orchestra together."

Emily motioned toward the plate of paper-thin ham, which had been fanned like a deck of playing cards. "You haven't tried any."

"Is that ham?"

Emily nodded. "It's almost like prosciutto, you really should try some."

"From pork?" Rachel asked.

"Technically, it would be from a pig or swine. Pork is the type of meat that comes from the animal that is called a pig when it is small or a swine when it is large." Emily said with complete patience, as though she had also just discovered the complexity of her own language.

"Then, no. I can't eat it." Rachel said

"Oh, are you a vegetarian? I'm confused. I know that you have eaten the chicken dishes that Madame Bernard cooked for us."

"I eat some meats. But not that."

"Oh. Several of the girls that I went to school with in London did not eat any meat at all. But I think they may have all been from India. Visited them a few years later during a tour of India that the Philharmonic did. Mother and I got to tag along. Ever had Indian food?"

She felt her face flush from the combination of wine and embarrassment. "No, I never have." After pushing a bit of potato around her plate, she asked. "Are you going to audition for a seat in Haydn's *Farewell Symphony*?"

"Certainly. It's performed so rarely. Are you?"

"I don't know yet. It is an interesting piece."

"I like the idea of it. As each member of the orchestra ends his part, they walk off stage—"

"Leaving just two violinists at the end. Do you think that could be us?" Rachel asked.

"I don't see why not, we can practice and audition together."

She remembered how they laughed that night.

Rachel sipped her wine and then looked at Emily. "Have you been everywhere?"

"No. And I don't want to go everywhere. I want to marry, settle in, and amaze my husband with my playing. I want a simple life. Playing professionally is not a simple life. I've traveled too often with my parents to want to keep on traveling like a Gypsy forever. So, do you want the meat or not?"

"You can have it all."

"Oh, all right then. All the better for me." Emily laughed. "How do you like the wine?" Emily asked, as she saw Rachel sipping it.

"I like it quite a bit. It's not quite as tart a taste now, as I thought when I first had a sip."

Emily laughed, "Do you drink wine at home?"

"Not like this. Like water."

"Do you like this wine?"

"Very much, what is it?"

"Simple wine from Valais."

"Simple wine...."

Emily laughed, wondering if Rachel was getting a bit drunk. "My parents became quite interested in French wine after my father toured with the Philharmonic through France. They are becoming more and more French in their dining habits, it seems. Wine tasting and all that. Some morning, I half expect my father to be testing some wine with his shirred egg and toast for breakfast. Does your family drink wine?"

"Occasionally."

"Well, I have a recommendation. You don't want to drink it quite as fast as you are drinking it now. You can get a bit ahead of yourself if you do that. Particularly if you are not eating a meal with the wine." Emily looked carefully at Rachel to be certain that she had not injured her feelings.

"Oh, was I...."

"You are just fine. I simply wanted to know if you drank wine at home. Because we have been invited to a party this weekend. I think there will be wine and maybe some other stronger things to drink. I simply did not want some good looking lad getting you tipsy and taking advantage, if you know what I mean."

"Yes, thank you. I really don't drink...."

"Well, Madame Bernard certainly does. She drinks Pastis with water after she thinks we're asleep. Late at night, you can hear a sudden thud as she lurches into a doorjamb or as a book falls off her lap. You must have seen her Pastis glass in the morning."

"Her what?"

"That tumbler, that smells like licorice in the morning, on the kitchen table."

"Oh, that. I thought it was some Swiss medication that she took," Rachel confessed. Emily laughed.

"French. Light green, clear from the bottle, turns milky when water is added. Nice trick for a bar. I'll show you some time. Do you like licorice?"

"Yes. Yes, I do. Do you really think she gets tipsy?" Rachel asked again, a bit louder than she intended.

Emily looked at Rachel. "Seriously. You don't drink, do you?"

"Sure I do. Once a week, at least."

"Communion?" Emily asked.

"What's that?"

"I forget that you're Czech. Do they call it something else? In church...."

Rachel shook her head. "I don't go to church. I go to synagogue. I'm a Jew."

Emily looked quickly to see if anyone near them had reacted.

Rachel looked at her and tears welled in her eyes. "Does that make such a difference to you, now that you know more about me?"

"Not to me, but it might to someone else here. Get your coat on," Emily ordered as she motioned to the waiter for the check.

CHAPTER 7

DIVISI

The instruction to play only one of the notes at a time.

Months after Rachel's introduction to raclette, she and Emily were walking to class. Each carried a violin case, had a small book bag on a strap over a shoulder, and ate a croissant as they walked briskly. The cobblestones were still wet with the evening dew and slick at the narrow stone stairs from Rue Bernard down to Rue de la Clef. Emily slid and caught herself. "Watch your footing."

Rachel asked, "Footing or step?"

"Americans say step. The English would say footing. Wherever did you pick that up?"

"Cinema, I suppose."

Emily teased her. "Film or movies as your Americans would say?"

"My Americans?"

"Yes, you adore them, don't you? There is something about America that intrigues you. I see it, but... I can't give it a name."

"Promise. Or the brashness. They seem to have so few conventions."

"Or maybe it is that you love Gershwin and have figured out how to bow it in a way that pleases the maestro. You'll have to show me."

Rachel grinned. "Why? Didn't you say you're only going to play for your husband?"

"But what if he knew music?"

"Would he really care?"

"I care, so show me!" Emily demanded.

"It's all so simple. All you need to do is forget that it is an American composition. There are lilts of the historic in it, but what makes it fresh is the transition and the lack of gravity that binds one phrase to another."

"So why does it come together so well?"

"Why do you care? You play it well."

"I just wanted your idea."

"You are a fraud," Rachel snapped.

"What?"

"A fake. Is fraud not a word?"

"It's a word, but what are you saying?"

"You pretend not to care, but you work hard at your music. As hard as I do. Why do you pretend it is of little matter to you?"

"I'm afraid, I guess."

"Of what?"

"Of not understanding all that I can, of not really exploring as deeply as I want to." Emily paused and sighed, "So, why does Gershwin work so well?"

Rachel relented. "I think it is in the imagination. Perhaps it is the youth of the country. It is not roped to tradition."

"Tied to tradition is the phrase," Emily corrected. "So, show me after class. How you can bow so quickly in the fifth and twelfth bars."

"Don't think about how to do it. Just imagine what you want to hear next and somehow your hand can make the turn faster than if you think through the steps of repositioning the bow's angle. I'll show you before class."

"Good. What's your favorite?"

"I wonder if I have only one favorite."

Emily huffed. "Well then, what are your three favorites and explain why? Pretend this is an exam, not a discussion. Perhaps then you can focus on the response."

"Emily, I was not ignoring you; I was thinking. Was it the piece that got me my scholarship and what my parents are most proud of how I play or what Yitzhak likes best, which is Vivaldi's Four Seasons or Mozart's Jupiter...?"

"Technically it's Mozart's Symphony Number 41...."

Emily nodded. "Yes, his last symphony. Truth be told, my favorites are the English romantics. Vaughn Williams."

"Which of his, in particular?"

"Fantasia on a Theme by Thomas Tallis and Elgar's Violin Concerto. Late Bach."

"Ever played Wieniawski?" Rachel asked.

"Me? No, he was too much the virtuoso on violin for me to try to play his work. Anyone who wrote to his own extraordinary skill level is beyond me. My father played his Violin Concerto Number Two several years ago in a festival, maybe it was in Paris."

"I'm still hungry. Want to get a piece of fruit on the way?" Rachel asked.

"We don't have time."

"I can eat as I walk."

"All right then, if you must."

"Good, the fruit monger's stall is just in the next block."

Emily scowled. "Not monger, that's more of a maker, like the iron monger. Fruit merchant or seller, would be better. Rachel, I wish I weren't correcting you so often, but English is quite precise. Not just in the vocabulary, which you are rather good at, but in the tone and accent. England is still a class society. The upper class has money and makes money. It goes to concerts and has a certain way of speaking. If you wish to float in that circle, then you must learn its manner of speaking."

"Why?"

"Because the language is full of snares for little rabbits like you."

"But it seems impossible. I study music and do well. Then I study English, but it is never good enough. Never."

"What is good enough? It's good enough to order food in a restaurant, or get a cab. But you sound more American and not above stairs," Emily said, bluntly.

"Above the stairs?"

"Yes, the upper class lives above stairs and the serving class lives below stairs. In the basement. Do you see?"

"You are very direct with me, but in a good way. I see what you mean. I see that I must work at improving. Can you coach me?"

"Yes, of course. For the price of a peach."

At the open market, the vendors were just setting out the sweet late season fruit from Italy. August was cooling in Geneva, but it was still summer in Italy. Rachel picked out two reddish peaches and paid for them. They ate them sitting on the stone rim of a small fountain in a square just before their school. Juice ran down Emily's chin and she quickly dabbed it off with her white linen handkerchief drawn from her light coat.

"May I ask you something personal?" Emily said, studying her peach.

"I can't promise that I'll answer," Rachel joked.

"What you said that night at Landault's. Are you a really a Jew or were you teasing me? Testing our friendship somehow."

Rachel frowned. "Does it matter to you?"

"No, but it matters if you might be losing your scholarship. It matters if your state stipend may end. Germany has just annexed your country…"

"I know. I can't think of anything else."

"What will you do if you have to leave school?"

"I don't know." Rachel held her violin case as though it were a living thing in need of comfort.

CHAPTER 8

CANNON

The music form that builds and layers over itself. It is similar to a round or a fugue. The child's song Row, Row, Row Your Boat and Pachebel's Cannon in D are examples.

It was close to midnight on Friday when a car alarm bleated somewhere near Sunset Boulevard and echoed off the hills. Emily tossed in bed, trying to get comfortable. She was too hot. She got up, went up to the kitchen in her light blue flannel pajamas, opened the deck door, and drank a glass of cold water from the refrigerator. Then she was too cold. She went to her music room, put the lap robe over her, and gazed out over the dark city.

A coyote in a far off canyon had found prey and a series of short yips alerted others to the meal. She was too warm again, tossed the small blanket on the floor, shut the deck door with more force than she intended, and paced in her living room. She considered playing the new CD of a Schumann work, balked at its romanticism, and noticed lights on at Ben's house. She phoned him as she turned on her computer.

"Ben?" Emily asked, even after he said hello and she recognized his voice. She hesitated. "Are you awake?"

"Yes."

"I mean, did I wake you?"

"No, is something wrong?"

"No. No, I have a question. About the account. You said the list was on the computer. How do I find it? I use e-mail, but I don't spend a lot of time just surfing. Isn't that it? Surfing?"

"Yes, that's the word. Close your e-mail. On the home screen, just type in 'Swiss Bankers Association' or 'dormant accounts' into the search bar. Do that now. See if you connect. I'll hold on, if you want me to."

"Please." She put down the phone and pressed the speaker button, closed one screen, and tapped into the search bar. "I think it is loading now." After a bit, a screen with an alphabet across it emerged. "I've got an alphabet now."

"Good, listing is by last name; should be easy now. The account on the list is in your name, your full name, Emily Finch Montgomery, opened in 1944—"

She shook her head slowly. "There is some mistake. I had left Switzerland by then."

Ben ignored her. "Your father opened it in December, 1944. I thought I told you that."

"My father? Maybe you did." Emily felt the room growing small and hot. "I won't bother you any more tonight. I promise."

As Ben was about to reply, he heard the buzz of a dead line and turned off his phone.

She tapped the letter "H" and waited. While the information loaded, the names of banks that Ben had been discussing became fresh again. She had seen these banks in Geneva as a girl. She knew their names. She could almost recall the look of their buildings. Which had the etched glass doors? Which had the heavy carved oak door? Which had a family crest above the name? Which names were in gold letters on old glass?

On her computer screen floated bank names. Some had new banking logos and a new look. Others retained the old names, rampant lions, and other mythical animals intended to suggest a protection of assets and a timeless stability. Then a few clicks of the mouse and the alphabet stretched across her monitor. Letter by letter, a directory. The instructions were clear. Behind each letter resided long lists of names.

She found Rachel Havel. Then she went to the "M" listing and found Emily Finch Montgomery. Both were there. Names and account numbers, what the balance was when the account became dormant, and a calculator to determine its current value. She ignored the calculator, stopped her search and turned off the computer.

Then she wept, stopped and forced herself to the rigor of practice. Midnight or dusk or three in the morning, this was the way she fought her demons. She opened the safe and took out the instrument that was Rachel's violin in Geneva.

Emily held it, smelled the richness of the wood and varnish, and was emotionally transported to Geneva. Suddenly, she was young again and there was nothing but her music and her future.

"Tell me about your instrument," Rachel asked as Emily tuned her violin and Rachel completed trimming a broken horsehair on her bow. They were planning to practice Haydn's Symphony No. 45, the Farewell Symphony. Both women had been selected as finalists for the violin section. The announcement of who would be the last two violinists to leave the stage was planned for the night of the performance, so all violinists in the orchestra continued to practice the entire piece.

"What about it? Why?" Emily asked, distracted from tuning.

"Just curious about its history."

"History? You mean who owned it before me?"

"Who made it?" Rachel asked crisply, as though that would make her meaning clear.

"It's not famous. Just a good practice violin that my father bought from a retiring violinist at the London Philharmonic. Probably could tell a few stories, but it's not famous or anything."

"How about your instrument?" Emily asked.

Sitting straighter, Rachel said, "My father and Yitzhak made it."

"No! I thought he just repaired concert instruments."

Rachel examined her bow. "He's a violinmaker too. Yitzhak apprenticed with him. It took a year to make this one at the shop in Josefov."

"I thought you lived in Prague. Where is Josefov?"

"It's a district of Prague now."

"What? I'm confused now."

"Papa says that most cities are like an egg cracked in a pan, they start and that village just gets bigger. But Prague grew together from five different villages."

"What are the others?" Emily asked distractedly as she waited for

Rachel to tighten her bow so they could practice together.

"Josefov is outside the walled city that the other four Christian quarters formed. The Castle Quarter is on the hill. You can see the red castle from all over the city. The Old Quarter has the Town Hall and the Powder Gate. It has the oldest buildings and a lot of them have gold on them. The New Quarter has more businesses. And the Little Quarter has the most wonderful park in it. The park goes up a hill and from the top you can see all over town. There is the Rozhelona, it's a miniature Eiffel tower at the top. But from my house, it is a short walk to the magnificent Charles Bridge. It's as grand as anything in Paris or London. Statues on it, wide and...."

Once her bow was fixed, Rachel started the practice session and Emily struggled to keep up with her. Emily concentrated on the music in front of her. Rachel thought of Josefov and how she missed her home, at the same time that her eye was on the musical score and her fingers moved flawlessly to it.

Josefov's Jews were not allowed into the trades and the commerce of the city in the Middle Ages. They lived on its edge and did work that was not controlled by the trades. And when they died, they were buried in the cemetery that held their fathers and mothers back to 1478. Graves were often twelve deep in the limited patch of a cemetery bound in by a mossy wall.

Stone markers clustered, one upon another, like crooked teeth of a dragon. The cemetery always seemed dark from the stains of moss and time. And it was chilled, even in summer. In early summer, the heart shaped leaves of the Linden trees swayed in the breeze coming off the river. The darker top and lighter green underside of the leaf shimmered. At the height of the summer, the bloom of the Lindens honeyed the air, and the hiss of bees hung over the cemetery. Then Rachel's father would ask her if the bloom were full, and when she said yes, they would inspect the mezuzah on the doorpost at their front door.

Even though the inspection was only required twice every seven years, it was at this time every year that her father took his small wood chisel and asked Rachel to help him as he carefully pried the brass mezuzah from the right side of the doorpost. When she was a toddler, she just held the two nails that fastened the mezuzah to the doorpost as he handed them to her. Later, when she could reach to her father's shoulder height, she would hold the mezuzah as it was pried free and carry it into the house for inspection.

Her mother would place a clean cloth on the kitchen table. Then her father would open the hinged door at the rear of the mezuzah case and gently remove the small parchment scroll that had two verses from the Torah. Her father would look at the letters on the outside of the scroll, and if they were clear and the parchment looked intact, he would unroll it and examine the letters on it. Then he would read the verses of the *Shema Yisroel* and *Vehaya* in a moderated voice, making the affirmation that the Lord our God is one Lord and the recognition of the commandment to love and serve the Lord.

If any of the letters on the scroll were damaged or if water had stained it or if heat had cracked it, her father declared it *possul*, unclean, unworthy. The scroll was either perfect or less than perfect, which was not acceptable. In those years, when damage was discovered, he replaced the parchment scroll immediately. When the mezuzah was nailed to the doorpost again, her father said the *bracha*, the blessing, and they resumed life.

Rachel could not remember a time that her parents failed to honor the verses in the scroll upon entering their home. A light kiss to the fingertips of the right hand and a gentle touch to the mezuzah---always the right side of the mezuzah, below the letter *shin*, every time, as it had been with their family since that brass mezuzah was made in the Middle Ages.

Rachel's thoughts turned to the smell of the fresh wood shavings in her father's workshop, a scent that was as crisp as new apples in cold air. Rachel loved to go into the ten by ten foot room that her grandfather and father had built before she was born. Because it extended their small home from the kitchen doorway, it was sufficiently warmed in winter not to need its own wood stove and offered an adequate draft in summer to cool the kitchen. Three years ago, a door to the street had been put at the front of the workshop to allow customers to enter directly and not have to walk through the house or into the rear and use the small door at the back of the shop. A small painted table by the door with a blue velvet cloth over the top sufficed as all the counter space that was needed to show any of the instruments that were suspended from the ceiling by wires.

She seemed to spend almost all of her time in the workshop or kitchen, doing her lessons or helping her mother, rather than staying in her small room or the comfortable parlor with the upright piano. If she closed her eyes, she could tell the season by small shifts in her father's attire. Every day he wore heavy pull-on boots and dark trousers. His white shirt without the collar and dark vest were standard. But in summer, the sleeves of his shirt were rolled above the elbow, in spring and fall a coal black muffler was wrapped around his neck, and in winter he added a black leather jacket to his wardrobe.

When she was small, he made violins and repaired the occasional instrument from the Prague Philharmonic. She would sit on a high stool and watch him work the wood, transforming it from a slab to several planks. Then he would study the grain again before the plank was planed, a bit more on one side than the other to line up the grain perfectly. Then the board was sanded and massaged until the perfect thickness was found, fragile enough to sing. By then the wood was barely thicker than a veneer and fragile enough for a child to break.

His stories about musicians he had known fed her imagination. She watched him reveal what he called hidden animals from the flat wood. Not by carving toys for her but by teasing her imagination to see patterns in the wood. Long, deeply alternating yellow and brown grain he called 'tiger stripes'. These 'tiger stripes' would be matched for the back of the violin. And occasionally there was a perfect piece of maple for the neck of the violin in which the end of the grain formed little 'bird's eyes' at the end of the neck, above the tuning pegs. All these colors and shapes came from a piece of dull wood. She had been intrigued by the delicacy of the woodworking tools that he used. They looked like children's tools. His smallest wood planes were the size of the silver thimble that sat beside her mother's sewing box.

The magic of the room surrounded Rachel as a small child. When she was three, her father fashioned a one-quarter-size violin for her to hold in his studio so she wouldn't want to touch the instruments left in his care for repair. He was startled when she actually played a few notes on it for a customer just a few months later.

"A mimic. A savant. A prodigy." That's what the customers called her. She was the girl that sat on a stool at the street entrance to the workshop. She was the greeter, the buffer between the anxious customer and her busy father. She was an oddity that brought some new customers to the shop to watch the child finger the strings and use the miniature bow. Even before she knew any real pieces to play, she replicated phrases and worked the scales with a remarkable accuracy of tone and timing for any amateur violinist, let alone a child.

By the time she was six years old, she had memorized the contents of each of the sixty-some drawers in the cabinet in the entry area. It held dozens of types of strings for violins, violas and cellos, as well as the usual small repair parts and a wide selection of rosins. From the time she was a child until she was a young woman, she would be the one to find what the customer wanted. By the time she had done that, her father was able to find a stopping place in his woodworking and could then sell the item to the customer. But only her father would discuss a new instrument with a customer, or design a custom instrument that he would craft in a little under a year, or repair a professional's instrument.

When the economy soured in the mid-thirties, new instruments were not in demand. New violins that her father had crafted hung in the workshop, unsold. Her father repaired instruments for the few private players who could afford repairs, but his primary income was from the many repairs for the Prague Philharmonic.

Although he knew that there were no buyers for any new instruments, he wanted to use this slow time to full advantage. He wanted to make one instrument with no compromises in it. This was the time to test his skills and challenge Yitzhak's skills. If he had learned as much as Mr. Havel thought, he could become a partner through this instrument, not merely an apprentice. But that question would not be answered quickly, for crafting this instrument would take a full year, if all went well.

After all repair work was done for the day, the master and the apprentice would spend the early evening hours crafting the new instrument. Her father was an artist. He worked with precision at every step. Yitzhak knew how to plane, how to sand, how to help, but now he was learning to envision the abstraction of the final owner's vision while the instrument was just blocks of wood and a jumble of parts.

At the start of the shaping, Yitzhak was trying to hurry with the medium plane when he heard Rachel at the door of the workshop. He looked up, without stopping the plane first. The wood reacted to the change in angle of the plane and an uneven curl of wood trailed behind the plane.

Yitzhak saw it first. "Oh no!"

Mr. Havel looked up from his work across the workshop. "Are you cut?"

"No, the wood...." Yitzhak could not speak. He stood frozen, staring at the uneven slice in the slab of wood and listening to Mr. Havel's heavy boots as he walked to the workbench. "I am sorry, I...."

"This mistake can be fixed. Taking this much off of the back piece in a week would have ruined this part. But now? Let me see." Mr. Havel took the plane from the shaking hand of the boy. Yitzhak had tears filling his eyes and turned to leave the workshop. Rachel stepped back inside the house, but listened to her father in the workshop.

"Stay, boy. Learn from this. If you ever need to look away, stop working the wood. If you are working the wood, do only that. This is not an occupation for daydreamers. Can you do that?"

"Yes, yes I can."

"Listen to the wood. It will take you where it wants to go. Where it must go. You are young. Later, you can guide it, once you learn its ways. Now, watch me and learn how to fix this little problem."

Quietly, Mr. Havel eased the plane at a slight angle and restored the symmetry to the wood. Yitzhak grew to understand more about the wood than he had known before the accident. Once the wood was again perfectly proportioned, Mr. Havel handed the plane to the boy. Silently he took the plane and returned to the methodical work with a new appreciation for the rigor of attention the work demanded.

Nature is unforgiving. Each piece of wood unique. They worked, anticipating that any pass of the plane or swipe of sandpaper could expose a flaw in the wood and show an unexpected turn in the grain that would take away from the perfection.

But day after day, there were no flaws in the wood. There were no more sudden lurches with the plane that gouged the wood. Each saw cut was on the line.

Fashioning the fingerboard was no easier. Finding the perfect line of the grain in the ebony wood to maximize the strength in the flat fingerboard was the first challenge. That took the better part of a day. When Yitzhak put away the tools and Mr. Havel filled his pipe, Rachel locked the front door and hurried into the back of the workshop to join them.

"What do we do tomorrow?" Yitzhak asked.

Mr. Havel struck a long match on the heel of his boot and brought the flame to his pipe. "We decide the width of the fingerboard and start to trim the sides."

"How are you going to do that?" Rachel asked, as a cloud of smoke swirled around her father's head. "You don't know who is going to play it."

"Well, let's imagine who might buy it. We'll consider the quickness desired by the player, the length of fingers and the size of the player's fingertips. Then there is playing style. How many violinists could play this instrument over its lifetime?"

Yitzhak guessed a dozen. Rachel nodded agreement. But a sharp rapping on the door to the street interrupted their speculation. Mr. Havel put down his pipe, went to the door and looked out the small window at eye level. He opened the door quickly and stood aside. The Concertmaster, a rotund man with a full red beard, rushed in and was quickly followed by an intense slim man wrapped in a brown wool coat, holding a brown fedora hat and clutching a violin case.

CHAPTER 9

MARCATO

This is a style of bowing in which all notes are strongly accented.

The Concertmaster motioned to the man to open his violin case on the velvet-covered table. "Mr. Havel, I need your help."

"Certainly, Mr. Bloom. What is the matter?"

"The matter is that our soloist for tonight's performance has a broken violin." As the man opened his case carefully, Rachel and Yitzhak came closer.

Mr. Havel walked up to the Concertmaster with assurance. "Let me take a look."

The man opened the case fully and handed Mr. Havel his violin. The A string was sagging but no damage was visible.

"Ah, tuning peg problem."

The stranger looked up from the violin that he was watching as though it were his sick child and said, "Yes, it split a few minutes ago when I was tuning it for my practice session. I can't see how you could glue it in time, but he says you have magic hands."

Mr. Havel shook his head. "Glue is not the answer. Not for tonight's performance."

The Concertmaster was flushed. "Well, can you fix it somehow? I have a—"

"Certainly. I can simply replace the peg. The other pegs are ebony. I assume you would want a matching peg for tonight. My apprentice has been roughing out a set of tuning pegs for a violin we are making now. I would be pleased to fit one to your violin for tonight's performance. If you want to retain your current peg, I could glue it tonight and then replace the original peg tomorrow."

"Excellent. I don't leave for Budapest until late afternoon. Will that give you enough time?"

"Yes, if you will wait here, I will come back in a moment."

The lanky man looked at the five violins hanging on the wall near the door. "These look new."

Rachel gathered her courage and walked up to him. "My father made them. If you wish to try any of them while you wait, please do so. I'm sure that this is interrupting your preparation for the performance."

"Yes, it is. Do you perform?"

Rachel blushed. "Just at my lessons, sir. But I have heard you before."

The man slipped off his overcoat and placed it on the stool by the door. "Have we met?" He balanced his hat on the coat. His athleticism made him appear to be in his thirties, but his gaunt face and white hair suggested that he was in his late fifties. His hair was full and brushed straight back from a high forehead. The high cheekbones and aristocratic bearing made his eyes penetrating.

"No, sir. You are Béla Bartók. We listen to your concerts on the radio. Of course we know who you are," Rachel said. "Are you playing your Violin Concerto tonight?"

"Yes, but I am just starting to write another one. I hope to preview it in a year or two, so listen for it on the radio, young lady."

Rachel smiled and said, "Then tonight's performance will have to be renamed the Violin Concerto Number One and you'll have to call the new one the Violin Concerto Number Two, won't you?"

He laughed and picked up a violin. He called to Mr. Havel, "Are you sure I can limber up on your new violins while you repair mine?"

"Of course. It would be an honor," shouted Mr. Havel who was leaning over the violin and sanding the ebony peg to fit. Rachel pulled a bow from off the wall and quickly tightened it for him. He took it with a nod. He ran the bow over the strings and tuned only one quickly. Then he played a Hungarian folk tune that he had incorporated into one of his compositions. Robust, rapid fingering, shifts in the tempo. Rachel watched, transfixed as his long fingers danced over the strings.

Rachel offered another violin after he finished the short tune.

"Perhaps this one might suit you better." It had a thicker neck and was slightly wider on the fingerboard.

Béla Bartók exchanged instruments and quickly checked the tuning, and ran the bow over the strings. "It's perfectly in tune," he said softly with amazement.

"I was playing it earlier," Rachel said. He nodded and plunged into the middle of the concerto, where the pace is rapid and the melody complex.

After a small sheen of sweat shone on his wide forehead, he stopped and handed the bow to her, as if dismissing her. He kept the violin at his shoulder and continued fingering it as he talked to the Concertmaster.

"How do you think they will receive me tonight?"

"Well, this is a popular work here."

"But there are sympathies for Germany here, aren't there?"

"Yes, but most of this audience won't know that you have refused to play in Germany since your premier performance of the Second Piano Concerto, in '33, almost four years ago."

Bartók snapped. "It has been five. Shouldn't you just say 'the week before Hitler was named Chancellor of the Reich'?"

The Concertmaster shrugged. "But most have continued to listen to your concerts on the radio, even though you have not performed."

"Well, at least I have a choice, not like Otto," he said, placing the violin on the desk and taking his own from Mr. Havel who had walked briskly from the rear of his workshop.

"And you think this will hold? I play hard, you know."

"Yes, I know your style. Test it, please."

Béla Bartók played again and pushed the limits of the instrument. It held tone and the peg matched perfectly. "Nicely done." He carefully placed the violin in its case.

The Concertmaster wiped his upper lip with a large handkerchief. "Thank you, my friend." He opened the door and the soloist got into the car that was waiting outside the door.

As he started to leave, Rachel whispered to the Concertmaster, "What did he mean about Otto? Who was that?"

"Otto Klemperer."

"The conductor?"

The Concertmaster whispered quickly, "Yes. Politics. That's why Béla refuses to play in Germany. After Otto conducted the Second Piano Concerto in Budapest, the Reich placed him on a 'leave of absence' from his post at the State Opera in Berlin."

"Why?" Rachel demanded.

The burly man scowled at her. "The Restoration of the Body of Public Officials Act. It removed Jews and anyone with anti-Nazi sympathies from public posts; ask your father about it."

"He'd do that for a friend?" Rachel asked.

"Apparently so." He turned from Rachel and called to her father, "About one tomorrow?"

"Yes, that will be fine."

The next afternoon, the Concertmaster came with Bartók's violin and Mr. Havel quickly seated the repaired peg.

"He was quite impressed with your work," said the Concertmaster.

"Ah, this repair was nothing."

"No, the violins he used for practice here in your shop; he was very complimentary. Said that the fingerboard on the larger one was the best fit for his hand-- better than his own concert violin."

"Very flattering."

"I told him you were working on an instrument that was utterly flawless. He said he'd like to try it after it is completed, so let me know. Maybe you have a buyer."

"Of course I'll let you know. Thank you."

After the Concertmaster left, Mr. Havel decided on a wider fingerboard to accommodate Bartók's long fingers and the strength he had from both piano and violin practice. Then he decided to maintain an arch in the wood that supported the fingerboard that would allow a medium sized hand to play as well. The decision was strategic and targeted not just to Béla Bartók's needs but to those who would play after him into the next century. The next week and a half was devoted to careful shaping of the neck.

Joining the parts was the next secret that he had to share with

Yitzhak. An off-angle in the neck where it joined the body would alter the tone, eventually undo the joints, let the strings rip out the tailpiece and ultimately destroy the instrument. Each joint must marry parts exactly to make the perfect curves and sensual body of the violin that would release the voice living in the wood. Piece was painstakingly glued to piece and abstractions took on form.

Perfect architectural balance was the requirement of a violin that was to stand the test of use and time. But that balance would be destroyed if the wood were not finished properly. Then the preservation of that balance came in the protective finish.

Rachel's father could replicate the voice from one instrument to the next. Some of the practice violins used by the current philharmonic members were made just for this purpose. Alignment of parts or finish. Balance or resetting the bridge. Whatever the problem, her father found the solution. She lingered in his workshop to listen and to see Yitzhak.

"You know how long my family has been making instruments?" he asked Yitzhak one night.

"A long time, sir."

"Six generations. For that long, someone in my family has made violins and violas. Once, one of my great grandfather's violins came to me for repair."

"Why?" Yitzhak asked, eager to learn about the failure so he could avoid it.

"The owner had left it on a table where his cat knocked it to the floor and a peg chipped. Once in my lifetime I had to fix one, but it was for damage. It was never from a seam coming unglued or the two matching parts of the back slab separating. Or the fingerboard cracking. Or the tailpiece rattling. Or the button breaking and releasing the tailpiece and strings."

Mr. Havel had started crafting the violin just after her birthday in the summer of 1937. She was seventeen and Yitzhak was a tall lad of eighteen. Rachel heard much that went between her father and Yitzhak over the months of the violin's construction. She recalled fragments from this period easily.

Papa tormented Yitzhak. "Is the heart of a violin in the wood or in the eye of the master?" Neither answer was going to be right.

"I don't know, sir. Maybe the wood?"

"Let me tell you about this wood, Yitzhak, and see if you think your hand is ready to work it without me. In 1786, maybe a dozen maple trees were planted around a house to shade it in summer and buffer the wind a bit in winter. North of Prague, scarlet leaves fell for 79 autumns from these trees. The year after they were planted, Mozart came to live in Prague.

In 1865, one of these trees was cut for firewood, the branches burned, but the grain was so perfect that the farmer who owned the tree cut it into slabs and put them away to age, to cure like a fine wine. Ends were waxed to allow the wood to age slowly, without cracking. Then my grandfather bought the wood. He too made violins and repaired instruments for the symphony.

The wood was in the attic then under the bed in the town home of my grandfather. Then my father had it in the attic of this house when I was your age. Then I started to cut it in 1934, but it was not ready. Now it is ready. You think you can do it alone?"

"No, sir. Maybe the answer was the craftsman?"

With a glint in his eye, Mr. Havel watched the boy. "In 1644, Italy produced a visionary by the name of Stradivarius. But if he just had old pine planks to plane away at and craft to a fiddle, then where would we be?"

Yitzhak guessed. "Nowhere? You need both."

"Right, at last. The perfect piece of wood needs special attention to let out its voice."

"How do you know what its voice will be?" Yitzhak watched as the older man took the back of a violin that was being repaired, tapped it, and smiled.

"You are starting to ask the right questions. Maybe there is hope for you. But it has taken centuries for the name Havel on a violin to mean a tenth of what the Amati Stradivarius or Guarneri names mean. Why should you think that you could be any good at that?"

"I want to know the wood as well as the craft. I want to know everything you know," Yitzhak said and then suddenly stopped, fearing that his interest had been insolent.

"I let you start here when you were just a 13-year-old, Yitzhak. You swept the wood shavings from the floor. Once I had to tell you what I wanted. Now, just a look instructs you. You are a good boy and a talented one. If you pay attention to the craft and not just my daughter, we can make a fine instrument together." Yitzhak blushed and turned to rearrange the tools that were in perfect order on the bench.

Over the next months, the raw woods changed after the small steel tool erased wood dust from the block. The maple showed its stripes and became a perfectly matched back for the violin. Other maple became the neck of the violin. Spruce with a fine tight grain was teased to almost a veneer-like thinness for the top of the violin. Ebony was transformed from a dull charcoal block of wood to a sharp edged fingerboard, shining and hard as polished onyx.

Yitzhak tapped the back, looking for the latent sound in it, searching for a tone close to G, as the master had taught him. But the instrument was not there yet.

The work grew ever finer. He used the plane and at the end of the day's work, Yitzhak sharpened and oiled it, and placed it in its space in the rack at the back of the workbench. No words. No instruction was needed. The apprentice worked the wood as taught, moving things, preparing things, anticipating needs. Now, he picked up the plane, no bigger than a baby's knit bootie. It was almost lost in his hand. Small shavings, more a scent of new wood than curls of new wood falling off, let him know how deep to go. Then the master took over.

Yitzhak sharpened the next tools and watched him use a plane the size of a walnut, and the next one was the size of a chocolate bonbon. After that, a plane the size of a thimble eased into the wood and made only dust. That was how close the tolerances were between good and fine. Fine to concert quality. Concerto to heirloom: a kiss of an angel was the difference.

Rachel loved eavesdropping when her father told Yitzhak the rules for violinmaking again and again.

"Making the violin is a disaster hiding in each movement."

"The back is two blocks, twins really, split and laid open. Thicker at the center, thinner at the edges to let the natural arch flow, glued together to be the back of the violin."

"There are fifty-eight pieces to make a violin. My name on the label that rests inside is the last, making it fifty-nine parts."

"Use strong light to check for any unevenness in the wood. Best done in strong summer light, not in the long grays of the northern European winters. Best done by feel."

"Hollow out the inside of the glued maple with a freshly sharpened gouge. The back will have a thickness of 2.3 to 4.6 millimeters, not any thicker than five sheets of good writing paper. Too thin, the tone dies too fast."

Yitzhak recited for the hundredth time. "And too thick, the tone is never born."

Eight months later, the new spruce top was paper-thin, and light from the candle showed through it on a dark night.

Cutting the sound holes in it was next. The classic f shape. The master measured and marked as Yitzhak rubbed soap along the blade of a hand jigsaw. "This is for the rough cut, and then I'll finish it with a small knife. That's its mouth, its expression, its face," Mr. Havel said after he finished the cuts.

"Follow the craft that leads you to your soul. That's what my father taught me. You don't make violins like furniture, you serve music."

On the wall Mr. Havel had written what the Protestant martyr, Jan Huss, had said at his death in Prague. *Pravda Zvítézí*. He believed it. He believed that 'truth shall overcome' and that there was truth in the wood as well as music waiting to be let out by the right master. First, the violinmaker and then the player. The master told the apprentice, "The music begins with you, your integrity to the craft; not even the best player can make this instrument sing more notes than you give it."

Now that the body of the violin was formed and the glue dried, it needed its finish. Mr. Havel's fingertips had been stained amber by the varnishes and solvents that he mixed and used. His special blend made the grain of the wood come alive-- accentuated the grain and exposed the colors of the wood, like a diamond that is cut perfectly.

First he stained it and then sealed it, just enough to protect it and still let it breathe enough to be a living thing. Then the sealed and stained wood needed to be perfect before the varnish was put on it.

"Rub the finish to satin with that cloth, then we'll test it," the violinmaker said. When Yitzhak had finished rubbing the dry stained and sealed wood with ordinary cotton cloth, the master handed Yitzhak a piece of silk. "Pull this over it."

"It's not catching at all," Yitzhak reported with delight.

"Now, then the interior of your wrist. Feel anything, any snags?" the violinmaker asked.

Yitzhak did not and smiled a smile of success.

"Then try a cotton tuft," the master said. With this test, a small imperfection was discovered. Yitzhak looked crushed.

"Simple, rub it in with a tatter of that bed sheet."

Now it was ready for the first of the twenty coats of varnish that would draw a deep chestnut from it. As the master applied the first coat of varnish he said to Yitzhak, "You know, I think the varnish is really too red on the Red Diamond Strad. I saw it about ten years ago. Too dark. We need to avoid that."

After the varnish dried, Yitzhak would test it for perfect smoothness and the master would adjust the tone of the next coat of varnish to develop depth but not harshness in the color of the violin.

Then, when it was perfect, Yitzhak added a chin rest and pegs for the strings.

The violinmaker had seduced perfection from raw wood and shared all of his secrets with Yitzhak.

Finally, it was ready to play. This would let him know if there were added adjustments to make.

Her father called Rachel to the workshop and turned to Yitzhak who was fitting the last string on the violin. "Congratulations. You have made a beautiful instrument. Why don't you ask her to test it for you? From the tone, we can decide if it needs more varnish."

Her father gave her the first moment with the violin and with Yitzhak, while making the excuse of going into the house to get coffee.

Yitzhak offered her the new violin carefully. She knew the violin was not hers to keep. It was a masterpiece. The best her father had ever made. The first violin Yitzhak had really helped to create.

But she alone would be the first to play it. Before the orchestra heard it. Before it had an owner. Before the Concertmaster and her father dictated its public voice.

This was her private moment.

Rachel's father left her alone with Yitzhak while she tuned and then played the new instrument. She heard the click of a cup against a saucer as he poured coffee in the kitchen.

"Do you think they can be trusted alone?" Rachel's father asked her mother with a broad smile as she poured coffee in the kitchen.

In the workshop, Rachel whispered to Yitzhak. "As long as I play, they think we can't talk or I can't look at you." She had overstepped her modesty and looked away.

"And how long can you play the new violin? How long can I look at you and want you to be mine?" Yitzhak asked.

"My whole life, if that's what you want."

"I want nothing else."

She hit a false note, intentionally, and stopped. She saw how he was looking at her. Suddenly, she kissed him and then tuned the violin again so quickly that no one in the kitchen had a suspicion. His dark eyes gleamed with a promise that she had seen growing over the winter months.

CHAPTER 10

CONCERTO

A musical composition, usually in three movements.

During the last weeks of January, 1938, Concertmaster Bloom arrived at the workshop every afternoon at four, brushed the snow from his heavy overcoat, and asked Mr. Havel to report on the state of the repairs of the Philharmonic instruments that were in the workshop. But the visits to the back of the workshop became more frequent; his coat was tossed on a chair in the workshop as he lingered. On a Wednesday in the last week in January, a visit ended in a quick chess game.

Mr. Bloom would arrive daily, promptly at four, and invite the game, even after all of the Philharmonic's instruments had been repaired. Mr. Bloom then brought in instruments that were in need of only the most minor attention. The visits were extended and often ended in a second thoughtful game of chess in the workshop as Yitzhak completed his chores.

One night over dinner, Rachel asked her father, "Why is he here so much?"

Her father placed his fork against the rim of the plate and looked at her directly. "At first, I thought he was just more interested in the repairs. But then he told me that his wife died in November. I think that he is alone for the first time in his life."

Mrs. Havel glanced at her husband. "It also lets him see the new violin being born."

Rachel balanced a forkful of dumpling just shy of her mouth. "Do you think he'll buy it for the Philharmonic if Béla Bartók doesn't buy it?"

"We'll see. It could be a good thing that he is interested. If it were not for the repairs that he brings us...." Rachel's mother passed bread to her and changed the conversation to something other than business and their dependence on the repair work.

On the last Friday in February, Josef declared the last coat of varnish sufficiently dry on the new violin to show it to the Concertmaster the following week, when he returned from a visit to his niece in Hamburg. As Yitzhak hurried out the workshop door, Mr. Havel placed the new violin into a case and propped the lid slightly open. As he turned to lock the workshop door for the night, he almost bumped into the Concertmaster who held the door open and tapped on it. "Mr. Havel? Have you a moment? I saw the sign that you were closed but your light was on and I had to come around to ask—"

Mr. Havel backed into the workshop. "Of course. I hope your visit was—"

"Today? Is it ready?" Josef watched the Concertmaster's eyes dart around the workshop for it and enjoyed his anticipation. He shifted from foot to foot, ignoring his black bowler hat, which was still on his head. His heavy beaver overcoat remained buttoned.

Inside the kitchen, her mother asked Rachel to see who had come into the workshop. Rachel glanced out of the kitchen to the rear of the workshop and quickly returned to helping her mother prepare for the Sabbath. "It's Mr. Bloom, mother." Her mother nodded without interrupting her work.

Fridays were for making two meals: the Friday dinner and starting the stew that would be the noon meal on Saturday. It all started mid-afternoon with the bread. Baking the two loaves of the twisted *challah* egg bread came first, one loaf for each meal. Then preparing all of the ingredients for the *chollent*, so that the stew could cook slowly until the next day for a warm mid-day meal on the Sabbath, when cooking was not allowed.

All this had to be accomplished before darkness fell on Friday and the Sabbath began. This was a time of anticipation for the family, careful timing, and a quick pace for Rachel's mother. Before, Rachel was delegated to help set out the china on the fresh white tablecloth; then she'd be released to join her father and stay out of her mother's way. Now she was a partner in the work.

Her mother taught her to make the braided egg bread and this act set the pace for the house. It was the invisible metronome that kept time and measured the limited moments before darkness fell and all work was suspended.

The first task was to stoke the wood cook stove hotter than usual. Rachel put a fast hand to this: a long match to shavings from the workshop that were a dry tinder, then slivers of kindling, then sticks of dry hard wood for a long burn, all set alight in perfect order.

Then, while the oven heated and came to temperature, her mother put the yeast and sugar into warm water to return life to it. Rachel gathered the eggs, sifted the flour into the big ivory bowl with the blue rim, and sprinkled in the salt. She made a well in the center. By the time she had completed this, the yeast was a living thing, which her mother poured into the flour with oil, more water and the eggs.

Rachel stirred the yeasty mass until the several ingredients began to have a new unified form. Then her mother kneaded the dough and set it to rise in a large bowl on the shelf over the iron cook stove where the heat of the oven gently found it.

When the dough had doubled, her mother split it into two parts, giving Rachel one and keeping one for herself. They stood next to each other and Rachel followed her mother's actions perfectly as she split the dough into three balls, lightly floured her hands, and rolled the balls into three strips. Rachel's mother braided them faster than she braided Rachel's hair in the morning when she was a child. Rachel had her dough braided by the time her mother had brushed the first loaf with egg yolk, and sprinkled poppy seeds on it. Then she put the egg wash and seeds on Rachel's *challah*, and both loaves went into the oven together. Rachel and her mother had a silent pact not to tell who made which loaf. Within a few months of bread making, her father really could not tell who made which.

When the bread went into the oven, they had just an hour left to get the *chollent* stew ready and make that night's dinner.

Rachel gathered the onions and potatoes from the root cellar and dropped the dried lima beans into boiling water. As she quartered the potatoes, she heard the deep laughter of her father and the

Concertmaster in the workshop and listened to the violin being tuned. Her mother never looked up from cutting the beef brisket into cubes on the counter, seasoning it with flour and paprika, and browning the meat in a hot pan before adding it to the pot of vegetables that Rachel had assembled. The covered pot of *chollent* went into the oven when the bread came out. Magically, this assemblage of ingredients would slowly cook in the hot oven overnight and become the warm Sabbath mid-day meal with the second loaf of challah.

Her father knew the sounds of the bread making. Even from the workshop, he knew that after the dull thud of kneading, there would be an hour of other sounds while the bread rose. Women were working now. He was to stay away, even though the scent of fresh bread now permeated the workshop.

As soon as the *chollent* went into the oven, everything else had to happen quickly and seamlessly. The cut chicken was tossed in flour and paprika and then fried. The diced potatoes boiled while the candles and wine glasses moved from the cupboard to the dining room. She heard the men talking in the workshop as she set the table. It would be just a few minutes before the potatoes were ready to be drained. The platter was on the counter waiting for the last of the chicken to be fried. The loaf of *challah* was already on a plate on the table.

Eva looked up from the stove when the Concertmaster gave a shout, "I must hear the voice. I want a violin with a rich velvet, a deep voice of an older experienced woman, not the shallow laugh of a schoolgirl." The Concertmaster turned toward the kitchen and started to blush behind his full red beard. He cleared his throat, and went on. "If it is good enough you may just find a buyer tonight, Mr. Havel."

Rachel was putting away the flour bin as her father leaned on the doorjamb and stuck his head into the kitchen. "Eva?"

"Yes, Josef."

"Are you free of Rachel for a few minutes? I want her to play the new instrument for Mr. Bloom."

"Why? Wasn't he just tuning it? Didn't he hear—" Rachel muttered, not stopping in the dinner preparation.

Her father lowered his voice. "Rachel."

She looked anxiously at her mother. Eva nodded. "Go along. I can manage dinner by dark. Go. If you are to play, it needs to be now, before Shabbat starts."

Rachel was never permitted to touch any instrument that her father was repairing for the Concertmaster. She could test some new instruments for her father, but never had she been allowed to play for anyone, not to demonstrate an instrument. And now she was asked to play her father's best instrument for the Concertmaster. And it was almost dark. She looked to her mother for guidance.

Her mother tugged Rachel's apron string and took the apron from her. "Brush the flour from your skirt before you go out there to play for Mr. Bloom." Her mother smoothed a stray hair back into place above Rachel's left ear, and hugged her. Rachel felt the rough warmth of her mother's dark shawl as it brushed her neck. "Show him how wonderfully you play."

"Maybe he'll convince Béla Bartók to buy it! Wouldn't that be wonderful?"

She ran to the workshop door, tugging at her skirt as a child but entered the workshop poised and calm, a young woman, full of confidence and skill wearing her dark blue skirt and sweater as though it were formal attire for the symphony.

"Mr. Bloom, you know my daughter, Rachel. I believe that she will be able to demonstrate the tone of the violin much better than I could. With your permission?"

"So, the child plays well enough for this instrument? Is this an insult?"

"She is very talented," her father said, a little too forcefully. "She has been playing almost as well as most adults who come here since she was a child of seven. By ten she was playing Mozart. Now, I think she is at a professional level."

The Concertmaster raised his eyebrows. "Professional?"

"Yes, if there were a hall where she could play." He spoke louder than he had intended and then cleared his throat as though to excuse his voice.

The Concertmaster crossed his arms. "Have her play then, let's see how good the instrument really is."

"Rachel? Play for the Concertmaster."

Rachel nodded slowly. Her father handed her the best bow in the workshop: fine white horsehair was drawn uniformly against the point of the bow and pulled tight against the base. She took it from him and slowly turned the screw. There was the perfect tension to the bow for playing. She had known what it was before she could even begin to explain it. All good bows were at rest when not in use. At the end of her sessions, the first thing she always did was to release the tension. Holding the bow by the frog, she would give it just the right number of turns to release it. Now it was instinct, without looking.

The Concertmaster challenged her. "Do you know what a Concertmaster does?"

"You are in charge of the orchestra, not managing a performance, but preparing all things to ready the orchestra for a performance. The conductor is responsible for the specific evening of music."

"Very well said. How did you know that, if you can't go to concerts?"

"I listen to our customers."

He tipped his head. "What else do I do, then?"

"You set the tone for the performance by making sure that everyone is on pitch. All tune to your pitch. And you make sure that everyone is ready. You are a violinist as well as the Concertmaster."

"Correct. Then why would I want you to play for me?"

"Because you can hear at a distance what you cannot hear when you play. The feel of the violin is more personal. The sound is more objective."

"Can you play for me now? Is it ready?" Mr. Bloom asked the child, leaning down to her level.

"Yes, sir, after I tune it."

"Didn't you hear me tuning a moment ago?"

"The weather is changing, so the tone is changing."

The Concertmaster watched her carefully as she went to the workbench where the violin was resting on a soft cloth. "Right you are. Is the weather changing for the better or worse?"

She reached for the arched neck of the violin. "Better."

"And how can you tell?"

"Because I looked north and the clouds were going to the west, to my left. It will be clear tomorrow." Rachel shrugged, as though everyone knew that trick.

"Clever child. Now, please. Let me hear you tune. In particular, I want to hear the A above middle C when you have finished."

She held it like a guitar and plucked it softly. A look of some distress quickly crossed her face and she loosened the second string quickly. Then she put the instrument to her shoulder and drew the bow over each string individually. A few seconds of testing and twisting the pegs brought the instrument to its full voice.

She looked directly at the Concertmaster. "Here is the A above middle C." She put the bow to the string and held it for several seconds.

"Hold it longer, my dear."

She held the note through three full bow strokes. The note was totally constant in tone and volume. A smile spread over his face and her father leaned back against the workbench. He watched as he tested Rachel as well as evaluating the violin.

"That was perfect."

Rachel smiled.

"But can you do it again?"

Rachel looked at him with some consternation, as though he thought that she would not be able to do such a simple thing. After repeating the perfect note through another three bowings, Rachel stopped but held the bow at the ready.

"What would you like me to play, sir?"

"Start with the scales, my little girl. You tuned it to perfection. Now let's see how you understand the instrument. From your lowest to the highest note in one seamless line of tone elevated by half notes."

"At what tempo?" Rachel asked, intending it to be a less prideful inquiry than it sounded. The Concertmaster met her eye and saw a confidence unusual for her age. He did not answer her with his voice, but with his finger tapping three times on the workbench before him. He did not tap an ordinary tempo. Nothing that would resemble a whole note or half or quarter or sixteenth or any of the standard

European tempos. Nothing that easy. He wanted to test her as well as hear the instrument. Rather he tapped so fast that the tempo was barely perceptible. A blur. A drum roll.

She set to thinking how she would make her fingers fly to that long a pattern as she adjusted the violin at her shoulder. She drew a deep breath. This was a new challenge to her. This was a Concertmaster who would know if she were touching perfection.

Simply, she touched the bow to the string and was fingering the next note before she actually heard what she had played. Never had she been told to run scales that fast. That absurd split of a note was usually reserved for punctuation on a piece.

It was a burst of light in a dark passage. Fast as a hummingbird's heartbeat.

So fast was the pace that the notes ran together in her father's ear as one note sliding from an imperceptible rumble almost beyond awareness to a high that came close to exceeding human hearing. Her fingers moved over the neck of the violin as fast as spring raindrops fell on the cut stones outside her home.

When she finished, she saw her father start to smile. Never had she been so challenged or had her touch been so light on the strings. Never had her bowing been that fast and seamless.

In a full life, there is a moment of perfection that will never be surpassed. A transforming pride can spark from that one moment.

Mr. Bloom applauded quickly, then tossed his bowler on the clean workbench and draped his heavy overcoat on the stool next to the bench. "Brava. Very well done exercise, my girl. Now play something for me. Play something I don't know. Surprise me."

CHAPTER 11

MUSICAL NOTATION

A system which uses words and symbols to represent in writing the music which is heard.

Rachel studied the Concertmaster's ruddy face wondering what she could play to surprise him. She examined him as she thought. His suit was black and the fabric good. A gold watch chain swept across his rounded belly through the buttonhole on his vest. The thick links were rich red gold. Antique. He was not a Jew. And so to play from her history to his future was her challenge and then it came to her.

"*Kol Nidrei*, Papa?" Rachel whispered and watched the Concertmaster for any recognition of the words in Hebrew.

Her father smiled and nodded. "Give him the other name of the piece."

"This is the Violin Concerto Number One by Max Bruch," Rachel announced formally.

Mr. Havel added, "The first theme is from the Hebraic song of penitence. It's taken from our *Kol Nidrei* chant that begins the ceremony of Yom Kippur. That is how we celebrate the New Year."

"What does that mean, *Kol Nidrei*?"

"The words mean 'all vows', as this is a time of reflection in our faith. Of seeing if we have met and will meet our promises to God. Does the piece meet your challenge?"

The Concertmaster tapped his knee impatiently. "Yes, yes, play now."

She stood straighter and introduced the piece as she guessed one might do at a recital. "Now, I will play for you the *Kol Nidrei*."

As the first note hung in the small workshop, time stopped. The long draw on the bow transcended the time and the place and distilled the strength and passion of four thousand years of promises made and vows kept. She compressed that emotion into nine and a half minutes through the voice of the solo violin played in the small room.

As Rachel played, the men watched and listened so intently that they did not hear the clang of the oven's iron door or hear Eva put the chicken and potatoes on the table. Josef saw Eva come into the doorway to the workshop twisting a kitchen towel in her hands. Josef held his hand out to her. She came to his side and listened.

This was not an invited moment; it was a presence that her mother was compelled to see. The food sat in serving dishes on the table, awaiting the family. But this night the dinner could wait a moment and music could prevail. It was not yet dark.

As Eva listened, she felt that her daughter knew the prayer service and ritual of *Kol Nidrei* with an adult understanding. She had explained to her daughter that there is power in the word and words of promise hold a power greater than any other words. *Kol Nidrei* is a legal fiction, an eradication of our imperfect efforts to keep promises to God. Eva felt this wash over her and tears filled her eyes.

The Concertmaster was silent and motionless as Rachel finished and let the bow fall to her side. She stood with the violin at her shoulder and spoke only to the Concertmaster. "Bruch was composing about Yom Kippur. That is the Day of Judgment when God inscribes your name in either the Book of Life or the Book of Death. An error in the past can prevent your name being written in the right book, so we recognize the power of a just God to forgive our failings, not just in the past but to recognize that we are not perfect. This is a powerful moment for us as we recognize the awesome power of a good God to forgive our unmet promises."

The Concertmaster took a deep breath. "So you pray for God to forgive you?"

"We know that God has power and mercy. We recite this more as a fact rather than a request for forgiveness-- as our promise to do better in the next year, realizing our imperfection in the face of perfection."

"I am starting to understand."

She took his comment as interest in the ceremony. "At the start of

Yom Kippur, the *chazanim* in the synagogue chant the *Kol Nidrei*. First, we approach God quietly with the statement of his forgiveness, then with increased conviction, and finally with a mighty roar of belief. The custom of recitation three times is from antiquity in which the recitation three times was required to be released from a vow."

"What is the meaning today?"

"That we are a part of thousands of years of knowing our God as a God of rules and logic and compassion. It reminds us of the power of words to hurt or to heal. To think on our words and deeds with more concern and caution. To live the lives we should. It is the gate to reconciliation with God. We open that gate by our song and the knowledge that we can do better. I think that was what Bruch was intending in his composition."

Turning to Eva, the Concertmaster said, "Your child has enchanted me even more than your tales of your customs."

Eva blushed and lowered her eyes.

"She plays with an extraordinary gift."

"Yes. I would have expected something by Bartók. Since this could be his violin, but no." He turned to Josef. "And who is teaching her?"

"Her mother plays piano to practice with her. There are lessons once a week from a family friend."

"She should be studying at an institute?"

Josef shrugged and raised his eyebrows. "How could she be? I don't have money for that and state stipends do not go to Jews."

The Concertmaster tapped his forehead with his fingertips in frustration as though he suddenly recalled the iron fetters on the lives of the Jews of Prague. Turning to Rachel, he asked, "Do you know the 9th of Beethoven?"

"The choral? Ode to Joy? Yes, of course; I can play it." Rachel looked past him to the window, measuring the failing light.

"Then do so now," he demanded.

Rachel looked quickly to her father who nodded to her concern. "There is not time tonight to play it all,"

"Well then, just a few bars so I can get another taste of the instrument."

As she raised her bow, Rachel said, "I can play it all, but just not tonight."

"Play the choral accompaniment, if you please."

She played and his eyes filled with tears, which then fell on the black wool of his suit coat. He drew a huge white linen handkerchief from his side pocket and wiped his face quickly and snuffed softly. "That was my wife's favorite piece. You understand the voice of that instrument. The choral is the voice of the human soul. You have married them tonight in a way that I have never heard."

Rachel nodded to him as she placed the bow on the workbench with care while she held the violin at her shoulder. Then with two hands, she lowered the instrument and placed it with great care on the cloth covering the workbench. She picked up the bow, released the tension on the bow, returned it to the bench, and gave a slight curtsey to the Concertmaster.

Eva looked at Josef. He knew her concern and nodded.

The Concertmaster pushed his handkerchief into his pocket. "She played it perfectly, but I want to test the instrument in the great hall. That's the only way that I will know if the voice of the instrument will carry true to the back of the hall."

"Certainly. That would be a good test."

"Can you come now to test the instrument in the great hall?"

"Now? Tonight?"

He nodded. "Put on your coats. Bring your wife. She may want to hear the girl play there as well."

Josef leaned over and whispered to Rachel. "*Golten hinteles.*"

The Concertmaster frowned. "What was that you said?"

"Golden hands. I said she had golden hands." He nodded to Rachel. "That's all for tonight, Rachel."

Picking up his coat, the Concertmaster looked at Josef in confusion. "How can you refuse this offer?"

Josef looked at his daughter in astonishment at her poise as she said quietly, "Our Sabbath starts in a few minutes. We cannot work during the Shabbat. I cannot play for you now."

Josef held up his hand to get the Concertmaster's attention. "But stay. Join us at table as we start the Sabbath. We would welcome you. Eva is a superb cook."

"Can she cook as well as Rachel can play?"

"Better," Rachel whispered as she passed him on her way into the house.

After prayers that he did not understand and a sip of wine, the Concertmaster took a plateful of chicken paprika and boiled potatoes from Josef. The Concertmaster discussed music and instruments. Rachel and her mother answered questions from the Concertmaster about her practice schedule and the range of her repertoire. The *challah* was eaten and wine glasses emptied. The Concertmaster relaxed and extended the invitation to play at the concert hall to the next evening, as there were no performances scheduled for that Saturday night.

The Concertmaster left with a full stomach and an agreement to return Saturday night just after dark. As he waited at the corner to catch the trolley to go home, he watched the Havel family walking to their synagogue for prayer.

The Concertmaster was early Saturday night, as Rachel hoped he would be. Rachel had invited Yitzhak to join them for dinner and hoped that the Concertmaster would allow him to go with them to the *Rudolfinum*. In that expectation, Yitzhak had borrowed his older brother's vest, which he wore with his usual black trousers and white collarless shirt that was unbuttoned at the neck. Mr. Havel wore his best dark suit with a black tie. Mrs. Havel had selected her newest dress, a dark brown wool with a pleated skirt, for the occasion. Rachel selected a dark blue dress with a white lace collar. Although it had long sleeves, she could move easily and felt it to be almost stylish, as she had recently hemmed it to mid-calf.

When they had finished a cold supper, Josef said the *Havdalah* prayer that ends the Sabbath as soon as there are three stars in the sky. Rachel put the twisted candle back into the cupboard and stacked the dinner plates. Eva said that washing them would wait until they had changed from their dress clothes.

The Concertmaster had driven his car from his home on the edge of the city to transport them to the concert hall. When he tapped on the front door, Mr. Havel helped the women into their long black winter coats and dispatched Yitzhak to get the cased violin from the workshop. Yitzhak carried the violin case and opened the front passenger door for Rachel. Once in, he handed her the case and closed the door. Yitzhak opened the rear door for her parents and sat silently with them. The Concertmaster drove the few blocks from their home in Josefov to the concert hall that he called the House of Artists. Rachel preferred its more formal name, the *Rudolfinum*.

The huge building housed the music conservatory, large and small concert halls, and was even used for occasional art exhibitions. Just off Jan Palach Square, it was built on the bank of the Vltava and named for Crown Prince Rudolph of Hapsburg when it was completed in 1884. In spite of the proximity to her home, the *Rudolfinum* could have been a thousand kilometers away or in another country for all the access Rachel had to it. Rachel had walked by it almost daily for her entire life. The pale green copper roof was her landmark, her compass in the city.

On some summer nights when her window was open and the wind pushed over the river bringing moisture into Josefov, Rachel really thought that she had heard music. Tonight, she would hear her own music there. She trembled and gripped the case tighter.

The building grew larger as the concertmaster drove to it. First, the moonlight showed only the pale green copper roof with the cap that always looked to her like a crown. Next, she saw the upper floors with the painted decorations on their windowless walls. She thought of this as a smaller building set on the larger lower floors. Next the solid blocky base was in front of them.

The Concertmaster glanced at Rachel. "You haven't been inside before, have you?"

"No sir."

"Well then, I suppose I should take you all through the front door so you can really see it and not through the artist's door in the rear of the concert hall."

The Concertmaster parked the car. Yitzhak opened the car door for her and she walked up the pale stone steps that led to the arched entrance doors, clutching the violin case in her right hand. The dark red stone of the building had faded to a darker haze in the moonlight. She felt that she was floating up the stairs as she gazed at the statues above the entrance. The exterior was decorated with statues of painters, sculptors, architects and composers. Although she could distinguish Della Robia from Donetello, her eye was keener for the composers. She knew them all. Bach and Handel. Schubert and Palestrina. Schumann and Orlando di Lasso. Mendelssohn and Vittoria. Beethoven and Cherubini. Mozart and Gluck.

Pulling out a large brass key that was on the gold chain draped over his vest, the Concertmaster opened the huge door with one hand. The entrance was dark when they entered. Josef had Eva hold his arm. Yitzhak followed Rachel.

In the massive lobby, their leather heels echoed against inlaid wood and marble until they came to the red wool carpet. Rachel smelled a scent that was new to her, a blend of perfumes, and some hint of coffee, perhaps they served it in intermissions at the concert hall. Some hint of citrus came from the wax that polished the oak banister to a shine.

The moonlight and the streetlights were sufficient to see the line of carved marble busts of composers that dotted the walls of the entrance. Rachel looked at the marble busts that were along the stairway. She tripped as she did not see the elevated surface of the carpet and then quickly regained her balance.

The Concertmaster turned on a light and the great brass and crystal chandelier burst to light. Rainbows spun from the crystal drops and danced on the cream colored walls. Rachel saw the ceiling fresco of cherubs playing instruments--colors so rich and deep that the blues and reds seemed to float away from the ceiling and the fleshy cherubs seemed alive.

They walked through the lobby area and into the large concert hall with colonnades on the south side of the facility

As they entered Dvořák Hall, Rachel imagined the horns and strings of the symphony in performance and barely heard the Concertmaster say, "Behind this hall is a smaller hall for chamber recitals."

SHARON O. LIGHTHOLDER

"You wish me to play in here?" Rachel held the new violin case to her chest, as though she were chilled suddenly.

"Yes, on the center front of the stage." The concertmaster motioned her to the small stair to the side of the stage and nodded. "Ode to Joy, I think it was to be?"

Her father took her coat and held the case while she took out the violin and bow. When the Concertmaster noticed her parents still standing with Yitzhak in the aisle, he took Eva's elbow. "Come. Come here and sit. The center front row is where you want to be. I'll walk around so I can listen to the tone at a distance. Sit here so I don't disturb you. Just drop your coats on the other chairs. Be comfortable."

Rachel looked at the back wall of the hall and began to play. Alone on stage. The most alone of her life. The most alive of her life.

Her parents and Yitzhak sat in the center of the front row of seats in the empty concert hall, leaning forward to catch every note and savor it. The concertmaster walked to the back of the hall as she played. Stopping, nodding. Walking to the center of the hall. Standing. Nodding. Crossing his arms over his huge chest. When she stopped, the hall held her sound for a moment longer and it wrapped around her as a gift.

The Concertmaster was the first to applaud, and continued doing so as he walked to the front of the hall. The others stood and applauded as well.

Josef grinned at the Concertmaster who nodded and smiled. "Yes, it is all I had hoped. That is a magnificent violin. Rachel was perfect. Absolutely perfect."

Josef turned toward the Concertmaster and spoke softly. "Then perhaps Béla Bartók might be interested in it?"

Shaking his head, the Concertmaster said, "I telephoned him at his home in Budapest this morning and told him how magnificent the instrument is, just after hearing it Friday. But he is not buying now. He has started selling some of his antique folk instruments. He did not say so, but I think he may leave Hungary. It is getting so unpleasant there."

Josef put out his hands in disbelief. "Then why did we do this test?"

"Because I was up all night thinking about this violin. This is an important instrument. A legacy instrument. And I am going to buy it from you."

Rachel put it carefully into the new case, balanced on the padded red velvet that covered the seat. "You want it?"

"Yes, I'll take it now, if you don't mind. I'm going back to my country house and want to show it to some of my guests."

"Should I leave the bow in the case with it?"

"No, I have several good bows at my country house."

She handed the case to her father who handed it to the Concertmaster.

"Let me drive you," the Concertmaster said as they walked out of the *Rudolfinum* and he locked the door.

"No, we can walk. Thank you for your appreciation of the instrument. It is the best I have ever made. The first Yitzhak helped me with. I don't know if there will ever be another like it. I'm pleased that it is going to be living in Prague, with you."

"But the cost? We never set a price," the Concertmaster said.

"You will make me a fair price. I know you."

"See you Monday. I have guests waiting for me now."

As they walked home, Rachel let the bow rest against the right shoulder of her coat as she walked, not unlike a soldier on parade. She was elated and distressed at the same time. Yitzhak was animated and could not stop talking about how well she had played, how tones that he had never heard in the workshop were disclosed in the hall.

As they turned the corner to the Havel home, Josef stopped and motioned for the others to be quiet. A black car was in front of their house. The Concertmaster was leaning on the fender, smoking a cigar.

Josef walked ahead of the others. "Yes? Is something wrong?"

"Not a thing. In fact, something just happened that is very right. I'd like to come in if you don't mind."

"Of course." Josef opened the door of his home and let his wife and daughter enter first. Each touched the mezuzah gently as they passed, then kissed the fingertip that had gently grazed the mezuzah. The Concertmaster followed them, holding the violin case. Yitzhak and Josef entered the house last.

Once inside, the Concertmaster simply handed the violin case back to Rachel.

She was flushed from the walk in the cool night. "Don't you want it?"

"I'm going to buy it if your father will agree to two simple conditions."

"What conditions?" Josef asked cautiously, as he took the coats from the women and put them on pegs by the door.

"First, I will buy it. It will be mine. But Rachel must keep it and play it. If she decides not to play it every day, she just gives it back to me. It is hers in trust."

"Every day?" Rachel asked.

He shook his head and looked at the low ceiling as though for patience. "Oh, I see, there is your Sabbath rule. Would you agree to play it every day you are allowed and able to play it?"

"Yes, of course, but—"

Josef held up his hand and frowned at the Concertmaster. "Wait, daughter. What is the other condition?"

"She must attend the conservatory in Geneva, if I can get a scholarship."

"Geneva? Why not lessons here?"

"Because things are changing here. Politics, you know. They are out of that fray in Switzerland."

Eva pulled her shawl tighter. "Why would you do this for our daughter?"

"I love music. People call me a master, but I know that I can't play as well as your daughter will be able to after a few months of professional instruction. I can't teach. I don't have children of my own." He patted the violin case. "This instrument needs a guardian. I told you before that it is a legacy instrument. It needs more than I could give to it. It needs a home."

"There are many collectors that can protect it..." Josef stopped when the Concertmaster stared him into silence.

"It's not just the instrument. You know how well she plays now, before she has had professional training." He turned to Rachel. "I have never seen a gift like yours. Never. I believe that I can arrange a stipend for you, but you will need a great instrument if you are going to achieve what I think is in you. One needs the other, you see." Over a pot of coffee, the men talked details of the bargain. Rachel agreed to the arrangement only after her mother nodded almost imperceptibly.

A week later, the Concertmaster visited again, but not to play chess. This time he arrived in the midmorning carrying his large, sturdy black leather violin case, which he set beside him on the sofa while he had coffee with Rachel and her parents. After exchanging pleasantries and talking about the latest practice session at the Philharmonic, he simply handed the violin case to Rachel.

"What's this?"

The Concertmaster smiled. "Open it."

Rachel carefully laid it on her lap and snapped the weathered brass clasps open and lifted the lid. Inside was not a violin, but two tan envelopes.

Rachel opened the larger one and pulled out more than a dozen pages of typed agreements with her name, Geneva Conservatory and addresses in Switzerland, and a blur of other words that she would read later. On the last page, there were blue ink signatures and red state seals and stamps. She handed the papers silently to her father who passed them to his wife.

Rachel looked at the Concertmaster and before she could speak, he barked, "Now open the smaller one."

This was not an orderly document but a collection of letters and receipts. "What's this?" Rachel asked before reading the assorted papers.

"That's your room and board for the year, so you can put your efforts into your studies and not have to tutor some untalented oaf for money, as I had to when I was studying. It's not fancy, but it is close to the conservatory and Madame Bernard tolerates practice at all hours."

Rachel held the papers and gestured silently before speaking, "There are no words to thank you for this."

"Be your best. Share your gift. That will be thanks enough. You do know that I will expect you to write your parents regularly so I can follow your progress."

"Of course," Rachel said as she closed the heavy case and placed it on the sofa again, next to the Concertmaster. He pushed it back to her.

"The case is for you. My wife gave it to me when we began touring years ago. It doesn't look as nice as the new case the violin is in now, but then a new case is more attractive to a thief than this one. This is specially padded and...look at this." The Concertmaster opened the small accessory box that was built to rest under the neck of the violin.

Rachel nodded. "Yes? Perfect for extra strings and rosin."

"And?"

"I'm sorry, I am not understanding."

"Things are not always what they seem. Watch this." The Concertmaster pushed on the red velvet bottom of the box and the base slowly pivoted up. "A false bottom. She had it built for us to carry extra money in, in case we were robbed of our wallets. I never used it for that. I carried a letter in it all those years from her to me when we were courting. Now it is ready for your secret, someday."

"I don't think I have any secrets. But it is a beautifully made case and I will be honored to have it."

"Good, then." The Concertmaster rubbed his hands together as if finishing some chore and stood up. "Well, I have other work to do, so thank you for the coffee, Fru Havel. My compliments."

"Thank you, thank you."

After the Concertmaster left, Rachel and her parents took a closer look at the envelope that held so many things and saw that it also included an open train ticket to Geneva and back, as well as a dark blue pass book for a bank account in Geneva.

STACCATO BOWING

The method of stopping the bow between each note to produce short crisp notes.

The cold August drizzle and light breeze off Lake Geneva swirled around Rachel and Emily. Cases in hand, they hurried as they walked from the conservatory to their rooms on Rue Bernard, named for some distant relative of their landlady. In the six months since her arrival, Rachel had changed. Although she still wore her hair long, she had abandoned the two braids trailing down her back. Emily had showed her how to make one braid and knot it at the back of her neck, like some French actress she had seen in a magazine. She wore the black beret Emily had given her pulled down over her ears. In the few months she had become slimmer and seemed taller.

Emily wore a light gray fedora that she had bought in France the prior year, thinking it was very Ingrid Bergman. Sensual. Feminine. The gray of her light wool coat matched the hat perfectly; as did the two other hats that she bought when she found the coat.

Tipping her head down into the wind, Emily pointed to a small café. "Treat you to a coffee?" Rachel held the door and they took a table at the rear of the smoky café. Emily ordered two coffees with milk and slid her case under her chair. Rachel balanced her case on her lap and undid the top buttons of her coat.

After putting her thin leather gloves on the table, Emily leaned forward on her elbows. "Any information today?"

Shaking her head, Rachel sighed. "I can't wait for term to end."

"Why? You know you can't just flit in and out of Prague now that the Germans annexed Czechoslovakia."

"Invaded is more like it—"

Emily glanced at the waitress. "Shush. I overheard Madam Ortal

∾ 87 ∾

telling an instructor they are imposing some travel restrictions. But I don't have any details on what that really means."

"Listen to me—"

The waitress put two steaming cups onto the small white marble table with a clatter. Rachel leaned on her violin case. "Let's not quarrel now. Maybe I can go back-- for a quick visit."

"Don't be a child. Your parents should come and stay with us here or with my parents in London, if they can get out." Emily regretted her candor immediately.

Rachel turned away from the table and reached for her embroidered handkerchief. She pretended to cough as she wiped her eyes. Rachel stared into her cup as she used the small spoon to crush the sugar cube in it. She thought of her father playing chess with his friend, Mr. Ravensbruk. Fresh coffee was brewed for their game. Small blue-gray ribbons of smoke spiraled up from their pipes. The smoke was the only movement for minutes at a time. The men were still as stones. They sat on work stools, leaning on a knee to get a better look at the board, balanced on the third stool in the workshop. Only a seasoned observer would know whose turn it was by noting a player leaning a millimeter closer to the board than the other. The men did not watch each other, just the board, as though it would self-animate at any time. Inaction and then a quick move. Inaction and a quick move. No idle chatter.

They invariably shook hands after a game. Then there was always a moment of silence. Then they would talk. After a quick discussion of strategy and compliments to the winner, Josef moved the board from the stool to the workbench. He carefully placed each of the chess pieces from the board to the workbench and then turned over the chessboard that was hinged at the center. It then became a box for storage of the chess pieces. Each chess piece fit into its own forest green felt-lined slot, white pieces on one side of the box, and the black pieces on the other side. Josef closed the box and pushed on the small silver clasp until it snapped shut. Then Josef placed it up on the shelf above the jars of varnish.

"Beautiful set," Mr. Ravensbruk said one day after their game. "Has it been in your family long?"

"I carved it as a gift to my wife's father when I was courting her. He played well."

"He passed away?"

"Several years ago. Odd how what you give away can come back."

Rachel let her spoon clatter against the saucer. "*Zugzwang*."

"What?"

"*Zugzwang*. It is a chess term meaning no move is a good move. That's how I feel. Like a chess piece trapped. One move is as bad as the next."

Emily nodded and muttered, "*Zugswang*."

They finished their coffee in silence. The rain had stopped by the time they left. A few blocks before Rue Bernard, Rachel nodded at the barren wooden skeleton of shrubs along the walkway that had small fragments of spent yellow flowers on them. "What are these called in English?"

Emily reached out to the waist high shrubs. She brushed her hand over the wet branches tangled like a wooden spider web. Water fell off in a spray. A few of the old blooms fell to the ground.

"Do you really want to know or are you just changing the topic?" Emily challenged. She knew Rachel's technique of avoidance by asking something that would seem too reasonable to be avoided but would swing the conversation away from danger or confrontation. She was good at it. Emily was going to let her get away with it this time. They needed to talk. But Emily would let Rachel decide when the time was right. Their friendship was strong enough to support silences or let chatter fill those silences.

Rachel did not answer her.

Emily looked at her in frustration, "Forsythia. Named by the British botanist William Forsyth. Related to the olive tree in some way that I forget."

"How do you always know so much?"

"We have them at our summer home, north of London."

"You have a country home? Tell me about it," Rachel asked in her effort not to talk about what she feared most.

"More of a small cottage. But there are a great lot of forsythia bushes on the property. Mother likes them to grow wild. And so they do in great tangles--looking like abandoned haystacks through the winter and then in the spring, the flowers come out before the leaves. There is this vivid swatch of yellow all across the eastern side of the property."

"I'd love to see that."

"You will." Emily continued, hoping that the sound of her voice could drive out fear. "Every year, mother would cut a great armful and put them in water in the house. She always knew just when to do it. Then in a few days the buds on the slender branches would simply explode in cascades of bright yellow blooms, hanging like little yellow Chinese lanterns. And that is how we knew that there was going to be a spring. These great fountains of yellow would obscure the dark branches. Sometimes she would bring out these grand Chinese vases. Almost a meter high each. Cream with indigo pictures on them of Chinese people riding in a rickshaw, others walking over a bridge, everyone going somewhere. She put them on either side of the front door for a party once. I thought it very elegant and daring. Who but my mother would have put the vases on the floor?"

Rachel demanded, "Why didn't we cut some of these this year?"

"You had just arrived. Besides, I didn't have a vase."

Rachel nodded as they turned away from the lakeside walk up their street.

A man on a bicycle passed them and stopped at their door.

"Oh God. A telegramme?" Rachel murmured rather than asked.

"Deep breath. It could be good news."

They walked a bit faster and found the man in the blue pants and black leather jacket just getting off of his black bicycle with the black leather saddlebags.

Rachel walked fast enough to intercept the man before he got to the door. "May I assist?"

He looked at the address on the yellow envelope. "Are you Rachel Havel?"

She nodded, extending her hand and taking the telegramme

quickly before her hand started shaking. Rachel bolted up the stairs to her room with the telegramme clutched in her right hand. Emily dug in her pocket and gave the man a five-franc piece and nodded thanks to him. He touched his index finger to the patent leather bill of his black wool hat and left. The chain of the bicycle was loose and clanked as he let the bicycle clatter down the small hill without pedaling.

Rachel had torn open the envelope as she ran up the stairs. By the time Emily got upstairs, the crumpled pale yellow sheet sat askew on the table that dominated their practice room.

"Rachel?"

"I don't know if I understand it, what with all the "stops' in it," Rachel said, pushing the yellow paper toward Emily

While smoothing the paper, Emily said, "Punctuation. In England, a 'full stop' is the punctuation at the end of a sentence. Telegramme offices call it just a stop. I think your Americans may use the same in telegrammes but call the punctuation a 'period'. Just don't read the word 'stop'."

Rachel let out one great sob and ran out of the room, still wearing her coat and hat. Emily read the blurred black letters on a creamy-yellow paper strips that had been pasted in uneven lines on the yellow paper from the telegraph company. The short strip with the date had fallen to the floor and there was a smudge of glue where it had been.

The message was simple.

Cancel holiday at home Stop
Will call when able Stop
Father

Before thousands of questions could form in her mind, a knock at the front door startled Emily. She was halfway down the stairs when Rachel opened the door.

A slender man in a camelhair overcoat and dark fedora stood in the doorway. A black leather attaché case was in his left hand. "Miss Rachel Havel?"

"Yes." Rachel pulled off her hat with a dramatic sweep, trying to do anything not to let her hands shake.

"Thank you, Fraulein. I'm from the German embassy. There is a need to have your passport checked by the embassy. It is a new rule. You can come to the embassy with your passport and student letters by the end of the week, or I can look at your passport now. I'm afraid that your student visa may be revoked if you do not cooperate," he continued in a monotone that suggested a veiled threat. "All passports of all German citizens who are Jews must have a 'J' stamped on them."

Emily hurried down the stairs, shoving the telegramme into her pocket, and stood beside Rachel. "Oh, when did that start?"

"I regret to say that has been a requirement for some weeks now, but my predecessor was a bit casual about this rule. I am not."

"So, I should take my papers to German Embassy?" Rachel asked.

"I thought I was clear. I am not interested in any further delays. If your papers are not in order now, you can come with —"

"Wait here. I'll get my passport now."

Rachel got her passport and student identity card from her room and returned with it quickly. While she was gone, the man had walked into the parlor and opened his wet attaché case on the small marble table. He opened an inkpad in his case and held a hand stamp. Silently, she handed him the passport and he stamped it without looking at her student card. He then put the passport on the table, put his stamp and inkpad in his case and snapped it closed. He stood, nodded, and turned quickly.

Emily opened the door for him. She caught the scent of a cigar and cologne. Perhaps Cologne 4711 or something like it, clean and sharp.

At the front of the building, a black Mercedes was idling and the diesel exhaust made a soft cloud behind the car. Small drops of rain beaded on the flat hood and on the window, obscuring the face of the driver, who was smoking a thin cigar. The rain had resumed.

The car door shut with a confident thud. The driver snapped on the windscreen wipers and started to pull away from the stone curb onto the gray stone street. The car braked suddenly and the window of the passenger side rolled down quickly. The thin man squinted against the rain and forced a smile. "Oh, you will let us know if you plan to leave the country or move to another address."

"Of course," Rachel said and returned his smile. He nodded. The car left as he was rolling up his window.

Emily shut the door as Rachel leaned back into the wall. Rachel stalked across the room to the wet table and picked up the passport. She waved it at Emily. "Useless now. Totally useless. I am a prisoner of that small blue letter in my passport. One watery blue letter, smudged slightly. Not even a real word. They don't even have the courage to say 'Jew'. The bastards."

They both knew that she could not leave without drawing undue attention to her movements. But, she could not stay forever.

Months passed like years. Lessons were unending.

Attention had to be forced to each lesson and hour of practice.

Emily stayed in Geneva over the winter break, not going home to London as she had planned. Somehow the rigor of practice for their spring recital blunted the terror of not knowing what was happening to her family and time built a bond of friendship.

Somehow the winter passed and the year turned to 1939. Then, there were hints of spring on the air some days and a freshness on the wind.

Brown buds on the barren forsythia branches were full and strained on the slender branches. Emily cut a few of the dark branches and slipped them into a heavy vase that she had convinced Madame Bernard to loan her. The vase was tall enough to let the spray of dark branches fan out and form shadow puppets on the cream wall.

In a week or so the warmth of the house would seduce the brilliant yellow flowers from the sticks, and each branch would be alive with a line of yellow flowers.

CHAPTER 13

MOVEMENT

A structural unit with its own key and rhythmic structure,
or a theme within a larger work.

The telegramme arrived just as she was going out the door to the conservatory. Rachel grabbed it from the deliveryman and went back into the house to read it. Emily saw him waiting at the open door, found a five-franc piece for him, and closed the door. Rachel read it quickly and handed it to Emily. Emily read every word, slowly, searching for the meaning.

4 mai 1939
From: Post Central Hamburg, Deutschland
To: Rachel Havel
7 Rue Bernard, Geneva, Suisse
Visa approved to Havana Stop
Will write new address Stop
Enjoy London Stop
All Our Love
Josef and Eva Havel

Rachel read the words aloud to Emily. "What is he saying? That I should leave now?"

"Yes, I think so!"

"But how? My passport is stamped. You were here when—"

Emily put her hand on Rachel's wrist. "First, you need money. Get as much out of your account as you can on the way to class. Then let me make a few calls. I'll see you in class."

Rachel nodded and put her passport and other documents into her purse. She went to the bank and cashed a check for most of the funds in the account. She saw the police come into the bank and she slipped into the bathroom. There, she shifted her money from her purse to her violin case and left the bank quickly. At that moment, she thought that she had everything with her of value in the world. She decided that the rest could burst into flames, but the violin was her life. Her small savings would ease the way to England.

She decided not to go to class and was returning to her room when she saw Emily at a distance, running up Rue Bernard. She called to her and Emily stopped and looked at her and then quickly around the street to see if anyone else had seen Rachel. Then, and only then, did she walk over to her at a fast pace, but not a pace that would attract attention on a brisk spring day.

"My God, here you are. I thought that the police had found you when you weren't in class," Emily stammered, wiping her red eyes. "The police came into class and ordered all of the German students to go to the office. And they were specific that they meant you and that new girl, Lisa, from Bonn. They want to see your passport, again. I was so frightened. Lisa did not come back to class. They took her away in a car. I don't know…"

"I have almost all of my money out of the bank now, and I'll leave all my things in my room, so you don't get pulled into it."

"They are looking for you by name. You can't go now," Emily said, crying.

"A car. Is there someone with a car? I could hide in the trunk." Rachel was talking softly and intensely now. Emily had regained control and was thinking.

"No, but if you were to take my passport and wear my hat, we look enough alike to…"

"To get you arrested, too."

"No, not if I didn't know that you took it. What if you stole it, and I reported the theft to the police in a day or two, after you were long gone?" Emily asked, wiping the tears from her face with the wool muffler that she had around her neck.

"Would you do that for me?"

"Of course. Anyway, my father is coming in about a week to play at the festival. He could just take me to the embassy for another one and who would be the wiser?"

Emily made it sound so simple until Rachel saw that her hands were shaking as badly as her own. "What if they arrest you instead of me?"

"You mustn't even think that way."

The mist from their breath was swirling about their heads as a car drove past them and stopped at the apartment.

"I can't just use your passport. I don't look that much like you."

"You have to. Your parents are at sea, traveling to safety, and you must too." Emily laughed a nervous laugh.

"The car!" Rachel said, motioning to the black Mercedes that had pulled to the curb in front of their rooms.

"Yes, I saw it, too. Go to Landault's. Order a coffee and sit in the back. Slip into the loo if you are concerned about anyone. I'll get there as fast as I can."

"Emily? Can you bring my mother's shawl from my room? Black wool. About a meter square. I just remembered it."

Emily nodded and walked to Madam Bernard's house. Rachel ran around the corner and then walked quickly to the restaurant near the university. At Landault's, Emily walked directly to the large bathroom and waited for Rachel to join her.

When Emily arrived, she handed her the shawl before saying anything. As Rachel put the shawl in the big violin case, Emily took her British passport, some French franc notes and a few silver Franc pieces and put them into Rachel's purse.

Rachel started to push her hand away. "What are you doing? I have money."

"You'll need French francs."

"Listen to me, carefully. Here's how you go to London. Train to Paris. The trip to Paris takes most of a day. You'll need the French francs to go to the WC or get a bite to eat. Then you have the train ride to Calais overnight. You'll arrive at the Gare Centrale in Calais, about six or seven. Walk north on Rue Royale toward the Place d'Armes, the big square. From there it's just over a kilometer north then the docks and the boat to Dover. Buy a ticket at the dock. It is well marked. Easy walk. Don't even need a taxi. My father will meet the boat at Dover. Take the money, silly goose."

"Your father—"

"Knows nothing about this; that's why we need to switch coats. He gave me this one as a present. Take yours off now."

Emily pulled Madame Bernard's heavy sewing shears from her purse. "Your hair." Rachel took the heavy shears from her. The shears bit into her thick braid and stalled less than a quarter of the way through it. Rachel tugged at the braid and cut again. Tears ran down her cheeks as she tugged and cut again and again until the ragged stub dangled under her left ear and the coiled dark rope lay on the white tile floor of the bathroom.

Rachel handed the shears to Emily who evened up the haircut. Rachel slowly leaned to the floor, picked up her hair and dropped it into the dustbin.

Rachel ran her fingers through her short hair. "Hurry!" Rachel watched in the mirror as Emily trimmed the edges. Within a few minutes, Rachel had a haircut that was slightly shorter than Emily's passport photo.

"Looks very stylish, if I do say so myself," Emily said with far too much enthusiasm, brushing the few remnants of hair from Rachel's shoulders to the floor.

"Thank you, Emily. Thank you for—"

Emily ignored her. "What's the tag in your skirt?"

"What?"

"Was that from Prague?"

"Yes, Mother made it."

"Then trade me. I know you bought that sweater set here, but your skirt needs to be English, more convincing."

Emily slipped out of her Harris Tweed skirt in chocolate and tan tones and put on Rachel's deep brown wool skirt.

"Not too hard, then, was it?"

"Emily, I don't know how to begin to thank you—"

"Not now. On your way. Father will meet you at the boat. Here, push your hair behind your ears, more like Garbo's. Nice. Very nice, if I do say so."

"It feels—"

"Be sure to hold your violin up when you dock in England. I'm sure that's the first thing Father looks for to find me in a crowd." The women exchanged coats. Emily put her hat on Rachel. "Be safe. Be well. See you in London. Not another word."

Rachel quickly hugged Emily, left the restaurant, and took a cab to the train station from Landault's. Emily threw the shears into the dustbin in the bathroom and waited several minutes before leaving the restroom.

The light rain had turned to a slushy sleet that had the cab sliding on the stone street as it stopped in front of the Gare du Geneva. Rachel felt unsettled as she handed the driver a crumpled twenty-franc note and left without waiting for change. It was too large a tip, but one the driver would not complain about to draw attention to her. He slipped the whole note past the opening of his black leather jacket and red wool muffler into the front pocket of his white shirt. She suspected that her fare was not going to show on the books.

As she went from the cab to the covered station house, her dark coat and hat were pelted with snow which began to melt as she stood in a short line and bought her one-way ticket to Paris. The woman selling the ticket did not look up as she took Rachel's money. But when she pushed the ticket through the small opening at the base of the glass window that separated them, she stared at Rachel. Rachel tried to smile, turned away quickly and walked briskly to the boarding platform. She wandered into the center of the crowd waiting on the platform.

The sharp echo of the train whistle in the enclosed terminal made her jump. The huffing of the train grew louder as it came into the covered station. The brakes shrieked as it stopped. The passengers left the train and hurried past the crowd standing on the platform. Rachel shuffled into the train with the others and found a window seat in an empty compartment.

Wet wool, smoke from cigarettes, and the blue-black coal smoke from the train mingled into an acrid wet scent, almost like that of a campfire on which water has been poured. Steam and carbon. Elemental. Primal. Others came into the compartment and she ignored them. Then the huffing got louder and the train jerked and started out of the station.

There was nothing about the train ride that would have appeared unusual to the other passengers. A young English girl in a winter wool coat appeared to be sleeping on a train trip.

An older man in a brown overcoat and brown fedora hat blew a small stream of fresh cigarette smoke that mingled with the scent of some garlic sausage from another traveler, perhaps from another day. On any other day it would have been just a winter train smell. Today, Rachel felt the edge of nausea. She pushed herself back into the red plush bench seat and pulled her coat collar up, partially covering her face. She turned her head to the window and into the cool draft that came from it into the sweltering compartment.

She closed her eyes, pretending to sleep in order to avoid discussion with anyone. She knew this journey, having made it once before, at least from Paris to Geneva.

Through her partially closed eyes, she would peek at the landscape as the train passed through the countryside. Snow outside hit the window, melted, and slid down in clumps. The heat and humidity from all the wet coats and people's moist breath steamed over the inside of the window.

Small silver rivulets of water formed at the top of the window inside the train compartment and slowly slid down, like the mountain streams that they were still crossing. She knew the sound when the rail left land and crossed over one of the dozen small bridges. It was a deep growling rumble that you felt, not heard. A low cello note. A dog settling into a night's rest.

The landscape was pale in the misty light. Skeletal trees lined the track shaking bony fingers at the train that dared disturb their winter sleep. She saw the cold metallic gray of a lake, angular mountains, rolling hills, and, then the land flattened.

Near the border, Rachel edged close to panic. It took all of her concentration not to jump from her compartment and run screaming down the corridor as the train pitched and lurched down the curves to the flatter land.

The window had steamed to opaqueness. Just like the window of the kitchen in Prague when her mother boiled water to wash her in the tin tub when Rachel was a small child. The windows of the kitchen steamed over and she felt that humidity and remembered when the black cook stove was fired high, to warm the room before her bath.

She pushed her thoughts away from the train ride and her fear. She thought back to bath days in winter, bringing all the details to her mind, making the good thoughts push out the bad. Her mother firing the stove, baking bread, and washing the small girl in a tin tub in the steaming kitchen. Her mother wrapping her in three towels. Her father carrying her like a sack of coal over his left shoulder and then tucking her into her own bed. Simmering in the warmth of the hot bath on a cold day.

From her half opened eyes, she saw the French soldier edging toward her. Moving slowly down the corridor, stepping into each compartment for a few moments. Stepping out and coming closer. She tried to stay in her memory of Prague as she watched him approach. But when he finally slid open the door to the stuffy compartment with a crash, she was slammed back into her fear of the moment.

"Pass control!" The French soldier in a dark blue uniform stood stolidly in the doorway of the compartment. All of the other five people in her compartment had started reaching for their papers or passports as they heard him finish up in the compartment next to theirs. All looked bored with the procedure. She tried to adopt their attitude.

Rachel put her purse on her lap and drew out the passport. She also sniffed and pretended to have a cold. If she had to speak, she thought the pretense of illness would mask her accent. She held a linen handkerchief in her left hand as she handed him her passport with her right. She hoped that he would want to avoid her and her invented cold.

She feigned a cough and looked out the window as he examined the passport, then stamped it and held it out for her.

Initially, she did not take the passport after he stamped it. She was tired and her mind was blurred by fear. It did not have Czechoslovakia's seal stamped in the cover. It was British.

"Pass!" He held it in front of her. She jumped and then took it from him and noticed a coffee stain on the cuff of his shirt. The moving train never stopped. She never spoke.

She left her purse wedged between her and the wall of the compartment and quickly shoved the passport into the right pocket of her coat. It was then that she discovered a wad of crisp folded paper money, crumpled at the bottom. She was afraid to look at the bills in the train compartment and tried not to count them. From the size of the bundle, she guessed there were twenty or more bank notes. She sat frozen until the train arrived in Paris.

At the train station in Paris, she left the train with the hurried and distracted look that travelers wear--purse and violin case in her left hand, her right hand jammed into her pocket. She tried not to look at the immense interior of the covered station, or the ornate carving in the marble. She left the arrival platform with all the others and passed a restroom on her way to the ticket booth.

She turned back and went into the restroom. Rachel found a French franc piece in her purse and dropped it into the porcelain dish next to the sleeping attendant. She groaned but did not wake.

"Madam." Rachel had to say it twice to wake the old woman who then hobbled to the rear of the large white tiled bathroom. She led Rachel to a wide oak door that had a slim panel of frosted glass. She unlocked the door with a small brass key that was on a long thin chain around her neck. It was one of the five large compartments with a toilet that faced the marble counter that held several washbasins. The attendant closed the door behind Rachel, who locked the door from the inside.

The stall was large enough for Rachel to take off her coat and hang it on the brass hook on the back of the door. She set her purse and violin case on the immaculate blue and white tile floor. Now in this total privacy, with a guardian outside the door, she looked into the coat pocket and found over a hundred English pounds, just over a hundred Swiss francs and several hundred French francs. She put the English bank notes in the false bottom of the small compartment in the violin case under the rosin and extra strings. She put half of the French franc notes in her purse and left the other half in her coat pocket with the passport. She put all of the Swiss notes in her other coat pocket. Then she leaned into the cold marble wall of the stall and let its coolness calm her. She used the facilities, put on her coat, and picked up her purse and violin case.

The attendant was at the door when Rachel opened it. The attendant laid a fresh white hand towel next to the basin at the end of the room. Rachel set her purse and violin case on the marble counter, washed her hands and left, tipping the attendant the last of her Swiss franc pieces.

"Merci, mademoiselle." The attendant had the singsong voice of the countryside.

Rachel went to the currency exchange booth, exchanged all her Swiss notes for French notes and bought her ticket to Calais. She waited as trains entered and left the station for what seemed like hours. Then, just after seven, her train left.

For the next four hours on the smaller train, again and again she read the same pages of a newspaper she had found in the station while her two fellow travelers slept. One snored while she shivered invisibly throughout the trip.

At Calais the train arrived just before midnight. The boat ferry would not leave until nine the next morning.

She crossed the well-lighted street from the station to the hotel, intending to get a room for the night. Standing in the lobby, she watched a couple register, leave their passports at the desk and start up the stairs. She could not turn over her passport to the desk clerk for registration with the police and then reclaim it in the morning. Too risky, she thought. She clutched her passport in her pocket and left the hotel and turned down a smaller darker street. She passed a bistro and heard late night laughing inside; then the door slammed open and three sailors stumbled into the street. She ducked into the darkness of a doorway and they passed without noticing her.

She returned to the small, dark train station in Calais, looked at the city plan on the wall, memorizing where the boat ferry dock was located and what streets would take her to it. She sat out the night on a small chair in the attendant's area of the bathroom of the train station. In the morning, she tipped the night attendant far too much for the privilege.

When the day attendant came on, Rachel fussed with her hair and appeared to be there for the brief and proper use of the facilities and then departed.

The early morning was cold, moist and gray as Rachel walked through Calais, from the train station to the docks. The dawn deliverymen ignored her and there were no other pedestrians, although she continually expected to see someone and be confronted.

Rachel confirmed the location of the dock and the boat ferry to Dover and then walked to a *boulangerie* that she had seen from the dock. She guessed that it had been open since six, like most of the bakeries in Switzerland had been. The warm breads were on the shelf and only a few pastries were in the glass case. The warm yeasty aroma still wafted into the street. Inside a blocky man in a white cotton jacket was stacking long thin batards of bread next to round boule, on a baker's rack to the left to the door. She suspected that the locals took their usual breads and that he knew exactly how many loaves to make. Who wanted a round, who a thin batard, who required a thicker baguette.

She bought a butter croissant for breakfast and two cheese filled croissants to take on her sea voyage. The man wrapped all three in paper that had wax on one side of it. She pushed all three into her purse as she turned the corner. The fewer people she had to talk to, the better her chances were of not being discovered for the fraud she was.

At the dock, the ticket seller had set up a small table and sat bored staring out over the harbor. Two soldiers stood behind him, smoking and laughing. She had to buy a ticket from him and thought again about feigning a cold to cover any accent. She thought against it and forged ahead.

"*Un billet.*" Rachel was able to just use the word for ticket, as there were no choices to be made, only one destination, only one class on this ferry boat, not like other luxury ships. She handed him a French franc note without looking at it and the man handed the wheat-colored paper ticket with blue ink on it to her and nodded toward the gangway. Rachel took the ticket and started walking to the ship. Then the ticket seller stood and walked over to the soldiers. He took a cigarette from a soldier, got a light from another and said something that made the one soldier laugh. The other soldier watched her closely as she walked up the short gangplank.

Once on board, she went to the rail on the opposite side from the dock. The cold and the smell of the salt air were refreshing and she pulled one of the croissants from her purse. She took a bite and let her thoughts go to the richness of the bread and the surprise at how hungry she was. At her first bite, flat flakes from the croissant fell on her coat and were as quickly blown off by the wind. Just as she was about halfway through the croissant, the unsmiling soldier came around the corner and walked in her direction. She decided to look only at the sea and avoid his eyes. But he stopped next to her.

"Miss?"

She turned quickly, dropping the last of the croissant over the rail.

"Yes?" Rachel answered flatly.

The soldier searched a moment for the English words. "Miss. The ticket man. He's cheating you. Perhaps you do not know our money too good. But you pay him too much for the ticket. Here, this is yours," he said as he handed her a ten Franc note and tipped his head in a short nod.

"Thank you. Thank you very much." Rachel accepted the note from him. He turned to walk away and stopped. Emily looked at him and froze. The soldier muttered and then looked back at her. She heard him say, "*Ils* étaient *erronés. Vous n∤avez fait rien. Rien!*" She understood his words. "They were wrong. You did nothing wrong. Nothing."

But he did not wait to see if she understood or not and walked away crisply. His last word, '*Rien*', echoed from the strength with which he said it.

The boat ferry left on time. In spite of the chill and light snow that had started, she remained on deck until she could no longer see France. The nausea that held her captive throughout the train travel left her on the sea.

At Dover, the docks were swarming with people. Handcarts loaded with baggage were being taken from the holds at dock level as she started down the steep wooden gangplank. She looked over a mass of faces, all strangers, wondering how she would ever find Emily's father.

Even as she watched her footing on the light sway of the gangway, she looked for him. She had met him just once, when he came to visit Emily at school. He had joked that it was good luck that two girls who were only children were fated to be roommates.

But as she looked for a man in a hat, all men seemed to have hats and be about the right age to be Emily's father. And there he was, at the foot of the gangplank. He was wearing a gray overcoat and gray hat. She remembered that he walked with a cane and saw him list to one side. He smiled broadly. He started to go toward her then stopped as if confused.

Rachel ran to him calling loudly, "Papa!" and embraced him before he could speak.

"Mr. Finch?" Rachel whispered as she held on to him.

"Yes." He started pushing her away, examining her frightened face. "Rachel isn't it? Where is Emily?"

Rachel held on to him for all her strength and whispered to Mr. Finch, "Geneva. She's fine. She sent me in her place.

"What do you mean in her place; where is she?" Mr. Finch snapped.

"She sent me to you. She said to tell you not to worry. She will cable you tomorrow if she can't get a telephone connection. Please, can we go now?"

"Of course, my dear," Graham Finch said loudly, as he wrapped a long arm around her shoulder and shuffled as he escorted her through passport stations and past the crowded baggage claim area as she carried only her purse and her violin case. She appeared ready to go to class rather than to a new life.

He found a boxy black cab easily. Rachel shivered in the back of the cab. Mr. Finch watched her as she cried softly, knowing that she was not going to tell him anything in front of the driver. Only after Rachel had passed the bright yellow bed of new daffodils in front of their flat and was inside the door of the apartment building did she really exhale.

During the slow walk up the one flight to the apartment, she assured Mr. Finch that Emily had crafted a plan that removed any suspicion from her and that she was safe. Only after finishing a breathless account of their planning on the landing, did Mr. Finch open the door to the modest flat. He called to his wife. "Nattie, where are you?"

To the immediate left of the front door was a small closet where Mr. Finch put their coats. Mrs. Finch called from the kitchen. "In here. I'll have your favorite tea in two shakes, Emily. I heard the cab draw up and put the kettle on." Her smile faded as she rushed into the living room, wiping her hands on her apron, and failed to see her daughter.

Mr. Finch took her by the arm and walked her to the sofa. "Emily has sent us Rachel in her place. Listen to what your daughter has concocted now."

As Rachel recounted her story, Graham put added coals on the small fire in the fireplace to the right of the front door and went down a hallway next to the fireplace. He returned in a moment tugging on a heavy tan cardigan sweater and sat in a wing back chair by the fire. He let his cane drop to the floor beside him and listened for added details as Rachel expanded on Emily's bravery and cunning in helping her escape before the police and agents from the embassy returned to the conservatory or trapped her at Madam Bernard's house. When the kettle boiled, Nattie jumped up and turned off the gas burner. She stood over the stove, staring at the kettle for almost a minute before she returned to the doorway. "Graham? Tea?"

"Please, dear. It was brisk on the docks. Odd late spring weather."

CHAPTER 14

PIANO

A musical instruction to play softly.

Aweek later, Emily arrived home in London. Claiming that her passport was stolen in a purse snatching at the cinema, she had convinced the British Embassy in Geneva to issue a provisional travel permit that allowed her passage only back to England. They would get it all sorted out back there, they said. Her first night back in England, Emily took Rachel out to a pub for a real English sausage and a pint of Watney's. Rachel tried to return the money from the coat to her but Emily refused.

The next day Rachel helped Emily unpack her trunk of clothes and books that she had brought back from school. Several of Rachel's better dresses and her two pair of trousers were in the trunk. Emily had obviously left some of her own clothes behind to make room for Rachel's. Emily pulled out a thick musical score and tossed it to Rachel.

"Open it," Emily said with a smile.

"Why? I know this score. It's one of our practice pieces from the conservatory, but this must be yours."

"Open it, anyway."

As she opened the folio, something dropped in her lap. It was her passport.

"Evidence of a crime!" Rachel said quietly, looking at the passport and starting to cry. Emily handed her a handkerchief.

"A memory, at least. Thought you'd want it. It was in your coat when we traded coats."

Emily pulled the journals from the trunk and gave them to Rachel. She stacked them on the passport, on the small stack of Rachel's things that Emily had rescued. Not much more than a breadbox of a life.

Rachel picked up the passport and thumbed through the pages.

"What good is this now? It's from a country that does not exist. It has that hideous 'J' in it." Rachel threw it across the room.

Emily picked it up and held it in front of her. "Look. Right now, it may seem irrelevant, but who knows how all this is going to work itself out?"

"But...."

"I know it must seem futile, but keep it for a while longer. Trust me."

"Why should I keep it? So I can go be with my parents? I don't even know where they are."

Rachel fanned through its pages again. The passport was missing an exit stamp that the Swiss would have issued. But they would not have issued it to the newly annexed German citizen whose passport had the "J" that the Germans stamped in it. It was the Swiss who had asked for this policy, to keep track of the flow of Jews into and out of Switzerland. And now she held the evidence that she had interrupted the perfect control procedure. The blue ink had smudged slightly when the slim man had quickly closed the pages after he had stamped it. That entry stamp was on a page alone. Rachel considered for a moment ripping out that page of her passport and erasing any history of Geneva at all.

But there was a part of Geneva that she could not abandon. Yitzhak had visited her there, shortly after her studies began. He arrived unannounced. Rachel discovered him leaning against the wall across the narrow winding street from Madam Bernard's, reading a newspaper, waiting for her to come home. She saw him and ran to him. They embraced and he came into the home.

It was three in the afternoon and a recital was set for four. Rachel gave Madame Bernard her ticket to go with Emily and made a great show of leaving with Yitzhak to go to the conservatory.

Madame Bernard eyed him as an intruding dog, walking sideways around him, trying to get his scent. She motioned Rachel to follow her to the kitchen, warned her that her board money did not include dinner for intruders, and no strangers after dark was her policy. Rachel nodded agreement and left with Yitzhak.

They had two glasses of white wine and walked through the narrow streets until they knew the recital was underway. Then they were at Madame Bernard's. Yitzhak kissed Rachel and used her key to open the door. Rachel took his hand and pulled him into the front room.

That was the day they made love. And then, at almost five, Yitzhak made scrambled eggs for them and pulled a few leaves of fresh tarragon from the herb pot in the kitchen window. He crushed the tarragon between his thumb and index finger as he sprinkled it over the cooking eggs. They ate. She washed the dishes and put the kitchen back to order as he watched her. He kissed her at the front door, and she smelled the tarragon on his hand as he brushed her cheek and smiled at her. He was gone before the concert was over.

No, there were parts of Geneva that had become her, shaped who she was. The passport stayed in the small stack of her things. As did a smudged mimeographed page of the loading instructions for those departing Hamburg on the *S.S. St. Louis* in May of 1939. Graham had been visited at a symphony rehearsal one afternoon in late May and handed the paper by an older man in a worn black suit. From the Red Cross, he said. A woman had given it to a Dutch sailor in Hamburg to give to the Red Cross in London. Graham's name and London Symphony were written on it in pencil with Cuba circled on the ports of call listing. No other message. No signature.

When Graham took it home that evening, a new pattern of watching and waiting began. First, it was a dash to the mailbox after the postal delivery. Then it became listening to the BBC reports on the travels of the *S.S. St. Louis* and its effort to take refugees to Cuba. The link between Rachel's parents and the ship was speculative until Graham read the passenger names in the *London Times* and confirmed that Rachel's parents were on the manifest.

After that discovery, all four would gather in the living room to listen to the BBC Home Service for news of the progress of the *S.S. St. Louis*. They followed Rachel's parents' voyage.

The small brown table radio balanced on the edge of the piano and boomed in the silent room: "Tonight our correspondent in Havana is reporting that the Cuban government has continued in its refusal to allow the 930 passengers on the *S. S. St. Louis* to disembark and the passengers on the ship are petitioning the President of the United States to intercede."

Another nightly broadcast: "We have been following the passage of these Jews escaping the grip of Germany on their lives. They left Germany with approval of the highest officials and with visas approved by the Cubans, but on arrival, they were held in the harbor, virtual prisoners on a luxury liner in Havana Harbor for almost a month. For a week, the ship sailed up the Atlantic coast of the United States, but to no avail. Now today, they have been refused entry by the United States as well. The Director of the steamship line has announced that the ship is returning to Germany."

Graham slammed his newspaper to the floor and stalked over to the radio. He turned the brown knob and the light went off on the front of the radio. All sat in silence for a moment before Graham roared, "The boat has turned back to Germany. What the bloody hell for?"

Mrs. Finch looked up from a button she was sewing onto the cuff of a white dress shirt. "Mr. Roosevelt's silence is absolutely deafening on this matter. How can he refuse to let the boat dock?"

"How can he let it dock without becoming engaged in this mess over here? God knows I'm not defending his being an isolationist. I'm just trying to explain it to you," Graham stammered, at once feeling cold and aloof, embarrassed and afraid for Rachel, knowing her parents were on the ship.

"Well, then I think the answer to all this is quite obvious. He is just not seeing it," Mrs. Finch said. "He needs to let them land, or maybe they can dock in Canada."

Graham chuckled. "Suspect he's catching an earful from Eleanor on this."

There were only a few moments that Rachel remembered clearly about the early summer of 1939. Every evening, they would gather around the radio and listen to the broadcasts of BBC, from America, from London, from Cuba, and the BBC Home Service, trying to piece together where her parents were and how they were managing.

In June, it made a brief stop in England before docking on June 17 in Antwerp, after forty days at sea. The passengers disembarked and were sent to distant places. Graham tried to find Rachel's parents through the British Embassy, the Red Cross, the musicians he knew in France, and a war comrade who was living in France.

In mid-July a man came to see her in London. He was cocooned in a dark brown suit coat and muffler, in spite of the balmy weather. He removed a derby hat as the door opened. He held the hat by the firm brim and shuffled the brim through his hands as he stood at the door. He was over sixty. His white hair had thinned to short wisps, but he was as shy as a schoolboy.

Mrs. Finch peered through the partially opened door. "Yes?"

"Is there a Rachel Havel here? I'm Jacob Weiss. Could you please tell her that I have something for her? A delivery."

Mrs. Finch opened the door and motioned him to enter. "I'll get her, please wait here."

But the man stood motionless just inside the door until Rachel came into the room. Rachel went to him and asked, "Mr. Weiss?"

He looked at the modern young woman in loose dark trousers and a pale blue blouse and searched her face. "Are you Josef's daughter?"

"Josef Havel? Yes."

Without moving, he looked at the floor and began a recitation that he had obviously practiced. "Miss Havel. I am Jakob Weiss. I left Hamburg with your parents on the ship, the *St. Louis*. I didn't meet them until we were coming back from Havana. I thought that I'd be going to Antwerp with your parents and everyone else. No one knew why we docked in England, but they put almost three hundred of us off the ship. And everyone else went to Antwerp. I heard some were sent to France. I don't know how they decided who.... I wanted you to know that we could not trade these appointments with others. If I could have, your mother—"

"Come, Mr. Weiss, sit by me." Rachel took his arm at the elbow and led him to the sofa. His hand held an envelope and trembled in a way that frightened her.

"All I know is that our names were announced in a meeting in the dining hall of the ship. Your father found me in that crowd, shook my hand, and wished me well in England. He said his daughter was here with a school friend. He told me how to find you. He didn't seem to resent my being picked. Your father found some letter paper and he and your mother wrote to you. He sealed the envelope and wrote your name and the philharmonic and Mr. Finch's name on it. He asked me to find you in London."

Rachel took the pale envelope from his shaking hand and thanked him.

The man quivered and started sobbing. "He never asked me to go on to Antwerp so he could come here. Your mother stood by him and shook my hand and wished me well too. How much I wanted them to be here, not me. But that wasn't allowed."

Rachel was seated on the sofa, but felt as if she were in a free fall from space, floating over it, hoping that gravity would orient her to this man and his message. The envelope was warm from his body, and crumpled at the edges. Rachel bit her lip while he composed himself. "Tell me again. How do you know my father?"

"From the boat. I couldn't have been with him more than a couple of minutes right after they announced...." The old man spoke very slowly, as it was clear that Rachel was only able to understand his presence there in small bits. "Then he asked me if I would get a letter to you. I said I would. And now you have your letter."

"Thank you. Is there anything I can do—?"

"Miss Havel." He stood and jammed his hand deep into the pocket of his brown tweed jacket as tears welled in his eyes. "Your father asked me to put this into your hand."

The pale blue green brass mezuzah from the doorpost of her home floated in this stranger's open palm. It was as she had remembered it, but different. There was a black piece of yarn, wrapped around the center and tied in a tight knot. To hold the back door of it shut. She reached for it, old brass, no larger than her father's thumb. She wondered if the yarn was from the fringe of one of her mother's shawls.

"How?" Rachel tried to ask, and only an unfamiliar whisper came out.

"I had taken the letter and was at the gangplank when your father called me and ran to me. He pressed the mezuzah into my hand and left before I could refuse this request. I never saw him after that."

Rachel had picked it up by the fingertips of her right hand and had laid it into the open palm of her left hand. She stared at it, not wanting to guess what it might mean. Rachel held the mezuzah in her left hand and looked at her name on the envelope that she had dropped to her lap. Rachel suddenly looked up, grabbed the stranger's sleeve. She held it until she could ask, "How were they?"

"Healthy. Many were seasick or so upset by coming back that they.... One man jumped off the boat in Havana to kill himself." Mr. Weiss patted her hand, "But that was not your parents. They held hands on deck. I had noticed them. I thought they might be recently married, you know. Even at their age."

Rachel nodded. "Thank you."

"Nothing. There was nothing we could do." And with that he stood, slid the hat on his head, a bit farther back than level, and then tugged it tight on his head. He patted her shoulder once and walked out the front door. When it clicked shut, Mrs. Finch came back into the room.

"Are you all right, dear?"

Rachel nodded and stared at the front door. She sat pressing the envelope into her lap with her right hand and holding the mezuzah tightly with her left hand.

"Do you want me to sit with you?"

Rachel shook her head as she stood. She went to her room, shut the door and sat on her bed. She sat very still and started to open the letter. Pulling the flap away from the back of the envelope with care not to tear it, as though it were made of spider webs. And then, she slipped out the one page. A short page, note paper, not proper letter paper. Sea blue ink imprint of the ship's name and black ink. Her mother's slim letters, followed by her father's blocky penmanship, and then their signatures.

S. S. St. Louis – Hamburg
Darling
We are together and well. Love to you.
Eva

Rachel bat Josef-
Be brave. Be loving. How blessed we are with you.
  Father
YOUR PARENTS
Evah bat Meyer
Josef ben Moshe

The words swirled as she read the page again and again. Why had her father used their Hebrew names? Nothing about where they were, nothing about how she could find them. No date, but it must have been early June.

She knew the message was rushed. Their writing was not as precise as their letters to her in Geneva. The paper was thin enough that even after it was folded in half again and returned to the envelope, the dark blue letterhead with the '*S.S. St. Louis – Hamburg*' glowed through the paper. The square envelope had only the '*S.S. St. Louis*' imprinted at the corner and her name in black ink. As she looked at it, it blurred, and only then did she realize that she was crying. She opened her Czech passport and slipped the note from her parents into the space between the flimsy pages and the hard covers.

She thought of her father's confident voice. The last time she had talked with him, months before, while she was still in Geneva. She knew the day exactly: November 11, 1938.

The office at the music conservatory smelled of pencil shavings, old leather, and strong stale coffee. Madame Ortal walked briskly to the telephone and pushed the hand piece toward Rachel. Madame Ortal's black cut glass beads clanked into each other with a sharp unpleasant sound, and her ankle length black dress made her almost invisible in the darkest corner of the room where she stood in silence during the conversation.

Rachel had no idea who could be calling. Fearful. Out of breath.

When she said "Oui?" as she had been taught to answer the telephone in Geneva, the operator said in German for the other party to go ahead. Her father was at the postal station in Prague where there were telephones for hire.

"Are you there," he asked, possibly not recognizing her French. "Is that you, Rachel?"

"Yes, Papa."

"Listen carefully. Is anyone able to hear you?"

"Yes, Papa."

"Then just listen. If anything happens, go to London. I will contact you through Mr. Finch at the Philharmonic. If not him, somehow through the Philharmonic. Just remember that as much as love connects our family, music connects us, too. We have that as our way to find each other in this madness. Remember that. We will find you. Your talent is a beacon for us."

"Yes, I will. But why?"

"Two nights, for the past two nights, the police and young hooligans came through the Josefov. Glass was broken and there were fires set... men were beaten. Worse things in Berlin and Munich...."

"But..." Rachel wanted her father to come for her, hold her, and make her unafraid.

"Listen carefully. Your mother and I feel it best to visit our friends in Hamburg. Nothing has yet happened there. And in the weeks since the annexation, it has been...."

"Should I join you?" she asked, knowing that Madame Ortal was listening, not wanting to say where.

"No, don't come back here. It is too uncertain. Listen, the Concertmaster has a cousin who knows people who might be able to help us find a way to leave. We will..."

"Can't you come here?"

"We can't leave Germany without an exit visa. Our passports have been stamped. Since we are now a part of Germany. But at least we can get to Hamburg."

"Stamped?" Rachel whispered.

"With a J-- Jew. We can't leave the country with that stamp. I don't know if they will try to get your passport or not. Don't wait. Go to London, any way you can."

"And leave school mid-term?" she whispered, hoping he could hear her.

"Yes, whenever you can, I'm sending you all I can to your account. Remember, music is universal and there is always going to be someone who needs a violin repaired. Or needs a good violinist. We are a small community and will be able to find each other after this madness is over."

She turned her back to Madame Ortal. "How can I contact you?"

"You shouldn't try. I'll always find you."

The line crackled before it went silent. She was ashen and her hand shook when she placed the hard black handset into the metal cradle.

Madame Ortal watched her and came closer. "Are your parents ill?"

"Yes…my mother. I may need go home and help care for her."

"Back to class for now."

And so she obeyed, for a time.

The months between that brief telephone call and the visitor from the ship had passed too quickly. Rachel slipped the letter from her parents and the faded instruction page with faint purple lettering into her leather journal and put the small mezuzah into the false bottom of the compartment in her violin case.

CHAPTER 15

SYNCOPATION

The direction to play notes between the beats.

Rachel held the squirming toddler as Emily shut the door behind them, took the *Times* from under her coat, and handed it to her father.

Graham took the paper. "Thank you, dear. Back so soon?"

Emily slid her wet coat onto a hanger and draped her dripping scarf over the coat's shoulder to dry in the closet. "The park is simply flooded." She unbuttoned the cream colored cardigan she wore over a light blue blouse and brushed the remaining raindrops from the cuffs of her navy wool trousers. She took the boy from Rachel and removed his wet jacket and knit cap while Rachel put up her coat.

Rachel made a direct line for the fireplace and faced it as she brushed the last of the rain from her charcoal sweater and trousers. She rubbed her hands together. "It felt cold enough to snow today. Think we'll have any snow by New Year's?"

Before anyone could answer, the child had fallen backwards on the carpet and sent up a howl. Over the next two hours, the young women took turns playing with the boy who seemed immune to any suggestion of taking his afternoon nap. By four, they passed him off to Graham who struggled unsuccessfully to entertain the neighbor's toddler. The boy squirmed and escaped from Graham's lap, slipping under the *Times* that he was reading aloud to the child in a particularly animated manner. The boy made fast but uneven progress toward the tray of cups and the teapot next to the fireplace.

Mrs. Finch called from across the room, "Graham, keep the lad away from the table lest he tip the tea tray into the coals, please." An uncommon sharpness was creeping into her voice.

"Certainly, my love." Graham failed to deter the child with a tap on his nappie-padded bottom with his cane. Relenting, Graham stood and scooped the chunky child into the air by the armpits. Fat legs ran in the air, heels pounded into Graham's thick brown cardigan sweater as Graham balanced on his good leg. "Got you now."

"Thank you," Mrs. Finch said with some relief. "It will be so much easier to watch him once the weather clears or it snows and we can take him out to the park."

"What do you propose we do with him now? The Prime Minister is going to be on the wireless in a few minutes, and I plan to hear him." Graham dangled the boy in midair.

Emily glanced up from her book. "We could eat him for dessert."

Mrs. Finch rescued the tea tray. "His mother *may* object to that."

As she carried it to the kitchen, Graham called after her, "Dear, where's the snow globe? That might amuse him."

She stormed out of the kitchen, wiping her hands on the white apron she had put over her dark green wool dress and returned in moments with a black-based snow globe of St. Paul's Cathedral. She handed it to Graham carefully so none of the porcelain chips in it would swirl.

After shaking it with a theatrical flair to focus the boy's attention, Graham began a narration of the snowstorm over the cathedral. The boy patted the globe and peered into it. However, his attention was diverted by a tapping at the door.

Graham placed the globe on the floor beside his chair. "Are you expecting anyone, Nattie?"

She answered from the kitchen. "No, dear. Maybe his mum's come home early."

Graham hoisted the child over his shoulder as he answered the door.

Two RAF flyers in wool overcoats filled the doorway. Raindrops glistened on their coats.

"Mr. Finch?" asked the taller of the two, in an accent that was clearly American.

"Yes, what can—"

Yitzhak saw Rachel at the kitchen door and pushed past Graham. "Rachel!"

Rachel looked up shouted, "Yitzhak!" She clung to him. Graham retreated to his chair with the boy. Emily motioned the American into the house as well and shut the door.

The American pulled off his soft cap and grinned. "Hi, my name's Harry. Harry Montgomery. From California. This here is Yitzhak Brod. He's from Czechoslovakia. As you can see, he knows Rachel. Met him when we both joined your Royal Air Force on the same day."

Emily put the snow globe out of reach on the mantel as the child squirmed free of Graham. "How ever did you find us?"

He surrendered his overcoat to Emily and moved toward the fireplace. "Wasn't easy. Last leave, we went to the Red Cross looking for Rachel. No luck. But then, we're walking downtown today and Yitzhak saw the poster in front of the orchestra. Yitzhak remembered your name, Miss Finch. So I asked the doorman at the concert hall if your dad still played there; he gave us your address since the phones don't work too well right now. We just came right over. Sure hope you don't mind. Do you?"

Now holding hands and looking at each other, Yitzhak asked "*Jak se máte?*" 'how are you.'

"*Dobro.*" Rachel answered that she was 'good'. And, after that, Emily could not follow a word that was exchanged between them as Rachel took his wet coat to the closet, they made their way to the sofa, and sat holding hands.

Graham started to quiz the American immediately. "What the blazes are you doing over here? You're not even in the war yet."

"*Yet* seems to be the question. I heard you were short of radio operators, and that's what I do. Been a ham operator for almost ten years now."

Emily took the boy from her father. "Ham?"

"Amateur radio operator. Wireless." Mrs. Finch took off her apron as she joined them, nodding. She reached for the boy, who kicked at her and twisted to be free of Emily.

Graham continued as though no one else were in the room. "Must have been a tyke when you started. Is your father interested in radio, too?"

Harry reached for the boy who went to him quickly. Harry hoisted the toddler over his head and planted him on his shoulders. He held the boy by the wrists and jostled him slightly as he answered Graham. "No, he's a farmer. Built the radio myself. Learned about radio from the pilots that flew the crop dusters. Made me a radio from a box of vacuum tubes and wires. Soldered it together myself."

"Really?"

"Yep. Astounded them, since I couldn't keep my mind on my chores for an hour at a time. Mom and Pop would come in and listen to me talk to people all over the world on this big silver carbon microphone. Then they'd listen to the radio, to BBC on my short wave. See, they'd never been out of California and Mom was fascinated by this." Harry went on to tell them about his farm, how he had to get the permission of the State Department to join the RAF, and about his training.

Dinnertime and Robert's mother finally collected him. After she left, all shared a light meal. By 10:00 p.m., Yitzhak and Harry were deep asleep in the front room on the sofas, while Rachel just dozed. Rachel did not cry until after the train left the next morning.

CHAPTER 16

HARMONIC

*A tone created when the bow of the violin makes contact with a string that is
lightly touched by the left hand. This special tone is neither the open string
nor a fingered note.*

It was a snowy Tuesday in January of 1940, barely three weeks after
they had rediscovered each other, when Yitzhak telephoned Emily's
flat in London to say that he and Harry had passes for the next 48
hours. He asked Rachel to marry him immediately, before he had to
return to the base and flights over Germany.

The call started a frenzy of activity. First, Emily and Rachel, who
had been practicing violin in casual sweaters and slacks, sent up such
a racket in the bedroom after the telephone call that Emily's mother,
ran into the room. "What is it? Are you alright?"

Emily hugged her mother. "Mum, Rachel's going to be married.
Isn't that grand?"

"That so? I do hope we will be invited to the—"

"Now, Mum. Here. At the flat."

Rachel nodded quickly. "It's true, Mrs. Finch. He just asked me.
It's going to be such a rush. They just got their passes and are arriving
tonight. Harry's coming too."

Mrs. Finch was a petite woman whose face flushed with excitement as she embraced Rachel. Mrs. Finch took off her light blue apron
and smoothed her dark blue dress with some formality. She brushed
back her light brown hair from her forehead and looked at Rachel.
"That's wonderful." Age sat well on her and eased her strength into
confidence. She calmed the worries of the girls by her presence. She
was suddenly a mother with two daughters.

Rachel put her hand to her forehead. "I need to find a Rabbi—"

Mrs. Finch put up her hands to calm Rachel. "Maybe Doctor Rosenberg can assist. He is of your faith. I'll ring him up in a minute; what else do we need?" Mrs. Finch started a list on a sheet of cream-colored letter paper. "Rabbi, dress, license—"

Rachel reached over to Mrs. Finch and took her hand, "Thank you for everything. Your help in planning the *simchah* is more than I could have ever imagined."

"What's a sim...ka?" Emily asked Rachel, stuttering, losing the last "h" in the process.

"It's means joyous event. That's what we call a wedding or any good thing," Rachel found joy in using her own language with a close friend. "Say it slower...sim, with the emphasis on kah. See how easy?"

Emily said it slowly and well. "Are you trying to give me language lessons now?" Emily asked in the teasing way that they'd developed at school. Some sisters have it. Few friendships are as trusting. Mrs. Finch laughed easily at her daughter's humor.

"No lessons for you. Just sharing with my friend."

"You just say that because I'm your only friend in London."

"You know you are so much more than just a friend. How did I get to London? Now the wedding. That is far more than any friendship could imagine."

"What's this going to be like?" asked Emily as Mrs. Finch went to call Doctor Rosenberg's office.

"Well, not nearly all the dancing and food and relatives that my parents would have planned. Just the ceremony. It's in two parts. First there is the *Kiddushin*. That's the sanctification. It's our contract, our covenant with God. In the *Kiddushin*, we agree to undertake that covenant as a couple."

Emily frowned. "What does that mean?"

"That we'll raise our children in the faith, keep a Jewish home, make joint decisions on big things, like how to educate the children, which synagogue to join...."

"Children? How can you even think of having a baby now?"

"How can I not think of it? I almost lost Yitzhak once. If it weren't for him knowing your name and finding your parents here in London...."

Rachel started to cry.

Emily shook her head and laughed. "So, I'm the link in this romance after all. I thought so."

Mrs. Finch returned holding her list. "I have the Rabbi's number. We can shop for your wedding ring after meeting with him. Or isn't that allowed?"

"It's allowed, a plain band without stones. I didn't even think of that. But, you are right, the *Kiddushin* is when we would exchange rings."

As she put on her coat, Emily asked, "What do you say? Do you have it all memorized yet? I have my vows memorized, even though Teddy is in North Africa and hasn't actually proposed."

"Our part is simple. We say, 'By means of this ring you are sanctified to me according to the Law of Moses and Israel'."

Mrs. Finch placed her hand on Rachel's arm. "Rachel, you said that the *Kiddushin* is just the first part of the wedding ceremony. What's the other?"

"The second is the blessing. It's called the *Sheva Berachot*. It blesses God for creating man and woman and the marriage both in the image of Adam and Eve and in the more heavenly image of the marriage. The groom is 'chatan' and the bride is 'kalah'."

Emily was wide-eyed. "What else do I need to know--not to be too big a fool for you and Yitzhak?"

Rachel nudged her. "There is just one thing that you need to remember. Can you say *mazal tov*?"

Emily tested the new word. "*Mazal tov*."

"It means 'good luck'. It's used for 'congratulations'. When the ceremony is going on, we'll be under a canopy. It's called a *chupah*. I'm going to ask if the Rabbi will let me use my mother's shawl for the canopy. It's all I have of her with me. I'll need to have four people to support the *chupah*."

"And then what happens?" Emily asked.

"We'll sip wine to represent our joined lives. Yitzhak will take a glass and crush it under his foot. That's when you shout *mazal tov*, good luck."

Mrs. Finch asked, "Why is the glass smashed?"

"A remembrance of the temple that was destroyed. That in joy there is sorrow, that nothing is permanent. Lots of meanings."

Rachel telephoned the Rabbi and met with him that afternoon. She told him that they had hoped to marry at the synagogue in Prague where Yitzhak's parents had married, as had Rachel's parents and their grandparents as well. But she explained that the ceremony needed to be the next day at the Finch's home.

By six that evening, the young women had polished the silver tea-pot and good spoons for the reception and changed into stylish wool dresses, Emily's was cream colored and Rachel's was a light blue.

Yitzhak and Harry arrived just after seven that evening. Nattie laid out a cold dinner for all to enjoy. After dinner, she whispered to Emily, who was drying dishes as Nattie washed them, and asked if Rachel was ready to be married. At Emily's blank stare, Nattie, stammering a bit, asked if her mother had told her what she needed to know for her wedding night. Nattie seemed relieved when Emily laughed and told her not to worry. Once the dishes were done, Nattie embarked on making a lemon cake for the wedding reception.

The morning of the ceremony, Mrs. Finch wore her lavender dress and pearls. She laid out her husband's best blue suit and a pearl gray tie. He was slim and of medium height. His thinning sandy hair was combed straight back and he leaned on his walking stick as he took Yitzahk, in his uniform, and Rachel, in a cream colored wool dress, to the licensing clerk and expedited the matter for them.

Emily helped her mother prepare the last details before changing into a dark blue wool dress that flattered the strand of pearls that she'd selected as her only jewelry for the event. By the time Graham, Rachel and Yitzhak returned, the house was ready for the wedding.

Dr. Rosenberg was the first to arrive. Rosenberg was over six feet tall, slim and was starting to develop the stoop that some tall men get from leaning down to make the world more comfortable. His thinning hair was combed with precision and lacquered enough to survive a light windstorm. His face was round, more suited to a smaller plump man. His eyes were eager and kind. His smile was wide and easy. He had selected a well-tailored pinstripe suit with a gray tie for the occasion.

Rosenberg was very deliberate in his actions in contrast to Graham's stick figure jerkiness. It was as though Graham saved all of his grace and coordination for his violin performances with the symphony.

Mrs. Finch thought her husband looked like the perfect English gentleman as he introduced Rachel to Dr. Rosenberg before the Rabbi arrived. Later, Mrs. Finch would tell Rachel how, when Dr. Rosenberg was a young intern, Graham was one of the war-wounded in his hospital. The men spent a great deal of time together and grew to discover similar tastes in music and a mutual admiration.

"Rosenberg is an Englishman who had the good fortune to be born here rather than in Russia like his parents," Graham said after introducing Dr. Rosenberg to Yitzhak.

When the Rabbi arrived with his wife just before noon, Dr. Rosenberg introduced them and chatted with her while the Rabbi spoke to Rachel and Yitzhak privately in the bedroom. When they returned, Rachel held her mother's shawl to her chest and walked with the Rabbi to the fireplace. He turned and stood with his back to the low crackling fire and motioned for Emily and Harry to join them. Rachel handed the shawl to Dr. Rosenberg who gave a corner to the Rabbi's wife. Emily and Harry quickly took the other corners and raised the shawl to become the canopy under which Rachel and Yitzhak stood.

Nattie and Graham Finch held hands during the ceremony. When Yitzhak discovered that the rings had been forgotten in the rush of the day, Graham Finch slipped the golden signet ring from his right hand and quickly passed it to Rachel. Emily held out her hand to Yitzhak who took her smaller signet ring from her finger. The golden rings, with an incuse griffon and sheaf of wheat, had been in the Finch family since the Crusaders went to convert the Jews and slay the infidels in Europe and Turkey. They exchanged rings. At the end of the ceremony, Yitzhak's foot came down hard, splintering the wine glass that was wrapped in a white handkerchief.

All shouted *mazal tov* as Rachel bat Josef and Yitzhak ben Solomon were married, although the London registry would call them Rachel and Isaac Brod.

After the ceremony, Emily and Rachel were dispatched to the kitchen to bring out the teacups and plates. Mrs. Finch followed, carrying a single layer lemon cake. She had cut a stencil and sifted confectioner's sugar to form a white Star of David on it. Emily grinned and whispered, "Clever girl, mum. When did you decorate it?"

"While you were setting out the china. Fetch the teapot, like a good girl."

Mr. Finch went to his cellar, as he called the bottom of the hall closet of their town home. Holding the neck of a bottle aloft, he called. "Sherry, anyone?"

Mrs. Finch cast him a glance and then retreated to the kitchen and returned a moment later carrying a silver tray with nine of the smallest glasses Rachel had ever seen. The deeply cut facets in the Waterford crystal caught the light like diamonds as Mr. Finch filled them.

The Rabbi was the first to raise his glass to the couple. "*Mazal tov*." Harry tapped the edge of Emily's glass with his. "Thanks for all this; he's a swell guy."

Mrs. Finch had the wedding couple make the first cut in the cake and then served the guests with a grace that suggested there were four more cakes in the pantry. Emily poured tea and delivered cups to accompany the cake.

Later, in the kitchen, Rachel helped Mrs. Finch wash up. "Where did you ever find tea?"

"I must admit it's not all that fresh. But then, you could probably tell that."

"Hardly! It tasted just like school. Good Darjeeling from India."

"It did seem awfully good, didn't it?" Mrs. Finch chuckled. "Must be a case of absence making the heart grow fonder."

Emily brought in a stack of plates and placed them on the side of the sink. She gave her mother a quick hug. "I think that the real triumph was your lemon cake. Just as good as when I was a child."

"Well, it took more chemistry than baking skills to reduce the recipe to the few eggs I was able to find."

"Well done, Mum," Emily whispered as she slipped out to gather more dishes.

"Mrs. Finch, you have made this a very special time for us. I can only hope that when Emily marries, she will have such love around her." Rachel said, holding Mrs. Finch's hand.

Mrs. Finch gave Rachel the same quick hug that she had just given her daughter. Emily came into the kitchen, a cup and saucer in each hand. "And what conspiracy are you plotting?"

"We were just planning your wedding, dear," Mrs. Finch teased her daughter. "Well, let's join the rest of the party, girls. The tea cups can wait until the morning." Mrs. Finch put an arm on the shoulders of both girls and then marched them out to the front room.

The Rabbi and his wife had left. Mr. Finch was pouring sherry into Dr. Rosenberg's glass from another bottle. "Well, now. Here's to absent friends."

"Graham, what an awful thing to say," Mrs. Finch chided.

"Well, it's the truth. That was the bottle that Chappie Roberts and I bought at the end of the Great War. He gave it to me after we toasted the armistice. We passed it back and forth every Christmas, toasting each other, the birth of our children, and promising to have a tot at all of our important events. We agreed that the last one standing would toast their good friend, schoolmate, and a good soldier. So here's to you, Chappie."

"Graham, must you be a wet blanket?"

He turned to Dr. Rosenberg. "Women. They don't understand the fellowship of men at arms." Mr. Finch went on muttering as he returned the old bottle to the closet.

Dr. Rosenberg said, "Women pray for peace and then they pray for us to regain the peace."

Mr. Finch asked no one in particular, "Who is it harder on? Them or us, I wonder."

"Dearest," Mrs. Finch called to her husband, "could you find the Kodak, so we can get some snaps?"

"Certainly. Be my pleasure."

Mrs. Finch then arranged various collections of the wedding party, toasting and pretending to eat cake from empty plates retrieved from the kitchen. Finally, Mr. Finch ordered Rachel and Emily to stand with the uniformed "lads", as he called Yitzhak and Harry. The four smiled at him as the last of the flash bulbs hissed and crackled.

Emily blushed at the awkwardness of her father as he invited the wedding party out to dinner to allow the newlyweds a few hours of intimacy.

CHAPTER 17
MARTELE

A bowing movement on a violin that accents notes strongly.

After Rachel and Yitzhak married, she remained in London with the Finches. The air strikes and nighttime bombing persisted throughout the remaining months of 1940 and into 1941, until the RAF got the upper hand in May. Every few months thereafter, there would be a rushed telephone call from Harry or Yitzhak announcing an afternoon in which they would be permitted off the airbase for a few hours. Rachel and Emily would grab their packed bags and take the dark green train. The four would meet at an inn hidden in a small town near the RAF airfield north of London. Once they arrived, Harry and Emily would take a walk into the countryside, linger over tea in a small shop, or see a matinee show at the cinema. They met up again for a late dinner at the train station before the last train left, going south.

For the next many months, life for Rachel was a blur of violin practice and volunteer work, wrapping bandages at the local hospital while waiting for the next call to meet Yitzhak. They somehow survived the uncertainty and chaos. In some odd way, life began to assume a new normality without the bombing raids. Evenings at the Finch's became a routine of listening to the evening BBC news report, dinner and a recital, with Graham playing the lead violin, Rachel and Emily accompanying him.

In March of 1942, Graham told both Emily and Rachel of an inquiry he had received from an elderly gentleman interested in taking violin lessons. Rachel took the job three afternoons a week. Half her earnings went to the Finches over their objections and the other half into her violin case.

Every few months, she would see her husband and try to squeeze as much out of those hours as possible. In January of 1944, she added a paid position as language tutor to a slim young woman who was going to the university and had as tin an ear for languages as Emily had.

In June of 1944, the Allied Forces landed at Normandy on the 6th by air and sea and pushed the Germans back. A week later, the Germans initiated a new terror on London. Bombs without bombers, they were called at first, then Buzz Bombs for all the racket that they made while flying, just higher than the effective range of the anti-aircraft guns at the shore and just faster than the larger cannons could sight on them. After a few days of unrelenting attacks launched from the French shoreline, the RAF discovered its vulnerability. The wind wake of a fighter plane diving within feet of the speeding projectile could put it off course and send it crashing harmlessly into open fields instead of the heart of the city.

Spitfires were the fastest planes in the fleet and the only aircraft that could outrun the pilotless bombs. All available Spitfires were redeployed to bases closer to London and pilots were reassigned to this new bomb-chasing mission. Radiomen were detached from bomber crews to support the Royal Observer Corps along the shoreline. Although the base was on restricted status during the transition, Harry had confided in their Commanding Officer that Yitzhak's wife was expecting and asked that Yitzhak be granted an exceptional leave before redeployment. Harry was stunned when he, too, was permitted to go to London and ordered to accompany Yitzhak in transit.

Just after five on a warm Friday night, Graham was alone in the front room of the flat. From the bedroom, he heard the muffled chatter of the three women fitting a new skirt for Rachel. The day prior Emily had found an excellent remnant of tweed and a pattern for a maternity skirt with a cleverly buttoned waistband and side gussets that allowed for expansion. Graham shook his head at the mystery of women, making a tweed skirt on a warm summer night, before Rachel even showed any sign of her pregnancy. He rolled up the sleeves on his light shirt, unfolded the *Times*, and settled in for a read.

There was a fast rapping on the door, and Graham frowned and dropped his paper beside his chair. He opened the door to see two grinning RAF airmen in their wrinkled summer khaki uniforms. "Come in, lads. You'll be a sight for sore eyes." He turned and shouted toward the hall. "Rachel, come here, quickly. The lads are here." Yitzhak held his arms wide. Rachel rushed to him, with the half pinned hem flapping at her legs.

Graham announced that he was buying drinks for all at the pub down the street and started rolling down the sleeves of his white shirt. Nattie patted his arm and suggested they have an early dinner first. Before dinner, Rachel slipped out of the heavy tweed skirt into a lighter pleated brown skirt and white short-sleeved blouse trimmed with lace. After a light supper, Nattie and Emily quickly changed from their daytime housedresses into new dresses that they had just finished sewing the week before. Both dresses were from the same pattern, buttoned up the front, and had shoulder pads; but, still, they looked quite distinctive. When they came into the living room, each twirled as if in a charity fashion show. Emily had selected a light floral pattern for her dress with a wide belt, while Nattie's dress was made from light blue cotton and trimmed with a white piping. As they walked toward the pub in the early evening, the light cotton fabric shifted in the breeze.

The night was clear. The little group walked quickly, laughing easily as they walked the two blocks to the Queen's Arms. Just before they got there, Emily slipped off her signet ring, and nudged Rachel. "Here, seems like you ought to be wearing this for tonight, even though you have your own gold bands now." Harry held the brass door handle of the dark oak door while all filed in. Graham found a table against the wall that was being vacated by two older men in dark suits.

Harry shouted over the din of radio music and conversations, each louder than the other. "Get settled in. I'll get the drinks." Smoke spun around the lights that hung from the ceiling, turning the room blue and gray. "Who's for a Guinness?"

Graham and Yitzhak nodded approval. Rachel shook her head. "Milk for me. I'd love a Watney's, but milk stays down a bit better just now."

Emily slipped into the chair closest to the wall. "Gin and French for me."

In order to be heard, Mrs. Finch put her hands to each side of her mouth. "Pink gin, if you please."

Rachel motioned for Yitzhak and Graham to sit in the chairs and took Harry's arm. "I'll help carry."

Harry leaned into the crowd of older men and a few women to provide a buffer so that Rachel didn't get bumped on the way to the crowded bar. Once at the bar, Harry turned to Rachel. "What is Emily having? A French gin?"

"No. Gin and French. It's gin with white vermouth."

"Oh. We'd call that a Martini in the States. "

"Odd. If she'd asked for a Martini in Geneva, she'd get sweet or red vermouth. "

"No foolin'?" Harry said.

The barman turned fast and more demanded than asked, "What's it for you tonight, lad?"

"Three pints of Guinness, one pink gin, a gin and French, and a glass of milk, if you got any."

"Milk? Sorry mate. Got a bitter lemon."

Rachel nodded. "That'll be fine."

Harry turned to her. "What's that?"

"Lemon soda. Tart. Quite nice, really."

"Yitzhak tells me that you have the best beer in Prague. Better than here." The barman looked at him with a sideways glance as he drew the pints of Guinness.

"A bit different. Lighter." Rachel watched the barman and moderated her words.

The barman slid the pints in front of them as fast as he pulled them from the tap on the bar and then spun to fetch down two short glasses into which he poured gin. Grabbing two bottles, he splashed some pale vermouth into one glass and a bit of red sweet grenadine syrup into the other.

As the barman slid the bottled soda and another glass in front of them, Harry reached to pull his wallet from the back pocket of his

RAF uniform. "How much is that?"

"Your money's not good here, Yank." The barman turned to the next customer.

Harry raised his hand to get the man's attention. "Sure it is. Listen. I didn't mean to hurt your feelings about the beer. Just joking. No harm intended..." Harry almost shouted to be heard over the din.

The barman grabbed the bar towel off his shoulder and mopped up a spill on the bar near Harry. "Look, mate. This wasn't your war when you Yanks came over here to fly with the RAF. But you're still here. This is my pub. I can stand you and your mates to a round o' drinks if I bloody well want to. Come back after the war and then I'll take a quid or two from ya."

Harry smiled, grabbed the handles of the three dimpled pint mugs into one hand and the bottle of soda with a glass put upside down over the top of the bottle into the other hand. Rachel took the two gin drinks and walked in front of him. As they were weaving their way across the crowded room, through the tight press at the front of the pub, someone started cheering and applause came from the back of the pub, drowning out Vera Lynn, singing on the radio that was near the front door of the pub.

They were almost to the table when they felt the explosion even before they heard it. The air was pushed out of their lungs just before the blast from the rear of the building spun them face first to the floor.

Glass shards from the mirror over the bar flew past their heads and the brick wall next to them tumbled into the street. As they fell, their drinks seemed to float from their fingers and dangle in front of them.

Parts of the splintered wood from the bar and paneling flew above them. As they fell, Harry grabbed Rachel's arm and pulled her into his side. As they hit the floor, he scrambled to shield her with his body and cover her head with his arm. As he glanced toward their table, the lights flickered out and he saw the brick wall behind Emily begin teetering dangerously before it pitched toward the table. Yitzhak turned and put his hands up, as though to hold the wall back. He shouted "*Zastavete!*" The wall toppled as a unit and then bricks flew from it after it had crashed over the table and onto the floor. Rachel heard only the dull ringing in her ears; not even a low cry from her husband. Before the dust from the crumbled bricks had settled, another explosion, possibly a boiler in a nearby basement, blew the reminder of the wall out into the street.

The blur of red and pink dust made breathing impossible even before the acrid black smoke started swirling in the pub. Some patrons at the back of the bar were screaming and others, coughing.

Harry slid sideways off Rachel. A small timber rolled off his back as he struggled to his knees. Glass gouged his left palm as he twisted up into a crouched position. In the faint blue light of the quarter moon, he saw that Mr. and Mrs. Finch were lying near the center of the street and struggling to sit up, as though just waking from a night's slumber.

Harry scanned the pub for Emily or Yitzhak, but he only saw a three-walled dollhouse with people in tattered clothing staggering toward him like sleepwalking scarecrows in a silent movie. Red and white smeared the wood fragments around him. Something like colored snowflakes drifted down from the gaping hole in the roof. Ash. Perhaps some paper.

He shook his head and some sound penetrated. Glass crunched under foot as people ran past him. Black smoke and white dust spun in the moonlight. He blinked to clear the soot from his eyes and heard the moan of the air raid siren that seemed very far away.

Harry's foot skidded as he tried to stand. He shook his head again to clear it. What remained of the roof seemed to flap as though in a windstorm. Rachel was moving very slowly. He took her by her shoulders and pulled her free of the debris. He saw that Nattie was stumbling for the far curb and pressing a fold of her skirt against her badly bleeding knee. Graham, who had lost his cane, was hobbling toward Harry. Graham pointed past Harry into the remains of the pub. "The wall's come down on 'em."

Harry carried Rachel across the street and propped her against Nattie. He turned and ran back into the pub, passing Graham and elbowing past several women who were running out, screaming.

Near the edge of the tumble of bricks, he saw a hand and a khaki cuff stained almost motor oil black in the moonlight. He dropped to his knees and began throwing bricks off Yitzhak's back into the street, until he saw Yitzhak's crushed head hidden under the splintered oak table. When he heard a scream behind him, he turned and saw that Rachel had followed him. He stood, grabbed her and pressed her face against his chest. "No. No, you don't want to see him, not like that." Graham arrived and took Rachel back to Nattie. He returned immediately to help Harry move bricks from the other side of the rubble until they saw Emily's broken arm and the way that her back had twisted.

Graham was weeping silently as he and Harry finished removing the debris that had pinned Emily. As the first of the ambulances arrived, Harry leaned close to her face, felt her shallow breathing, and jumped up, shouting for the men in uniforms who were arriving to get a stretcher. With Graham standing guard, they gently lifted Emily onto a dark canvas stretcher. As they ran to load the stretcher into the first ambulance, Graham wiped his sleeve across his face and took command. He pointed at the ambulance and shouted for Nattie to go with Emily. He ordered Harry to carry Rachel, who looked like she might faint. He said they would all meet at the hospital reception if they got separated. Nattie ran to the ambulance and crawled in just as it was starting to move. Harry scooped Rachel into his arms and started down the dark street after the ambulance to the hospital almost four blocks away.

Rachel was only half aware of Harry carrying her and of Graham walking beside her, holding her hand. The metallic taste in her mouth made words impossible to form. The stinging in the back of her head seemed to come and go with each footstep that he took. She could not understand what Graham was saying to her or where she was. She moaned and passed out as Harry lurched up the steps of the hospital.

The reception area was chaos by the time that Harry carried Rachel into the admission area. The niceties of names and addresses would have to wait until later. All the injured were issued a numbered tag and sorted for the degree of urgency their injuries posed. Admission papers coded to the tag number were shoved at anyone seeming to have any information on the patient. Because Rachel was unconscious and Harry had shouted that she was pregnant, a matron placed her on a gurney. As she started to wheel it toward the emergency room, the nurse pointed to Harry's ankle where raw bone was visible through his torn pant leg and his shoe was filled with blood. She ordered him to sit on the floor before he passed out. After applying a compress, she gave him a numbered tag and had him lean against a wall until called.

Graham took both admission papers from the matron, rolled them, and held them like a baton as he hobbled over to Harry. The huge room was crowded now with others from the pub looking for their friends and family. They had small splatters of blood on their legs and knees, and were oblivious to their minor wounds.

Harry was taken away on a gurney after about an hour. Graham sat in a hard backed chair against the far wall of the crowded admissions room and watched for the numbers to be posted on a large chalkboard. He knew the numbers for Rachel and Harry and wondered what number Emily might be and where Nattie was. Once a number was scratched on the board, family could go to the scarred oak desk and get a status of their condition and turn in the admissions paperwork.

When they put up Rachel's number, Graham went to the desk and listened carefully to the stocky matron. "She has a serious concussion. The cut on the back of her head is superficial and nothing to worry about. But because her husband said she is in her first trimester, we think it best to hold her overnight. You can find the ward number in about an hour." Graham nodded and knew that it would be pointless to explain that her husband was dead or ask after Emily or Harry in this madhouse. His only comfort was in knowing that, if there was anything humanly possible to do for Emily, Nattie was doing it.

After almost another hour of waiting, the number issued to Harry was posted and Graham was told that Harry had been admitted for treatment of a torn retina, ruptured eardrum, as well as the torn tendons in his ankle. Shortly after that, the waiting area seemed to thin and there were a few empty chairs. Nattie found Graham easily when she walked into the glaring brightness of the waiting room. He saw that her knee was bandaged and that she was holding the corner of a paper in her hand and looking around the room. He stood and waited for her, knowing from her numbed movements that Emily had not survived.

When she stopped in front of him, Nattie simply shook her head and reached for her husband. "Our dear sweet Emily…." Graham smothered her cry into his chest and burrowed his face into her neck. After the silence of their loss surrounded them, Graham helped Nattie into a chair and sat next to her, holding her hand so tightly that his knuckles went white.

Graham whispered to his wife, "Are you certain that she's… It is so confusing here." Mrs. Finch sobbed and nodded her head. She let Emily's admission paper drop to the floor. Graham picked it up and added it to the roll that was crumpled in his hand. He tossed the papers on the empty chair beside him and put his arm around her shoulder.

"Nattie, wait here, dear. I'll be right back."

She clutched his hand. "Where—"

"Just to get a pencil or a pen. I suppose they will need these papers to get on with what they must do."

As Nattie watched Graham walk to the desk, occasionally using the back of empty chairs for support, she thought that he looked smaller, more frail somehow, than she had remembered from just a few hours earlier. When he sat down, he smoothed the papers on his leg and started to write with a stub of a pencil. She watched as he completed the paperwork for Harry, simply noting that he was in the RAF and putting the Finch's address in parenthesis as a point of contact. Nattie put her hand over the paper where he was about to write on Rachel's form. He frowned and looked up.

Nattie spoke very softly. "You recall when you met Rachel at the boat?"

"Of course I do, but—"

"I have often thought how selfless that was of our girl to put herself at such peril for Rachel. To save her life by trading places."

"Yes, but—"

"Perhaps she means for us to continue that charade."

"I am not understanding…"

Nattie held his hand. "What if Rachel had died and Emily had lived?

The Germans could strike her off their list, you see?"

"No, I don't see; because that's not what happened."

Nattie picked up the admission papers "But what if it had? If we were to just exchange these two papers, we could bring Rachel home. We could protect her and her baby."

Graham whispered. "Are you mad? We can't do that."

"Of course we can. We can continue what our Emily started."

Graham sat motionless for long seconds. Finally, he squeezed her hand. "If King Edward could abdicate the crown and abandon England for the love of that Simpson woman, I would expect Rachel could leave her old life to protect her child, wouldn't you?"

"Yes, I do. And if we are mistaken, we simply say we confused the two papers."

After turning in the altered admissions papers, they were told of the ward assignments for the two survivors.

When Rachel awoke, she saw Mr. and Mrs. Finch seated forlornly on small white metal chairs beside her bed. Nattie saw her stir and nudged Graham who had fallen asleep with his chin on his chest.

Nattie stood and placed her cool hand on Rachel's forehead as she struggled to speak. "Hush, darling. Be quiet and let me tell you what has happened to your friends," Mrs. Finch began.

Rachel gasped and put her hand to her mouth "The baby…"

"…is fine, you are going to be fine and have a fine baby just as you and Yitzhak had hoped." Then in whispers, she and Graham took turns telling Rachel what had actually happened while she was unconscious. And they offered her a new name and their home.

Graham said finally, "I want you to be certain of what you want. I can always go and reverse the names on the hospital papers."

Rachel whispered hoarsely. "The baby would be your grandchild?"

Mrs. Finch said softly, "Yes, certainly, my dear. We promise to treat you as our own, in all ways, unless of course you decide otherwise."

Rachel nodded and held her hand out for Mrs. Finch to hold. Tears fell easily from Rachel's eyes and then the silence was broken by heaving sobs. Mrs. Finch leaned over the whiteness of the hospital bed and held her until she slipped back into sleep. Mrs. Finch stayed with her while Graham went to fill out the forms for the funeral directions for the young woman named Rachel Havel.

Harry had regained consciousness by the time that Graham came to see him on his way back to get Nattie. Other men in the ward were making rough sleeping sounds.

In the next room, a child cried the soul-deep low cry that only a child has permission to do for pain that should be reserved only for adults. Nurses in starched uniforms and small starched caps rustled past the door. It was just past midnight.

"Harry? It's Graham. Are you awake yet, lad?"

"Yes, sir," Harry mumbled. His jaw was bruised and a bandage covered his right ear, eye and forehead. His head was flat against the mattress. A bulky bandage was on his right leg.

"The others? How are they?"

Graham put his hand on Harry's shoulder. "You know Yitzhak died, don't you?"

"Yes, yes, I guess I did."

"And there is something I need you to understand. Can you listen to me very carefully?"

"I'll try."

Graham leaned down and spoke very softly. "My wife and I made a decision that you need to know about. It is a decision that is going to be difficult to understand, but I rely on you as an officer to honor this request for confidence. Am I clear?"

"Not really, what?"

"Will you give me your word as an officer not to repeat what I tell you?"

"Sure."

Graham leaned close to his left ear and whispered. "My daughter, Emily, has died. Rachel will become Emily from now on."

"Rachel?"

"Stop and listen. Rachel is now our daughter. Her name will be Emily starting now. They will exchange identities. Do you understand?"

"Rachel is dead. Emily is your daughter now?" Harry repeated softly to Graham, but Graham didn't know if he was starting to hallucinate or if he truly understood. Harry started to sink into sleep. Then he lifted his head, and asked "The baby? Is the baby okay?"

"Yes."

"Thank God. Rach…Emily and her baby–" Harry turned his head and was asleep.

Graham left Harry to the nurses and went back to get Nattie. To his surprise, Rachel was sitting on the edge of the bed and Nattie was buttoning her stained blouse.

Graham frowned. "What do you think you are doing?"

Mrs. Finch took Rachel's elbow. "They are short of beds. They say she just needs rest now. Help me." Graham took the other arm and steadied her as she stood. Then the newly formed family went to their flat to weep.

As she crawled into her bed, the new Emily tried to make sense of the day. She understood that the rituals of religion and language could divide nations and people. How we are born and how we die are the same. But how we celebrate those moments and how we marry somehow divides us. But what connects us is life, she thought. Life. The life inside her. Love. As she started to calm herself for sleep, she had only the energy to look forward.

Her unborn child made her decision to go forward possible. That child informed and gave meaning to every moment of her life. She'd never really known her own limits: shy in some parts of her life, confident and assertive in her music.

But now. She could and would do anything for this child.

After Graham left, the nurse gave Harry another shot and he plunged into the restless sleep of the damned and drugged. Drugs and pain were of equal strength. When the drugs finally took over, his grief submerged him into a dream of endless flying glass and rolling red clouds after a storm of lightning. Then the tulips, red and yellow, started to fall like parachutes from a sky of lemon yellow and covered the hill behind the barn at his farm. The tulips became a thousand toy tops spinning slower and slower, rocking back and forth, like the sound of a pan lid spinning in smaller and smaller circles on a stone floor. As he tried to regain consciousness, the room began to revolve faster and faster and the sound shrieked higher and higher until it was no longer a sound but something else. Then it was that Harry realized dimly that he could hear from only one ear.

Only later would Harry discover that the explosion was from one of the rockets that he and Yitzhak were being reassigned to repel. The newspapers called the new terror the Buzz Bomb and initially translated its German title as Revenge Weapon One. Later, others called it the Vengeance Weapon One. It continued to menace London in the summer of 1944 after flying over the channel at 350 miles an hour. Finally the weapon called *Vergeltungswaffe Eins*, became the V-1 rocket in the papers.

CHAPTER 18
FERMATA

The direction to hold a note longer than normal.

Morning came. Mrs. Finch pulled a beige shawl tighter over her light floral housedress as she watched a young woman sleep in her daughter's room. The dreams that Emily had were gone from the room and grief floated like a fog, filling all the empty places. She watched the injured Rachel stir and moan deeply. She knew what a mother must do to protect a child, even the child of another woman.

"Wake up, my darling. Listen for the birds," Mrs. Finch said softly to the sleeping stranger who was now her daughter. "Wake up now."

Rachel awoke as Rachel.

"Mrs. Finch? Nattie? Good morning."

"Good morning, 'mother'. Say it, even in private," Mrs. Finch gently taught her. "Good morning, 'mother'."

"Good morning, mother," said the new Emily and then gulped in her losses like seawater, choking and sobbing, fresh from the hurt of the loss of her husband and friend. How could Mrs. Finch give her language lessons after the loss of her child? How could she become someone else when she did not know where her mother was? Her father? How cold were these English? How stiff their upper lip? The new Emily propped herself up on one elbow to face the inevitable morning. Her thin cotton nightgown clung to her and the sudden chill of her sweat evaporating made her shiver.

Mrs. Finch picked a light pink dressing gown from the closet and held it, like a bullfighter's cape, inviting the sleepy woman to enter it. "Come, my darling. First, breakfast. Then if we are going to complete this charade, we must get your hair and clothes right. You look too, well, too European."

The robe was her daughter's. It had her scent on it. Mrs. Finch caught the gentle essence like jasmine at a distance, like late summer. That was her daughter. Like late summer. Long days of ease. Long limbed and agile in the water. The escapee from boarding school uniforms, the girl with the easy laugh. A child who awoke smiling. At ease with herself. Talking to her parents more as an equal than as a child.

Mrs. Finch pulled the robe to her breast and crushed it to her. She buried her face in the neck and folds of the dressing gown. She inhaled as deeply as she could, as though this one moment was all there was in the world to capture all that ever was of her daughter.

The new Emily sat up on the edge of the bed. Tears ran down her face. The girl wondered if there was a word in English for the parents who have lost their child, like orphan is the word for a child who has lost her parents. She could not ask. Mrs. Finch sat beside her. Wilted. She took the young woman's hand.

"You know. Once, Emily and I were walking. It was summer at the lake, and she said something I want you to know. She said that the one great advantage of being an only child is that we, meaning she and I, could make up our own rules. What she intended was to convince me to abandon discipline by mutual consent. And we could do this." Mrs. Finch stroked the younger woman's hand, as she had done to her child when she was fussy. "We had a conspiracy of women. We were without witnesses or rules when her father was away. We were alone with each other. We enjoyed each other's company and complemented each other. She was brave in ways I was not. She was wise in ways I will never be. I think at some level, her father knew that he never could be her conspirator as I was. And I think that he will take to that role with you in a very special way."

"Are you sure that we can do this?"

"No. Not at all. Maybe we made a very bad decision. But all I know is that there is one name on Herr Hitler's list that he can't even think of harming now. Rachel does not exist. Herr Hitler will never know your child. Your passport stamps and their records make it appear that you are still in Switzerland. Who would imagine a London wedding of a conservatory student who is officially in Switzerland? You simply adopt Emily's documents. We have welcomed you into our lives."

"How do we fool your friends? I need to beware of Emily's friends and avoid them."

"What friends? Graham always was one for having our family time just for us in the country. He was always putting up the front that we needed our privacy. But, in actual fact, the war, his war, took so much out of him that our time in the country was usually garnering his strength so he could go back and play his role well. Emily was off at boarding school, then the conservatory. We visited her. We traveled alone, apart from the orchestra people that were so much a part of our day-to-day life here in London."

"But there must be someone who knows Emily here."

"Certainly, but only superficially. You can recuperate here; then go to our country house. It's quite secluded. I don't think Emily has been there for at least three years." The new Emily slipped her arms into the sleeves of the dressing gown held by Mrs. Finch.

"Last night, after we got you to bed, Graham asked me why our daughter had to die. He didn't ask why it was not you instead of our child. I don't know and will never be able to answer him. She was so talented and loving. Giving and bright. I didn't have an answer for him. I'm not sure that I do now, but I have an idea. Maybe, just maybe, something can come of her death. Maybe her name can give you the freedom to live the next part of your life in a way that you choose. She always felt her destiny was to help others, but she thought it was through her music. Perhaps her destiny was to save you and your child. I'll never know." Nattie sniffed and clapped her hands once. "But I do know that you need your breakfast and we need to start making you look a bit more like…her. Graham has eaten and is off to the hospital already, so we have the flat to ourselves."

After breakfast, Mrs. Finch cut Rachel's hair with the care and precision required to match the passport photo of Emily. With a new haircut and breakfast settling well, Nattie tucked Emily back into bed with orders to rest until noon. Dr. Rosenberg visited daily for the next week and then pronounced that the danger to the baby had passed, she could resume light walking for a week, and then approach her pregnancy without restriction.

When Dr. Rosenberg left, Mrs. Finch smiled. "Let's take a slow walk to visit Harry. Graham says he asks after you every day. Select a dress more…English than your usual ones. The one with small lavender flowers on a sea of cream should fit you. It reminds me of our family trip to southern France, when…."

Rachel started for Emily's wardrobe but stopped and looked back at Nattie. "Can you really call me Emily?"

"Yes, yes, I can. I must."

When they arrived at the recovery ward, Graham stood quickly and motioned Rachel into his chair to the left of Harry's bed. Graham took Nattie's arm and they went into the hallway.

"Emily? Is that you?" Harry asked with his head flat against the mattress, not moving. The right eye was covered with a bandage from his high cheekbone to the edge of his hairline. A smaller bandage covered the right ear. His cast was elevated on two pillows.

On her way to the chair, she leaned over and whispered in his left ear. "Yes, you are right to call me Emily. Is your neck—"

"It's fine. I just have to hold my head still. The eye, the retina is detached. They don't want me to move."

"Oh, I see," said Emily feeling stupid and embarrassed at her comment, and then she sat silently blushing.

"Just for a few days. As soon as they can, they'll move me to another facility. The leg is going to be about four weeks in the cast, then I'll be learning to walk again before I can even think about going back to my unit."

"Another hospital?"

"No, more like a nursing home, I guess you call it. The hospital is so crowded, they need to move us out as soon as possible if we don't need immediate medical care."

"Why don't you come to the flat? We can tend to you there, if the doctor agrees."

"I couldn't."

"Why?"

"I can't impose."

"Why? We're all numb and sad and the world has changed in a way we never imagined. But we must now look after each other."

Mrs. Finch came in from the hallway and overheard the invitation. She stood behind the chair, and put her hands on the young woman's shoulders. "I know Graham would want you there. And, besides, I fear that he is a bit overwhelmed by all the women in the house crying at the same time."

For the first week at the flat, he was restricted to bed except for bathroom trips. Mrs. Finch cooked meals that Emily served on a tray and fed him so that he moved his head as little as possible. Dr. Rosenberg monitored his healing and provided progress reports to the Royal Air Force flight physician.

There was very little conversation and many deep silences in a home that had been filled with music and laughter only days before. No one knew what to say, so they all practiced at perfecting the new Emily: coaching her, helping her absorb as much of the family history and local information as possible, and avoiding the callers from the orchestra who were dropping by to express their concern over Emily's injury and the loss of her school chum in the bombing.

Over the next two months, Harry's ankle healed well enough that he was able to discard his crutches and walk with a cane as he helped with the household chores. As the leaves began to turn in September, Emily and Harry began taking walks to the park near the flat.

With each of his official visits to Harry, Dr. Rosenberg monitored Emily's weight chart and prenatal diet. He complimented Emily on how well she was adapting and becoming more like Emily. Soon, it became shorthand, a code, a game for the doctor to say, "How becoming you are today, Emily."

Late in September, Dr. Rosenberg surprised Emily when he asked to see her passport and school photos. Emily fetched the British passport from her room while Mrs. Finch pulled out several photo albums. He examined the pictures and looked again at Emily.

"You are too perfect. That's what has been bothering me. Emily had a small scar over her eyebrow. You don't, and you should. So if we are going to continue this little masquerade, I would like to prescribe a little cosmetic surgery to add that scar. Since I've already put my practice at peril in doing what we have done so far-- that odd certificate that I signed, I think it only right that I perform the surgery."

"What would you do?" Mrs. Finch asked, before Emily could.

"Simple removal of a small wedge passing through the eyebrow. See how the eyebrow was not complete in these earlier pictures, there is a break in it, and it is a continuous element later and noted on her passport as a small scar, right eyebrow, although you don't see it clearly."

Harry said, "I never noticed it."

"Pencil. Eyebrow pencil. She was very vain about it," Mrs. Finch said.

"Well?" asked the doctor.

"Yes, you are right. I need to have a scar."

Two weeks later, Dr. Rosenberg stopped by the house and found Harry, Emily, Nattie and Graham all in the front room listening to the BBC home service report. He listened to the end of it, and then blurted out, "I need to motor up to the north and see an elderly patient. Near your country place, Graham. Thought Emily might like the trip. It might be a good time for that eyebrow to get fixed. And besides, I thought perhaps Emily might want to visit the Jewish cemetery? I'll be going quite near it on the way up."

"Yes, thank you for thinking of me, Dr. Rosenberg. But I can't go in, you know..."

"Because you are expecting?"

"Well..."

"That's custom, not a requirement. I asked my Rabbi before I even considered inviting you. In these circumstances, he approved of the visit."

"Are you sure?" Emily asked.

"Yes, yes I am."

"Then I would. Yes."

"Mind if I come along? I'd like to pay my respects." Harry asked Emily, but looking at Dr. Rosenberg for permission. He nodded. Harry glanced at Emily, who nodded. The drive was long and silent. A sudden windstorm the day before had stripped the trees of leaves, making the drive seem winter bleak.

An old black iron fence rose out of a pale granite block wall that was waist high. As the car passed it, Emily knew, even before Dr. Rosenberg turned into the driveway, that this was where her husband lay buried. She sank deeper into the tall back seat. This was the Jewish cemetery outside London.

The old marking stones were gray and a light green on one side from old lichen and moss gone dormant in the winter. Snow dusted the ground and there was a light breeze to blow away their steaming breath.

"I can't thank you enough for arranging this ... his burial, when we were in the hospital. I don't know if I could have managed it, even if I hadn't been hurt," Emily said.

"I think you can manage just about anything," Dr. Rosenberg said. "You are a very strong young woman."

"Is Emily buried here, too, as Rachel?"

Dr. Rosenberg spoke very softly, although they were alone. "Officially, her paperwork's gone missing. In truth, Graham had her taken to the village churchyard by their country house. Family plot there. They'll put up a stone after the war. Won't be dated, though."

The car stopped on the gravel lane just before the black iron gate. Harry got out of the passenger seat and tugged at the sliding bolt that held it closed. The hinges groaned as he pulled open the gate.

The doctor opened the car door and held her arm as she walked through the gate. Harry walked several paces behind them.

They went and stood silently in front of the grave. It was not the only fresh one there. Some tombstones had small pebbles on them.

Emily walked away from the grave, further into the cemetery. Dr. Rosenberg picked a pebble off the path and placed it on the headstone. Stone on stone.

Harry and Dr. Rosenberg walked back to the car and waited for Emily. Once she was alone, she too placed a stone on the marker. When she came back to the car, Dr. Rosenberg took a small glass bottle of water from the trunk of the car. He poured water over her hands and gave her a towel. She dried them and stood a moment in the cold air before getting into the car. Harry stood at the rear of the car and watched Dr. Rosenberg wash his hands as well, then place the towel and water in the trunk and shut it carefully.

Dr. Rosenberg turned to Harry. "After visiting a cemetery, it is important for a ritual cleansing. Don't worry. This does not concern you."

During the drive to the country house, they were silent. Once there, Harry lit a fire in the fireplace and it warmed the small cottage quickly. Then he took the large picnic basket from the car and spread a lunch on the table in front of the fire. They ate.

Dr. Rosenberg quickly cut and stitched her eyebrow and left her resting on the sofa in front of the fire. Harry walked him to the car.

"Anything I need to do?"

"Be there for her. This is so hard on the young. The loss, not the nick I put in her brow."

"Can I ask you something?"

"Certainly."

"Why were there pebbles on the grave markers?"

Dr. Rosenberg smiled. "Wish I knew. As a boy I heard a story that in old times a shepherd would count his flock in the morning and put a pebble for each in his pocket and count them again at night. So too, God cares for each of us as his sheep. But then, maybe it is just a way to show respect—a reminder that the grave is visited, that they are remembered."

CHAPTER 19
LUFT PAUSE

The direction to insert a short pause in the music.

Emily awoke Sunday morning to the glare of the screen saver on her computer after falling asleep while reading her journals. What sleep she had was not restful. Ben and a dozen other faces she had known in Geneva, Prague, and London invaded her peace. In just a few days, Ben had moved from being an unknown neighbor, to an annoyance, to potentially a threat. Now she expected him to hover over the repairs and invade her life even more, if that were possible.

She put the water on for tea, and then she looked at the deck and smiled to herself. Emily remembered what her mother had said. 'You have to break an egg before you can fry it.' She smiled. The smallest chuckle escaped and startled her. She was accustomed to quiet in her life except when she planned a sound and brought music and conversation into the house. For years she thought that her mother's saying had to do with following the rules of cooking. Only later did she understand that some opportunities come from tragedy. Sometimes pain precedes pleasure. There are moments of understanding that can come only when their time is ready. Some understanding is only a façade. It is a fiction when it is intellectually understood but not known in the recesses of the soul.

She knew the damaged deck was cracking open a secret. And she did not know what the repercussions might be. Or how far the disclosure would go. She spent Sunday morning in practice. First violin, and then tai chi in the living room.

At four, Ben came to Emily's house and reported on his telephone calls with the project manager, the schedule for repairs over the next week, and repeated his apology. As he was almost out her front door, he stopped. "I'm picking up some take-out Chinese tonight. Join me? We'll eat early."

"That's a lovely offer, but—" She looked at her warm up suit and shrugged.

"Good. My place. I'll do the dishes. Name your three favorites. I'll fill in the rest."

"Oh, so many choices. Mongolian beef, I think that and sweet and sour pork—" Emily chuckled.

"What's funny?"

"I guess pork is out."

"Thanks, I'd never be able to explain that to Ellen."

Emily nodded quickly. "Something with lots of vegetables. You know, those little baby corn cobs. You decide the rest."

"Great, I'll drive down for you about six."

"Just walk down; the air will do me good."

She returned the journals to the safe. She smiled as she recognized that wonderful blend of joy and terror that she usually felt before a demanding performance. Readiness. Anxiety. Adrenaline. She found herself checking the clock too frequently, deciding what to wear, changing her mind twice, and pacing near the door just before six.

She heard his footsteps on the flagstone and opened the door just as he was about to knock. He was dressed in a starched blue shirt that was open at the neck, with cuffs rolled up past his elbows, charcoal gray slacks and black loafers. He glanced at the pale linen tunic over matching linen slacks and the Italian sandals that were mere threads of leather across her feet. "It's going to be chilly after dinner. Want to get a coat?"

She nodded and pulled her pale London Fog raincoat from the closet by the door. He watched her slip it on before he could offer to hold it for her. He puzzled how she looked so elegant with only a single strand of dark wooden beads for jewelry. She picked up a house key, slipped it into her pocket, and closed the door behind her.

They walked slowly up the narrow road to where it ended in Ben's driveway. She knew the house. An architect built it in the mid-sixties on spec, after the old wooden frame house on that lot had burned. The design was modern. Rectangles stacked on each other, offset, like a controlled logjam in natural wood.

She remembered when the older home burned. Some said it was torched for the insurance, and not a victim of the fire that was pushed by the winds. She never knew how that had ended, as the owner never returned.

She shuddered when she remembered the fire. It all started in Bel-Air and then swept into Brentwood in 1961. The first week in November.

When she thought of the fire, it always jogged her memory to the night before the fire. That night was the clearest in years. She and Harry sat on the deck wrapped in heavy woolen shirts and drank coffee late into the night, snugged deep into their Adirondack chairs. They sat, still as stars, in a way that only lovers know.

The stars that night shimmered, like they did in the desert. Emily had sat on the deck and watched the city slide into the night, long after Harry brought her a lap robe and went off to bed. As midnight approached, she saw the first of the Leonoid meteors streaking across the velvet black sky. She came in and locked the doors behind her. She started to check on Barbara in bed and caught herself. Barbara had just moved into her student apartment near campus in Claremont. She smiled to herself.

In the soft glow from his electric alarm clock, Emily saw that Harry was asleep. She felt his warmth as she slipped into the cool bed, finding him, as one's foot automatically seeks the one cool place on the sheet on a too hot night. His being soothed her.

They made love before dawn and by 5:00 a.m. the wind was tugging at the trees next to the deck. Dry branches snapped and skittered across the deck, fracturing the silence of the night.

By the light of morning of November 6, 1961, the Santa Ana wind had developed into a hot, dry, blowtorch. Static electricity made Emily's hair crackle with each stroke of the brush.

Days before, a cold polar air mass began its trip to California. It started out frigid and wet. As it swept across Utah and Colorado and Nevada, it lost its moisture. Thirsty plants and trees and wild growth robbed the air of its water as it came south.

The sun and the spin of the climate invited the wind to wildness as it sped across the flat of the desert and found the mountain pass that let early settlers find Los Angeles.

The compression of the fast wind through the mountain pass was like cranking down the nozzle on a garden hose, shifting the gentle spray to the hard blasting water that shoots the last of winter's leaves down the street or the unwanted cat out of the yard.

It gained more speed as it fell to the lower elevations, dropping a mile or more. As the air fell into the basin, the heavier atmosphere caused friction and rubbed the dry air even hotter.

The fire started small and turned bad from the first hour. Instead of just burning a hillside, the wind scattered chunks of burning brush to the next few hills to the west. By midmorning, it was out of control. By noon, the wind was topping fifty miles per hour. Trees were tipping out of the earth on the hills where they had been over watered.

Then there were three fires. Bel-Air was the first. The second fire, arson, started in Benedict Canyon. Then Topanga, south of Mulholland Drive, burst into flame.

She pictured it back then when wild grass lined steep canyon walls. There were no roads to move the fire trucks. No firebreaks. Gravel and dirt roads led off to the few homes that spotted the canyons. Roads without signs. Houses without numbers.

Most of the houses had wood roofs of shake and shingle, wood split to slabs forming a natural roof. When burning, the flat wood slabs went airborne and flew up in the thermals hundreds of feet into the smoky air, then were shoved by air currents and finally pulled by gravity to fall again.

Miles away, the burning brands fell to earth. Three miles easily. If it fell on a driveway, it sputtered out. If it fell on a roof of wood shake or thinner shingle, another fire started. And so it was that the fire played leapfrog throughout the city.

The fire crews fought with water. Then the burning homes melted plumbing and the hydrants went dry. The water flooded impotently down streets.

She still recalled the streets that formed the margin of the fire: Linda Flora. Chantilly Road, Stone Canyon and Stradella Road. Mulholland Drive and Kenter Avenue. St. Mary's College lost two buildings. Evacuees met at UCLA.

The sound of airplanes that day was like being in London again. B-17s were dispatched from Van Nuys airport first. Only one was ready. An hour later a second was in the air. Planes came from Carpinteria and Chino, Goleta and Hemet. All through the southern California area, pilots risked death to save others.

Flying low into the blindness of the smoke, hoping the hills were where they remembered them to be. They dropped Borate on the flaming hills, avoiding the few houses. A load of flame retardant would kill a person, dogs, horses. It would collapse houses.

Even hidden in the smoke blackened sky, the sound was like that of bombers over a London in flames. She trembled and sat on the deck, rocking in the chair that did not move. Rocking, until Harry found her, pulled her into the house and then put her in the car. Harry drove east for almost half an hour before she stopped shaking. When they arrived at Claremont, Barbara was at the curb in front of her college apartment. Barbara grabbed the small suitcase and cardboard box from the back seat and dropped them on the sidewalk. She helped Emily out of the car. As soon as the door shut, Harry sped west to their home. Through the rest of the day, he stayed on the roof and sprayed water on the hot embers as they hit the roof or trees near the house or the deck. He sprayed the hose on his face and hair to clear the ash and then wrapped his wet tee shirt over his face like a bandit while he listened to the planes that he once manned when they carried bombs, not Borate.

Harry knew from the whine of the engines that the needles on the rpm gauges were past red line, but the pilots persisted and the dive, dump and climb maneuver was repeated over and over. Finally, the borate had slowed the fire's progress. The smoke thinned just before dark. The Santa Ana wind calmed and let the fire finish burning up the steepest of the hills until there was nothing left to burn. Then it went out slowly, swirling smoke up to erase the stars. Red flame and embers were still scratched across the northern hills of the basin, but at least they were not speeding toward the ocean. He waited out the long red night on the roof with a gallon of orange juice on one side and the garden hose on the other. And in the morning, the house still stood. The transistor radio carried the news that police lines were set up and looters were being arrested. The telephone poles to the west had burned and the telephone lines went down. Power was out for almost a week.

All she wanted to remember of that fire was that Harry was on the roof with the garden hose, spraying off the ash when Barbara drove her home the next day. Later they discovered that there were almost 500 homes lost: both mansions and modest homes, part of St. Mary's College. The lot that Ben's house was later built on was only a mound of black and gray remains.

It smelled like the beach with dead embers in fire pits. The smell of acrid smoke and white ash lingered for weeks. That winter the blackened hills let rain run faster and clean deeper. By spring, the smell of the smoke was gone and the ash had washed away. That spring, new types of flowers were on the hill above the house and a new home was being built on the scorched earth.

The home was rebuilt using contemporary plans and some former official who'd served in the government of the Shah of Iran purchased it. He remodeled it, put statues of well-upholstered women along the driveway and painted the home a deep pink. The overall effect was reminiscent of a pile of hot dogs.

Then some writer bought it with royalties from his first book and option money from the studio, repainted and remodeled it. But the film was never made and he never produced a second book, never quite got the screenplay right on the one book that did sell, and so he moved back to Ireland. She wondered how long Ben and his wife would live there, or if she would outlast them too.

She saw Ben watching her. Adjusting his pace to hers. Not quite knowing if he should extend his arm for her to hold or simply walk next to her. She enjoyed his concern and confusion. She thought it was interesting that she was old enough to be his mother, and realized she actually could be his grandmother. Yet, here she was...going to yet another dinner with an interesting man.

As she entered the home, he took her coat, hung it in the closet and then rushed to a rack of stereo components. She glanced around the home as she followed him. Lean Danish modern furniture and the two bright abstract oil paintings almost gave the living room the feel of a hotel lobby. No clutter or real signs of life, except for the row of Chinese food containers on the teak dining table.

He put the needle on the record turntable. Music flooded throughout the house from hidden speakers. "Four Seasons." She recognized it as the 1957 recording by the Los Angeles Philharmonic Orchestra even before she saw the album cover on the coffee table. The corner of the album was worn down to the pale raw cardboard. She had played the violin solo on the recording. She was in the orchestra for the 1949 version as well. He pointed to the dining table with some pride and grinned as he motioned her to a chair.

CHAPTER 20

SHARP

The notation that directs the player to raise the note a half step.

Ben had arranged the two straw place mats across from each other on the richly grained teak dining table. Sleek stainless steel cutlery and brown Dansk ware plates were at each place. Closed containers of Chinese food and large serving spoons were balanced precariously on three large platters running down the center of the table. An open bottle of Riesling wine was on a coaster. A handful of cellophane wrapped fortune cookies were in a soup bowl next to the wine.

"My goodness! How many are dining with us?"

He pulled out the chair for her. "Just us. I got carried away. Good thing I like leftovers." When he leaned over the table and opened all of the white glossy paper containers, the complex sweet and spiced aroma filled the room. He motioned at the platters. "Please, help yourself." He remained standing to pour the wine as she spooned steaming white rice onto her plate. "Would you like water?"

"Yes, that would be nice."

He hurried into the kitchen and returned with two tall glasses of water. Ben quickly covered his plate with rice and smothered it with ample scoops of sweet and sour chicken and three other dishes that he named but that she had never heard of before. As soon as she finished centering a large scoop of Mongolian beef on her rice she relinquished the container to Ben and reached for the sweet and sour chicken.

"This is such a treat. I really cannot remember the last time I had Chinese food."

"We could make this a regular event once Ellen gets home. She loves the Chinese food from this restaurant."

Emily nodded her head as she took a small bite of the steaming beef.

After a bite and sip of wine, Ben relaxed and asked her about Harry and their life in Los Angeles. She would have been hesitant if she had not faced this question time and time again. Now she had a rehearsed story that she was delighted to tell him. It was the same rendition that she had told her daughter as a bedtime story and used for that oral history report that she did on the early days of radio. "The day after VE Day, Victory in Europe, that was May of 1945. We were back in California by then. Barbara was still a baby, not yet walking. Harry called the radio station during his lunch hour at the airfield where they were still test flying planes for McDonnell Douglas. He applied for a job at ECA. That's KFI now."

"The radio station?"

"Yes, with victory in Europe, the world had a potential of getting put right again. Harry wanted to get into radio fast, before all the other radiomen were back from the war." Emily went on telling Ben the parts of her life that had been in newspapers over the years, parts of her life with Harry. All very practiced. Nothing new. But in an instant, she remembered the hollow feeling when she heard their light gray Plymouth pull up to the curb, not knowing whether or not Harry had got the job. Emily was silent and almost heard herself calling to Harry from the open door of the house, even before Harry was out of the car.

Ben took a sip of wine and asked, "And?"

Emily blinked quickly and remembered that day with a flash of clarity. She picked up her water glass and took a slow sip. She could see it clearly. Harry jumped out of the car, slammed the door, and ran into the house, but then wanted to string out the story as long as possible when she asked him if he got the job.

He started slowly, "First the guy asks me how I started in radio, and I tell him the long version of how I made a crystal set with a cat's whisker and an ear piece to get the static at the start."

"And then, what did you say?" Emily had asked breathlessly.

"Told him that in Fresno, I'd get a San Francisco station on a clear night. Then I built a ham set and went into radio training in the ROTC at Fresno State. Then to the Army Air Corps after a stint with the RAF in England before we were in the war."

"And?"

"And, well, I knew that Earl C. Anthony created a radio empire, at first bearing his initials as the call sign: ECA. There was a major battle between Mr. Anthony and Don Lee in San Francisco. Lee sold Cadillac cars in Los Angeles and San Francisco and Anthony sold Packard cars in both cities as well. Anthony owned ECA and KECA in L.A. and Lee owned KHJ in Los Angeles and KFRC in San Francisco. I never mentioned KHJ."

"And then what happened?"

"ECA was only beaming out of L.A. but the guys in Frisco thought that both their cars and radios were under attack. They assumed that Anthony was going to broadcast from Frisco. I knew that KFI built an antenna up there in the thirties and it's still looming over the Packard dealership up there with the KFI letters and call sign on it. Told him what a slick move that was, even though they never used it, and how the folks in Frisco teased Lee about it."

"What does that have to do with your interview?" Emily demanded.

"Honey, it's all about calling a bluff. All about looking like you're 'in the know'. I called his bluff. Told him the pay I wanted, and he matched it."

"No!" Emily shouted and threw her arms around him.

"Hook, line and sinker, he bought it all. We're in the money now!" Harry laughed as he gave her a big hug and the laughing woke the baby.

A new voice was calling her. "Emily?" Ben's voice was calm but insistent.

Emily smiled, and took another sip of her water before continuing. "Well, after Harry worked in radio a couple years, he moved over to Columbia Records: January, 1948. I don't imagine you knew how long it really took to recover from the War. In England, they were still rationing meat years after the war officially ended. Here we were recovering, readjusting. New homes were being built and paid for by the mustering out pay and the VA home loans. Even Hollywood had some recovering to do. We couldn't even cut records until 1948. They were made of shellac, and it was all used for the war effort."

"I thought they were vinyl."

"That's later. Harry told me all about it in excruciating detail. The studios needed shellac to make the master. Needles cut into a plate of shellac making deep grooves for lower pitch and shallow grooves for higher tones. Better than wax. Then a master record mold was made of metal and then vinyl records were pressed by the metal mold into records. Like making a coin. First 78 rpm records, on the thick brittle plastic, then the long-playing 33 1/3 rpm vinyl. LPs we called them. Long Playing. Do you remember that?"

"Sure, but there is nothing to compare to the precision of the Compact Disk. Laser precision. Imagine trying to get a record to play in your car on a long drive."

"Tape. That worked in cars. Eight track and now cassettes. Didn't they have tape for recording then?"

"No, Germans had it during the war. Wasn't until 1947 when ABC first used it on a radio show, Bing Crosby's show. They were still using captured German Magnetaphone tape while 3M figured out how to make it here. Took until the fifties to get it into studios here. Acetate. Clarity kept improving until it was as good as the hard masters."

As Ben finished the last of the rice, he asked, "Did you ever go to the recording sessions to watch?"

She nodded. "I'd watch and listen to music being recorded while waiting for Harry to finish engineering the session. I parked myself on one of the cold tan metal folding chairs with Barbara. Reading Golden Books to her snuggled on my lap. Then, it had to be perfect, all in one take. Later, with tape, you could have an error and then just record that part over again. A good engineer could splice the correction and the final would sound perfect. But the earlier sessions ran late into the night. Paper coffee cups started to leak at the bottom about midnight. Then about 1:00 or 2:00 a.m. Barbara would be sleeping on my lap. Harry would pick her up, and we'd go home."

"I know you were recorded, but how did that start? Through the Philharmonic or through Harry?"

"I worked in film and records, not just for the Philharmonic. Played violin for a lot of singers at the Capital Records building in the early sixties."

"That round building that looks like a stack of records?"

"That's it. Harry told me that the stylus on the top blinks out the word 'Hollywood' in Morse code."

Ben laughed and shook his head. "Only in Hollywood." He reached for the bowl of fortune cookies and held it in front of her.

"Oh, Ben, I couldn't manage another crumb."

"Tea or a coffee?"

"Thank you, no. This was simply perfect, but—"

He walked to the rear of her chair and slipped it back as she stood. "Then let me walk you home before it gets any later."

CHAPTER 21

CRESCENDO

The direction to play in a manner that gradually increases the volume of the music.

As Ben walked her to her door, he pulled three cellophane wrapped fortune cookies from his pocket and held them for her. "In case you change your mind."

Emily laughed as she took the cookies. "Thank you…again." Once the door was shut, she dropped the cookies on the table by the door and put her coat in the closet. The lavender sachet in the closet seemed stronger than usual. She leaned into the closet and inhaled deeply. She spun and marched directly to the safe and pulled out her journal. She sat on the love seat and leaned back. As she opened the cover, she was in London again.

It was a rainy day in early October. As she read, she placed her hand on the side of her flat belly as she remembered how large she felt by her seventh month. Harry had let himself into the flat with his own key. She was reading and looked up when the door opened. He stood by the door after he shut it, almost at attention in spite of the cane and black patch over his eye. Rain glistened on his dark coat and dripped from his billed cap.

She patted the sofa next to her, and straightened her maternity smock. "You must tell me. What did you find out today? Are you released to go back to your unit now?"

He put his wet coat and hat into the closet. On his way across the room, he put a small shovel of coal on the fire. He stood in front of her. "I'm being reassigned to an Army unit in the States. Won't let me fly combat anymore."

She sighed. "I'm glad for you to be away from all this, but I will miss you awfully." She watched him as he sat down next to her and then looked away. The scent of lavender followed him. As he leaned forward and put his hands on his knees, she noticed a hint of talcum from the barbershop on the back of his collar. "What is it, Harry?"

"Where are they?"

She nodded toward the closed door that led to the kitchen. "Just starting dinner. What is it?"

"I don't know where to start..."

"Harry! We're friends. You can tell me anything."

He looked at his hands and spoke very carefully, "You know that I greatly admired your husband. He was my best friend and as brave and decent a man as I've ever known."

"I know how close you were."

He clenched his hands on his knees until his knuckles went pale. "Will you just hear me out before talking?"

"Hear you out?" Emily asked, unclear on his meaning.

"Listen before you say anything?"

Emily nodded.

He faced her. "Yitzhak and I were good friends. You were his life and everything centered on you. He loved you and I have never, I mean never, seen a person as happy as when you told him he was going to be a father. He would have been a wonderful father." She started to say something, but he motioned for her to wait. "I know that you don't love me or even know me very well. But I am going to ask you to marry me."

"I'm sorry, I just couldn't."

"Why not?"

Emily sat straighter. "It's not proper."

He strained to hold his voice down. "What's proper about anything now? About war or his death or any of this?"

Emily started to say something, then leaned back and stared at Harry.

"Emily. Just listen to me. Trust me as Yitzhak's friend."

"I do trust you, Harry."

"Look, here's what I'm thinking. I don't have a girl back home. Nobody's gonna think anything of it if I come back married."

"What?"

He held his hand up to silence her. "All Yitzhak wanted in life was for you and the baby to be safe. I don't know when the war is going to be over, but I can make you both safer. Marry me and come to America."

"I can't."

"It's not like you gotta love me. Or be with me... in that way. I'll take you to Reno any time you say."

Emily frowned in confusion. "Reno?"

"That's where you go to get a divorce. To get unmarried. What I'm trying to say is that you don't have to stay married to me if you don't want to. When the war is over, or any time at all, I'll help you get back to Czechoslovakia if that's what you want. Or to England. Or if you want to stay with me, I won't bother you, not ever. Not unless you want to be, you know, really married to me."

"But Yitzhak—"

Harry leaned forward and put his hand over hers. "I want my friend's child and his wife to be safe. I want a family as much as Yitzhak did, but—"

"Don't you want someone to love you, too?"

"Sure I do. But I haven't met anyone yet that fills the bill. We are here now. There's this war bride program. We can marry now and you can go to live on our farm with my father until I can get home. You can be an American, just like that. Your baby can be born an American."

"Harry....tell me the truth. Do you want to marry me?"

"Yes."

"How could you love me? I am another man's—"

"I've always loved you," Harry said, looking at his hand on hers, "But you were married to my friend, and there are rules about that. I want you to take your time and decide if you want to really be married to me or not."

Before she could answer him, Graham slammed through the door from the kitchen and pointed at the front door with his cane. "Come along. Be quick about it!"

The sound that followed Graham from the kitchen window began as the distant buzz of a fly on a summer afternoon, shifted to a wasp hissing, and then it became a motorcycle's chatter. As Harry helped Rachel from the sofa, the air raid siren started its wail. Emily grabbed the two violin cases they kept at the end of the sofa. Mrs. Finch snatched the battery torch from the table by the door. "The stove? Did I—"

Harry lurched toward the kitchen. "I'll check. Go on."

Graham pointed for the women to go down the two flights into the cellar of the building. He and Harry trailed behind, using the railing for support.

The cellar was empty when Nattie pushed open the door and snapped on the switch to the hanging light bulb. Most of the apartment's tenants had fled to the country; the rest were away, working late, or ignoring the siren, so the cellar held only the four of them. Graham and Nattie claimed the far bricked corner of the cellar and sat on the green blankets they had stored there beside their spare lanterns and candles. Emily and Harry sat next to them on small wooden storage crates, leaning forward to avoid the moist mossy wall. Emily took Mrs. Finch's hand. "Harry has just asked me to go to America with him."

"I asked her to marry me," Harry corrected her gently.

Graham whispered to Emily as though others were not present, "You don't have to marry him, you know. We'll take care of you as if you were our very own."

"Yes, I know. Your generosity—"

"Generosity?" Graham roared at her. "Nothing of the sort. There's a war on. Nattie and I are only doing for you what your parents would have done for our daughter in the same circumstances."

"But..."

A thud shook the cellar and the light jumped on the cord and then swayed, making their shadows lurch against the wall. "There's nothing to discuss," Graham barked over the creaking timbers.

Mrs. Finch patted Emily's hand. "What do *you* want?"

Before Emily could answer, Graham interrupted, "No, you are not going. I will not lose you too." And then Graham gained his composure and spoke in carefully measured words. "I'm not upset that you might marry him. I just want you both to know that you don't have to marry to have your child well cared for. We have considerable..."

The light on the wire above them swayed again. Emily's face went in and out of shadow. "How can I live here? I'm a fraud, and the lie will be discovered. I'll never know all I need to know."

"Such as?" Graham said curtly.

Emily ignored him and continued, "But in America, who will know if my English is English enough. An error can be dismissed as my just being that odd Englishwoman. The Americans won't notice it if I don't know how to act at church, or know the history of a building, or catch the joke, or know one of your associates, or recognize one of Emily's school chums on the street." Drops formed at the corner of her eyes. Graham looked away as Harry put his arm around her shoulder.

Mrs. Finch took Emily's hand and asked, "What do you want for your child?"

"To be safe enough to grow up. To be brave. Never to know how afraid I am." Emily crossed her hands over her rounded belly and began to cry.

Nattie pulled a small lace trimmed handkerchief from the pocket of her sweater and handed it to Emily. "I think that your child has a very brave and a very good mother. If you have the baby here in England, I can help you with it. There is so much to learn. I remember how much I wanted my mother to have helped me as a new mother."

"Yes, but the war. You lost your child to it. God alone knows what is happening with my parents."

Graham barked louder then he intended. "I mean, can you really enter into this sham of a marriage?"

"Harry loves my child enough to give us a home." Emily took Harry's hand. "I think he is a very good man and I trust him."

"That isn't what I asked," Graham shot back.

"I loved my husband, and I still do. Harry knows that and is still willing to be the... the vehicle of our deliverance from the war."

Graham challenged her. "There is no escape. This war is having an effect in America as well."

"But they are not running to the underground shelters when that horrid whistle sounds, waiting like we are for whatever happens. They are not being bombed. There is food enough. There aren't even many children in London now. They are in the country or being shipped to Canada to live with people they don't know so they won't be killed here."

Graham cleared his throat. "The war won't go on forever."

Harry slapped the edge of the crate next to him. "When will it stop? Give me a date."

Graham got up and stretched his leg that was cramping. "If only we could see the future. If only life were played with a straight bat."

Emily looked up at him. "This isn't about me. It's about my child. How can I stay?"

"Well, then go you must. But you'll not be rid of us that easily. I always wanted to be the doting grandfather. You'll have to put up with that at least." As Graham looked away, Nattie saw him roughly swipe at a tear to hide it.

Emily hugged him. "What a lucky child my baby is. What a blessed child to have so many wonderful people all caring."

Mrs. Finch embraced Harry. "Well, then if she's set on marrying this handsome Yank, you both will have all our love and support. Won't they, Graham."

He blinked for a few moments, then smiled. "Certainly, my dear. I knew we could not keep her with us forever. But it is just a shock when the inevitable occurs."

The wedding at the civil clerk's office was fast and informal. Graham and Mrs. Finch signed as witnesses. Harry guided her through the blur of paperwork at the Embassy. Then she had a new passport with United States of America written in gold on the cover, with her married name and a new picture of her inside the green cover. The number of the passport was punched through the edge of her picture, all the way through the clean new document, in a pattern of small holes.

In mid-October, Emily's transport was arranged, billet secured for her passage in November to the new world on the hospital ship, *Lady Nelson*. Harry left for America the next day on a troop ship, and she remained in London without him.

Graham practiced violin with her every evening and she felt the baby growing. It seemed to her that the baby kicked harder when they played. As the departure date came closer, they played more and more difficult pieces. Her last next to last night in London, she and Graham played Partitia for Violin No. 2 by Bach, which Graham claimed was the most difficult of all violin pieces to play well.

Dinner her last night in London was too quiet and the tick of cups to saucers and forks to plates replaced their usual spirited discussions. As they finished, Graham said, "Let's just put the dishes to soak and have a performance tonight."

Emily glanced at him in surprise. "Tonight? Is there time?"

He nodded. "The night train is not leaving until eleven. We have plenty of time."

Nattie muttered, "Leave the dishes?"

"Tonight, Emily and I should play something special for you. A violin concerto, don't you think?"

"That would be very nice, but the—"

"The dishes can wait until after we play. I don't want her hands softened by dishwater before we play a long work. Or you could do them in the morning when we are out of your hair."

"What did you have in mind?" Emily asked.

"Brahms...Violin Concerto."

"Which one?" Mrs. Finch asked.

Graham and Emily looked at each other in silence and then laughed. Any attempt to talk simply made them laugh harder. Mrs. Finch left the table in a huff and carried her plate to the kitchen. Graham followed her, struggling for composure and wiping the tears off his cheeks with his dinner napkin. He gave her a hug.

"Sorry, my dear. Just musician's humor. Brahms only wrote one violin concerto, so it does not have a number."

"Well, you could have said as much at table. Go get ready. I'll clear the dishes by myself." Mrs. Finch turned to the wall and wiped at her tears before they fell.

"Do you mind us playing tonight?"

She waggled her hand over her shoulder, keeping her back to them.

"No, not at all. Leaving the dishes for after you both are on the train to Liverpool will give me something to do other than just worry after you. Go, tune up now. I expect a stellar performance."

Mrs. Finch cleared the other dishes and silverware from the table as Graham set up the music stands, placed the music on them, and then tuned his violin. When Mrs. Finch came in and took her seat at the center of the sofa, she glanced at Emily's book bag and a small suitcase, which were set by the door before dinner. During the performance, Mrs. Finch steeled herself not to look at the bags. She did not want this haunting her.

Glorious music filled the silence that they all felt. It united them. It grounded them. It was the first time that Graham had played at home with his rosewood bow with the gold tip.

At the end of the recital, Graham and Emily nodded to each other as Mrs. Finch applauded.

Graham watched her put away her bow and violin with the ease and love that he knew she would bring to her child. Graham tapped the back of his violin with his fingertip to get her attention. "Don't latch your case yet."

Graham twisted the knob and released the tension on his rosewood bow. The gold at the tip sparkled as he handed it to her. "Think there is room for this one?"

"But..." Emily started to object.

Nattie smiled at her husband. "Graham wouldn't tell you this, but it's the bow that he was awarded by the Philharmonic Board of Directors. What was it they said? 'For his excellence in his mastery of his instrument'? Yes, that was it. He asked me if he could give it to you, and I agreed wholeheartedly. It couldn't have a better home."

Graham simply placed it in the top of the case, turned the peg to hold it, and latched the case shut. "A remembrance."

Emily found herself in tears. Graham blinked hard and went for his coat. "No time for that; get your coat. We need to get to the train station."

CHAPTER 22

MEZZO PIANO

A musical instruction to play at a medium soft volume.

T he first day of November, 1944, was marked by an early snowfall
as the night train pulled into the station at Liverpool just after
dawn. Graham took Emily to a small restaurant near the station where
he ordered a breakfast of scones and tea before taking a taxi to the
docks.

A dry snow fell gently and dusted the eves of the sooty row houses
like white icing trim on a gingerbread house. The snow formed small
cones on fences and pier pilings in the harbor, and sat like a hat on the
red postal box beside the military sentry station at the entrance to the
pier.

It was just after 8:00 a.m. when the sentry, wrapped in a heavy
overcoat of green wool, motioned their taxi to a slot on the loading
area of the pier. The snow lay on the thick ropes that moored the *Lady
Nelson* to the dock. The white ship, with the red cross marking it as a
hospital ship, seemed to blend with the snow which slid off the lines
into the cold dark water. The other gray ships sat patiently under the
dusting of snow while the hospital ship seemed to shift and tug at her
lines as though eager to be underway. Great hoses ran from under the
dock to ship fittings for diesel and for drinking water. The gangplank
had a canvas roof that was keeping most of the snow off the wood
tread.

Emily pulled her violin case and purse from the taxi while Graham
carried her suitcase and book bag for her. Graham walked her to the
foot of the gangplank, set the bag and suitcase on the wet dock and
hugged her. He held her for a second too long. Then he leaned back on
his cane and looked at her with a full smile. Emily nodded to a sailor

who had noticed her pregnancy and picked up the suitcase and bag for her.

"Off you go now. Off to your new life, with all of our prayers," Graham said.

"Thank you, Graham, thank you..."

"Just this once, could you call me Father? I know you'll always be Joseph's daughter, but just this once..."

"Goodbye, Father."

"Thank you, dear."

She walked up the swaying gangplank, following the sailor who was carrying her bags. She gave her name to the soldier with the clipboard at the top of the gangplank, showed him her green passport, and was handed a packet of papers with her cabin assignment and a key. She walked closer to the rail to wave at Graham.

A young woman on the dock shouted. "Rachel."

Emily dropped the packet and leaned down to pick it up. As she gathered the moist papers from the deck, she trembled and wondered who could have found her out.

Before she stood up, another young woman ran to the railing, waved vigorously, and shouted down to the dock. "Shelley, I'm up here. I'll meet you at the top of the gangplank. Hurry up! It's cold."

The young woman saw Emily collecting the papers and stopped to pick up one page that was skittering toward the railing and handed it to Emily. "Here you are."

"Thank you," Emily said to the woman who had her other name. After that, she never saw either of the two women again.

She went to her assigned cabin on the E-Deck, where the sailor put her suitcase under the lower bunk nearest the door and handed her the small book bag. The slight odor of mildew and the richness of diesel fuel overwhelmed her and she felt nausea tempt the tea and scones. She stood quickly, put her hand to her mouth and breathed deeply. Then she knew that she needed fresh air and tried unsuccessfully to open the small round porthole. She grabbed her violin case and purse and went back to the top deck, where she watched the dock come alive with action.

The *Lady Nelson* had been in harbor only four days. During that time, old men, replacing the hardy longshoremen who had gone to war, pushed crates of provisions on small hand trolleys across the gangplank that was level from the dock to the cargo hold of the ship. First, taking great slabs of frozen beef and crates of tinned food from the United States off the ship, then stocking the hold with trunks and luggage for its passengers going west, across the Atlantic to Canada.

It had taken only two days for unloading provisions and then loading the wounded, evacuees, and brides for their passage. If the weather held, the crossing would be only eight days. If they had to dodge the weather or German U-boats, it could be twice as long. Provisions for twenty days were in the cargo hold, along with food and medicine for the passengers. Contingency planning. Stocking the hospital ward for the ship came last, as the number and type of wounded returning to Canada varied from trip to trip.

It was mid-morning when a small black lorry came to the dock with a dozen children and two stout middle-aged women dressed in gray wool suits and coats with matching gray hats, tight brimmed and practical. All came up the wide wooden gangplank to the C-Deck with small dark brown suitcases made of cardboard and canvas.

The gangplank was covered with a canvas awning that ran its length. Now, the snow was melting on it and it was dripping water into the sea below it. The snow had blown onto the wood and had melted into a slippery slush. If it weren't for the small raised wooden crossbars, there would have been almost no traction for the children who marched up the gangplank.

The children, who were used to walking in step, like little soldiers, started up the gangplank which was swaying dangerously under their cadence. A sailor yelled, "Stop, hold it right there." Then he motioned for the first five or six to walk up while the others were frozen in place. The gangplank continued to pulse and sway. A small girl started crying, and the matron called her back to the end of the line and picked her up and carried her up to the deck. When they were all on the deck, the matron had them line up and march off to their large dormitory that had been converted with bunk beds from a dining hall.

Now these little troopers were going to pack into the bunk beds and sleep their way to a new life, away from war.

An hour later, a second lorry arrived with ten more children and one more guardian similarly dressed and appointed. The sailor on guard at the gangplank made sure that they came aboard in small clutches of two or three at a time.

A town bus, red and stark, rattled onto the dock just as the first of the cargo holds had been shut with a loud clang that echoed in the cold. By then the diesel soot from other ships entering or leaving harbor had dusted the snow with soot, and by tomorrow, it would be a gray slush, pushed into the sea by the old men with their wide brooms.

Twenty more women and three toddlers, with piles of additional suitcases, were left upon the dock by the town bus and crept their way up the gangplank. Then a large green truck with green canvas over the back pulled up and soldiers in green uniforms carried stretchers of men from the dock directly to the other cargo hold. Only later would she discover that the hospital ward was below, covering a full deck, and that entrance though the cargo door made their access to the hospital deck simpler.

By 3:00 p.m., a rumbling, throaty vibration pulsed through the ship as the first engine started. A belch of blue-black smoke came out of the stack and swept down over the dock. Then the second engine was started and the rumble steadied as the ship established a humming pulse.

By 4:00 p.m., the gangplank had been lifted away from the side of the ship by a crane and lowered to the dock. The snow that had collected on the canvas cover slid into the seawater between the ship and dock and vanished. The sun was gone and the sky dull.

Then the mooring lines were dropped from the ship down to the dock with a crash and a thud, and the tug pulled the bow out away from the dock.

The engines growled as the tug let loose its towing line and the *Lady Nelson* left port. Two battleships led the convoy. And behind the *Lady Nelson*, three frigate-class warships followed, wafting smoke into the gray sky. Snow hit the deck and started to collect as the temperature dropped.

A wind blew the diesel exhaust fumes from the smokestacks back over the ship, swirling around it, creating a fog bank. And then they were on the open sea. Land was a smaller and smaller slice where the eastern sky met the dark water.

Emily fought nausea. For dinner, she just had bread and milk. She did not sleep easily in the cramped cabin with the perfumes and smells of wet coats hanging on the hooks at the back of the door. And the sounds of strangers sleeping. And the pitch and bucking of the ship.

Waking abruptly, she was uncertain where she was. Then she realized. She was in a small cabin with three sleeping women and too much luggage. She pulled on slacks and a sweater and tugged her overcoat and life jacket off the pegs on the back of the door. She pulled her violin from under the bed. Air would help and it was only an hour or so until first light.

Air on deck. The sea was calm and their progress swift the first morning of their voyage to the new world.

She walked alone on deck in the biting air. She pulled the scarf from her pocket and tied it over her head to keep the freeze from her ears. The deck was still wet with night dew that had frozen into a silver skin on the metal fittings at the bow of the boat. She walked with the horizon in sight until her stomach calmed. Then she went to the empty dining room in the stern.

When they had arrived, the dining room was a reception room for passenger instructions: signing in, getting materials on the boat rules and instructions on which lifeboat one should report to for drills, a paper on how to put on the life vest, and a book of chits for meals. But it was quickly transformed for the dinner service.

Dinner the first night out was light. A buffet of sliced meats and cheeses and breads was set out against the starboard bulkhead and after the passengers got their paperwork, they got plates and made sandwiches. The children quickly spilled glasses of milk. Stout coffee mugs were substituted for milk glasses for the remainder of the voyage. Then the passengers tried to sleep in the cramped staterooms, getting used to the incessant rumble, the faint smell of diesel fumes, and the gentle rock of the ship at sea.

Meanwhile, the dining room was transformed. By morning, the tables were covered with white linen and set with heavy silverware. Ivory plates stacked in a pillar almost a meter high were at the end of the buffet table.

She set her case on the large table under the formal photograph of King George VI and dropped her lifejacket on the floor.

A uniformed sailor with a holstered gun on his hip walked up to her. "You can't be in here now, Miss. Security."

"I can't be in my cabin!" Emily retorted and then pointed to her stomach.

"Sorry, but you can't be in here."

"Why not? All I am going to do is practice my violin. I need to every day."

"Really? Well, you can't be in here alone."

"How can you tell me that?"

"The rule is that no passenger is to be in here alone. I'm on watch."

"Then stay with me while I practice." Emily simply turned and opened her case and fingered the new bow in its safe case, and pulled out her practice bow and twisted it as she turned to the sailor.

"Are you going to leave?"

"Do I really need to?"

"I guess I could do my reports in here with you while you practice."

"Thank you. Instead of practice, would you like me to play something?"

"Like what?"

"Greensleeves? The ten minute concert version."

"Oh, that would be wonderful. I'm going off duty in a few minutes and ought to be going to bed now, but I never can sleep the first day out."

"You've crossed in this ship before?"

"Ah, yeah. Been on her since I joined up in 1941. Got back on her after she got the refit two years later. Became Canada's first hospital ship, she was. Got room for five hundred eighteen lads and a medical staff of seventy. Far cry from carrying those on holiday from Canada to the West Indies, it is. Did you see the red cross and the number forty-six on her? Well, she's a hospital ship as well as a convoy vessel. Seen action in the Mediterranean and the North Atlantic. Don't much like the idea of her being painted white. Too much of a target if the German submariners don't see the red cross that goes with the white paint. But she's a survivor. She's a lucky ship."

"What do you mean by that?" Emily asked, as she tuned her violin to the new humidity.

"The Jerries have already torpedoed her once. When we was in harbor in Castries in Saint Lucia. Caribbean. U-Boat, think it was U-514. Some reports credit U-161 with the shot. Snuck right into harbor and got her at dockside. That was in 1942, tenth of March. Me mum's birthday. That was before she was a hospital ship. Got refitted in America. Mobile, Alabama. Yanks did a fine job on her. Better than new. Yeah. She's a trim vessel. Gets 15 knots at open sea from her twin turbines, 438 feet with a beam of fifty-nine feet, loaded draught of twenty-four feet, just under eight thousand tons. Yeah, she's up for any weather and any challenge. She's a fine ship, indeed. They got two of her sister ships as well. Total losses at sea. *Lady Hawkins* was torpedoed off the North Carolina coast. That's mid-way up America's Atlantic coast, and then they got the *Lady Drake* off Bermuda, both in 1941. So, she's a lucky ship."

"I'm glad to know that she is a lucky ship!"

"That she is indeed. In a couple a ways, really. Going to be good berths in the merchant marine for us after the war, and serving on her is going to be a top recommendation. Love the sea. Me pa was a sailor, too. Don't you worry a bit on it; we'll get ya home to Canada right smart."

Emily nodded and started to play.

The man started to write his report, then sat back in his chair and relaxed, almost going to sleep in the chair by the door.

At seven, a horn went off. The first of the two short blasts made her jump. The sailor who was her audience stood quickly and nodded to her.

"Lifeboat drill. Hurry," he said as he rushed out the doorway. She put the violin in the case, twisted the bow slack, and put it into the case. She struggled into the lifejacket, snapped the case shut and ran out of the warm dining room into the blustery morning. She went to the lifeboat station that she had memorized from the map on the back of the cabin door.

By then, the air was clean and there was no smell of land or diesel or anything man-made. The sun had melted the ice and the wind had blown much of the moisture from the wooden deck. She listened carefully as the sailor at the lifeboat station explained very slowly how to put the bulky jacket over your head and tie the long cotton straps that fell from the sides of the vest. The women struggled to get them over their heads without mussing their hair and tied each other's lifejackets over heavy winter coats. Several held their hands over their ears against the bitter wind. Emily had somehow managed to get the lifejacket on correctly but gladly accepted help in tying it.

A ten-year-old boy stood against the bulkhead holding his lifejacket. Then he threw it on the deck and raced a few meters toward the stern of the ship, then spun and ran back. He ran into Emily before he picked up his lifejacket from the deck.

"Is he with you?" the sailor conducting the drill asked sternly of the matron in the gray coat.

"Yes, lad's not following this in English, so I'm afraid that we're going to need to do a bit of pantomime for him," she said taking his shoulders and turning him to watch the drill and not the seagulls that were still following the ship. "Czechoslovakian refugee."

Emily heard this and turned, almost against her will. She stared at the boy. The matron took her stare for displeasure as he had run into her.

"Hasn't a clue where his parents are. One of the little lads that got brought to London from Prague. Hoped they could live safe during the war. What did they call that? *Kindertransport*, I think, something like that--the trains that rescued the children from the German occupation of Czechoslovakia."

"How awful for him," Emily said.

"Well, at least he's getting to a safer place for a while. We've registered him with the Red Cross, so if his parents turn up they can find each other. There was a man who spoke Czech at the mission in London-- told the lad all about what's going on. This Canadian fisher couple is going to take him in for the duration. When his parents are found, then the church group sponsoring him will arrange passage back for him."

"And if they aren't found?" Emily asked.

"Well, he'll probably really have to learn English then. Doesn't know a word now."

"Not a single word?"

"Not that we can tell. Just that Czechoslovakian gibberish. No one can make up or down of it."

"I might be able to help. I went to school with a girl from Prague. I may recall a few phrases."

"How wonderful. Can you join us, then, for breakfast after this awful drill?"

"Certainly, what's his name?"

The matron looked at her roster of names and scanned it before shoving it back into the pocket of her winter coat. "Jan, it is. Jan, " she said pronouncing the hard 'J' as in January.

"Jan," Emily called to the boy with the softer 'J', sounding to the matron like 'yawn'." The boy turned around with a look of expectation. Emily looked at the deep longing in his eyes as he heard his name, his real name, for the first time in weeks. His need pushed Emily past introductions, past formality, she leaned over and held out her hand to the ten-year-old.

"*Jak se máte?*" Emily whispered, asking him in Czech, 'How are you?'

The boy yelled, "*Co?*" What? he asked himself in disbelief. Jan grabbed her hand, tears running down his face, staining the lifejacket. "*Dobro*," 'Good', he said as simply as he could, coughing back tears.

Emily simply stroked his hair until his tears stopped. She let the other children go into breakfast first and waited with him on the cold deck until they both were ready to be with other people. Then she held him to her side and walked him into breakfast, Jan to her right side, violin case in her left hand.

As they entered the dining room, young men in starched white coats were putting large silver pitchers of water and smaller glass pitchers of orange juice on each table. Tall tumblers and stocky glasses sat empty, awaiting the diners' directions. Cups were set upside-down on their saucers, waiting for stewards to fill with real coffee or real tea for the adults. It was an unanticipated abundance.

She did not remember everything at the buffet, but the sheer range of the food and elegance of the cruise ship was breathtaking. The number of choices was confusing for the small charges, who wanted one of everything. People pointed and asked and a steward served generous portions of whatever was requested. Porridge and scrambled eggs. Potatoes diced and fried with onion. Dried herring and kippered herring at the end of the buffet line. Toast and strawberry jam. After the passengers were all seated and eating, the stewards came to pour water, juice and the hot drinks, to the embarrassment of those who had poured their own beverages.

Near the end of the meal, stewards placed a large bowl of fresh oranges on each table. They were encouraged to take a couple and peel them later for snacking during the day. Emily cried, as did several other women, at the rediscovery of fresh fruit after having only tinned fruit for over two years.

Emily's recollections of the dining room were more overwhelming impressions than memories. Fresh linen and dark wood. The glitter of silver and baskets of fresh oranges set upon each table. White bread and dinner rolls. It was all too much luxury. Too much for her hollow heart to embrace. Too much for her tenuous stomach and fear. But the small boy. That's why she came back. That's why she kept arriving before mealtime, so they could talk before the richness of the smells of food brought on the nausea.

And then the weather turned harsh. Three days out, the clouds went solid black and threatened rain or snow momentarily. The blue deep waves turned darker and darker until the sea was almost black, and the trenches between the wave crests deepened, and the ship began to pitch.

On the fourth day they finished breakfast and Emily and Jan went to the deck to look at the sea. The sea was shaded in giant charcoal waves with black tones at the base of the swells. The wind was strong enough to pull spray off the face of the swell and make of it a bubbly smear of gray.

Then the most marvelous thing happened. The sun slid between two different banks of clouds, and in the margin between two fronts, it slanted sharply into the sea. In late morning, suddenly, the swells gave up a secret. From their dark base, they narrowed and peaked to a clean crest. In the top of each swell was a slice of turquoise, darker at the base, and then transparent at the top. Clear for a moment, before the wind captured the top of the swell, spun it into a creamy froth, and blew it across into the trough of the next swell. But for a few magical minutes, while Jan and Emily were alone on the wind whipped deck, the ocean was sprinkled with bright gems over a dark sea. Turquoise, almost iridescent, emerald tips toward the horizon, and tourmaline and tea-colored quartz crystals, as the sun teased color from the crest of the swells.

Later that day she was confined to sickbay. Seasick and morning sick, she asked if the boy could visit and indeed he did.

Her memory of that time was simple. Nausea had overwhelmed her. Less and less food staying down. The sick bay room, Jan, her violin case, lifejackets and white sheets. The visits lasted all day. The matron would deliver him after breakfast, pick him up for lunch when Emily had her intravenous feeding, and then again, the matron would pick him up for the second dinner seating. He would reappear again the next morning on schedule.

In their days together, she told him stories and let him talk, let the bottled up language rush out. Then her stories were more in English than Czech. One day he was allowed to bring his lunch on a tray to eat with her. That day became a child's tea party in English while the clear fluid dripped into her vein. Soon he was fluent in the words and manners for proper dining. Then their time was spent exploring words for living and asking and finding ways to work around words that were not in his mind, inventing linguistic bridges to his future.

'What is that called?' "Please hand me that thing.' He learned enough English to survive at dinner with the other children and to start a life in his new home. He reminded her of what courage was. They talked and planned and she gave him the address where she was going on the farm outside of Fresno in California, and he gave her the address of where he was going on the outer banks of Canada. They both wrote their addresses very very carefully and exchanged them with formality and shook hands.

She recalled their discussion of the foods that the Americans had donated to the ship. Neither she nor the boy had ever tasted a Fig Newton or sipped a 7-Up. And then in the morning, it happened. The rumors were too intense to ignore. Nurses were speculating when land would be seen. There was a ship's pool, and whoever guessed the closest time to when the Captain sighted land would win the pool. Doctors in sickbay started pulling paper scraps from their pockets and looking at the wall clocks too frequently. Then a paper slip would be crumpled up and tossed in a wastebasket as the time passed and the slip documented a losing time. More than two hundred pounds sterling was the prize for the time that landfall was made. But, for her, the prize would be setting foot on solid ground when they docked in Halifax, Nova Scotia, Canada, to the north of New York.

The excitement had reached the children as well. Jan ran into sickbay and told her landfall was very, very soon. The nurse nodded when Emily asked if she could take the boy on deck, but was told to return after the horn sounded to transition to her stateroom to pack. She struggled into her coat and went on deck.

It was bitter cold with the salt air cutting through the boy's coat and the two green blankets she had taken from sickbay to wrap around him. Her thick coat did not control her shivering either. When land scratched a brown slice into the blend of blues that were the sea and sky, the horn on the ship sounded a long blast that rattled her teeth. She pulled in the smell of freedom and let out a breath full of all of the fear she had ever known.

She returned Jan to his group, checked out of sickbay, and packed her things quickly. What seemed like hours later, the ship finally docked and was still, although the engine drone continued. She waited for Jan at the foot of the gangplank and took his hand as they walked down Pier 21. A band on the dock played *Sentimental Journey, Goodbye to Piccadilly*, and *Oh, Canada,* the Canadian national anthem. Then they played some tunes she didn't recognize. When they left the dock and went into the huge warehouse at the end of the pier, there was an interpreter from the Jewish Immigrant Aid Society to help the matrons with the paperwork for Jan and the other guest children. There were collection barrels for the Red Cross and Boxes for Britain ready to be loaded for the return trip.

She remembered that she left Halifax by bus, took a train to New York, then to Chicago, and finally started to Sacramento in California. One of her first discoveries in America was the enormous scale, vastness, beauty, and grandeur. She did not know what to make of the curiosity of some travelers on the train who looked at her silently and then out the window again or the generosity of other travelers on the train who would hoist her luggage to the overhead rack and seemed embarrassed when she thanked them. More than once, a family opened a wicker basket and handed her half of a sandwich without asking. Wheat fields in the Dakotas seemed larger than countries in Europe. Prairies strained the limits of sight. Mountains loomed for days as the train approached them. And the quiet. It was so far away from London. There was no shadow of a U-boat lurking. There were no air raid sirens in the night.

California was only sweater cool on the day of her arrival in Sacramento. Harry had been flown back to California from the east coast and been medically discharged. He met Emily's train in Sacramento and drove her to his farm in a gray 1938 Plymouth with a rounded trunk that looked like a turtle to her. After chatting rapidly about the sea voyage, Emily fell asleep for the rest of the drive to his farm outside Fresno.

They arrived just past eleven at night. He woke her as he turned off the paved road and onto the gravel road that led to his house, which glowed in the distance. All of the lights in the house were blazing when she arrived. Harry honked the car's horn and the foreman got up from a chair on the porch and helped Harry carry the bags into the house.

Barbara was born in Fresno General Hospital, three days before

Christmas in 1944. Harry asked that she be named for his mother.

Six months later, a letter arrived at her Fresno farm from Jan's foster parents in Canada thanking her for teaching him so much English and befriending him. His letter to her in Czech was enclosed. They corresponded for years. The Children's Overseas Reception Board found his parents after the war. He returned to his parents, who had fled to France. Letters came from Lyon, then Paris when he was in university. He enlisted in the French army and was wounded in Algeria. He returned to his parent's home in Lyon, worked in their small shoe repair shop, married and had three boys.

Two months after their arrival in Fresno, Harry had a job with McDonnell Douglas in Santa Monica, doing radio work on the new planes that were still in production. Maybe he couldn't fly combat, maybe his hearing was not good enough to let him train others, but he could be sure the radios going to war were good enough to save lives.

CHAPTER 23

PORTANDO

Two or more notes that are smoothly connected in the same bow direction.

L ate in the evening, Emily carried the fortune cookies into the
music room, ate one, and read the fortune. She crumpled it and
dropped it beside her. It shed no light on how complex her deck repair
would be or when it would end, but she resented the uproar and shook
her head. She opened a journal wanting to disappear into her past and
remember her sea journey from England. When she tugged at the light
lap robe, the journal slipped and several letters slid to the floor. She
picked them up slowly and then read the one on pale blue stationary,
her mind knowing each word by heart.

> *Dearest Emily,*   *March 13, 1945*
>
> *We are well and hoping that this finds you the same in your
> new home in Los Angeles.*
> *We celebrated your mother's birthday by toasting our daugh-
> ter and granddaughter with the same bottle of sherry we drank
> from on your wedding day and then spending a day in the country.
> She swears that she saw a skylark but I think it was a bit early in
> the season for the sighting. As it was her birthday, I didn't protest,
> but I note that she did not enter the sighting in her birding log.*
> *We had occasion to be in the south of London for a performance
> last month, so we are trying to return some normalcy to our days.*
> *As your husband last inquired on my take on the new V-2
> bombs, please tell him that Jerry seems to have a keen new strategy
> in his war against us. Of late, we have taken to calling these rock-
> ets Doodlebugs. But unlike the noisy V-1, the damn new rocket, just*

cuts off the engine, silently drops to earth and blows up something. The south of the city seems to be taking the brunt of this just now.

You will be pleased to know that your husband's fellow pilots here have had some success in shooting down these beasts or knocking them off course with their fighter planes. The area near Canterbury in Kent was having them fly over with such frequency they're now calling that area Doodlebug Alley.

Much Love, G.

Actually, your father got it right this time. It was a possible sighting and I don't make entries into my bird diary lightly. I wanted to thank you for the kindness of your gifts and let you know that the tinned ham is going to be the centerpiece for the annual party of the symphony this year. I want you to come and play for me again. I miss your "Motzard" and your laugh. I want you to come here yet respect your desire to remain there. Perhaps I can convince Graham to pack for a trip to the States, as he is now calling America with great familiarity.

I hope the baby has your laugh.

I can see her father's eyes in the wonderful picture that you sent.

Love,

Your mother

After putting it beside her, she picked up a letter written on a creamy onionskin paper that had been folded and unfolded again and again on the same creases. The paper was almost transparent at the folds. This letter began with the fine blue lines of Mrs. Finch's pen, and ended with Graham's scrawled black ink at the bottom of the second page.

London   *Spring 1949*

Dearest,

I thank you for the phonograph record that you sent over. It is magnificent.

Easter will be with us soon and I find my thoughts going to our faith. I found your Book of Common Prayer where you left it at the city house. You left in too great a hurry to have packed your prayer book. So I am sending you a new one and keeping yours here for when you visit.

I have been doing a great deal of reading lately about the relationship between the Anglican Church, of which you are a member, and other great religions of the world. As you recall, we share with Judaism the great belief in one God and in a system of justice based on God's laws and his great mercy.

What informs Christianity and Islam is the monotheism that began, I believe, with Judaism.

I also believe what separates us is not the word of God but the way we have heard this word. Goodness shall follow those who do good, not those who are good. Your father and I believe that good-ness is not a passive state but one of action, if grace is to come from it. The Sabbath is central to our religious experiences and the Law of Moses guides us as well. Your friend from school showed us so much of that grace and strength.

I have discussed with our family priest your ongoing religious practice in America. He reminds me that there are no Protestant churches quite like ours. So you may not know quite the same ritu-als, as you are English.

Consider refreshing yourself with the tenants of faith in the Catechism in the Book of Common Prayer and with the flow of the service. The Protestant Episcopal Church in America follows this form of worship closer, I believe, than other churches.

As interesting as the forms of worship are, I believe that a child needs to have a central ethical precept that has a name and support of a community. What name this has in your new home is for you to discover.

You and yours are in our daily prayers, and our hourly thoughts.

With all love,

Mummy

*PS Your recording of the four concerti grossi of Vivald's Opus
8 that others call Four Seasons has us breathless. I am wearing
out the copy you sent, bragging on and on about you to others at
the orchestra. When it is released here, I am certain that all will
purchase it the first week. Proud of you.*
    G.

The first time that Emily read the letter, she threw it in the trashcan. How dare Mrs. Finch dismiss her faith, she had thought. How
dare she presume that the charade was forever. But then, Emily retrieved the letter from the trash and read it again. Permission or a
sentence? She was unsure of its meaning or of her future. She refolded
it carefully and returned it to its envelope.

Only later did Emily realize that in that letter she was provided the
instruction and choice to hide in plain sight. To be different and know
things differently because she was English, not Jewish. She was given
permission to have a religion that captured the ethical basis of how to
act, but with the addition of the notion of a prophet as the Son of God,
not a messenger of God.

The letter was burned into her memory. Did Mrs. Finch think she
needed to hide forever or was it permission to tell the truth? Was it
a guide to the truth or a bridge to reconciliation? Did she mean her
lie was eternal or open to remedy? Was the loving letter a crutch or a
challenge? She read it over and over again during the years that she had
held it, protected it, prayed over it.

She read it again and went to bed, wondering if she would ever
know what was intended in that letter. Sleep not coming, she turned
on the small television in her bedroom and listened to the audience
laugh at Leno's jokes, as they had to Parr's and Carson's and others in
the darkest part of the night.

CHAPTER 24

FORTE

The direction to play in a manner that is strong or explosive.

Construction trucks arriving and departing, men shouting, and the shrill whine of saws filled her Monday. The construction noises and cement trucks on Tuesday were sufficient for Emily to call a cab and go to Pasadena to wander The Huntington for the day, walk in the gardens, lunch in the tea room, and savor its galleries of paintings until late afternoon.

Late Wednesday afternoon, the knock on the door came as Emily was making soup. She left the vegetables on the cutting board and answered the door, after wiping her hands on a new dishtowel. Ben had a sheaf of papers in one hand.

"Come in, I'm cooking. What's all that? More papers about the deck?"

"No, the new cement footing is drying now, and the bracing looks good. All the timber is on-site and ready to put in place. They just need the city inspection for the cement and then they can replace the timber. After that they can paint as soon as we get a few dry days."

"That sounds fine. Is that something I need to sign?"

"No, these are banking documents." He placed them on her table and sat on her sofa, waiting for her to join him. "I want to show you my latest discovery on your account."

But she did not come to the sofa as he expected. She stood at the door and turned to him. She did not close the door or move to her usual seat on the sofa. She gripped the dishtowel in her hand and shook it at him in a rage.

"How dare you? How dare you come into my home and push your agenda on me? Didn't we end this on the phone the other night?"

"What..." Ben was confused and sat forward with his arms out-stretched. She shut the door with enough force to qualify as a slam.

"Don't sit there with that innocent smile. How do you have the nerve to come into my home and upend my life?" She slung the towel onto the table in front of him and spun to go to the kitchen.

"By telling you the truth?" Ben called after her.

"Who asked you to?" Emily shouted over her shoulder.

Ben sat back on the sofa as though slapped.

She caught her breath, spun and stomped back to confront him. "Precisely what gives you the right to invade my privacy?"

Ben started to say something, but she turned and stalked across the room, like some caged animal, cruising past Ben but never looking away from him.

"It's just like the bloody witch-hunts in the fifties. Sneaking be-hind my back. What are you going to do to me next, start a whisper campaign? Going to get me blacklisted, so I'll never work in this town again? Too late for that. Too bloody late. I have my money. My house is paid off. I don't have to be careful now. Do you have my FBI file, too? You can't make my life how you want it to be. It's my life. So why don't you just put a sock in it and push off."

Ben stood and walked toward the front door.

Emily rushed past him and opened the door so fast that the handle hit the wall. Ben stood still and shoved his hands in his pockets.

"If that's what you really want."

"Yes, and take those bloody papers with you!"

"No, they're not about me. They're about you. And if you won't let me help you, maybe there's somebody else that you'll let be your friend or your lawyer or your banker or advocate to get what's yours."

Emily swept the papers up from the table and shook them at Ben. "Why should I? Why should I let you or anybody else turn my life up-side down for some money?"

"Hell, if you don't want the money, burn it, give it to your grand-daughter for a wedding present, or to charity. Throw it off your deck for the squirrels to play with for all I care. But if you do nothing, they have won again. Stand up to them. Say it was wrong. Don't let them get away with it."

"Them? Aren't you just making everything into your own crusade? Not every problem in the world is related to the Holocaust, now is it?"

"I'm just trying to fix something that was broken," Ben said controlling his anger.

"Fix what? This was a banking error. That's all."

"Emily," Ben said softly, trying to reason with her, "this was no error. This was how Hitler financed his war and how companies still profit from that. We can stop that."

She threw the papers on the table and they fanned across the waxed surface and skidded to the floor. "That's extreme, Ben. Why don't you take a look at your motives? The fact is that this was all over long before you were born."

Ben went down on one knee to gather the papers. "Facts? Look at the facts. Jews in Europe had a net worth over $12,000,000,000. That's billion, not million...before the war. That included those in ghettos with a net worth of just a couple hundred bucks. That's where the German treasury got the money to wage war. That and slave labor in mines and munitions factories. Confiscate property. Sell assets. Work deals with industry. After the war American soldiers found a cave at the foot of the Alps. It was the Merkers salt mine. Over 400 tons of artwork was hidden there. Over 337 tons of gold was there. Most of it ingots marked with the Reich's seal, and 3,000 bags of currency waiting to be laundered."

"So?"

"So, that gold exceeded the value of the entire German treasury before the war. It wasn't really gold from the treasury. It was gold from the camps. From fillings and wedding bands and pocket watches."

"That's old news..."

He stood and put the papers in order without looking at her. "Did you know that the life insurance industry in Germany and other countries made a mint on policies that were cancelled for failure to pay a premium when the owner was in a camp? Even fully paid policies were not paid to heirs or beneficiaries because there were no death certificates issued from the camps. Billions of profits for the companies. One

Swiss bank set up an account in the name of a S. S. officer, Melmer. The Nazis sent laundered money to it as a front for the German government. They hid the deposits and kept all the interest. As long as no one claims it, all that is raw profit for the Swiss banks that held these accounts. Don't tell me that it is over. There are still businesses making money off their victims."

"Ben, I'm not a victim. I'm alive and have a life. Take these papers away."

Ben held the pile of papers and took a slow breath. "We're all victims in some way. It forms our age, shapes our time. Look at the 18-year-old skinhead in Munich or San Diego. It permeates our foreign policy. It let us question *why* in South America when people were disappearing by the thousands. Look at why the U.N. troops are in Albania. That's the start of genocide, and the world sees it for what it is and is responding. We can say 'no' today. And we are. Yes, it surrounds my life. But you are not a cause. Not you. I was just trying to be a good neighbor. A friend."

"My friend? What friend would bring me those? Take them."

He turned and started for the door. "They're not mine to take."

Emily slammed the door after him and locked it as Ben scuffed across the flagstone path to the road. She slipped the CD of Vivaldi's Violin Concerto No. 5., 'The Tempest', into the CD player. The volume was high and as Emily sat on her sofa she let the music wrap her tight.

She thought of one word: "*Kaddish*"

The name of the prayer in every Shabbat's service affirming God's mercy and wisdom. She wondered how the name of this prayer became so strongly associated with mourning and death when it is so life affirming. That is what her father argued with Mr. Zablinski about after he sat *shivah* with him for the death of the elder Zablinski for those long ten days. Then say *Kaddish* for one year. Every day the men went to pray at *schul* or at home. Always ten men. The minion.

She puzzled on it again. How can a woman who has no loss visible to the world have the right to mourn? She stood and paced in front of the sofa.

What was her *keriah*? By what ritual would she begin her grieving?

How could she cut the garment of her new life? What could she cut for her silent grief? How easily she remembered her mother taking that small knife and cutting the lapel of her own dress and then cutting the dress of her aunt, when they heard of their own mother's death. How easily she recalled the moment. The *keriah*. How could she embrace that ritual without opening too much of herself to a world she still did not trust?

What stone could weigh heavier than the invisible one she carried in her chest? How could emptiness weigh so very much?

Daily for a year and on the anniversary of the death: the *Yahrzheit* candle. The memorial candle that is lit on the anniversary of a loved one's death. The candle that is lit on the celebration of *Yizkor*, the memorial service related to Yom Kippur, the last days of Sukot, Pesach and Shavuot. She remembered.

Emily questioned herself. Did her silence strengthen the tradition within her or merely deny heritage to her child. 'Did I give her life only to deny her history?' Emily asked herself in a whisper.

CHAPTER 25

DECRESCENDO

The direction to play so that the volume gradually gets softer.

Kike. That was the new word she learned when they were house hunting in 1947. She and Harry found a run-down house that they could afford in the hills.

Don was the slim man with the thin moustache from Midtown Realty who drove them to see the house. He gunned his shiny Buick too fast up the twisting street and braked too hard in front of a white house. As he opened the car door, he said, "Here we are. A kike owned it. But I'll get it cleaned special before you move in. He still has a couple of boxes in there."

"Let's see how it looks before we get into any details," Harry said crisply.

They walked toward the door and Emily looked down the hillside over the city while the realtor found the key to this house on his big key ring. She was in love with the view and if the house were in any way salvageable, she wanted it. She winked at Harry and he knew that he should try for it.

Don went to the door and unlocked it. He left his huge key ring in the lock, and the keys clattered as the door opened. He stepped aside, "Go ahead, look around. I'll have a smoke out front. You know, the old guy that lived here never put in a deck, but think of it with a deck, how perfect it would be for a party? A barbecue. Wonderful view."

Don walked out and leaned on the front fender of the Buick. The summer sun was blinding off the chrome. He tapped a Camel on his thumbnail before he lighted it with a silver Ronson butane lighter. Harry heard the snap of the cap on the lighter and then turned to Emily, "Come on."

He entered the house and was in the middle of the living room before he noticed that she had not come into the house. She was on the porch. There was a mezuzah still on the doorpost. Small and pewter. She wondered if the owner had moved and abandoned it or if he would remember it when he came for the rest of his belongings. "Well? Aren't you interested?"

Emily was startled by his voice, and quickly walked into the house without saying anything. Then she came up behind Harry as he turned off the faucet at the kitchen sink and looked out the window, over the city. She put her arms around him and said softly, "Harry, I feel like I'm home. I don't know how this could be better."

"Before we set up house here, let's see if the rest of the plumbing works. Let's go downstairs." And they held hands as they explored the rest of the house. On the bottom floor, there were cardboard boxes with neat labels on them. "A workshop for you?" Emily asked.

"Could I?" Harry asked, as they went up the stairs to the next floor and he looked under the sink and ran water in the bathroom.

"Why not? The house is huge. Where would we have our bedroom? There are two rooms here, on the middle floor. But the room off the living room is so...."

"No," Harry said flushing the toilet in the bathroom and nodding approval of the plumbing.

"No?" Emily stood at the door and looked hurt.

"If we get the house, I want to make a music room for you there. It's the best room in the whole house."

Harry vaulted up the stairs and went to the bright room on the top floor. He stood in the center of the room and spread his arms, "Isn't it perfect for a practice room?" Harry asked and Emily beamed.

"Yes, yes, it is," she agreed.

"Well, do you want the house, Emily?"

"It's wonderful. But what was he saying about the owner?"

"That he was a kike?" Harry's smile vanished and something that she had never seen replaced it. A set to his jaw and narrowing of his eyes that frightened her.

"Yes, what is that?"

"That means that he's a Jew. It's a crude word. Forget it." Harry stalked out of the room and stood at the kitchen window with his hands planted on the counter, watching the sky for a moment. Emily came and stood behind him.

"I never meant to complicate your life. I'm sorry."

"I'm not angry at you. But he..."

"Let's buy it and make it ours. Make it how we want it. Make it a good home."

That afternoon when they were signing paper after paper, the realtor said, "I could add a restrictive covenant to the deed, if you wanted."

"Restrictive covenant?" Emily asked.

"Prohibits sale to Jews or Negroes. Keeps property values up. This deed doesn't have it at the present time. Property hadn't changed hands since the house was built in the 20s."

"I don't want it. Just a regular deed," Harry said.

Don interrupted, "But that is the regular deed for this area. Now this is going to be a very expensive area...."

"I don't want that in my deed. I want my house to be the way I want it. Clear?" Harry said, not looking at Emily.

"Sure, it's your money," the realtor said, and drew up the rest of the paperwork.

When they moved their furniture into the new home, Emily noticed that there were nail holes where the mezuzah had been. When he painted the trim on the house, he filled the nail holes and sanded the wood almost smooth. But she remembered that once there was a mezuzah on the doorpost.

After they started making the mortgage payments, Emily wanted to help pay for it. She went to the formal auditions for a chair in the philharmonic, and applied for work in the studio orchestras.

She remembered when the new home was straining their budget. Barbara had just started the first grade.

It was late summer. The wind coming off the desert was hot. It wasn't the heat that bothered her. It was the dry air. She enjoyed the smell of coffee as she was making it and left a pan of water on the stove to boil and bring some humidity to the kitchen. By the time she had made the toast and scrambled the eggs, Harry brought Barbara into the kitchen on his back.

She looked at him, his black hair, still wet from a shower, was combed straight back, and his cheeks were pink from a close shave. His white T-shirt was hanging loose over his gray slacks.

Both were laughing. He sat at the kitchen table, elbows on the table. Barbara's elbows were on the table too, waiting, like old married people. Emily served their plates and went back to the kitchen to get the coffee.

She knew why her daughter smiled and laughed when she saw him. He was nothing but unconditional love and support for her. Small moments like this crawled into the corner of her eyes and surprised her. She disguised the small catch in her throat with an easy cough.

"Hey, you okay in there?" Harry called.

"Sure, just the weather."

"Want me to come get the coffee?"

"No, I'll bring it right out."

She loved her kitchen. She loved the fact that she could make coffee the way he wanted his coffee made. That she had discovered how to make scrambled eggs the way he wanted them. Her cup of tea was half gone and next to it on the saucer was her toast. She rarely ate breakfast with them. It was their time, she told herself.

"Did you know," Harry asked Barbara with great formality, "that your mother is the best cook in the entire world?"

"I know that," she said with the confidence that only a child can have.

"And how did you discover that?"

"You told me so, Daddy."

"Well, it's the truth. Do you know that when you are old enough to drink coffee, your mother makes the best coffee in the entire world?"

"Maybe I won't drink coffee when I grow up. Maybe I'll drink tea like Mummy does."

"Well, are you a lucky girl to be able to have a choice?"

"Yes, I am a lucky girl," she teased.

"But for this morning, do you know what I am going to say?"

"Drink my milk?"

"That depends," Harry said, finishing up his scrambled eggs.

"On what?" Barbara asked with a bright smile.

"On you," he said with even a larger smile.

"If I drink all my milk right now, can I go with you today?"

"And play hooky? I don't think so! I don't think that the studio would pay for both of us to go to work, anyway."

"But it's more fun to be with you, Daddy." She tipped her head forward and her thick black hair fell over her eyes. He brushed her hair back with his fingertips and saw a pouting face.

"Honey, eat up. I'm driving you to school, and I want to be on time. Emily? Em? Are you going with us?"

"Yes, I have to go out to get strings. I need them settled in before the next audition."

"What about your bow? Some of the hairs on it are broken and hanging loose. Is that a problem?"

"It can wait another three or four weeks. I can trim the loose ones. If I am careful in practicing with it and use the practice bow more...." She watched his mood change and stopped speaking to watch him.

"I don't want you to be careful," he said too forcefully and startled the child. "I want you to be brave and dangerous and adventuresome and everything you want to be when you practice." When Harry enunciated 'adventuresome' his tone changed to humorous and he approached Barbara for the mock attack. She knew it was coming, finished her milk quickly, and prepared to be tickled.

"It can wait," Emily said, as he picked up the child and started a noisy piggyback ride to their bedroom. He left Barbara in the bedroom and came back to the kitchen.

"No need. Get ready, I'll rinse the plates."

Emily went into the small bathroom. She looked in the mirror in the bathroom and saw that the wind yesterday had made her eyes as red as they felt. Grit was in the air and her hair snapped with electricity when she brushed it, even in the morning when it was still cool and the sound of the wind had not yet come to the city. She ran warm water from the tap and washed her face and then her eyes.

Harry had just finished shaving and the bathroom smelled of his shaving soap. Clean, sweet, almost lavender. She inhaled. Something in that aroma made peace for the day. Let her know that she was safe. Reminded her of London. She could hear them talking softly, then a small laugh.

"You about ready?" Harry called to them, knotting his tie, but not cinching it up tight. He picked a gold tie bar from the small dish on the top of the dresser. He squeezed the spring open, slipped it across the tie and released it. Emily slipped out of her light cotton bathrobe and into a pale blue shirtdress. She buttoned the pearl buttons and put a wide white belt on quickly. The white leather pumps completed the look. On her, the single strand of pearls did not look like costume jewelry. Her hair was just at shoulder length and turned under in a pageboy cut. She smoothed her hair with her hand again.

"Any word from the Philharmonic?" Harry asked her as she came into the bedroom. The auditions for the symphony were taking much longer than she had anticipated. And that was irritating her. The tests and trials and practices were stretching into six weeks. As much as she wanted the position with the symphony, even as a substitute performer, she needed income.

"Not yet. I am hoping that they will make a decision within the next week or two. They have the phone number. But no call yet."

"But you've been out a lot, too."

"Do you think I should be looking for another job as well?"

"Not unless you want to. You said that you wanted to teach, but I don't know how you could do both with the practice schedule that the Philharmonic would have. Look, my job with the studio has gone from part time to full time. I don't want you to wait to get what you need for the violin."

"Maybe just strings for now. I can just trim the bow hair. Our savings...."

"Are going to be fine," Harry lied to her and smiled broadly to make it believable. "Look, you have to be completely true to what you want to do. Get Barbara moving, will you? I'll be in the car."

She still lived with a fear that he would never understand. She knew about his full time job. The opening was made possible when they fired his boss. Blacklisted. Harry entered each day with an optimism that she never would understand. She was silent in a way that closed him from her world.

"I forgot to give you this last night," Harry said, handing her a matchbook. He opened the thick paper flap and turned it to her so she saw the writing on it. "It's the address of the music store that most of the studio of musicians use. They do repairs and can put new horsehair on the bow for you."

"It can wait."

"Damn it. Can't you at least go there and get an estimate. It's only a block from the studio. I'll drive that way after I drop Barbara off, and so you can see where it is. Then you take the car."

"If you're sure," Emily said as he gave her a kiss on the forehead.

He was more confident of her driving than she was. He taught her to drive on the farm. He sat on a log and whittled while she discovered the tolerance of the clutch. How to brake and then push the clutch before the engine died. He trusted her, but going up the steep hill to their house still required a white-knuckle grip on the door handle when she drove.

The wind had increased during the morning and was moving in small bursts. Dirt and twigs snapped at the back of her legs as she walked to the car that Harry had pulled out of the garage. He drove, first to Barbara's school, then to the studio, where he got out; she slid across the worn seat cover and drove off.

She liked looking at Los Angeles. She had grown up with very different colors. Gray skies, deep green countryside, old buildings made of native stone or finished off in shades of ocher or tan. Black and gold.

Her new city was brighter, full of yellow, orange, and terra cotta. Smells of desert plants came into the city, sweet and tart on the wind. Clouds were rare, gray skies even more unusual. The sun was too bright, but she enjoyed that difference as well.

She remembered the burgundy letters of the sign above the music store from when Harry drove past it. She drove back to it and parked across the street on the curb just as the owner opened the store.

CHAPTER 26
PIANO SUBITO

A musical instruction to play suddenly soft, a change.

Cheap rental violins hung, like hams, from wires in the window to the left of the door. The awning that was over most of the sidewalk gave shade to them so the varnish did not crack or the glue melt in the heat. Practice violins she said to herself softly, seeing their defects from afar. Student violins. As she slid out of the car, she cradled her violin case like a child against the wind, and then she walked across the street to the music shop.

In the window to the right of the music shop door there were a variety of brass instruments suspended from almost invisible wires that floated in front of movie posters of musicals. Before Emily went in, she looked past the displays in the window to the interior of the store. It was tidy although crowded with instruments. To the right was a long glass counter in which there appeared to be smaller instruments and repair materials. Covering the back of the shop were orderly racks of sheet music. And to the left, there were several drum sets and a battered upright piano.

The handle on the metal doorframe was also aluminum and formed in the shape of a treble cleft. The backward "S" was smooth and warm to her touch. The door opened easily and a small metal bell on the inside clanged. It was a miniature cowbell that had a white Alpine flower painted on it, a souvenir of Switzerland.

At its clatter, a short rounded man with thinning ginger hair looked up from the pale green cloth bound book of accounts that he was reading on the glass counter. He had a stack of papers to the left of the book. He put the cap on his gray Parker fountain pen and took off small gold-rimmed reading glasses and set them on the papers.

"Good morning. What can I help you with?"

"Strings. I need new strings for a violin. Can I see your selection?"

"Of course. We have a range from practice strings for students all the way up to professional grades. But the way you carried your case from your car suggests that you have a long and fond acquaintance with the violin. So, I don't think the strings on the counter are what you'd want."

"Really?" Emily asked, laying her violin case gently on the glass counter.

He pulled a narrow drawer completely out of an oak case and brought the drawer to the counter, turning it for her review. "I don't leave these out for kids to steal. I think you want professional strings."

"You are a real Mr. Sherlock Holmes," she said and laughed easily.

"You can tell a lot about people by the way that they handle their instrument. Even in a case. Take those student violins in the front window. Every summer I spend putting them back together so that another bunch of children can try to destroy them."

"Aren't there some that actually enjoy playing?"

"Sure. But most of those kids don't come here for their rentals or their lessons. They have a teacher come to their house. Those instruments in the window are for the kids in music class who selected the violin simply because mobsters put machine guns in violin cases in the movies."

As they spoke, Emily went through the drawer and selected four paper packets; each was about an inch and a half square and contained one coiled violin string. Each string was of a different dimension, drawn of metal to capture the perfect vibration against the perfect instrument.

He opened the first paper packet and pulled out a silver circle and handed it to her with care. It was the G-string. It was the thickest of the four violin strings. It was a wire wrapped around a wire. The base wire, which was hidden, was about the thickness of the D-string. But this wire was wound round with silver wire. The wrapping wire was thinner than a human hair, pulled so tight that it became one and formed a new wire. The lowest tone on the violin came from this string. Open, unfingered, it had a wonderful rumble that she measured in her mind and felt in her chest. This string was so beautifully and invisibly wound that it was easier to discover the wound silver by running a fingernail up the string, as the eye did not always see the wrapped wire. Red thread was wrapped at the base where it would attach to the tailpiece. Good color. Well crafted. She nodded and he opened the next envelope.

Then she looked at the D-string, almost as thick, mere wire, not wound with another wire. This sound was going to produce the D just above middle C on the piano, and it was her favorite sound. It was the perfect sound. Although the concert tuned to the A, the D was her anchor, her sound. She nodded. Silver color. No abrasions or oxidation on the string. It held the light perfectly. She nodded.

The A-string, thinner than the D was also silver toned. She nodded and he opened the last paper packet. It was the thinnest string, the E-string. The highest note, when not fingered on the violin. Fingered, it went up to the high B.

"You want me to put them on the instrument for you? A dollar for all four."

"No…"

"Fifty cents?"

"No, I can't…. I'll put them on myself. But I would like you to give me an estimate on rehairing a bow."

"Of course, you have it with you? We have a very good black hair that is available as well as a mix of black and white. But from the strings that you just selected, I suspect that you'll want all white hair. Am I right?"

"Yes, yes, you are. Just the finer white hair."

She looked at him again before trusting him to hold her bow.

She opened the case and felt the familiar scent as much as smelling it. Felt the sharp medicinal smell of the mothball crystals that she kept in the small box under the neck of the violin. Felt the clean woodsy comfort of the cedar chips that she also kept in her case to discourage small insects, and keep them away from the bow hair. Amateurs or the lazy players who did not do this often found that silverfish or other insects were nibbling away at the good hair and destroying a bow's integrity. Daily use did not let anything get started on the wood of her instrument, as she had seen mold or rot take hold on instruments stored improperly for a long time.

"Camphor?" he asked, not being able to place the blended scents.

"Cedar chips and mothball crystals. I use both."

As she opened the case fully, it lay flat on the counter. The violin was in the half closest to her. The two bows were held into the top of the case by small leather-covered pegs that turned. She did not give him the better bow, but handed him her practice bow. He took it carefully and examined it well.

This bow was made of Pernambuco wood, *bois de Fernambuc* as her master teacher called it. Rosewood frog. Small mother of pearl eye was inlaid in the rosewood. Rounded silver tip. Extremely well cared for. Any professional player would envy it. But then he glanced at the bow that remained in the case and was breathless.

That bow was ebony, and the perfect wood glimmered. The frog was ivory, so old that it had turned to the color of tea with milk in it. The tip was a small gold rose. An award from a competition he speculated. Both bows had white hair. Excellence. Simple excellence.

The violin looked like a Stradivarius. Red varnish, in the old style.

"Where are you playing now?" he asked her, knowing this was a professional player.

"I'm not. I'm still going through the auditioning process for the Philharmonic."

"Still? Most of the string section has already been selected. The bass, cello, all finished for this year down to the final auditions and interviews this week and the next. Viola this week, violin next."

"Yes, I was told to come back but have not yet had the call for the time."

"Ah, so that's why you want the new strings. To sharpen the instrument's sound. But why not get the bow done at the same time?"

Emily looked away. She was not going to let him see her struggle between her wants and her pocketbook.

"You working now?"

"No, my husband…"

"I asked about you."

"No, no I'm not."

He stared at her and took the measure of her trade for the next few years. Then he offered, "You want me to check? See if you are going to get a call?"

"Can you do that?"

"I know a few people. What's your name?"

"Emily Montgomery. Emily Finch Montgomery. And you are?" Emily asked extending her hand to introduce herself, being too English and formal.

"Martin. Martin Greg. Glad to meet you." They shook hands in an awkward way, almost embarrassed after they had touched. He laughed, "I'm the man with two first names. That's what I tell the school children who come here."

"Why don't you just look around for a minute and let me call a friend of mine." Emily went to the rack of sheet music and looked at the titles without reading any. She tried not to listen as he went to the telephone on the wall. He picked up the black receiver of the telephone and spun the dial. It seemed as though she heard every tick as it circled back to its place. He asked for someone; she did not hear the name. He laughed, spoke quickly, thanked him, and clicked the black receiver back into the silver hook that held it.

"Next Wednesday. You're in the final four. They just started calling this morning and no one answered your phone. Obviously, because you are here. I'll write the address for you. Act surprised when you talk to the girl who will call you."

She nodded. "What do you mean the final four? That it is the fourth interview?"

"No, there are only four of you left for the one remaining chair."

"Oh my, I thought there were more of us."

"What did they have you playing at your last audition?"

"Vivaldi and Beethoven mostly-- some exercises, responses to direction mostly."

"Do you believe in first impressions? Ever take a chance?"

"Sometimes. Sometimes I do."

"Well, sometimes I do, too. How would you like to play your favorite piece from your last audition for me? No more than five minutes. And for five minutes of music, I will do the bow for you as a gift. Because if I like what I hear, I know that you will come again and again and again."

"Now?"

"Yes."

The bow that needed new horsehair remained on the counter and she took Graham's bow from the case. She tightened it quickly, with the eight twists of the screw at the base of the frog. She laid the bow back on the case and pulled out her violin. Holding the back of it to her, she plucked each of the four strings. She then put the violin to her shoulder and drew the bow gently across each of the four strings. The E was slightly flat. She turned the fine tuner near the chin piece of the violin. Tested and approved.

He sat back on a tall stool and folded his arms. He leaned back against the wall. Even the way she tuned was different.

She played the opening movement of Vivaldi's Four Seasons. It was bold. Starting at a gallop. No warm up. No approach, just the full force of the bow against strings. The opening hard, solid, fast notes set the pace and tone of the first movement. Unforgiving. It was perfect or it was not. This was perfect. It was strong, clean, and crisp, even on old strings.

And then the music shifted into something smooth and mellow and rich. Five minutes had passed. She knew it. She knew her musical scores precisely. She knew to the quarter second where the conductor should be in the score. She knew which conductors would have the orchestra playing ahead or behind her mental version of the perfect timing for any composition. She knew when the five minutes had elapsed, but stopping there would have left the movement incomplete. It would have been unsatisfying, abrupt, and rude.

But he had not stopped her.

She played to the end of the movement. Well over three times the time required. Never once referring to sheet music. Never once pausing. No hesitation. Only pure Vivaldi in a music shop.

He nodded.

She stopped.

The violins hanging in the window quivered and a set of drums close to her vibrated. Then there was a long silence---almost a reverence.

"You are not cautious with your playing, are you? But you are cautious with people."

"Sometimes. What made you say that?" Emily gave the automatic twists to the bow to release the tension.

"Because you trusted me only with your practice bow. Not the one you would use in the audition. Am I right?"

"Yes, yes, you are." She blushed as she twisted the screw the rest of the eight precise times to completely release the tension on the bow. She put the good bow in her case and left the top open. She took a linen cloth from the neck of the case and quickly wiped away the invisible powder of resin that had come from her bow.

"Well, how about I do the practice bow right now, and if you like it, I do the other one for you when it is ready to be redone. Today, everything is free, if you promise to trade here in the future. Do we have a deal?"

"Yes, yes we do." Emily closed her purse.

"My gift to you. Today and today only," he said mocking the shouting car salesmen on the television late at night. Trying to get customers from the wealthy few in the city that had the early television sets. "Who else could hear Vivaldi. Live. This very morning in the city? I think that I am going to enjoy doing business with you for a very long time, Mrs. Montgomery."

Taking the bow, he walked to the back of the store where there was a workbench positioned so that he could work and still see into the store if the Swiss bell on the door clattered.

"Come back and watch. You'll see then I am as good at what I do as you are at what you do." She folded her case shut and latched it, picked it up and followed him to the back of the store. There was a small kettle on a hotplate. Steam was drifting from it. The humidity made the dark room inviting and relaxed her. Her skin was dry, in spite of the lotion she had rubbed on hours ago. The humidity was welcome.

She saw a small index card tacked to the corkboard above his workbench. Small neat letters in blue ink printed a request from a Mr. Bloom for 'a teacher for my son in the violin'.

"May I take it down and copy it?" Emily asked, motioning to the card.

"Just take it, pretty lady. If the job don't work out, bring it back and I'll put it up again. Bloom works near here. Runs a deli. Nice man."

She had hoped that the card would have a telephone number. She wanted to discover more about this possible teaching position before she arrived on his doorstep. But there was no telephone number. There was, however, a small, neatly printed line at the bottom of the card that said, "Ask for Mr. Bloom, Old New York Deli" with an address on Fairfax.

"Do you know this address?" Emily asked him.

"Sure, that's where we get corned beef sandwiches sent over. It's down two blocks and then a right. Big sign. Not much parking there, so you might want to leave your car where it is."

It was just after one when he finished with the bow and putting the new strings on for her.

"Need any rosin?"

"Colophony?"

"Of course, I use pine rosin. I cook my own, as well as selling commercial grades. Have a distributor that makes turpentine in North Carolina. He sends me the residue, unprocessed, so I can do it the right way. I make a harder block of rosin for violin than cello."

"How good is it?"

"The best. Not as acidic, better for the violin finish. I'll give you a sample; you decide another day." He said as he placed a small block, the size of a domino and the color of amber, on the counter.

She slipped the small block into the storage box in her case, snapped the three clasps shut, and took her violin case with her. She walked out into the wind. His directions were simple and precise.

Grit from the sidewalk blew against the back of her legs as she walked. Her hair blew, snapping against her cheeks. She turned the corner and the wind suddenly stopped. Blocked by the building. She shook her head quickly and used the reflection of the glass to run her fingers through her hair and restore order to it.

CHAPTER 27
CANTADA

A sung mass, a sacred choral, recited pieces, often as interludes.

She walked into the delicatessen. Twenty booths of dark red vinyl lined the walls of the room. Each had customers. Half of the ten tables scattered in the middle of the room were occupied and the other tables had dirty plates, which were being removed in a clatter. To the right of the door, by the cash register was a large glass case trimmed with stainless steel. It glinted in the brightness of the day. At eye level on the stainless steel top of the case were baskets of bagels and loaves of white, rye, and pumpernickel bread. The case was filled with neat rows of sliced meats and cheeses and with metal tubs of herring, both pickled and in cream, and trays of lox and bins of dried fish.

Take out sandwiches were being ordered, still.

The counterman wrote the order on a paper bag and passed it back to the boys at the meat slicers. After pastrami, corned beef, roast beef or turkey was sliced it was weighed. Then it was put on a plate and passed on with the bag to the sandwich boy who assembled it, wrapped it in waxed paper and put it into the brown paper bag. The cashier rang up the bill from the notes made on the paper bag. Customers ordering a dill pickle had it put into a waxed paper sandwich sack, turned over on itself three times and shoved into the sack, with the hope that it would get back to the office before the pickle juice ran out of the waxed paper and dissolved the bottom of the brown paper sack.

The heat of the day did not follow her into the delicatessen. It was cool and calming in spite of the noise. Next to the door was a small wooden stand with a rack on its side holding menus.

A waitress with vivid red-orange henna hair, made even more vibrant by her sherbet green uniform, rushed to the front of the delicatessen, grabbed one menu from the rack and asked her, "Just you?" in a mildly accusatory manner.

"Oh, I'm not here for lunch. I wanted to see Mr. Bloom."

"Why?"

Emily pulled out the card, as though it were an identity card or passport "It's about music lessons for his son."

"Well, wait over at that table there. I'll get it cleared off in just a minute for you. No need to order anything, but we're just finishing up the rush from lunch, so if you could just gimme a minute...."

"Thank you. Thank you, I appreciate that."

She wanted lunch but was not going to buy it.

She was hot and hungry.

And she wanted a job so that she didn't have to feel like she couldn't buy a drink and sandwich when she was hot and hungry.

The remnants on the plate were familiar. A blintz on one, just the corner, a smear of sour cream to the side. A blur of blueberry stained the edge of the plate. On the other plate, crumbs, possibly from a latke, a potato pancake. A small dab of applesauce dangled from the rim of the plate.

A skinny man, pale, in his sixties, pushed a small chrome cart to the table and put the dishes into the cart, one by one. She was invisible to him. He pushed the cart to the next table and as methodically pulled plates from the table to the cart.

The woman with the electric red hair rushed by again and left a menu.

"Is he here?" Emily asked, attempting to wave the menu away.

"Five minutes away. He covered the lunch crowd. Doing the bank run now."

Emily sat silently, watching the sandwiches being made and glasses of tea being refilled.

Then, a short man with black curly hair and deep-set black eyes stood in front of her. He was stocky, wearing a white shirt, open two buttons at the neck, with the sleeves rolled up two turns at the cuff. Black pants, black shoes and carrying a white apron that he put on the back of the chair as he stood there.

She looked up and asked, "Mr. Bloom?"

"Shelly said you came about my card for a music teacher…"

"Shelly? Is she…?"

"Yes, the rude waitress." He motioned and two glasses of iced tea appeared at the table.

"Oh, I didn't order anything. There is a mistake."

"It's hot outside. It would be rude to drink tea in front of you. Please?" When he asked her, the 'please' had an accent to it that felt familiar, old world.

She looked at him to see if there was any resemblance to the Mr. Bloom so long ago in Prague. Only the kindness and alertness in the eyes.

"Mr. Bloom, may I ask where you are from?"

"From? I live here."

"No, I mean, has your family always lived here?"

"In Los Angeles? No, lot of 'em went to New York since, shortly after the Russian Revolution, Minsk became an unpleasant place for Jews. Distant relatives. My side of the family was dumb enough to go to Berlin. I got here after the war. Why?"

"For an instant, I thought you might be related to another Bloom my family knew, long ago in Europe."

"And?"

"No." Emily laughed at herself for even considering the possibility.

"So, had lunch yet?"

"No, I just came about your card…"

"So, you're the music teacher, then?"

"Violin. Yes."

"But, have you taught it before? Yes?"

"Yes, I have. Private lessons only. Never a class of several students. My last student went from knowing nothing of the violin to reading music and playing before others in six months."

"English, are you? And why are you living in Los Angeles? Got a family?"

"My husband is American. We have a daughter."

"And does she play violin?"

"No, she wanted to learn piano. We've rented one to see how sincere she is. I play with her now. Children's songs. My rendition of Three Blind Mice is really quite splendid."

"And where did you learn to play violin?"

She sat straighter. "I studied in Geneva and London. I played with the London Philharmonic. But I must tell you that it was during the war and it was not a permanent seat. I am currently auditioning for the Los Angeles Philharmonic Orchestra."

"My son, Avi, would be your student."

"Just one child?"

"Yes, but a special child. Look, do you have some time? Now?"

"Yes, I guess I do? Why?" Emily looked at her violin case. "Do you want me to play for you now or meet him?"

He shook his head and laughed a deep rich laugh. "Have lunch first. Talk to me. Let me tell you about my son and about why this is not just teaching music to a boy. Then if you want to, you can meet him. And we can talk terms."

"Yes, that might be a good idea."

"Okay then, I'm going to have lunch now. You should join me so I don't feel like a big hungry rude man." He held up his hand and the red headed waitress started toward them. He opened the menu that she had left on the table and handed it to Emily. It's all very good. Can't miss."

"The tea is fine, thank you."

He ignored her. "The matzo ball soup is good today, but then it's good every day! I'm going to start with a cup of that and have a plate of scrambled eggs with lox and onions. If you are really hungry, get the pastrami sandwich, it's that high." He gestured broadly, extending his thumb and the tip of his index finger as far apart as they would go. She laughed. "And there's lentil soup every day. Every day, just as my mother cooked for us."

"Your mother's recipe?"

"Yes, the lentil is mourning, she'd say. It has no mouth to cry and it is round like the cycle of the world and of life." Mr. Bloom moved his left hand in the air as she supposed his mother had when she had said those words. Lightly for such a big man. Emily knew that it was his mother speaking to him decades before.

"I'll remember to try your mother's soup next time I'm in here," Emily said.

"You will love it," he said to Emily, and in the same breath he turned to the waitress and said, "Shelly, scramble me some eggs, with lots of lox and less onion. Lentil soup for her, small matzo ball for me. Pastrami on rye for her."

"I could never...."

"But your husband could." He smiled, nodded to the redheaded waitress. "Make the sandwich to go." He turned again to Emily. "When did you study?"

"My formal music training started when I was eight. I was playing long before that. Your son is how old now?"

"Ten, almost eleven."

She nodded. "I remember how my lessons went. How some parts were a joy and others dreary. My mother taught me at first. Then I had a family friend, then a private teacher every day after school. Then to the Music Conservatory in Geneva, but the war came. I played in London before I married Harry. Then I started playing professionally."

The soup arrived. He cut the large round matzo ball into quarters, ate a steaming quarter quickly and then looked up at her. "I wanted to ask where you went to school. You are well spoke. Where did you go to school?"

"In Europe and England."

"And that is why you don't sound like people around here. English is not your first language. That is your secret?"

She froze and tears began to pool in her eyes. It is about to end, she thought. The first honest moments in years could begin with this moment.

"What?"

"Music! Was not music your first language? Am I right?"

"Yes," she almost whispered.

He finished his small soup before she started hers. He took the saucer under the small bowl and moved it to the side by his fork. A cup of coffee arrived for him and the empty bowl and his tea glass were taken away.

Emily took a spoonful of her soup and looked at him. "How did you come to be here?"

"After Berlin, we moved like Gypsies through France and Spain during the war. Then to New York for a time. When my wife needed clean air, I found a small deli out here, near her brother and near the ocean. Just meats, no tables. Small place in Santa Monica. We bought it. The ocean air did her good. She died two years ago, right after Avi lost his voice. Then I moved to Bunker Hill to be near my cousin. We bought this place together. He works in jewelry making near Pershing Square. But enough of me."

Mr. Bloom poured sugar into the black coffee from a glass container on the table and stirred the coffee without looking at her. Then he looked up again and said, "I want to know you first. I don't just want a teacher for music. I want my son to be around a woman who wants to be around him. He can't talk. Used to be able to speak. He's a bright boy and understands and writes well. I want to know if you can manage with that. Sometimes he gets frustrated and has a temper."

"Sometimes I get frustrated, too," she looked at the plates as the waitress slid them to the table.

A mound of glistening rich yellow scrambled eggs had diced onions and chunks of lox stirred throughout the eggs. Rye toast was on a smaller plate with a sprig of parsley, looking like a palm tree.

"You haven't asked me why he doesn't speak," said Mr. Bloom scooping a mound of eggs onto his fork.

"No, I assumed an accident of some sort...."

"There was no accident. He was the only Jew in school. The older schoolboys tormented him and once dared him to drink some tequila. They handed him a bottle, but it had lye in it as well. It was meant to be a cruel joke. To taste bad. But it scarred his throat. Now he cannot talk."

"How can you live here after that?"

"How can I not live here? This is where my wife loved the sea and where my son was born."

He shook pepper over the top of the eggs and then cut a chunk out with his fork. He ate quickly and tore his rye toast in half with his square hands. The waitress came and filled Emily's iced tea glass again.

"How could you look at those people and forget?"

"Who said I forget?" Mr. Bloom shouted, then looked around the room quickly and spoke too quietly. "Look, I forgave them." His eyes were suddenly red-rimmed with grief. His eyes filled and sweat suddenly covered his face. She saw that the pain was fresher than he wanted it to be. "I had to keep living. I had the boy. But, no. I won't ever forget. And my being here won't let them forget either. I don't know who they were. But they know I am here." Mr. Bloom mopped his wet face with a paper napkin and crumpled it on the table next to his coffee cup. He looked into his plate of eggs as though there were an answer lingering there.

"Why music lessons?" Emily asked softly.

"You may open his eyes and his talent. Give him music. Make him know that he is talented, if he is. Let him hear a woman's voice again; that is not in our family." He hesitated. "I am not just looking for music lessons. Violin lessons."

"Why violin?"

"My wife said a violin sounded like a human voice. Because he has no voice to speak the Torah at his bar mitzvah, he needs a voice to express himself to our community. If he is good enough, I want you to teach him the *Kol Nidrei*-- there is music to that prayer. Then, I want him to play at the synagogue, just like I heard in New York when I was a boy."

"Music in a synagogue?"

"No, not during prayer. After the Shabbat had ended. A recital. The music moved me. It spoke to me in a way that I remember 'til today."

"I'm confused. You want him to play during his bar mitzvah?"

"No, I'm not explaining myself. The bar mitzvah is our time when a young man puts aside childhood and joins the faithful. He proclaims his intention and ability to live by adult rules, God's rules."

"Oh."

"Usually a young man would chant or recite a verse from the Torah. Sometimes give a lesson. But you have to be able to talk."

She frowned, trying to understand. "But…"

"Our Rabbi will question him privately. They are doing lessons together now. He hears. He understands. He is a smart boy. He just can't speak. That way he can join the adults and become a man. He can have his bar mitzvah. But that is private. He wants to do something more involving the others of our faith. More public. So, I thought of this. He has time to learn."

"I see. I see what you intend now. Two different events. Thank you for being so patient with me."

"He won't be an easy student. Still want the job?"

"I still need a job, and he sounds like a fine boy."

"He's an angry boy. You don't look like you need the money?"

"We're buying a house. I want to help with that."

He nodded. "So? What now?"

"Would you like me to play for you?"

"Yes, I would like to hear you play. But you have the job, if you want it. I don't need to listen to you to know that you are the right teacher."

"Could I meet him today?"

"No, he is with his uncle now. He'll be back next week. Could you come back tomorrow and play for me?"

He finished his eggs quickly and drank his coffee slowly, watching her as she finished her soup.

"This is very good soup. I thank you for ordering it for me," Emily said as she finished it. He saw the strength that she had. Something in the way she ate reminded him of his wife. Small, precise portions. Neat. Perhaps it was her manner or perhaps it was his longing.

She finished and started to open her purse. He frowned and shook his head. He stood as she scooted the chair away from the table.

"What time tomorrow?" she asked.

"Your husband works near here or you live near here?"

"Both."

He motioned to the waitress to bring over her bagged sandwich. "Would you both like to have dinner here tomorrow and play after dinner?

"We don't eat out often; perhaps I could come during the day?"

"Sure, about ten? There is a small office in the back, we can have privacy there."

"I'll be here at ten."

"Thank you for finding me."

He shook her hand and watched as she walked to the door and into the hot wind of the city. He ran after her. "Wait, I don't know your name."

"Emily. Emily Finch Montgomery."

He clutched his apron. "I can't wait. Can you play now? In the office?"

She followed him through the kitchen chaos to an eight by eight office with a scarred desk, a stack of bills and three cases of paper napkins against the wall. She set her violin case on the desk and pulled out her practice bow. It was fresh and had no rosin on it. In that condition, it would simply slip over the strings in silence. She pulled the amber block of rosin from her violin case and ran it over the new hair to develop the friction needed to seduce sound from the strings. Eight then nine passes over the bow hair. Now she tuned again.

"Would I have noticed it being off tune? Is it so great a difference that I'd know?" he asked of her.

"No, but I would."

She played the first few bars of Greensleeves, to get a tone of the instrument, and ensure that the bow was properly tense and prepared. Then a small melody by Ravel.

A touch of Beethoven's Ode to Joy.

And then, after a pause, *Kol Nidrei*. The lamentation and the joy of the promise it holds.

She ended.

She ran the fresh handkerchief over the face of the violin and wiped the neck of the violin, the fingerboard, even the pegs that she had touched in tuning it. Slowly, soundlessly, she placed it in the case. Silently, she gave the bow the fast twists of her wrist to release the tension and locked it under the leather bar that held it in the case.

She scrupulously avoided looking at Mr. Bloom. Her back was to him. Tears streamed down his face. He wiped at his face clumsily with his square hands and then with the apron.

He tried to sound gruff. "What kind of violin do you want him to have? Tell me, and I get it. If you want to buy it, I'll give you money today to get it."

"Why don't I meet him first?"

CHAPTER 28

MODERATO

A moderate tempo.

Emily met Avi.

He did not try to speak, but his bright brown eyes indicated that he understood her clearly. She remembered her first lesson with him.

The day was overcast. She drove that day. Her violin was in its heavy black leather case next to her and a new pale tan leather portfolio of music was under it. Next to her things on the front seat was the violin in a new case for the boy. Martin had selected it as his best rental. The new leather of that violin case perfumed her car with a rich male scent. The earthiness gave her familiar comfort as she began this new adventure.

She ran the back of her hand over the new case as she drove to Bunker Hill and then touched the same fingers to her own cheek. The new leather scent was as rich as his RAF flight jacket when he pulled her close to him--that day when they rediscovered each other.

And then she caught herself. Now was now. Not the war. Yet scents pulled her back to London. Out of order were their deaths. No closure. No order to the life she was living now. Just parts and pieces strung together by the succession of minutes, growing into days, and months to years.

Emily began their first lesson. "Congratulations, Avi. Today you are starting on a voyage of exploration not only of your skills, but also of gifts from the past to me and from me to you. I can tell you anything you want to know about the music and playing that I know. Tell me; nod for me all you want to know, so I will know what to help you discover. How to play?" He nodded.

"How the instrument is made and how to care for it?" He nodded.

"About the music?" He was motionless and she waited for a minute that seemed longer. "Its story, what makes it work?" Avi stared at her and she waited. Finally he nodded.

"Sit back and listen. I'll play and then tell you why I played what I played. Perhaps I'll tell you more than you want to know about how the instrument is built and why it works, if you let me. Each time we meet, I'll tell you a story about music. You can know the why of music, not just the how. I'll teach you to read music of others in musical notation. And then we'll have fun making our own music."

Non-verbal modeling was the first step in learning. Or 'monkey see, monkey do' as Barbara called it. Very little need to talk. Sentences said hung in the air. She remembered her snatches of instruction and how she had used the same words with hundreds of students after Avi. But how fresh they seemed with him.

She remembered how she started her lessons with him on their first day together. "You know," she said, "when I was in my first orchestra in Switzerland, the conductor was Italian, the first violinist was Polish and so we let the music speak for us since we couldn't speak to each other. Maybe you will be able to let this instrument talk for you, too."

The language of the lessons resonated in the silence when she thought of her time with him.

The skeleton of those days echoed in her. Her words met his attentive eyes.

"Your hands learn their parts alone and then they work together. Watch how the left hand holds the violin and fingers the notes while the right hand and arm manages the bow."

"Before you can really know how to care for the instrument you need to anticipate the weather. Really, heat or cold, dry or damp can change tone a half note or more. It changes how the instrument acts and reacts. So keep your violin at room temperature, don't leave it in the sun, think of your violin as a stick of butter, don't let it melt or freeze."

"You may need to raise the bridge in the dryness of winter and lower it again for summer."

"Strings need to be cleaned after playing to remove any rosin that the bow has left there. If not, the tone will be changed. Any rosin on the varnish will eat it, so use a dry cloth to remove it after each playing."

"The bow should be relaxed when not in use. It keeps the stick from warping; release the tension after you are through playing."

"The bow should be re-haired annually, for your birthday."

"Listen: first the ear to the music, then the eye to the sheet music, then bow to strings." The boy struggled to read the music and was very mechanical at the start of the lessons. Then he started relaxing and listening.

She played and he parroted her actions and approximated her sounds, roughly at first but he advanced quickly.

"Hold the violin in front of you like a guitar, then shift to a rifle. Good. See how it is cupping into your chin. Perfect."

"No, no, no, you are not sawing wood in that piece; the rapid bow movement needs to be a light touch, loving."

"Hold your posture and move the instrument to you. Let it become a part of you. Don't just stick your chin out, or lift your shoulder. That's no way to look, and it's not comfortable in the hours of playing."

"Vibrato is the adjustment of the note to give it more depth. Moving the finger is possible, the hand better, moving the arm is best. Use the largest muscle you can to do any of the changes."

As he advanced and showed even more promise, there were practices devoted only to the bow.

"Before you play, let's find the balance point on your bow. If you know where the center is, by weight, not distance, and you focus your playing on that center, the bow weighs less and you can play longer than if you were to try to play on the end of the bow only. Now, pick up the bow in both hands, hold it in your left and point your right pointer finger at me. Good. Now, slide the bow over your right finger with your left hand until it balances on your pointing finger. Good. Remember that point. That's what you want against the strings. That's the one place where it will weigh the least and you can play all day without getting tired."

"The job of the right hand and arm is to hold and move the bow.

But, it is subtle. Every finger has an assignment in holding the bow. It's not like sword fighting. Or shoveling dirt."

"First, relax. Pretend that you have a feather in your hand or water and you need to shake it off. Do that and relax."

"Now, here's a pencil. Pick it up off the table the way I do. Pretend you are picking up something large and heavier than the bow: a softball or a potato. Now with your very open hand use the thumb and tips of the middle fingers-- only the tips, to pick up the pencil. There is a natural bend to all your fingers. For now, your pointer and pinkie are on vacation. Now roll your thumb until the nail touches the hair of the bow. Good."

"That square of wood near where you hold the bow, that part of the bow is called the frog. It holds the bow together. It has a screw in it to tighten the hair and make the bow curve when you twist here. Funny name, frog."

"Before we make music, we'll make noise. There are three things that will affect the sound. Bow placement closer to or farther from the bridge, speed and pressure of the bow against the strings."

"Elbow first, wrist and fingers last. Feel the changes in your chest and shoulder and throat before you can even hear the sound."

She pushed and he pushed. She layered the learning, each lesson building on the last. The boy followed with effort in catching the mechanics and ease in getting the patterns.

"Listen to the rhythm."

They did scale patterns. Then intervals, diatonic and chromatic. Then chromatic variations C to C#.

"Here's a better way to finger that note."

After he demonstrated confidence in standard bowing, there was more on the bow work:

"The bow strokes have names. They are *martele*, for the strongly accented. *Spiccato* has the controlled bounce or brushstroke. *Sautille*. Watch, the bow bounces but the hair does not leave the string. Ricochet. *Saltando* is a ricochet with ending notes. *Sul Tasto*. *Flautando*. It means over the fingerboard, where you wouldn't normally play. *Sul Ponticello*. Near the bridge-- makes a glassy sound. *Tremolo*. Be tremulous, use short rapid up and down strokes, drum roll. Watch how the bounce of the bow sounds like a drum roll. Staccato. Play a note and stop before playing the next; put tension in the arm and control it. *Pizzicato* is plucking a string with your fingers and not the bow at all.

"Don't force it. Relax. You are not making sound. You are releasing the sound that is living in that instrument."

Avi looked at her inquisitively.

"You are not making the music. All you do is release the music God put in it. And that is the part that takes as much heart as ear and the commitment of every part of your body. Balance on the left foot for a better *spiccato*? Know how to develop a controlled spasm of the arm for staccato because you can never consciously decide to start and stop your arm that fast."

"All you are doing is pulling away the curtain of silence."

"Schumann was impulsive and meditative. Listen to his inner voice before playing. Think. What was he saying?"

"I use music to render my interpretation of the voice of someone else. I play from my memory when I allow their music to be my voice."

Avi was able to perform each of the new techniques. Granted, his playing was at a superficial and mechanical level, but she found his progress impressive. She began to explore the strategies to allow his playing to mature and integrate the mechanical techniques into a unified whole.

"There is a certain athleticism in great performance. The endurance of practice is not for the weak. Chopin was no longer strong enough to play his Polonaise after he was smart enough to write it. Brave enough to conceive the plan but not strong enough to execute it."

"Here's a memory trick I use; hum before you play. Not like the pianist, Glenn Gould, who hums out loud in concerts, but to yourself."

One night, when she came home after a lesson, Harry was already home, and had picked Barbara up from school and fed her dinner. She was silent as she cleaned her violin.

Harry watched her as she opened the violin case, removed the violin gently, and slipped the moistened sponge into the small rectangular storage box that sat under the neck of the violin when it was in the case. There was a combination of feelings that he did not know how to name. Delight in her talent-- envy or, perhaps, jealousy about the violin.

He tried to blink away the feeling. How could he be jealous of a violin?

But it wasn't the violin; it was that the violin was her connection to a past and a lost love and a ghost that haunted him. Like mornings when there was crushed tarragon in the scrambled eggs.

He knew the ghost visited her. He could see it in her eyes. He could tell, sometimes, by the way she played. He knew the violin was her past. He also knew that it was her future.

CHAPTER 29

RETARDANDO

The direction to gradually slow down the pace of the music.

O ther letters from the back of the journal were on the floor. Emily
picked them up and read each one slowly.

July 1951
Dear Emily,

*Again, your generosity overwhelms us. Thank you for the ham.
Many shared it. We pretend to be country folk. But, if truth were
told, we are very much city dwellers. London is our heart and breath,
and as they say, it is the heart and brain of our empire. Only when
those times during the war are too much with us, do we retreat to
the country for a moment of fresh perspective. In a manner, I do hope
that you and yours will retreat occasionally to a grand city and to
the country to get those other perspectives as well.*

*I do know what you mean about him. It is something that others
may not notice that is the one precious element that you hold most dear.
Before the war, I often thought that what most endeared me to your
father was his smile. Not the look of his smile only, but that he had the
disposition that allowed him to smile when all was looking rather bleak.*

*Now I am dealing with the other side of that coin. During the
war there was a frightful lack of fresh foods. Only now do I understand the privation that we somehow muddled through. At any rate,
your father has just had the last of his teeth removed by National
Health and a set of the most absurd dentures installed in place of
his own teeth. Not that I would ever mention it, but I am saddened
that the war took his smile from him both in the losses which we have
endured and in the physical sense.*

I want you to know that your father has made arrangements for your child to attend any university that she selects. He was quite proud of my entrance exam to university, although I never actually went due to our marriage. But I want you to be prepared for his letter telling you about his grand financial plans for the security of your most precious child. This is something of which he is most proud and wants to tell you in his own time and manner.

Love,

Mum

11 November 1952

Dearest Emily,

It is with the deepest regret that I write to you to advise you that my beloved Natasha died last night. After surviving all of the war and its grief and losses, her heart simply stopped.

I wanted you to know that she went into that good night with the grace and ease with which she lived her life. She soldiered on when it was beyond me.

We had finished listening to the evening news, after having a particularly fine day together. She was telling me how fast our Barbara is growing. Almost eight now, and that it will be a blink of an eye before she'll need her own account in Switzerland, just as you had for school. The BBC evening news was just finished and we were about to listen to our phonograph. She just put her teacup to the side table, nearest the fireplace. Then she leaned back in her chair and slipped away.

Our seasons seem so short at a time like this, but I will tell you, I can recall every glorious second with her and how she made my life whole and rich and worth the living.

If there is a heaven, she will be there for us. And it will be a better place for her presence there.

I never knew a braver or better person in my life. I will be eternally grateful that she brought you into our lives.

Much Love,

Your father,

G.

CHAPTER 30

CANTABILE

Playing in a singing style.

It was mid-morning on Thursday when the telephone rang. Emily answered it on the second ring.

"Hi. It's Ben."

"Yes?" Emily said softly, still embarrassed at her outburst at him earlier in the week.

"I have tickets to the opening of a new exhibit at the MOCA."

She was silent. He cleared his throat and continued. "The Museum of Contemporary Art. I thought it was the 14th and Ellen would be back. So, I was wondering if you might accompany me. It's informal."

"Tonight?"

"I apologize for the late invitation. I was thinking of ducking it. Ellen and I belong to the museum. This is a complimentary sponsor thing. Small eats. Chardonnay. Not as good as yours. But the chance to see an exhibit and have it explained by a docent. Ellen always gets it. I need the tour. Anyway, she's out of town and I thought you would take pity and let your neighbor make a peace offering of a night out."

"What time?" Emily asked.

"Pick you up at seven. Reception starts at eight. Home by ten, unless you want to go out for a late dinner."

"I eat early now. But, yes. I would enjoy the exhibit. I read the review in the *Times* Calendar section last Sunday. I appreciate your calling. I'll be ready at seven."

"Want to go to the Water Grill before? Won't be a stylish late dinner, but it won't be crowded either."

"How formal?"

"It's L.A. casual. Pick you up at five thirty. I'll call now for reservations."

Ben was still driving his wife's sedan. During the ride Emily kept trying to find a way to apologize for her anger the other evening. She never found the graceful moment for which she searched. Just off Pershing Square, Ben turned and they drove past the Biltmore into underground parking. When they emerged, the Water Grill was just opening and was alive with activity in that 'almost ready for the audience' moment.

As they walked into the trendy restaurant, Emily felt the energy, admired the tall ceilings, and the sparkle of ice at the oyster bar.

He was formal with her in the restaurant. Protective. He held her chair, made recommendations from the wine list, ordered a glass of Puligny-Montrachet for her and a Pinot Grigio for himself. They sipped and looked over the pages of new, exotic, classic and inventive seafood. She ordered a classic Dover sole. He selected a seared Chilean Sea Bass on French salad greens. Brilliant. Fresh. Inventive. Architectural plating. Perfect.

"You know," Emily started to say and hesitated.

"What?"

"I was going to bore you with something."

"I doubt if you could bore me with anything." Ben laughed.

"I remembered when a really big night out for the three of us, when Barbara was a child, was going to Cole's PE Buffet, over at Main and Sixth. You might have been there. It's been open since the turn of the century. When we were young, I thought the colorful Tiffany glass lampshades were plastic. Later I discovered that they are real. Still there. That was where the old Pacific Electric trolleys, the Red Cars, had their garage. Or we'd eat at Clifton's."

"The cafeteria?" Ben asked as he took a sip of wine.

"Yes, on Broadway. We'd all eat for less than the price of this glass of wine."

"It's a new day. Enjoy."

"I am. Thoroughly," Emily said, taking another small sip.

"What was the best thing at Clifton's? I've heard of it but never been there. Is it still open?"

"I think so. I loved their macaroni and cheese. Not a low cholesterol event. Barbara loved the pumpkin pie. I remember one night she and Harry decided that they'd go back for a second slice of pie each. And then splitting a third. They enjoyed that moment; I savor it over and over. The way they laughed."

"I think sometimes that you love everything."

"No, not at all," Emily snapped back quickly.

"Really? Name one dinner you hated," Ben challenged.

"Easy. Jonathan Club. In the same building as Cole's, the old Pacific Electric Building. Exclusive. Oil money started it. Ballroom, a men's club really. When I went there, I was getting some award-- can't recall what it was, about 1974. There was a reception on the ninth floor in the rotunda before dinner and the awards. All the men in the orchestra went up in the mahogany elevator, like penguins in their tuxes. I went up, in a silk evening gown with the other women and some waiters in the service elevator. I hated that."

"I apologize. What I said was unfair."

"No, I just don't dwell on things. Good or bad, that's how I am."

After dinner was over, they went to get the car from the underground parking. The valet was swift and they were in the car again for the drive of a few blocks to the reception.

When they passed a new restaurant that had replaced the "Rhapsody," which was one of the few Hungarian restaurants in southern California in the 1960s, she remembered working in the dark restaurant from 1959 to 1963. The work at the Philharmonic was steady, but she was not yet a senior member of the orchestra; she was still growing. She played when and at the salary they determined. And the private lessons were infrequent, but a minor source of income. Barbara was going to go to a private college.

After Max, her friend at the Philharmonic, decided to go to New York with his boyfriend, he recommended her to the owner of the restaurant where he was a strolling violinist on the Saturdays when he was not playing at the Philharmonic. They called her with an offer and she took it. Max warned her that her good violin was not safe there. Waiters bumped into you, as did the clients, after too much Bull's Blood, the raw red wine that they served in green bottles without labels. She bought a slightly used violin from Martin and some sort of peasant dress from a costume shop off Vine.

The engagement at the restaurant expanded to include regular Friday nights and Sundays. Then the Sunday afternoon grew to early evening as well. Dinner was included, so instead of eating there every night that she played, she arranged for Harry and Barbara to join her once a week.

Her favorite music to play at the restaurant was Béla Bartók's String Quartet No. 4. Of course she played an occasional mazurka, bits of the Hungarian Rhapsody, Franz List, and Brahms' Hungarian Dance. Some pieces got old after a while. But Bartók never did; his work was too demanding. This was a job, not for the music, but for the money. She began playing for the money and not herself after several months. Then during the summer there was a late Sunday night, just before she would stop playing at nine. The crowd was not listening. There was too much wine on the tables and a large after-party crowd had come in to the corner table.

They ordered quickly and talked too loud across the big round table for eight. Her interest was wandering from the mazurkas and she was thinking about the film she and her daughter had gone to the week before. *West Side Story*. She was thinking of the music to the film and simply decided to play it, improvise it by memory after listening to it once. And she did, not in the order of the film, but in the order of her recollection. The meter was difficult as it was a 12/8 meter and not a common one to most American players. But to her and at the restaurant, there were other sensibilities and other histories.

The loud group at the large table stopped talking and eating foods seasoned with too much paprika. They pointed to her and listened with a new interest. She ignored them and fell deeper into her explo- ration of this new music. She revised and played major themes again and with a different emphasis. Then she wanted a rest; Harry would be there soon and she wanted to clean and case her violin before he arrived.

The large party had eaten and was leaving just as she stopped play- ing and started to walk to the rear of the restaurant. A man stopped next to her on his way out-- a confident man who wore a black turtle-neck sweater over black slacks. He had a square face, dark hair just turning silver at the temples and a Palm Springs tan that made his wide smile even brighter.

"Tell me. Do you usually play *West Side Story*?"

"No, I just saw a preview of the film."

"And? What did you think of it? Some of my dinner companions worked on the film, that's why I ask." The man looked directly into her eyes as he asked.

"I thought the movie was incredible. But the music, the music that Leonard Bernstein wrote, was as powerful as his composition in *On the Waterfront*."

He chuckled. "Most people think that Elmer Bernstein wrote that."

She was very sure of herself. "He didn't, although he wrote a lot of other great music for film. But this was brilliant. Sondheim's lyrics are stunning. It is going to touch people in a new way. This is a major composition that will get exposure as the other contemporary compositions won't...."

"I sense that this is not what you do for a living?" He made a broad gesture around the restaurant.

"No, I play with the Los Angeles Philharmonic."

A slim woman in a blue silk dress shouted from the front door. "Come on! The car's here."

"Great rendition. I'll bring Lenny by the next time he's in town. He'd love the way you played it." He patted her shoulder and hurried to catch up with the others.

Emily was jolted into the present when Ben asked himself, "Where is it that Ellen always parks?"

"If we park below the Plaza, we can take the Angel's Flight up to the museum." Ben parked below Hill Street and they walked to the inclined railroad.

As they approached the archway to the funicular, Ben stopped and put his hands on his hips. "Always looks like a Chinese pagoda to me. What's that color? "

She shrugged.

"I'm glad you suggested this. I always park above the MOCA and walk down, kicking myself for missing a chance to ride Angel's Flight. It's my secret adult amusement in the heart of the city." Ben laughed as they stepped onto the platform to wait for the two red and black cars to trade places. As one went up, the other came down the hill, passing each other on a double track in the center of the trip up the steep hill. "These two cars remind me of the trolley cars in San Francisco," Ben said.

"But these were built just to accommodate this incline, built with angled benches so the passengers wouldn't slide to the rear. Look, the uphill end of the car is a full ten feet higher than the rear."

"This is fun."

"It wasn't so much fun when I used to teach violin to a boy who lived at the top of the hill. He lived in an old Victorian home that had been converted into a boarding house. I'd usually take a bus to Pershing Square, and then walk to Hill Street and up to Angel's Flight. It's the shortest railroad in the world, but in the summer, it felt like a lot more than 267 steps. Goes up a grade of 33 1/3 degrees. That's steep."

"You really counted the stairs?"

"Musicians count everything. Sure. Fare was a nickel then, in the 1950s. Round trip for a nickel. If the weather wasn't too hot, I'd walk. Counting distracted me. Sounds silly now, but a nickel meant something then. We were saving everything we could for Barbara's college. Neither Harry nor I got to finish college. The war. And she was so bright that we knew she'd go. But we never expected to be paying for graduate school, too. So spending a nickel was a decision."

"Did it look like this back then?"

"Yes, beautiful restoration, even down to the names on the cars."
"Names?"

"Sure, look at the bar on the top of the car as it stops here. See this one that is coming is Sinai. The other one is Olivet. Biblical."

They waited in the cool evening for the car to stop for them.

Emily thought back to the day that Avi changed. "Memorize by humming to yourself," she had said. Then one day, months later, he was humming. And he could almost speak. Emily was distracted and noticed that Ben had asked her something.

"Sorry, I missed that. What did you say?"

"Nothing important. Hop in."

The ride was smooth and was over too quickly.

At the top of the hill, Ben stood and gave her his arm as she rose from the low wooden bench. They left the car and stood aside to let the others go ahead of them into the Plaza. Ben paid their fare at the top. A quarter each. Ben had a dollar bill and told the young man in the booth that he was paying for the next two riders as well, whenever they arrived.

He took her arm and started to walk past the fountain at the spectacular California Plaza. She admired the work of Arata Isozaki: his use of pyramids, cubes and cylinders to make MOCA distinctive. The copper sheathed barrel shape that connected the wings was even more spectacular in the lighting at night from the Plaza. She stopped suddenly.

"Are you okay?" Ben asked, looking down at her feet, wondering if she had turned an ankle on the paving stones.

"No, I need to apologize. I should have called, but I couldn't find a way to start. So I need to say I was wrong and that I should not have...."

"That was then. You had a few good points about my nose and not sticking it into the business of others, although you didn't put it quite that way." Ben smiled at her. "You're making me think a lot, Emily."

"As you are making me think a lot on things I have not visited for a very, very long time."

But for the evening they drew a line of truce on any discussion of banks or papers or causes and tried to understand an assemblage of abstract sculptures formed of tires and things that most would assume to be trash and construction materials. It was evocative of traffic accidents and lovers. They left the exhibit early and went back to the Plaza, enjoyed another glass of wine and talked in the cool evening. Then they went down the hill on the same car they rode in earlier in the evening. "There's a funicular, not unlike this one in Pittsburgh. Did you know that?" Emily asked.

"No, really?"

"Discovered it on a concert tour that took us there. The Duquesne

Funicular. Built to carry steel workers to the mills from where they lived. Much longer than ours. Again, commerce fuels the transportation."

"There's one in Prague. Just for the sheer aesthetics of it. Goes up a park to a miniature Eiffel tower. Well, now that I think of it, there is a restaurant halfway up. Would that count as commerce in your definition?" Ben chided.

"Possibly. I'd have to see it before I decided."

"I would have thought that you played in Prague."

She shook her head. "Born there. My parents were on tour. I haven't been back since I was a child." Emily looked out over the plaza and watched the lights play on the water from the fountain.

"Did you travel much with the Philharmonic when you were with them?"

"No, just domestically. Not overseas," Emily said in a way that was almost curt.

"Why not?"

"I had a child at home. Others were more interested in travel. Harry used to kid me that once I got to America, nothing was going to get me over the border again. Not even to Tijuana for the shopping."

"I see."

"No, that was not the full truth. I never got a new passport after I arrived here. I never planned to ever set foot outside the borders of this country. Europe to me was more bad memories than good. Names of places I had loved had been transformed to places of battle or air raids. Horrible associations. I didn't want my daughter to have to deal with me if I pulled away that scab. I can't imagine how unpleasant I would be to know. And for me, going out of the United States was opening that wound again. Even thinking about it. It took me to an awful place."

"What do you mean?" Ben looked at her and all the teasing was gone.

"It wasn't quite like depression. But it was close. I knew that there were times that the war overwhelmed me. Harry knew it and somehow found a way to shield Barbara from my distance, my foul moods.

Not so much depression as we read about it now. Not the black cloud. But something else. An emptiness. Churchill's black dog. There was an ecclesiastical word in the middle ages, *acedia*. It was the emptiness of monks or scholars. The mental prostration of the recluses who pondered too much on the sadness of the world, of a collective grief that shrouded them-- not a personal grief."

"And how did you manage it?"

"Harry wouldn't let me be sad. He was nothing but an optimist. Nothing but promise and tomorrow. Yankee ingenuity. You know that thing they say about the glass. Harry would see the glass as half-full and think that he got to keep the glass. Whereas, I am a half-empty person, expecting the glass to break. Thank God he was able to buoy me up. Some surprises still found me, as much as I avoided the sadness of the war."

"Like what?"

Emily thought for a moment. Which of the many moments could she share with him? What might make sense to him? Emily did not look at him when she started to tell it. "Like when the new ambulances in the late 1960s started using the European sirens. Before then, American sirens used to be one solid high pitch. The European siren used the high then the low tone, the warble. It was too much like during the war...." Emily smiled and continued. "Harry told Barbara not to worry because it meant that help was on the way."

"I see what you mean. He turned your terror into her hope," Ben said. "I'm sorry I never got to meet him."

"He would have liked you. He would have enjoyed how you push me."

"I don't push you!" Ben protested.

"Of course you do."

Ben saw that she needed silence for a few minutes. He just walked with her. He watched her enjoy the beauty of the California Plaza.

He watched her travel through time to another Bunker Hill, and then interrupted her. "I think that's our tour guide, over there."

Where?" Emily asked and Ben pointed to a lean woman in her twenties wearing leather pants and a loose black shirt. She motioned for a few others to join her and then began a brisk walk into the museum. Emily was only half listening as the guide made some links between the abstractions and classic perspective painting, reviewed names of artists and their works, provided an opportunity to donate to a restoration fund and reminded them of a scheduled children's exhibit in the plaza before she thanked them for their visit and escorted them out the door. As they walked into the plaza, she gathered another group to tour the exhibit.

They walked across the plaza, and Ben asked Emily if she remembered the term the guide used for the point where all of the lines collided on the horizon.

"What term? Vanishing point?" Emily asked.

"No, the other term."

"I really wasn't listening to her," Emily said simply.

"Then, why'd we go?"

"You wanted to."

Ben glanced at her. "What about you?"

"What about me?"

Close enough to touch, but then the fog rolled over it, or distance, or invisibility... There was a vanishing point to Emily that he was trying to find.

"You mean centric point?" Emily said after a long silence.

She was hiding in her silence.

"Yeah, I guess that was it," Ben said and then muttered *Clumah*.

Emily heard him. She knew that the word meant 'silence' in Hebrew. But she did not know what Ben meant by the word. She stared at him and tried to find his meaning in using that word. Quietly, they walked to the car.

After driving in silence for a mile, Ben said, "I wish Ellen could have been here tonight."

"It was an excellent tour."

"Yeah, it was. I guess I just miss her."

"My husband once told me that nothing in nature is still or straight. Time has proven him right. What he never told me was that time is variable. It is either geologic when I think how much I miss him or lightning fast when I watched our daughter grow up."

"How did you know?" Ben asked. "How did you know that you loved him?"

"Because of an accident."

"An accident?"

"Yes, small enough in hindsight, but it frightened me so at the time. He was sharpening a plow blade in the barn. Something broke. Metal cut his cheek. High up. His shirt was soaked with blood by the time he got to the house. Barbara was screaming and crying during the drive to the hospital while he held a towel against the cut. And we thought some metal might be in his eye. So he was in the hospital overnight."

"His absence...."

"No, not just his being gone or my worrying about him. He had this awful habit of leaving his wet towel on the foot of the bed after he showered in the morning. I'd huff and carry on, and he found it funny to tease me. 'Let the squabbles be about something other than us'. I think that was his idea. Then he was gone--in the hospital overnight and suddenly there was no wet towel in the morning. Stupid as it sounds, that was the moment that I knew that I loved him, not just for his enormous kindness to us and ... well, that's more than you wanted to know, isn't it?" Emily blushed and gazed at the passing cars.

"I knew I loved Ellen by the way I relaxed when she'd touch my hand. She'd just reach over and hold my hand. No, just touch my hand, really. And I always knew everything was going to be all right. I don't know how I could live without her."

"Life goes on. Whether you want it to or not. A child makes you braver than you are. Whether they are small or grown. Harry knew he was dying. Cancer, but not long and lingering. Short and nasty. He told me that after he died, I should put one rosebud in a vase and when it faded, so would my grief. After that, all I was allowed was good memories."

"Almost like *keriah*." He watched for her reaction. Seeing none, he continued. "The tearing or rending of a garment when hearing of the death. It starts the healing. Did it work that way?"

"Nothing is that simple, but it helped. I did buy other roses."

"Is that why you have roses by your front door?"

"Might be. Hadn't thought of it that way before."

In spite of herself, Emily was starting to like Ben. His pushing her. Her rediscovery of herself.

Truth followed slowly, like an aged cat stalking a sliver of winter sunlight or the cat that came to her music room window with the silent meow, unbidden.

CHAPTER 31

MEZZO FORTE

A musical instruction to play medium loud.

Before the urban renewal and renovation of Los Angeles in the six-ties, the Bunker Hill area was in decline. Stores were closing. Lots were left vacant when the old homes burned. Decaying mansions were converted into boarding houses. This was where she taught Avi to play the violin. Bunker Hill was the place where she had helped Avi heal.

Avi lived with his father, Mr. Bloom, in a room at the top of the Angel's Flight. She stood with Ben drinking wine in the night near a fountain and could see the empty space where the boarding house had been, where she had taught the boy. But that was before the two funicular cars were put in storage, and earth-movers sculpted Bunker Hill from the anthill of people that it was to the landscape and urban art that it is. He watched her as she vanished again. She was there, but not there. Centric point. Vanishing point. Silence.

Emily thought back to the late fifties. Young men were back from Korea. New cars were on the road. New energy was back in L.A. The G. I. Bill had a lot of young men going to school at Cal State L.A. and at Long Beach State College, studying electronics and getting ready to make a future. New homes were being built on the windy margins of the city and being bought with V.A. Loans. New movies were being made and new soundtracks cut. It was a busy time.

Emily had the nickel in her hand as she got off the bus at Pershing Square and walked the half block up Hill Street to the Chinese red pillars and entrance at the base of the Angel's Flight. She waited for Olivet, her favorite of the two cars.

Bunker Hill's cluster of old Victorian homes was showing its age by the time she came to know it through Mr. Bloom. The grand old

homes were like old rich society matrons, down on their luck. They
had sold off the good jewelry and were wearing the gaudy, flashy stuff.

Mansions were cut into rooms for tenants and became boarding
houses. Paint had long ago peeled to let raw wood bake like a bone in
the desert sun. Weeds were taller than the concrete chunks that lit-
tered some of the vacant lots.

Once there had been homes. Some had burned to oblivion. Fine
French and English cuisine cooked in the large kitchen and served by
maids was replaced with boiled cabbage and potatoes and an occasional boiled beef left on boarding house tables.

Once she gave lessons to a mute and gave him a new voice.

Once neighbors sat on their front steps every Thursday afternoon
knowing that she would play a piece from 2:30 to about 3:00, before
the boy would play for her. The music floating from the open window
of the second story of the boarding house perfumed the afternoon.

She recalled it and it was fresh again. She was there in the past, she
walked through the hot afternoon and nodded to the neighbors. Some
carried a glass of water to drink on the cement steps to their boarding house, others carried small wooden chairs out onto the browning
lawns of late summer. Word spread through Bunker Hill of her 'free
concerts', as they were called. By late summer almost all of the neighbors of Mr. Bloom would sit on the front steps or on sills of the open
windows to hear her. First they were discreet. Later they would applaud. Some would see her on the street on her way to the lesson and
ask her to play some favorite.

Emily remembered one day in particular. Mr. Bloom had asked her
to stay later than usual. He wanted to talk after the lesson. That day
she waited a moment longer than usual at the Angel's Flight before she
entered the red and black car. There was a quiet longing in getting here
and now a new feeling, coming like sweat to the brow, unexpected.
One of impending loss. a vague fear that made her linger a bit longer
before leaving the red car. Of words which have not been said and
perhaps should have been said.

During Avi's lesson, the shade of the late summer afternoon would
slowly crawl up the side of the house where they lived. In summer,

when the late afternoon sun hit the music stand, it was time to end the session. As usual, Mr. Bloom had been in the next room listening and had a cup of tea ready for her and a small sweet cake from his store. She never knew what the treat would be and took tea even when it was too hot and humid for it to be enjoyable, but there was something about the English tradition that Mr. Bloom tried to replicate for her. To honor her English tradition.

"Come in. Come in," he smiled as she passed by him. Small beads of sweat were on his brow and his white shirt had the sleeves rolled up the usual two turns. "Have a seat and I'll be right with you. Your usual tea is ready or I could go down to the corner market and get you a cold drink, perhaps?"

"Tea, please. Even in the hot weather it seems to suit me."

Mr. Bloom poured it and set the small pot on the yellow Formica-topped kitchen table. The plastic seats and backs on the four chairs matched it, almost a canary yellow, made even brighter by the chrome of the legs of the table and chairs.

She continued, "He has been doing so very well that I am anxious to see how he will develop his bowing on the piece I left for him. He's so talented and so angry at the same time that I tried to challenge him. It's a small Bach piece. He is playing so very well. It may be almost time to consider a new instrument for him. I really think that he is better than his violin, that he is hearing more and more nuances and that a better instrument will aid in his continued growth."

She laughed. And when she laughed, he saw in her a release, a freedom to match the openness that he felt with her.

"What? What's funny?" Mr. Bloom asked.

"I'm going on and on. I don't know what it is, but today I just feel happy. His playing was fantastic today. It brushed aside anything else. I'm so proud of Avi."

"Oh, he practices and works very hard on what you teach him. Maybe you are seeing your success. Would you like an almond tart with your tea?"

"Yes, that would be nice; they smell wonderful." She looked at him, without saying anything. She was questioning his new manner.

He was not his usual calm self. He was uncertain but continued in a rush of words.

"My cousin Abe from New York is visiting."

"How nice for you."

"I wanted to talk to you, Mrs. Montgomery. As a person, not Avi's music teacher. Not as a client who pays for his son's lessons. A decision. I want to talk about a decision to you."

"I see." She looked into the teacup as though the answer were floating in the cooling amber of the tea.

"But I did not intend to offend you," he said softly. "If you think I am too forward."

"You did not offend me."

"But, you seem…." he said.

"You surprise me, that's all."

"Can we talk now? It's okay?"

She looked at her watch and nodded.

"My cousin is moving to Israel. He wants us to go with him. He's been talking about it since statehood in '48."

"But isn't it more expensive to live there? You have your restaurant here. You have a life here."

"I cannot think how hard it will be to let him stay here. His resentment is growing. I see it in him. I have thought about taking my son and starting a new life in Israel. It's a new country and I am ready for a new life. It honors hard work, and I do that well. It also respects the arts in a way that can be good for my son."

"You would go? Just like that?"

"Not just like that. Lots of nights of not sleeping to decide this."

"Why? Why uproot him now?"

"I just don't know if he can learn to speak again or not. I am writing to doctors there now. Going into another culture and language may be too much, or maybe it is what he needs. But I think about it more and more. And…."

Emily sipped her tea and waited.

Mr. Bloom took his beefy hand and pushed up the sleeve of his white shirt, past the turned up cuff, which she was used to seeing, summer or winter. He pushed up the sleeve to where his arm was pale, past the tan of his wrist to where there was a number on his forearm.

Smeared blue ink. A tattoo.

Mr. Bloom ran his index finger over the numbers lightly, as though they would rub off under any pressure. "This is why I am going. Not the camps, not that I lost all of my close family. No. You see this number. Mine ended in a six."

Emily looked at the number and there was an eight at the end. "But?"

"I changed it to an eight, a tattoo parlor in Long Beach, at the pike, you know the carnival area by the roller coaster. Where the Navy guys, the sailors, go to get some girl's name or an anchor on their arm. All I wanted was to make my six into his eight. Just by closing the loop at the top, just a few dots of ink."

"I'm sorry, I don't understand. Why eight?"

"My father's number. He was behind me at Auschwitz. I was tall for my age so they put me with the men, not the boys. My father told me not to look at him or act like we were related or they would separate us. He had a friend stand between us in line so we wouldn't talk to each other or touch."

She nodded her head very slowly.

He swallowed hard. "I won't let him be forgotten. I learned rebellion there, at Auschwitz."

Emily frowned slightly. He continued, "You think there was no rebellion? Well, there was hope at the front gate. We had to pass under a sign. It was in iron and was an arch over the road that we went on into the camp. The iron letters spelled out in German *'Arbeich mach frei'* -- do you speak German?"

"Not well."

"It means, 'work makes you free'. A lie, but that was what it said."

"But, I don't see...."

"The blacksmith made all the letters and welded them on this big arch. The 'B' was welded in upside down. He was a Jew. This was his small act of rebellion, but enough to fire something in my father and in me."

"I see-- I see that spark in you."

"He wanted a homeland. Now it is possible. This is as much his dream as it is mine."

"Is it your desire, really?" Emily asked.

"Yes, I need to put my energy into my religion and my son. Not my rage. In my heart, I know that I watch the kids that come into my deli and I see boys of a right age, and I think, 'could he have been the one who hurt Avi'? I see rich blonde boys come in wearing college jackets. You know, the ones with the letter on the front, and wonder 'did they do it for fraternity prank'. I see the old Mexican man in the back doing dishes and wonder 'did his brother or son do it because Avi is a Jew'? I need to put hate out of my heart. And that can only start with me. This is my best way to do that."

"But if you go to Israel, there is one thing that I ask of you with all sincerity," Emily said. Looking into his eyes. Reaching out. Holding his wrist in her hand.

"And that is?"

"Continue his lessons. He is not just a good student. He is a genuinely gifted musician. Soon he will need a better teacher than I am anyway."

"He learned more than music from you, I think. He smiles again. He was humming as he played a few nights ago."

"Humming?"

"Yes, clearly humming. There is a joy that is returning to him."

"If he can hum, can he speak again?"

"My God, I didn't even think about that. He has never made a sound since the accident. Since he was hurt, but if he can hum, maybe there is new hope."

And there was.

It began with the sounds that existed before language, the sounds we still make in joy or sorrow or passion. These sounds stayed with him. The vowel sounds and the cries.

Surgery at UCLA followed by speech therapy let him start to talk again. He rejoined the world of words...raspy, halting at first, but clear later. Words began coming with confidence and the world again was open to him.

In the late fall, they decided to make their move. There was a last lesson and gifts of new music books to take with him. The boy thanked her with a whisper and left the adults at the kitchen table. Mr. Bloom looked out the window over the fading red Victorian house next door into the distance where the wheat-colored sunset was starting to form over the Pacific Ocean. He let his shoulders droop. "We will miss you."

"And I will miss you and your son. You both have become a very special part of my life."

"Can I write to you?" Mr. Bloom asked and suddenly wondered what he might say to her.

"Yes, yes, I would be pleased by that. "

"There is something in your voice. What is it?"

"If it isn't too much trouble…" Emily began and then stopped.

"What?"

"A small stone. If you could send me a small stone."

"You want a stone from Israel?"

"Yes."

"Yes, of course. Write your address for me. Here is some paper. I'll put it in my wallet right now."

"Yes, just like that. No questions?"

"Why would I need to ask you questions? I trusted you with my son. Why do you think I would question your request now?"

"Then you don't care why I want to have a stone from Israel?" She seemed relieved.

"Of course, I care! Of course. But once in a blue moon I can mind my business."

"You're living for tomorrow. I'm still trying to understand today."

"I don't know who you mourn, but I want to help let the pain pass. And if a stone for their grave will help…."

"Who said it was for a grave?"

"You didn't say what it was for. It would have been so simple to say if it were for your garden or to throw in a pond. But your silence." He folded the paper and put it in his wallet when she stood to go, and he walked her to the door for the last time.

Mr. Bloom stood in the open doorway of the red Victorian boarding house and watched her walk to the top of Angel's Flight. Case in hand. Violin safe against the sun and dust that the late afternoon wind was swirling at her feet and pushing at the hem of her pale cream dress. The car, Olivet, took her to the bottom of the hill. She walked past the Chinese red pillars to Pershing Square and took the bus back to her other life.

The stone never came.

After a week in Jerusalem, Mr. Bloom and his son were on a bus going to a kibbutz at the edge of the Negev desert where they were going to help grow oranges and where there was a music teacher. When the bus of recent arrivals stopped at a military checkpoint, a man on a bicycle peddled past it slowly and threw a Molotov cocktail through the open window of the bus. The simple tool of terror, just a few ounces of gasoline in a discarded wine bottle with a wick made from a strip of cloth from a shirt too old to wear any longer made a firebomb. His cousin was burned, his left arm and chest, but he lived, and when he could, Abe wrote her of this. It was four months later.

After she read the letter, she laid it on the *Los Angeles Times* that she was taking to the trashcan on her curb. She pulled off the shiny tin top and dropped the papers into the can covering the morning's orange peels.

She never mentioned their names aloud again. There were other students. She recognized their names in the Calendar section of the *Times* on Sunday when they toured in concert. Some visited her when they were in L.A. But of all her students, her thoughts were the most vivid and frequent of Avi and his father.

CHAPTER 32

LEGATO

To play smoothly.

After the show at MOCA with Ben, Emily could not sleep and tried not to put a name to the fear that she felt. She submerged herself in the rituals of return, took off her silver bracelet, let the wide band rest on her bathroom sink while she put away her clothes. She hung up her black silk pantsuit on its own hanger, and pulled on her flannel pajamas. The evening sandals went to their place on the rack on the floor of the closet. All in order, she thought, as she started to brush her hair. Then she noticed the silver cuff and slammed down her brush, put the bracelet away, and resumed brushing her hair with unnecessary vigor.

Was it being at Bunker Hill again? Was it riding Angel's Flight, the wine, the conversation? Was it that Ben had met her family and asked after Barbara? What had she told Ben when he asked about Barbara tonight?

"Barbara's a teacher. Always has been, in the broadest sense. She went to a liberal arts college here in L.A. Now when she teaches history, she uses family films for the McCarthy era discussions. At first I thought it exploitive. Now I see how really bright she was to challenge the college into adding a curriculum on the blacklisting and the House Un-American Activities Committee Hearings. Who ever thought we would have lived through something called an era? We were just trying to be true to our art. Mine was easier as I played the music of dead revolutionaries. It is hard to imagine now, but to his contemporaries, *Motzard* was outrageous." Emily had slipped into the old pronunciation but Ben seemed not to notice as he laughed. Now he is traditional. Anyway, it got her a job right out of graduate school and she continues to teach.

After years of avoiding the class, at Barbara's insistence the prior June, Emily had joined a panel discussion titled "Blacklisting and Red Scare of the 1950s."

After Barbara had introduced the panel members, consisting of her mother, a director who hadn't worked since 1954, and a couple of young tweedy professors, she gave her usual introduction to the new audience. Barbara's stockiness became authority. Her mastery of the history and context of the era was impressive. Barbara stood at a pale oak lectern in a clear bright spotlight. She had a poise that Emily had never seen before.

"Blacklisting was a powerful conspiracy between the government, private employers and the press to silence public debate in the 1950s. The House Un-American Activities Committee. HUAC, was established back in 1938 as backlash against the New Deal. By the late forties it was popular to go 'Red hunting', so the committees grew. There were a dozen more committees at all levels of government. Many of the states and some cities had Un-American Activities Committees. In 1948, the Alger Hiss case showed the government's ability to root out communism.

"Fear followed and by 1951, Hollywood was running scared. The Blacklist was an informal agreement between motion picture studio heads and the government, after a meeting at the Waldorf-Astoria Hotel in New York. What was the deal? Simply that these private businesses would not hire or employ those who may be considered subversives by the government and objectors to this process were taken to court or ruined by the press.

"The Hollywood Ten were writers called to testify at the House Un-American Activities Committee in Washington. Those who did not testify and recant earlier statements, statements we know now to be protected by the First Amendment, were jailed. Over 150 others were jailed for a year or two. Over 10,000 lost jobs. 'You are too good for the part.' was code for not being hired because you were on the Blacklist." Barbara virtually spat the word and continued.

"Many writers used 'fronts' to sell their scripts and treatments to studios for less than they were worth. In 1956, Robert Rich failed to show up and claim his Academy Award, because there was no Robert

Rich. The writer was Dalton Trumbo, and he was on the Blacklist. Later he was given credit for *Spartacus* and other films that he wrote.

"By the mid-sixties the Blacklist had been lifted, but most artists had lost the best years of their careers and never were able to restart. In 1961 Ring Lardner got screen credit for *The Cincinnati Kid*. Just this spring the Screen Writers Guild West restored the true credits for ten more writers on twenty-four films.

"Actors had no such ability to hide in the shadows. Their face was their meal ticket and there was no invisibility that they could find. Not in America. Some went to Europe. Some directed. Some died. How did it impact my family? I was about ten when I remember two FBI agents in suits coming to my house and asking my father questions late on Thanksgiving Day. Later I asked him about this and here's what he wrote for me before he died."

Barbara picked up a paper and unfolded it. She put her reading glasses on and looked at the back row of the auditorium. She held the paper in front of her and read from it with slow precision.

The agent asked, "Why are you having a meeting today?"
My father said, "A meeting? It's Thanksgiving! A potluck."
"Who all was here?"
"Anyone without a better offer. Mostly studio friends."
"What did they talk about?"
"The women talked about raising kids, Dr. Benjamin Spock's theories, and prices. Milk was pushing a dollar a gallon. Gas just jumped to twenty-two cents downtown. Men talked about cars and work and writers they knew. About what President Eisenhower was doing. And women, when their gals weren't within earshot. A couple of kids were playing a record player downstairs in Barbara's room. Want to know the records they played? Perry Como. Eddie Fischer. Tony Bennett's *Rags to Riches*. Nat Cole's *Pretend*, and a few others that we had in the house."
"Was it an organizing meeting?"
"Organizing? Hell, most of these clowns could barely organize a meal. That's why Emily did the turkey and others brought whatever they brought."

She took off her glasses and looked at the audience again. "That was what my father told me about that day. Here's what it looked like."

The lights dimmed and she showed the family film of Thanksgiving Day, 1953. Scratchy black and white images formed and people smiled at each other and waved at the camera and ate and drank and talked.

As the film Harry had taken so long ago was played before strangers, it startled Emily as all of her memories from the day were in color.

The shirt that Harry wore that day was his knit brown golf shirt with the pale yellow trim on the collar. Barbara was nine years old again and in pull-on tan slacks and a sweatshirt with Mickey Mouse on it.

CHAPTER 33

SOSTENUTO

Play with a sustained smooth style.

Suddenly, Emily found the quiet night in her silent home was full of images of her daughter on Thanksgiving Day in 1953. Not the film, but the day the film was taken.

November rain had been unusual in California. But that Thanksgiving Day, great thunderheads formed over Palm Springs and somehow climbed over the mountains to the Los Angeles basin. At four in the morning, there was a terrific thunderstorm and rain, making it humid, laying the foundation for a nasty argument when Emily tried to comb Barbara's thick curly hair. After she was bathed, her hair was neat and held in a clip over her right ear. Her dress was straightened, white anklets turned over once perfectly, and her shiny Mary Jane's were buckled.

She was ready to go to be the hostess of their Thanksgiving Day party. It was really too early to dress her, but there was so much work that Emily needed to do in the kitchen after she got the turkey in the oven. Harry had to set up the card tables and the bar. If the rain continued, the party was all going to be indoors.

As Emily went to the front of the house to bring in the morning paper, Barbara followed, found a puddle, and jumped in it with both feet. Emily gasped as a wall of groundwater, full of mud and grass clippings splattered her leg and drenched her dress. Emily looked at her daughter, standing with brown water hiding her new shoes. The rain started again and Barbara simply put her head back, opened her mouth, and stuck out her tongue.

"Mommy, taste the rain!" Barbara squealed and stomped her feet again in the mud puddle in delight. Emily did taste the rain. Harry came to the front door, leaned into the doorframe and just watched them with a broad smile.

Emily walked behind her daughter, held her small shoulders in her strong hands and tossed her head back again.

The lightning was over the Pacific Ocean by now, and its low rumble could still be heard. The smell of ozone and freshness surrounded them. The two had tasted November rain together. And they listened to the moment of silence when the rain stopped, just before the city took a deep breath and life began again.

When Emily turned, she saw that Harry was smiling and then he held out his arms to them. Sometimes, when Emily thought of that, she held her breath. As though she could capture the silence again of that one moment when the world was everything it needed to be.

Emily bathed Barbara quickly as Harry set up the card tables. Then he dressed Barbara, this time in play clothes and tennis shoes, while Emily showered and dressed again.

By eleven the deck was dry enough to use and the clouds were thinning. By noon, the day was cool and perfect. By one, the house was full of noise, rich scents and anticipation for the feast promised for two o'clock sharp.

Barbara showed her paint-by-the-numbers oil painting portrait of a horse to all of her father's friends. The kit from which it was made was simple. There was a pre-drawn silhouette of a horse head outlined and defined in a spider web of pale blue-green lines. Each shape had a small number in it that matched a small plastic cup of oil paint. It was all the rage. Barbara decided not to confine her painting within the lines and the effect was closer to impressionism or pointillism than realism.

"Is it safe to talk in front of the kid or is she working for J. Edgar?" a newcomer to their house asked Harry, only half-joking.

"She knows that the guys who wear the dark suits in summer are taking our pictures for Uncle Edgar," Harry laughed.

"Hey, I'm serious. What with the schoolteachers telling kids to be good Americans and rat out your Commie parents, now defined as union members. I'm serious, I didn't know that there was going to be a kid here."

"Actually, she runs the place. She's really quite a remarkable child. Takes after her mother," Harry bragged. "Excuse me, I need to get some film of Emily in the kitchen."

Harry experimented with his new Brownie 8 mm movie camera throughout the day. Hand cranking the big silver key on the side of the brown leather camera and then holding down the button on the top while aiming it at people who were used to being behind the camera, not in front of it. There was a constant ticking sound of the film running through the camera so as Harry came up to people, his presence was announced, like a rattlesnake, and they turned and usually smiled and waved or offered those exaggerated expressions and gestures common to home movies. Her memory was a swirl of overlapping conversations that she only half heard from the kitchen.

She was the cook and Harry was the reluctant barman and avid filmmaker that day. The bar had the usual quart bottles of Cutty Sark and Johnny Walker Red Label scotch whiskey, Seagram's Canadian whiskey and Gordon's gin. Two smaller green bottles of vermouth were on the counter as well. A bottle of pale, dry vermouth for making martinis and a new bottle of Martini & Rossi red sweet vermouth, not so much for anyone to drink, but so Harry could tell his story of her confusion of the gin and dry vermouth drink he called a martini with the sweet red vermouth she called a Martini. Almost everyone had heard the story, but Harry told it again, and somehow turned it into a celebration of his luck in marrying an English woman during the dark days of the war. After telling the story twice, and mixing the first drink for everyone, Harry abandoned his bartending for filmmaking.

Emily somehow fit everyone's hot dishes into the oven to warm after the turkey came out. Harry carved the turkey and set slices on a platter that Emily put on one of the three card tables in the living room, each covered with a white bed sheet pretending to be a tablecloth. There was an assortment of unmatched dishes holding favorites from all over America. Herb dressing and pickled crabapples from the North. Stuffing of cornbread and dirty rice, sweet watermelon rind pickles, mashed baked yams with melted marshmallows on them from the South. Hot creamed pearl onions, cold pickled beets with onion slices and dinner rolls from the Midwest. Smoked salmon and apples and pears from the West. Mashed potatoes and gravy. Three types of cranberry relish. Black olives.

Barbara stood at the far end of the tables and somehow had appointed herself to offer everyone a scoop of the lime Jell-O salad with pineapple chunks and cream cheese in it that the redhead from Fox brought.

On the deck, the dented red Coleman cooler was full of ice and cans of Pabst, Schlitz and Budweiser beer and bottles of Coca-Cola, Nehi orange, Hires root beer, Canada Dry ginger ale, 7-Up, and grape soda pop. They lost the beer can opener over the edge of the deck at the last party, so this time it was tied to the handle of the ice chest with a long brown string.

Most of the conversations that Emily remembered were not attached to anyone. Women in two distinct groups talked either about fashion or if Dr. Spock's approach to raising children was too permissive. Men talked mostly about new cars that no one could afford, politics and the studio. And then after a plate of food and a few drinks, the women joined the men in their conversations.

At first it was social and business. Several people asked Emily what she was working on for the Philharmonic.

"Bartók's Viola Concerto," she said simply to the first person who asked and that satisfied them and they wandered off. What she wanted to tell them was how pleased she was that the Concertmaster had finally succumbed to her hinting. Although a viola was featured, rather than a violin, she had nagged and nagged to get it performed. What the Concertmaster never knew was that the royalties from the work were the only retirement Bartók had been able to leave for Ditta, his widow. He had died of leukemia, before the work was completed. Only the masterful work of Tibor Serly brought it to life from the notes and sketches that Béla Bartók left. She never told anyone how she sobbed into the newspaper when she read of his death in September of 1945. Barbara was less than a year old and she started crying when she heard her mother cry. Emily thought of this moment as her last link to Prague and her family.

She could almost hear them.

"The investigating committees are just working though their partisan agenda, 'Attack the New Deal' programs, and Truman's liberalism by putting a pink tint to it-- smear anything with the fear of Communism."

"Just look at the timing of accusations and hearings. They are made to coincide with opportunities to embarrass or derail local or state elections, union elections. If you can't win on the issues, just win by laying your opponent out as the devil. Miller has it right. Silence is the damnation of the normal man, in Salem and in Los Angeles. Speak out back then and the devil was tempting you to cross God. Speak out now and you are the tool of the Red Menace. You may not speak to proclaim your innocence, as we know that to be a lie, but confess anything and repent and that becomes the new truth."

A tall man in a Hawaiian shirt pounded on the door. "What's the password to get into this den of iniquity?" He had two bottles of gin cradled in his arms.

"Have you now or have you ever been a member of the Communist Party?" Harry shouted toward the door.

Emily held the door open. "Just in time, Jake, we've got way too much vermouth."

"Where's your date?" Harry asked. "Stand you up?"

"Meeting me here. Had to go into work this morning."

"It's Thanksgiving, for God's sake."

"That's what I told Alice, but you know working women," Jake said, winking at Emily as he walked out to the deck with the gin.

The deck was swarming with young actors and older writers and their unwitting dates who thought there was just going to be free food without the continuation of the office politics. Young men were balancing plates of food and eating as they debated important things. Too-thin women sat on chairs and balanced half-eaten plates of salad and cottage cheese on slim legs.

Mike, from the legal department at Fox, was half leaning into and half sitting on the rail of the deck and layering turkey on a roll to make a sandwich. He bumped a martini glass that he had balanced badly on the railing and it disappeared into the brush below. Emily pulled him away from the deck railing and plopped him in a chair. "That could have been you, Mike. Have a seat. I'll get you a 7-Up."

Mike never stopped talking to the man next to him. "Selling out any other name to save your own skin. That's the strategy." The other man, who Emily hadn't met before, continued the same concern, "So? What's new? They did it in the Spanish inquisition and the Salem witch trials. Look at *The Crucible*, Miller's new play, opened in January to awful reviews. Saw it in June. Hell of a play! Really one of the best I've seen in the past ten years."

"Open casting when it comes to L.A.?" a blonde asked, wondering if there was a part in it for her, or if they ever would make a movie of it.

"Set in New England, just about the time they invented Thanksgiving. Pilgrim looking costumes."

"Not my type," the blonde said and lost interest.

"Girls accused of being witches save their own skin by naming others as the devil's tools," Mike continued.

"Sounds like one of the costume dramas Warner Brothers was making a few years back," the blonde said, visualizing the casting.

"Not this play! It may look like Salem a couple hundred years ago, but the issues are right out of the front page of the paper. Corruption of the powerful and how silence has the force of evil."

"Is Arthur Miller really that overt?"

"No, of course not. You can't speak up against the oppression in the Soviet Union for fear of being labeled a Communist or a sympathizer. He uses the metaphor of the witch burning trials."

"I get it, symbolism," said the blonde. "And speaking out obviously makes you a Communist or a witch."

"If you answer yes, you will be asked to give names," Mike said.

"And if you don't play that game by confessing?" the blonde asked.

"If you don't, they will read a list of names for you to confirm or deny. There is no way to be silent." Mike looked up at Emily as she put her hand on his shoulder. It did not calm him.

"It's a game, isn't it?" Emily asked.

"Sure, give up your First Amendment rights to protect the

Constitution. The best Nazi is an anti-Nazi. The best fascist is an anti-fascist," Mike snapped as he took the dark green bottle of 7-Up from Emily and she turned to go back into the house.

Mike called after her, "Let them cut down the forest and then see who complains that there are no trees. Slash away!"

Emily went into the house, trying to get the ring of the anger out of her ears. But there was no escaping the politics of the day.

Then from inside the house, there was shouting, "I know a new parlor game! Anyone want to play?" George, the screenwriter with the beret was yelling.

"No. No one likes any of your games. Pin the tail on the director last month was too stupid for words, even your words can't do it justice."

"Word game...." George persisted

"Meaning he has it all worked out? So you can't play."

"All right, I'll be the moderator.... Need two teams: one in the house, the other on the deck." George waved his arms for quiet then continued. "For the first question, what is the one trait that Joe McCarthy and Dick Nixon share? Hint, go for the subtext not the obvious."

"Both are lawyers," shouted a blonde in shorts from the house.

"That's text, not subtext. No credit. Another player?"

"Both look like they've been on a three-day bender."

"Good, but not the exact point...think tough-man thematic," George prompted.

"They both need a shave. Look like thugs in Houston's cowboy movies," said a stocky woman from make-up at MGM.

"You win. The prize is never to have to kiss them. The next is a team effort. Gather in a huddle and make a list all of the writers you can think of who have been silenced for their political position? Not just politically, but artistically exiled," George clarified.

"What's the prize?" asked a slim man balancing a plate with turkey and dressing on it.

"My new Parker pen to the person selected by the winning team," he said patting his pocket.

"Dead or living?" someone called.

"Dead, or the list would be too long. Write, man, write."

Both teams whispered and scribbled.

The front door had been left open and a tall woman with auburn hair and blue eyes stood in the doorway looking for someone. She saw Jake and waved at him.

"Alice!" Jake called. He left the team on the deck and walked across the suddenly silent room to her.

"What's going on, Jake?"

"Just a parlor game to let their food digest so they can drink more. George's idea of a game, I think. Let's grab a plate. I waited to eat with you."

While others wrote lists on paper, Jake and Alice picked through the remains of the buffet and walked out on the deck. Harry introduced himself as George yelled, "And now to decide the winner, give me your lists of exiled, silenced and roasted writers." He took the lists and scratched off duplicates until he smiled and stood to report the results.

"Who won?" asked the tall man in the Hawaiian shirt.

"Hold on. Here are the names on both lists. Dante, for the *Divine Comedy*," he intoned as though he were announcing the Academy Awards for the year.

"Which wasn't funny to some," someone yelled in a Groucho Marx imitation.

Undaunted, George continued with the listing, "Victor Hugo, Daniel Defoe, Cervantes, Ben Johnson, Milton, Emile Zola, Rousseau. No credit for the Hollywood Ten. And it is a tie to that point. The winner goes to the team with Voltaire. Team House."

A stocky man in tan shirt with rolled up sleeves and khaki pants stood and recited carefully and sincerely, "Voltaire had to escape France to Geneva and later from Geneva to the village now called Ferne Voltaire which is at the border of France and Switzerland. Wonderful bar there. Papa and I...."

"Jack, for that invented drinking bout with Hemingway, you forfeit the prize pen. But I'll leave some passes on the counter for anyone who is interested." Mutters and laughter followed George as he went to the counter, and dropped a few passes to movies that most of the people there had already seen. Then accounts of other writers started, almost as gossip.

"So, who is the latest to flee town?"

"Bertold Brecht."

"No, not Bertie?"

"He escaped Hitler and now he's escaping Hollywood. No irony there."

"He's really repatriating to Germany?"

"That's what I heard. Our ex-pat is going to re-pat. Thinks it's safer for him there now than here."

"When's Bertie leaving?"

"Why? Looking for a good party?"

"Hear about Chaplin? They've pulled his paperwork. He went for a visit to Geneva and now can't come back into America."

George went to the deck for a beer. Barbara was specializing in opening beer cans with the pointed opener tied to the cooler, more than were actually needed at the moment. She handed George a beer and he nodded appreciation to the child and joined another cluster of writers and actors on the deck.

"The WGA is not doing all that much for us publicly," an older man said. "How's stuff at SAG?"

"Screen Actors Guild? For the love of Mike, Ronnie Reagan is still its president and is going over lists with the FBI all the time. I'm scared to death that I'll end up on one of the lists."

"Like Chaplin?"

"Well, I don't mean the short list for best actor, I'm not waiting for my Oscar. Not this year."

"How's the blacklisting sorting out now?"

"Over half are writers. Still blasting the 'unfriendly witnesses' with his shotgun of venom."

"Another mixed metaphor like that and I'll call WGA to pull your card," George threatened.

"Before the HUAC can?"

"Sure. What can the House Un-American Activities Committee do to you? You're just a working stiff."

"But why ask if they already know the names?"

"It is not a fact-finding, but a ritual slaughter designed to expose and vaporize people."

"You know, in some ways, I really miss the War. Really. We all were on the same side then. War Bonds. Saving fat and tin foil from cigarette packs for the war effort. You were fit or you were 4-F and couldn't be drafted. It was simpler then."

"Yeah, I remember putting little plastic name tags on my kids in grade school in New York so if there was an invasion we could identify their little bodies. No, I'll take the cold war any time. As inconvenient as it is," said a man a bit older than most of the people at the party.

Emily went out to the deck to remove Barbara from the cooler and passed a lawyer talking to a blonde starlet, "Sure, they have a technique for women as well. The men are dupes, and the women are sluts or nuts. You need to know their strategy before you talk to the press at all. If you get called, call me before going to any meetings. And if you ever want to have lunch…well."

Jake and Alice seemed to be having a fight at the far end of the deck. It was the overly civilized type of argument in which words are terse and quiet enough not to be overheard, but strong enough to bring tears.

Emily took a reluctant Barbara, who was staring at Jake and Alice, into the house. Then Alice turned, put down her plate and walked through the room and out the front door carrying her purse.

Jake started to follow her. Stopped and had a bite of food and then went into the house.

"Is Alice all right?" Emily asked as she was washing grape soda off Barbara's hands at the kitchen sink.

"I guess. She didn't see much humor in the 'writers in exile' game and we sort of had a little fight out there."

"Shouldn't you go after her?" Emily asked.

"Barely know her, and if she's gonna boo-hoo over some game, and get all fussy over my friends, well, maybe it's better that she let me know now. Go after her? Naw, I think I'll go after more turkey. This is great, Emily."

Over by the music room, two men in their thirties, looking too much alike to be coincidence, were talking. Emily overheard only a snatch as she walked by with a drink for someone. "In Eperney, there is a rose bush at the end of every row of the vines that grow the grapes for champagne. The roses bloom and fade and warn of disease. If the roses become ill, that is a cautionary sign that the vines are at risk. A sentinel plant, they call it. What cautionary note do we have for a world about to go mad again? What canary in our coal mine warns us of the madness of a McCarthy?" asked one of the men in a black silk shirt to the other.

The party ended late and the next day was a quiet family day.

At noon, Harry made the perfect turkey sandwiches on white bread with just enough mayo and cranberry sauce. He took three sandwiches out to the deck and called Barbara, who was in her room playing, to come to lunch. On her way past the kitchen, Barbara picked up the movie camera, walked to the far end of the deck and started filming them.

There they were, captured on film. Harry and Emily in their chairs, looking like movie stars. Sunglasses on. White shirts, khaki slacks, barefoot on that warm Friday. Sandwiches on saucers, balanced on the wide arms of their Adirondack chairs. Perfect day. The film showed Harry waving for Barbara to come to him and get her lunch. The camera was still whirring as Barbara laid it on its side and ran to Harry. She hopped into his lap and took a bite of the sandwich that he held out for her. That part was filmed sideways. That was a day of laughter and sun. The three laughed and the camera's spring ran down and stopped as they ate. But the laughing lasted all the rest of the day.

The best day.

At dusk, they went to Grauman's Chinese Theater and saw *The Robe*. It was the first film in Cinemascope. The first film to escape the square format and go to a stretched format. It pulled the audience into the film.

Harry was right when he guessed that if the picture got better so, too, would the sound. That started a wonderful inventive time for him. Barbara was almost nine in Harry's film and on the edge of that explosion called adolescence. This was Emily's day, the day after the Thanksgiving fuss. The day alone with her family. The day Harry always made special for her.

CHAPTER 34

DIMINUENDO

A musical instruction to play gradually softer.

The hollow fear was not new to Emily. She remembered how it had startled her in the past. Not just tonight with Ben, at the MOCA reception at Bunker Hill, but years ago in Los Angeles as well.

The morning had been nasty. Mother and daughter fought, as usual, over teenage things. Barbara's hair being too puffed out, mascara too black, eyeliner too dramatic, and her bright orange mini-skirt too loud and too short.

After Emily had backed the MG out of the garage and put the top down, Barbara complained that her hair would be mussed and put the top back up. Halfway to the event, Barbara announced that they were taking a friend to the Senior Brunch. Seething, Emily followed Barbara's directions to the home of the boy who was her co-editor on the school paper, Goody Richmond. Fortunately, he was slight and limber enough to squirm into the jump seat in the rear. Emily was frustrated that Barbara had not yet found the time to take the driving test at the Department of Motor Vehicles and had let her learner's permit expire.

The graduating class of 1961 had its spring breakfast at the Blue Hills Tennis Club on the edge of Los Angeles. Emily dropped them off at the entrance, put the top down, and quickly left the club to run errands. As she turned onto Santa Monica Blvd., Emily saw note cards, bound by a rubber band, sliding in the passenger's foot well of the car. Emily downshifted and pulled into a parking lot to rescue the cards. Barbara was scheduled to give a speech, but had forgotten her notes. Emily snatched the note cards from the floor of the car, shoved them into her purse, and drove back to the tennis club. When Emily went into the dining room of the club, they were refusing to serve Goody. Emily froze. The club was restricted. Emily never thought of that.

She heard Goody say to the slim man assembling the breakfast plates in the buffet line, "Really, all I want is a new plate, I can't eat bacon, so I don't want it on my plate. Just the eggs will be fine." The waiter in his crisp white coat stepped back from the serving duties at the buffet line and whispered quickly to the manager. The blue-suited manager moved rapidly around the white tablecloths and silver chafing dishes full of scrambled eggs and hash browns, bacon, sausage, ham and small New York steaks, sweet rolls, croissants and dinner rolls. As he approached, he interrupted something Barbara was saying to Goody.

The manager took Goody's elbow. Come with me, young man. I'm afraid you'll have to leave." He began to escort him from the buffet line.

Barbara held her plate in front of her and turned toward the manager. "What do you mean he has to leave?"

"He is not welcome here," the manager whispered.

"He was invited. He is a part of our senior class."

The manager spoke very softly, hoping she would lower her voice as well. "He is not invited to be at this club,"

"Why not? Tell me! Why not?" She was insistent. Goody was quietly moving toward the door and motioned for her to stop. She did not.

The high school football coach, who was balancing a heaping plate with one of everything on it, came up behind Barbara. "Just what's going on here?"

Barbara pointed at the manager. "He said Goody had to leave."

"Why?" The coach placed his heaping plate on the table of pies and cakes and fresh fruit before turning to face the manager. The coach looked significantly taller to the manager than he did when he was going through the buffet line. The manager started shaking his head 'no' and backing away from the coach. The manager seemed to be struggling to find the words to explain his dilemma to the coach. How was he going to say it? How was he going to explain that the Jewish kid had to leave the restricted tennis club without causing further commotion?

If not, how was he going to explain to the club members that a Jew had brunch at their restricted club. Members would, no doubt, discover this breach and fire him.

The manager was pointing toward the lobby. "There has been some misunderstanding. I think it might be best for us to go to the office and...."

The coach did not move. "There's no need to go anywhere. I think you should apologize, get him a fresh plate, and let him enjoy his breakfast."

"Well, I'm not sure that...."

"Well," Barbara asked in her too loud voice, "can he eat here or not?"

The manager had small beads of sweat forming on his upper lip. "I would rather that he left."

Barbara took a step toward the manager. "Would you rather that I left as well?"

"I believe that you would be welcome here."

"Because I go to church?"

He sighed. "Yes, exactly, thank you for being so understanding."

"I understand what you said, but I have no intention of accepting your offer. You are a bigot." She held her plate and went to the lectern that had been set up for the awards ceremony following the senior banquet. She tapped the microphone with her index finger and it let out a sharp squeal. "Since Goody... my co-editor of the newspaper ...has been asked to leave the tennis club because of his religion, I would invite you to reconsider your continued attendance at this restricted club. I know that I have lost my appetite."

She walked back to the buffet line and handed her plate to the slim waiter in a starched white coat. And then the coach picked up his plate from the table and handed his plate to the manager. And then the football team captain, Frank, left his plate on the table and walked out of the room. Several linemen stood up from their mounded plates and looked at the captain for leadership before reluctantly abandoning their food and the promise of dessert.

Then the manager started waving his hands in front of him to stop it all. And the room stopped. He went to the microphone and announced 'a misunderstanding' and welcomed Goody to visit the buffet.

The manager took Goody a new plate and personally escorted him to the buffet line. Goody pointed to one of the sweet rolls and then returned to a chair near the front of the room with his plate. Barbara followed with a new plate and calm was restored, but not for Goody. His ruddy complexion had paled to a sallow off-color. Barbara saw his hand shake as he started to drink from the water glass at the table. He put it down and she put her hand over his. Emily walked up behind Barbara with her speech notes.

"Hi, Honey," Emily said. "You forgot these." Barbara took her notes from her mother and looked for reproach. She knew she had been rude. She also knew she was right.

"Hi, how long were you...."

"Long enough." Emily leaned down and hugged her daughter. "Want to stay or go?"

"I think I need to stay for a little, don't you?" Barbara asked Goody.

"I think I'd like to go soon," Goody said to Barbara, after he chopped at his sweet roll with his fork but didn't eat any.

"I'll be right outside when you're ready," Emily said and left to wait in the MG.

Emily was surprised when she saw Barbara laughing as she and Goody came out of the club. She overheard her daughter telling Goody, "It worked. I think we really scared them."

"God, I was the one who was scared. I thought the manager was going to punch me when I didn't leave."

"Really?" Barbara said calmly.

"You expected him to cave that easily?" Goody asked, as he crawled into the space behind the bucket seats.

Barbara smirked as she tied a scarf over her hair. "Cowards usually do."

Emily drove Goody and Barbara to Hamburger Hamlet in Westwood. They were going to eat and walk to a movie. They would call a cab after the movie. Emily stopped at the Richfield gas station at the foot of the hill to put gas in the MG. While the attendant filled the tank, she looked at the note cards that she had shoved in her purse. They were blank. She wondered if Barbara had intended to give her speech, but never asked her.

A week later at the Department of Motor Vehicles, fear came to Emily from an unexpected encounter.

Barbara was standing in line ahead of her, pretending that she did not know her mother in public. She was reading the latest issue of *Mademoiselle*, flipping through the pages quickly to look at the new clothes. The late summer issue featured fall clothes. A quarter of the way up the long line Barbara started reading one of the fiction pieces, became mesmerized by the craft and freshness of the fiction, finished the short story, and was just starting to read a poem when a woman rushed up to Emily and gave her a Hollywood hug, fast and insincere. Barbara looked up from her reading and looked over her shoulder at the invasion.

"Well! What a surprise seeing you again after all these years," the woman said. Emily looked into the face that she did not recognize. Emily looked at the stranger and took inventory quickly: oversized sunglasses hid her eyes, bouffant blonde hair teased to transparency, deep tan, with lines starting at the corners of her shimmering pink mouth, not from smiling but smoking. "It is you, Emily, isn't it?"

"Yes, but..."

"I'm sure that you don't remember me. I was a dishwater blonde and about twenty pounds heavier in school. I was only there until I could get back into the good graces of my mother and come home. I was only in Geneva for a little bit." The woman kept her sunglasses on.

"But you remembered me?"

"I'm Vanessa," she said, putting her hand out to shake hands, very formally in contrast to her earlier manner. "I was in your music class for a short time. You and that other girl were such pals that I had to look and see which of you was really here. Got you two confused even back then."

Barbara watched her mother abandon her poise and attention to others that was so much her hallmark.

"And you remembered me?" Emily asked as much as stated.

"Your manner. But the signet ring. Very classy. That was what brought it all back to me. That's what made me decide that it was you and not your friend," Vanessa said, too loudly for Emily.

"Why ever would you remember my ring?" Emily looked at her small ring.

"Because you slapped me with that hand. All I remember was looking at how angry I had made you and wondering if that ring had cut my cheek," Vanessa said in a matter of fact manner that had Barbara staring at her and not moving forward as the line moved.

"I am so sorry, but I have no recollection of…."

Vanessa tugged at the hem of her short dress. "I know exactly what I said. I've thought about that moment a thousand times. I even told my therapist how bad I felt about it."

"I can't imagine it was so bad; that was so long ago," Emily said, hoping that the line would move forward. Barbara stared at her mother.

"We had a spat over letting just anyone move to America. It was right after the Germans had stamped the passports of the girls at the conservatory. I said that I thought that President Roosevelt was right not just letting anyone in. We were just coming out of a depression with barely enough food and jobs for Americans. We had food lines in the cities then. I know. I stood in them with my mother before I won a scholarship to study in Geneva. I'm not old money. Just a very lucky girl who never meant to offend your friend, or you. I was stupid and young. Who could have known what was going to happen?" Vanessa started to cry. Tears welled in her eyes and her mascara started to run and traced a black line down her face.

"Geneva was beautiful. That's the part I try to remember," Emily said, wanting the meeting to end.

"You were a good friend to her. I tried to apologize, but you both left school. My therapist would probably say I need to thank you for that awareness." She pronounced the word 'awareness' as though it were a magical word with lots of eastern mysticism surrounding it.

"I don't know what…." Emily was confused and on the edge of panic.

"What was her name? Your friend? Ruth?" Vanessa asked, dabbing her face with a Kleenex pulled from her white wicker handbag.

"Rachel."

"Do you see her or write any more?"

Emily shook her head. "She died in the war. Her whole family did." Tears formed in Barbara's eyes as she watched her mother.

Vanessa took Emily's hand and patted it. "I'm so sorry."

"So am I."

Vanessa walked away.

Emily turned back to her daughter. Put her arm around Barbara's shoulder and pulled her close to her.

Emily asked her daughter quietly. "You okay?"

"Mom, I didn't know...."

"That was then," Emily said, giving her a quick squeeze. But Barbara did not leave the moment as Emily had hoped.

"Your friend died in the war?" Barbara asked.

"Several did, but Rachel was my closest friend. You've seen her picture on the mantel. You are a very fortunate young lady. So don't frown like that; I want your driver's license picture to look a lot better than mine."

Together they waited in line for the photograph to be taken of Barbara for her first driver's license. Barbara told Emily about the short story that she had read and offered to let her mother read the magazine that she always inhaled as soon as she bought it at the drug store.

Emily thought of another time and of her decision to live for the present and future, not the past.

Barbara was in the second grade when it happened for the first time. Emily took Barbara to a birthday party for a boy in her class. What was his name? Todd? Terry? The mother was Marty. That's all Emily remembered now. Marty. Not the last name. She could see Marty's face as she opened the front door to let Barbara into the birthday party and a balloon exploded behind the door.

The sound was like a sharp explosion, like a shot. Short. Crisp. Emily froze and waited in that fractured second for an explosion and shards of glass. When the sound was empty and there was no explosion,

Emily let one sob of raw terror escape as she backed into the wall and slid to the floor. Barbara threw herself on her mother and cried in that small muffled way that children do at fear, not hurt. Barbara held on to her mother until Emily caught her breath and held her.

Marty looked at them huddled in the hallway of the house and did not know what to say. But what she did was all that needed doing. She simply shut the door to the living room and put one hand on Emily's shoulder and her other hand on the child's. Simply touched them until silence became safe again.

Marty left them and returned with a glass of water for Emily and a Kleenex. Emily did not know what to say as she took the glass of water. Her hand was shaking. She could not stop shaking and was breathing too deeply to trust a sip.

Marty was kind and smoothed the child's hair.

"Ready to go into the party?" Marty asked Barbara, who looked at her mother. Emily nodded for her to do so. Barbara picked up her present for the boy and went into the far part of the house, following the sound of laughter. Emily looked at her hands as she let go of Barbara. Her hands shook and she leaned her head back into the wall until she absorbed its strength and calm.

She decided that this party was just another performance, just another façade. That it was now. And would never be London again.

Marty came back and sat in the hall next to her. "I'm sorry. It was the sound, wasn't it? It made Frankie jumpy this morning when we were blowing them up and one popped. Was it the war? But I never thought of the women that were coming. I should have remembered that you were in London then."

"Thank you," Emily said as she straightened her hair and got up. She went into the family room where there were helium filled balloons floating into the ceiling, and balloons that the children had blown up were rolling around on the floor. Inviting more explosions. Calling up memory.

Emily decided, at that moment, that she did not have to react. She was not able to let fear go, but she decided not to show the depth of her fear. And now, she could decide that there was no need for fear.

CHAPTER 35

TREMOLO

Rapid up and down bow strokes.

Friday was cool enough for Emily to choose her heavy fisherman's sweater and black wool slacks after her practice. With rain on and off throughout the morning, she lit the gas log in the fireplace. A perfect day for making bread, Emily thought, as she kneaded the rich yellow dough. This had become her practice on Friday afternoons, shortly after Barbara left home. Some note of remembrance always came to her when she made her mother's recipe. One loaf for tonight and the other for tomorrow.

Today she was flooded with the memories of her childhood, the sounds of the solid iron clang of the oven door of the wood-burning cook stove and the yeasty smell of the kitchen in Prague. The sharpness of coarse salt, the bitter heat of horseradish, and the sweetness of the wine of the Sabbath-- all were fresh again. She was almost through kneading the dough when a knock at the door startled her. Only Ben knocked on the door. Everyone else used the doorbell.

She quickly glanced around the kitchen. The soup pot was on at a very low simmer, and the bread would be fine if she just tossed a towel over it so it did not dry out before she could return. She threw a fresh white dishtowel over it and went to the front door, wiping her hands on the thicker kitchen towel.

She opened the door to discover Ben holding a bouquet of white carnations with three blue irises and delicate ferns. The cellophane wrapping around it dripped water on the front door stoop and splashed on his shoes. He smiled broadly. "Hi."

"Hello, what's the occasion?" Emily asked, wiping her hands on the dishtowel.

"I pick up flowers every Friday on my way home for my wife. For Shabbat. It makes it even more special. Since she's out of town until Sunday night, I thought you might like them. Want to join me for dinner tomorrow night? I can cook after sunset."

"Is that an invitation to dinner or to more questions?" Emily asked cautiously.

"Just dinner."

"Fine then. But have dinner here tomorrow night. I warn you, it's simple food. Soup and bread. And I'll throw you out if you misbehave."

"What time?"

"Anytime after five, that will give us time to watch the sunset from the deck, if the rain clears."

"I'll walk down about 5:30, if that's okay. But you are not going on the deck until the inspector clears it after my guy finishes, and we know that it's safe for you."

Emily took the flowers from him. "Yes, yes, see you tomorrow." She watched him pull up the collar on his raincoat and start down the hill before she shut her door.

She returned to the kitchen and finished kneading the dough. Instead of weaving it into the braided bread as she had done as a child, she took the rich egg dough and made two round loaves of bread. She thinned a beaten egg with water and brushed the wash on the top of the dough before putting the loaves in the oven. She checked them when she smelled the sweetness of the browning bread from the music room, a minute before the timer buzzed. She tapped one of the deep amber-brown rounds, slid them on a rack to cool, and thought that the hollow sound was very much like longing.

Saturday came without the brightness that Emily wanted. It rained heavily throughout the day. Emily checked the weather forecast occasionally on her computer after being frustrated by the ongoing radio reports dwelling only on traffic collisions and power outages. Putting on her raincoat she walked on the slick deck twice in the morning to check the hillside. She was relieved to see that the new ice plant was holding firm and the hill was not eroding. Shortly before Ben's prompt arrival at 5:30, she changed into a dark blue cotton blouse, casual slacks and a matching blue cardigan sweater.

The winter evening was mild enough for just a light tan V-neck sweater over his black Polo shirt and slacks. Ben held an open bottle of red wine in his right hand and a bottle of white wine in the other. "I forgot to ask which you'd want. So I brought both, a Chardonnay and a Merlot."

As she closed the door, Emily took both bottles to the kitchen while Ben hung his raincoat in the closet. She motioned toward the kitchen cabinet that had the wine glasses in it. "Let's start with a glass of Chardonnay while the soup heats." He followed her subtle direction, got two glasses, and by the time the wine was poured she had adjusted the heat on the stove.

"We should be able to get the deck fixed and cleared for occupants well before the wedding. You still are going to have it on the deck, aren't you?"

"Yes, Susan and Ray called earlier today to check on the progress. They'll be back Monday night."

"The more I tell my wife about you the more she wants to meet you. We think you are interesting."

"Really? How could I be interesting?"

"Actually, I think she's getting jealous of the time we're spending together."

Emily laughed and then saw his concern. "Well, I certainly want to meet her as well. Isn't long distance really expensive?"

"We don't really use the telephone that much. Between our work schedules and the time difference between here and Switzerland, we mostly e-mail each other and occasionally set an appointment to talk on the phone. Isn't that ridiculous?" Ben gave a crooked smile, then paused.

"What is it, Ben?"

"Emily, I want to be a good neighbor to you." Ben watched her as she took a very small sip of her wine, then put two woven placemats on the counter where he had perched.

"You know, it's been a very long time since I had a real neighbor or friends like when Harry was alive." Emily pulled silverware from the drawer and arranged it on the placemats without looking at Ben.

"It changed when your husband died? Sometimes that can be a...."

"No, it was before that. Most of our friends were writers or at the movie studios for some reason or another. And the mid-fifties and early sixties were very difficult for many of them. Some lost their jobs. Some moved to London. Some avoided us either to protect us or because they were afraid. But now, I've outlived most of them," she said with a small laugh. "Let me go check the soup. It should be about ready."

She ladled soup into large flat soup bowls that Ben carried to the counter for her. She set a small glass dish holding a half-cup of a deep green mixture between the placemats. There was a spoon on the glass saucer under the dish.

"Have you ever had *pistou* before?" Emily asked.

"Is this it?" Ben asked, pointing to the soup. Emily laughed and pointed to the small glass dish of thick green sauce almost like Italian pesto.

"When you put it in the vegetable soup, the soup is then called *pistou* as well. They make it in the south of France." Emily put a large spoonful of the green sauce into the center of her bowl of soup after she slipped into the tall bar stool next to Ben. "It's probably a cousin to Italian pesto, you know, that mix of basil, garlic, olive oil, and Parmesan cheese. But this has hot red pepper in it as well."

"Is the soup French?"

"Yes, just a good vegetable soup with leaks, tomato, carrots, new potatoes, string beans, zucchini, small white beans and a very small pasta in it. Put a little of the *pistou* in the middle of the soup and have fun with the explosion of taste. Think of it as French salsa."

Just then the buzzer on the kitchen stove broke the calm of the evening. "The bread. I always set the buzzer so I don't dry it out." Emily got up to get it and brought back the warm bread on a wood tray. She picked up one of the rounds of bread and tore it in half. She nodded for Ben to rip open his round of bread as well. They used the wooden tray as their bread plates.

Halfway through the soup he looked at her differently. Then he took a chance. He took a small sip of wine, set the glass down and looked directly at her. "You're observant, aren't you?" Ben was testing her with the ambiguity of his question.

"Observant?"

"Jewish."

"What now?" Emily snapped.

"Nothing," he laughed. "I was just wondering if we had more in common than just being neighbors."

"Why?"

"This meal. It is just what I would want on a Saturday night. Temple last night. Temple this morning. Now, a simple meal and thoughtful conversation after Shabbat ends, when I see three stars in the evening sky."

"Well, you didn't see any stars tonight!"

"Don't evade me. You prepared this meal yesterday. This is a day of rest and refreshment and rejuvenation. A day to spiritually refresh ourselves, not work. You are used to the 'third meal', aren't you?"

"Oh, Ben. Do you really think I am Jewish because I like to eat early?" Emily dug her short nails into her left palm as she stirred more *pistou* into her soup.

"Maybe not you. Was Harry? Why are there nail holes in the trim by your front door? Painted over but there was a mezuzah there once, I'd bet on it."

"Yes, before we bought the house; it was gone when we moved in. I guess Harry didn't patch the holes as well as he thought he did." She forced a laugh.

"Maybe your parents?"

"They never came to America."

She suddenly felt stricture in her life and held her breath. Could he have discovered who she was or that her parents died at the camp at Terezin just a few miles from Prague, where her family had picnicked in the summer? Could he imagine the madness that allowed them to die so close to home after sailing to Cuba and then back to France only to end up there?

Did he know how she wept at the *Life* magazine pictures of the living cadavers in filthy striped rags leaning on the thick necks of rud-dy Yanks. The Yanks looked too young to be there and embarrassed as their tears cut lines through the dust on their cheeks and made dark patches on their uniforms? How 'gas' for years meant prussic acid, the gas of the chambers? How did you even spell it-- Zyklon B or Cyclon B--let alone think about it. No, gas was not gasoline and why else would she have used the word 'petrol' long after anyone could have cared that she came from England.

"What church do you go to?" Ben asked her.

She picked a flake of crust from her sleeve and put it on the coun-ter. "When Harry was alive, we went to a Protestant church. He used to call it the N.W.D. church."

"N.W.D.? I'm not familiar with that."

Emily took a small bite of bread. "Nearest walking distance. That was his joke. That's how he decided where to take Barbara to church. I rarely went," Emily said. "But you go, don't you? That's why you were walking in the rain yesterday afternoon, rather than driving. Going to synagogue?"

"Yes, I was. It's about forty-five minutes each way, and opportu-nity for reflection before I *daven*."

"*Daven*? Are you testing me again? Yes, I know the word. It means to pray. To worship." She waved her finger at him. "But that doesn't mean what you think it means. All that means is that I have lived in Los Angeles for a very long time and have a very wide and eclectic circle of friends. I speak fluent French, but that does not make me French."

"Yes, I can see that. L.A. has a Jewish population that is huge. What is it? Third largest of any city, and maybe that includes the whole coun-try of Israel?"

"That can't be."

"I think I read it recently."

"And in the recording and movie industry, when I was working full-time, maybe those who were Jews were just more comfortable in being visibly Jewish than if they worked at a department store. We had a lot of friends in this house over the years. It was like a little United Nations some weekends. Maybe what I liked best about those times is that we didn't try to label each other. Differences were respected. Often celebrated."

Ben knew that he had offended her. "If I was out of line…"

"If we're going to be neighbors, then let's be good neighbors and respect our boundaries." Emily gave him a look that told him he had crossed the line but the breach was not without the possibility of repair.

"Like that poem by Carl Sandberg?" Ben sipped his wine.

"You mean Robert Frost. How good fences make good neighbors?"

"Yes, that's what I wanted to say."

"Have you ever lived in the snow?"

"Not really, just vacations for skiing."

"The rainwater gets into the cracks between the balanced stones. When it freezes, ice can topple stones from a rock fence. It wedges them apart. Harry said that poem was about mending the fence together. I thought it meant good neighbors honored distances."

"If I'm wrong, I deeply apologize. Know that I am your neighbor and would like to be your friend. I know that you have visitors. I see their cars parked in front of your house. But if you ever need a real friend…"

"Actually, most of my visitors are not friends. I still teach, coach really. Just a few master students. I consult with the Los Angeles Philharmonic. I review new recordings for *Stereophile* magazine, which accounts for the stack of new CDs by the stereo system. All free. I am not a very good model for retirement."

Ben relaxed his shoulders in surrender. "I think you are a great model. What are you reviewing now? I need to expand my musical horizons." He poured the last of the white wine into their large glasses.

Emily relaxed into the litany of the impersonal, the objective. "Midori has an excellent CD, Bartók's Violin Concerto Number One and Number Two in B Minor. Zuben Meta conducting the Berliner Philharmoniker."

"New?"

"No, Sony Classics. Excellent remastering makes it worth the new review. Also, I am reviewing another surprisingly good work with antique instruments. Violins from the Baroque era used to play violin work from that era. Hyperion issued it. Elizabeth Wallfisch plays. The style is a bit jerky for my taste, but she is superb. The sound is a bit off from what I know. The A is at 440 and I tune at 400… Sorry."

"For what?"

"Being boring."

"Not you," Ben said and laughed. "What else are you doing?"

"An overview piece for the *Times* on violinists of this century. Profiles of Isaac Stern, Jascha Heifetz, Mischa Elman, Fritz Kreisler, Nathan Milstein, Ruggiero Ricci, David Oistrakh, and a few others. I'm going to contrast their approaches to the classic violin pieces. The sonatas by Franck, Bach and Brahms."

"Perlman?"

"No, these are the old masters. I think he is in their league now, and he is still growing. I'll reserve his work for another article. He's simply remarkable. Joshua Bell is a young violinist that I want to write about too. Very promising future."

"Who else is upcoming?" Ben asked finishing his soup.

"I want to do a profile on three women. Midori, Hahn and Mutter. Midori, the Japanese prodigy, is in her mid-twenties now. Her Bartók is magnificent, especially the Violin Concertos, but I think she is still developing, as remarkable as she is. I'm currently listening to her Elgar recording. Rich, daring, emotional. I think she will eventually rival Heifetz for perfection and that clear Stradivarius sound."

"Really? Why the others?"

"Hilary Hahn, extraordinary. She's an American girl, just eighteen. Her talent is already mature, confident and lithe. And Anne-Sophie Mutter…"

"The German?"

"Yes, Von Karajen's protégé, now just thirty-something, with enormous skill and depth. There's a lot to enjoy in the new talent."

"Whose Four Seasons solo is closest to yours?"

"The recording itself or my vision of it?"

"The ideal."

"Mutter's. Clearly inspired."

"Are you playing now?"

"I won't play professionally anymore." Emily looked at her hands and was again grateful that her arthritis was limited to the little finger of her right hand. The bowing hand. The finger turned in at the end joint. Lately the arthritis had been calm, but last year her finger was red and throbbed most of the winter. But like most things, Emily just waited it out and prevailed. She paused and then added, "Occasionally, I'll play for a charity fundraiser or if an associate asks a favor."

"Friends?" Ben asked with a sly glance.

"I don't have that kind of friends anymore. Real friends. And I do miss that. I miss it deeply. There is something very challenging about losing your friends. Death, grief, reordering of life. All were very difficult for me after Harry died. I did not know if I wanted to stay here. But Barbara was in college then and moving seemed more than I could handle. There is a certain momentum. No, I think the word is inertia, which holds you to a place, almost like emotional gravity. This is my place. I don't want to live anywhere else. My friends moved away to be with their children or go to the desert or go to assisted living homes. Some simply forgot who they were, or who I am." Emily had said more to him that she intended and surprised herself with the candor.

And her lie.

She feared performing now. She always had. She still feared discovery. But she still longed for a reunion that would never be. She tried to stand still in the vortex of pain and fear and made them manageable by not moving, not confronting, not facing down her demons.

Ben saw sadness drift over her and wanted to swing the conversation back to a happier tone. "What did you like playing the most during your time with the Philharmonic? No, let me ask it a different way. What is your favorite piece of music?"

Instantly she thought of 'Smoke Gets In Your Eyes'. Dancing with Harry after Barbara was born and they were safe and starting their new life. How he held her, like she was special and frail and he had all the strength that either of them would ever need. Emily shook off this memory.

"That I played professionally?" Emily asked, stalling, finding distance again.

"That you played or just enjoyed. I just caught myself. I don't want to ask you as a lawyer. This isn't a deposition. So, tell your neighbor who is interested in music and you, what gave you the greatest pleasure?"

"Let me think. Geneva, London, the States...." Emily thought back to Geneva when she wrestled with the same question.

"When I was a student, my favorites were Vivaldi, Vaughn Williams, and Mozart's 'Jupiter'. In London, I played with the Philharmonic. It was good work, but not up to the reputation of the London Philharmonic, far too many stand-ins, like me. Again Vivaldi."

Emily paused and did not speak what came to her next. It was music from her past, her faith. *Kol Nidrei* in Prague and Los Angeles. Bernstein's *Kaddish*. In his symphonic expression of the Jewish prayer she began to feel grief emerge from years of numbness. Still she could not mourn, but this was the start of the pathway to her *keriah*, the ritual of tearing of clothing, the beginning of mourning. This music was a start on the *Sheloshim*, the thirty days of mourning, but how could she find the end of it?

"Vivaldi? I could have guessed that."

Emily twitched slightly, jarred back to the present. "Yes, but in my music, in my performance, I still do not feel that I have found the fullest expression of Beethoven's Symphony Number 9 in D minor, Opus 125, 'The Choral'. That's the one ending in the Ode to Joy. Schiller wrote that dream of peace and brotherhood. Beethoven put sound to it. What I hear in my mind when I read the score is never exactly what I hear in concert, whether I am playing or in the audience. Van Karajan's conducting has come the closest, but there are dreams that we all have of a perfection that evades us."

"But you have had so many extraordinary performances."

"But you know, I think my best work, the work I was most satisfied with was never performed." Emily cleared away the empty dishes and rinsed them quickly before sliding them into the dishwasher.

"What?"

"When I finally was able to play Bartók well, I was selected to play a piece by Haydn. It ends in a violin duet. My closest friend and I hoped to play it together. We never did. But in our practice, I found myself as an artist. I discovered a confidence that let me live my life… in music. Perhaps that final practice that we had was the closest to perfect happiness that I ever knew as a musician." Emily was silent for a moment, looking at her hands, then she looked at Ben, "And maybe that's a larger truth, that at the end of the day, the personal prevails over the professional."

"Do you have a recording of it? I don't know the piece."

"No, but there are a couple of new CDs that I'd like to play for you over dessert. I made brownies. Would you like coffee?"

Ben smiled. "I think I'd prefer some red wine. I'm not driving anywhere, and it goes great with chocolate."

"Really, I must try that."

Ben poured two small glasses of Merlot and watched her as she took a pan of brownies and cut two pieces. They ate in the living room and listened to music without speaking for the next hour.

After Ben left, Emily opened the safe again and fanned through the letters. She touched the leather binding but did not open the journals. She watched the lights of the city blurred by the rain and then went down the stairs to her bed and slept.

She woke. It was just after eleven. She knew the only thing that she could do to be herself again, was to confront herself.

She picked up the telephone receiver and dialed three numbers before she slammed it down. She went upstairs and looked out the front window. Lights were on at Ben's, and she dialed his number from the portable telephone in the kitchen. He picked up the phone on the first ring.

"Ben, this is Emily."

"Yes?"

"Did I wake you?"

"No, chatting with my wife on the Internet."

"Could you come by tomorrow morning?"

"Sure."

Emily was silent.

It was then that she decided that the life that she had lived was hers, fully and completely. But there may be other decisions that her granddaughter would want to make about how she lived her new life as a bride in a Jewish home, and what she told her children, when she had children.

Ben broke her silence, "Emily?"

She looked at her hands. They were the slender hands of an old woman. She saw strength still, but thought of parchment, ancient, creased. Her hands were older than she had ever seen her mother's hands, which were still plump and firm in her memory. Flour on them as she gave her the shawl. Fat fingers, 'sausage fingers' her father teased before he called her golden hands. Sausage fingers, as she teased Barbara, when she was a baby before such things had meaning.

"What, Ben?" Emily said in a faint voice. She remembered the feel of the rough wool of her mother's shawl the last time her mother held her, hugged her, wished her well, surrounded her with love.

"What time?" Ben asked, listening to her carefully.

"Ben?" she asked softly, ignoring his question.

"Yes."

"Ben, is it true that if I hire you as my attorney, you can't ever tell another person what I tell you?"

"Generally. Unless you tell me you are going to kill someone or commit a crime. Are you?"

"No," Emily forced a small laugh as she searched for the right words, "I want to discuss a serious matter in confidence. I want you to help me decide if I should do something that will change my granddaughter's life, and possibly harm or at least change my relationship with my daughter."

"For this, you may not need a lawyer."

"Who do I need then?"

"Maybe a friend?"

"Can you be my friend?"

"I think I am already," Ben said calmly. "Emily? Do you want me to come now?"

"It's still raining."

"Do you want me to come now?"

"Yes," she whispered and hung up the receiver before she started crying.

CHAPTER 36

TONE

A musical sound of a certain pitch.

Emily let Ben in while still in her bathrobe, put on a pot of coffee, and changed into her warm up suit. Through the remains of Saturday night and into Sunday morning, over cups of coffee, Emily told Ben the truth.

All of it. Not just the logistics of her life, but how abandonment of her name and religion had weighed on her. How betrayal and necessity tangled in her thoughts. How protecting her past was limiting her future. And that she felt that the lie that she had held for season after season was no longer hers to hold.

Emily thought that there was a moment in the fall and again in the spring of crystalline clarity, when the city was different. There was a sharpness or brittleness that lasted only a moment. That was the moment she awaited.

In the fall, the brittle light is of death and the dryness of bones, and in the spring it is of the birth and bone-draining commitment to life that mothers make. One of those moments of clarity arrived. Not in the light, but in the soul, and, with that, Emily knew that she had a choice, a moment of decision, and that the moment would not come again. She found her choice as inevitable as the migration of geese that she had watched season after season from her deck.

She told him the truth about where she was born and how she was raised. How her friend had helped her escape from Switzerland and how she had assumed the name of her friend in England when the real Emily Finch was killed. That Harry married her to rescue her unborn child from a war. That she grew to love him and made a new life in America.

That she had maintained a façade of being raised English to distance others and that she had lived a lie for what she thought made some sense, day by day, and that there was never a good day to tell the truth. What then was this shortcoming, this *chet*, her sin? How had she missed the mark so far when she tried so hard to keep her child safe? How could that harm her granddaughter?

Then she was silent. And the silence was absolute and pure.

Ben reached for her hand and held it lightly as he asked, "So, what do you want? *Misphat*, justice? *Tzedakah*, righteousness or charity?"

"*Teshuvah*. Repentance. Returning," Emily whispered as though the sound of the words would scare the nightmare away.

"Why now?"

"It seems different now. With Susan marrying a Jew, her study to convert, to be a 'Jew by Choice', as she called it. The odd irony of her *Gerut*, her conversion, is that she is not the outsider she thinks she is. There suddenly was a shift in the balance. I used to think that the legacy of my violin was its voice, how well it was made. Now I see that its real legacy is in its story. Now I need to find a way to tell Susan and Barbara who I am."

Ben listened for several hours, made more coffee and passed Kleenex and held her hand across the table.

"All be told, I'm a fraud. Simply a fraud. From the simple to the profound. Saying plaster for Band-Aid, spectacles for glasses, rubbers for overshoes. Ordering Guinness stout or a wine when I really just wanted a good pilsner, a Budweiser, but was afraid I might pronounce it in the Czech manner. All a sham that I kept on too long. How could I be silent so long?"

"Maybe the better question is why did you ever start it?"

"Because," Emily said, finally trusting herself, "it was during the war. My parents were lost to me. Only later I discovered how they died. I can only hope that no one ever knows that bone deep fear. Ben, I was hiding in plain sight. No trust at all in myself that I ever could survive here. Not a moment of sleeping through the night, always waiting for some off-hand discovery that someone who had an affair with Emily was going to show up, or someone that my father helped years ago would appear and know me for who I really was. There was a close call … or two, over the years."

He asked questions and had her balance the harm of the truth with the good of her transparency. How she had traded her life for her child's security.

When she told him that she had decided what to do, Ben stopped her. "Before you tell me, I need to tell you something."

"What?"

"When you called, I was talking to my wife. She found out something that I need to tell you. I know you told me to stay away from the banking records, but I didn't have a chance to tell her yet. She discovered that Graham had made Emily the trustee for her child. Barbara was the intended recipient of the funds. Not you or Emily. I know that might be confusing, but it was listed in the trustee's name, not the real owner. So, you still could have the money go to Barbara and not have to disclose your true past. You don't have to…."

"Ben, I know what I need to do. My decision was never about the money."

"I wanted you to know that there was no issue of who Emily was or was not, only of who Barbara is; her name alone triggers the release of the account now that she is an adult. You…Emily, were simply the trustee."

Emily nodded and looked at him and patted his hand.

Ben said softly, "I'm your friend, but I'm also a lawyer, not your conscience. Let me be certain that you know that there still might be an immigration violation here. I don't think so because you had adopted your name before marrying in England and coming here as a war bride. Do you want me to do some research into it or get you a lawyer who deals in immigration law? There may be a slim potential that the Immigration and Naturalization Service might get—"

"Ben! Stop it." Emily asked in a tone usually reserved for small children, "Do you really think they want the publicity of harassing an old lady who simply escaped Hitler in the middle of a war with all their issues now with terrorism in the Middle East and refugees and humanitarian relief in Kosovo, with Mexico and drug traffic?"

"Yes, I see your point, I was just being overly...."

"You were being a friend. And I thank you for that from the bottom of my heart."

"I just don't want you to feel scared or endangered...ever again." Ben looked at her and waited.

"Ben, I guess what I really fear, when I am honest with myself, is that Barbara will hate me for not being honest with her long before now."

"If she didn't hate you for all the British language pretensions that you've told me about, for yelling at her in front of her school friends, to be sure to wear her rubbers, she'll get through this just fine."

Emily laughed at herself, "Really?"

"Really."

"Thank you, Ben."

As Ben got up to leave, he turned. "Do you remember the word, *zachor?*"

"To remember?" Emily said tentatively.

"Yes, to remember. Remember who you were when you decided that Barbara's life was so important that you put your life aside for it. Both of your lives have inestimable value. Your family is strong enough to see that."

"*Zachor,*" Emily said as the door shut behind Ben.

Now she was alone.

CHAPTER 37

FINE

The end.

Emily gathered their coffee cups and washed them as the sky brightened into a clear Sunday. She thought that the truth is like a bone, skeletal, bleached white by time, unbendable, and impractical.

She squeezed two large oranges and took her glass of fresh juice out to the deck. Less than halfway through her juice, the rain started again and forced her retreat to the house. After three hours of energetic violin practice, Emily showered, wrapped herself in an oversized towel, and went back to bed. She thought it through again. Still wrapped in her towel, she called Barbara and then Susan and asked them to dinner the next evening.

She dressed casually, wrote checks for the December bills, and edited her review of a new CD. Late in the afternoon, she remembered that Ben was going to go to the airport to pick up his wife.

She changed out of her casual shirt and slacks and dressed in charcoal wool slacks and her new silk blouse, just lighter than cream. As she walked to the kitchen to get her rose scissors, she turned up the cuffs so the rose thorns would not snag them. After she cut several roses from the low bushes by the front door, she carried the pale pink flowers to the kitchen, shook the raindrops from them, and put them in a simple vase. She shivered from the chill in the air and slipped on a cardigan sweater before walking up to Ben's house. She caught him just as he was backing the sedan out of the garage. He turned off the car and opened the door.

"Hi, Ben. I thought Ellen might like to have some fresh flowers when she gets home."

Ben took the vase from her. "She'll love them." Ben turned toward the house but stopped and faced her. "I want to be a good neighbor to you. I am sorry if I am making your life more difficult."

"It's my life, Ben. How could you make it more or less difficult? Now it is going to be up to Barbara and Susan...and Ray to decide what to do with what I am going to tell them."

"Do you want me to be there?"

She shook her head. "No, I need to do this alone. Now, go put the flowers away and bring your wife home."

Emily gave him a hug and turned to go home. She knew what she wanted to write in the journal that she had started in Prague, but not the precise words. She got the journal from the safe and sat on the love seat.

The last light of day glowed red over the ocean. The lights were starting to weave the pale amber and gold net over the city. Emily wondered how she could say what she felt. How could she explain that the life of a lie is just long enough for the truth to defeat it?

All she needed her daughter to know was the complexity of the tapestry of her life and the simplicity and strength of truth. But for her granddaughter, there was more that she wanted.

She uncapped her pen, convinced of the value of her truth but wondering at its cost. She wondered how she would tell them of the Havel family of Prague. Perhaps she could start by telling Susan the name of the woman in the photograph, Rachel bat Josef, of her mother Evah bat Meyer, of her father Josef ben Moshe, and of her husband Yitzhak ben Solomon. That she is Rachel, that Emily died in the war and her family helped her survive as an English rendition of herself.

She started to write something and stopped as she recalled the scrap of paper pinned to the wall in her father's workshop. She saw it clearly in her recollection, black ink from her father's precise letter-ing, *Pravda Zvítézí*."

She printed the words *Pravda Zvítézí*. And below it, her translation, "Truth shall overcome."

Emily capped her pen and returned the journal to the safe, next to her passport that still held the last letter from her parents. Perhaps she should start with that letter. She could read it to her daughter, granddaughter and Ray. Then she would explain the names in the letter. This is how she would start to tell them of their history.

She shut the safe, stopped before spinning the dial, and opened it again. She pulled out her violin case and laid it on the love seat. She leaned over it and removed the violin that her father had made and set it carefully beside the case. Then she opened the storage compartment in the case and tossed the extra strings and small cake of rosin to the floor. She pushed down on the velvet-lined compartment and the lid to the false bottom sprung open. She reached in and removed the small brass mezuzah that had developed a pale green patina. The frayed strand of black yarn tied around it fell apart at her touch.

Emily held the mezuzah in her left hand as if it were a bubble, ready to evaporate into the air. She brushed the fingertips of her right hand against it very gently before bringing her fingertips to her lips as she had done as a child.

She felt something that barely had a name as she stood. A lightness. An ease that had not been hers in a very long time. She smiled as she took the mezuzah to the living room and placed it on the center of the coffee table.

She went to the kitchen put a small block of Jarlsberg and a few Wheat Thins on a plate. She pulled the wire cheese-slicer from the drawer and then put it back again. Not slices, but chunks, that was what she wanted. She selected a small paring knife from the dark oak knife holder on the counter and laid it across the plate. After walking to the far point on the deck that wedged into space, she looked out to the Pacific and balanced the plate on the railing. She closed her eyes and listened to the hum of freeway traffic and the occasional squeal of brakes. When she turned her head slightly, the breeze obscured the city sounds. And then above her, there was the sound like the sound of a child breathing on the edge of a dream. A wedge of geese flew above her, followed by another to the west, and a third wedge trailing behind, almost lost in the last of the rain clouds. The blaze of the sunset had passed and the last light made them shine almost silver against the pewter sky.

She shivered and hunched her shoulders. Her wool sweater rubbed her neck, just under her left ear. When she pulled the tip of the silk collar over the wool, she thought of her mother, of the roughness of her wool shawl. She inhaled deeply as though she were on the bow of ship approaching a new world and smelling land after too long at sea.

She took the knife from the plate and held her breath as she pulled the silk tip of the collar away from her neck. In a motion as fluid and precise as her bowing, she lifted the small knife and cut cleanly into the thin fabric. She had acted as she was taught. *Keriah* completed, her mourning begun. She smiled and returned the knife to the plate.

She thought of Susan and of tomorrow as she watched the wedges of geese pushing to where they must go. Pushing home.

Postscript

This novel began when I visited Prague in 1996 while the multinational negotiations were in progress concerning the return of "dormant accounts" from Swiss banks to their owners. Chance meetings with American and Czech dignitaries, the Prague Spring music festival, time at the Pinkas Synagogue, and my imagination led to the "what if" questions that fueled this fiction.

Ultimately, the Swiss Banker's Association called for claims due on January 23, 1998. Of the 21,000 listed dormant accounts, 9,000 were resolved through this process. The average account increased ten times in value from the end of World War II to the distribution of the account to the account holder or their heirs.

On January 18, 2001, the American and French governments agreed that the French Government would establish a commission to compensate the victims of anti-Semitic persecution in France who may have had bank accounts during the German occupation of France.

On February 5, 2001, a new claim process was authorized by the District Court in New York State. That legal action allowed claims by Holocaust victims as a class-action lawsuit against the Swiss government and its agents for actions taken by the Swiss government during the war.

The Claims Resolution Tribunal of the Holocaust Victim Assets Litigation against Swiss Banks and other Swiss Entities set deadlines for claims in 2001 and 2005. Over 32,000 claims were filed. Over $515,000,000 has been restored to its lawful owners or their heirs from dormant accounts.

Respectfully submitted,

Sharon O. Lightholder